PRAISE FOR ALEXEY PEHOV

"Toothy, gritty, and relentless. Alexey Pehov sneaks up on you and fascinates with the wry voice of a young Moorcock."
—E. E. Knight

"Bestselling Russian author Pehov translates easily in his English fantasy debut. Protagonist Shadow Harold proves modest and witty enough a narrator to carry the series."
—*Publishers Weekly* on *Shadow Prowler*

"A book that most fantasy readers will want to read and explore . . . In short, if you like reading fantasy, you'll love reading this book."
—*Graeme's Fantasy Book Review* on *Shadow Prowler*

"The second of The Chronicles of Siala is as mesmerizing as *Shadow Prowler*."
—*Booklist* on *Shadow Chaser*

"Employing all the standard trappings of the genre, this sequel to *Shadow Prowler* enjoys a freshness of vision that elevates it beyond standard fantasy fare."
—*Library Journal* on *Shadow Chaser*

TOR BOOKS BY ALEXEY PEHOV

Shadow Prowler
Shadow Chaser
Shadow Blizzard
Chasers of the Wind

CHASERS OF THE WIND

ALEXEY PEHOV

TRANSLATION BY ELINOR HUNTINGTON

TOR®
fantasy

A TOM DOHERTY ASSOCIATES BOOK
NEW YORK

CHASERS OF THE WIND

Copyright © 2005 by Aleksey Pehov

English translation copyright © 2014 by Aleksey Pehov

Originally published as Искатели ветра (Iskateli vetra) by Издательство Альфа-книга (Izdatelstvo Alfa-kniga) in Moscow, Russia

Map by Maxim Popovsky

A Tor Book
Published by Tom Doherty Associates, LLC
175 Fifth Avenue
New York, NY 10010

www.tor-forge.com

Tor® is a registered trademark of Tom Doherty As sociates, LLC.

ISBN 978-0-7653-7015-0

Tor books may be purchased for educational, business, or promotional use. For information on bulk purchases, please contact the Macmillan Corporate and Premium Sales Department at 1-800-221-7945, extension 5442, or write to specialmarkets@macmillan.com.

First Edition: June 2014
First Mass Market Edition: May 2015

Printed in the United States of America

0 9 8 7 6 5 4 3 2 1

I would like to thank Trident Media Group and especially Robert and Olga Gottlieb, whose efforts made this book possible. My wife, Elena Bychkova, who worked on this book as I did. This book is dedicated to you, the reader. Welcome to the new world.

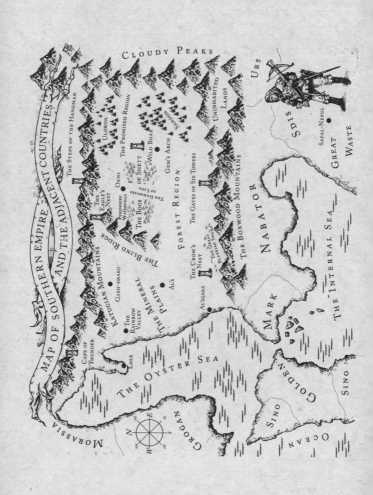

He who chases the wind will find the storm.

CHASERS OF
THE WIND

PROLOGUE

Luk had been unlucky last night. He'd had to take over someone else's shift, and as a result he hadn't had nearly enough sleep. Huddled against the early morning chill, the guard jiggled his legs and chafed his cold fingers in his mittens. Every other second his thoughts turned to the grand party that had been organized for the fifth barracks in honor of the Feast of the Name. Most of the garrison was planning to start celebrating early this morning, but here he was occupied with this nonsense.

"Screw a toad," muttered the soldier.

If the commander was so afraid of absent enemies, then why didn't he order the gates to be closed? These past few years, the vast forty-yard-high wings had stood wide open even during the night and not a single rat had dared to sneak through. What was the point of strengthening the watch if it would be far simpler to just lower the portcullis?

Damn that stupid commander! Damn the sergeant! Muttering curses under his breath, Luk moved along the wall from the Tower of Ice to the Tower of Fire. Along the way he gave a nod to his friends, who were drunk on hot shaf (a weak, spiced alcoholic beverage, infused with hops, thyme, chamomile, goat-weed, and linden), giving half an ear to the usual little jokes and remarks addressed to him, lazily straggling and then moving on somewhat quicker when they reminded him of his debts. Luk had no love for returning money.

The Gates of Six Towers was the greatest fortress in the world, constructed by the Sculptor himself, and it guarded the only passage through the western region of the Boxwood Mountains. The famed citadel had withstood many an onslaught over its thousand-year history, but had never been taken. The army of Nabator had broken its teeth against the gray stones and lost many warriors in the process. Causing the fortress to surrender would require something more forceful than steel and bravery.

While the Gates exist, the soft underbelly of the Empire remains safeguarded.

Luk watched as two women exited the Tower of Rain onto the wall. A Walker and an Ember. The mages were conversing about something, and the guard paused, reluctant to interrupt their conversation. He turned away toward an arrow loop, scrutinizing the scene before him.

He had been born in a small prairie village, and even now, six years after he first saw the snow-covered peaks, he never tired of marveling at the beauty of the mountain heights. The Gates, situated between two ridges, bridged the entrance to the lowlands, where the route into the heart of the country began.

In former times, multitudes of caravans had made the journey to the south. Weapons, silks, carpets, spices, horses, and hundreds of other wares passed through the Gates to distant countries beyond. But that golden age had long since passed, and the route had dried up. Only the local herdsmen, as well as the scouts that the commander kept sending into the nearby ravines, ever dared to venture along the old route and ascend into the inhospitable mountains.

But something strange had been going on with the scouts recently. The second squad of northerners was already late, even though it was long past the deadline when they should have returned. The commander was taking his frustration out on the captains, and they, consequently, were taking it out on the sergeants and the common soldiers.

The guard, unlike the officers, secretly rejoiced that the squad, in which the red-haired Ga-Nor served, was still wandering around the neighboring environs. Luk owed the northerner money. But he didn't have very much money at the moment. He'd blown too much of it on the dice last time. Almost all of his wages had disappeared into his debts, into other people's purses, screw a toad! All there was in his purse right now was one sol (a small silver coin), and that was not nearly enough money for Ga-Nor, but he had to find a way to pay him back; the northerners were a straightforward people, and if everything wasn't just so, he'd get it right in the choppers.

The soldier leaned out of the arrow loop and spat with relish. He followed the spittle with his eyes, hoping it would land on some heedless idiot, but to Luk's intense disappointment, there was no one standing under the wall. For the hundredth time since that morning he swore an oath and then resumed his contemplation of the landscape.

A small town was spread out in front of the Gates. The humble dwellings were constructed of round stones and clay, which had been taken from the banks of a nearby mountain river. The families of shepherds, wool merchants, and silver miners lived in the settlement. The villagers were not frightened to be living on the very edge of the Empire. The fortress was impregnable; the soldiers experienced. None of the mountain tribes would bother them here. They had already taken it on the nose more than once, and they knew that they couldn't seize the Gates. It would be quicker to gnaw a passage under the mountains than to tear down the mighty walls of the impregnable fortress.

Despite the fact that it was early summer, the air smelled slightly of frost. Rays of sunlight painted the snowy heights of the mountains with rose, and the peaks were shrouded in clouds. The sun was slowly climbing up from behind the eastern range. Another minute passed, and the sun began to shine so brightly on the summits that Luk screwed his eyes shut and once again called on his toad.

When the guard opened his eyes, he saw that two skinny mules hauling an old caravan had appeared on the empty morning road. From such a height the caravan was no bigger than the palm of his hand, but Luk could clearly make out a woman sitting on the driver's seat.

She was dressed almost entirely in rags. She looked just like a stuffed scarecrow. The soldier frowned in confusion. Had one of the villagers taken it into her head to set off for El'nichi Ford? It was fifteen leagues away. It would be stupid to haul wool to the fair, which had been arranged in honor of the Feast of the Name. To have any chance of trading goods, she should have set out six days earlier. Now she was just wasting the labor of her animals for nothing. Even if she hurried, she'd get there far after the trading had ended.

A strange caravan. He didn't recognize it. And that old woman. More like a beggar than anything else.

Luk frowned, trying to recall if there was anyone in town who had two such emaciated mules, not to mention a caravan with a blue top. A quick rundown of all his acquaintances' names and nicknames gave him nothing. If the guard could trust his memory, he'd never seen such a piece of junk. And after all the time he'd served here, standing by the Wing, the soldier knew everyone who did business at El'nichi Ford quite well.

One of two things was going on. First, she could be someone who traveled to the town while it wasn't his shift. Secondly, the unfamiliar wagon could have come out of the pass, and therefore, from Nabator itself.

The strange wagon still had about two hundred yards left until it reached the Gates when he called out to a friend of his who was chatting with two other guards.

"Hey, Rek!"

"What?" he responded petulantly.

"Take a look."

Rek grumbled discontentedly, but all the same he turned in the direction indicated. For several seconds he watched the road apathetically and then he turned his gaze on Luk.

"What of it?"

"Do you know her?"

"No."

"Neither do I. You think she came from the pass?"

Overhearing something about the pass, the seated soldiers leaned toward the arrow loop.

"The captain should be informed," Rek said uncertainly.

"You go inform him yourself," muttered Luk. But then he replied, "Shout down below, get them to check who it is and what she's doing here."

Rek turned away from the arrow loop, brought his hands to his mouth, and bellowed to the guards standing in the exterior courtyard of the fortress. At that very instant, a captain emerged from the barracks with the twenty unfortunate wretches who were doomed to work on the holiday.

Meanwhile, two guards stepped away from the wall and slowly made their way toward the caravan. Another dozen, mostly just curious, stood by the Wing. The woman tugged at the reins and said something in reply to the soldier's question. Luk would have paid a lot of money to hear exactly what was said. But a moment later he saw eight men emerge from the caravan. Six of them were dressed in chain mail and armed to the teeth. But it was the sight of the other two that froze the blood in Luk's veins and sent shooting pains throughout his stomach. They were wearing white robes!

Necromancers from Sdis!

The guard wanted to call out, to catch the attention of the Walkers, but fear made his voice seize in his throat. Unable to rip his gaze away, he watched as the warriors, dressed in the colors of the kingdom of Nabator, killed the surprised soldiers and started running toward the fortress.

A battle broke out below.

Something snapped, howled, hissed, and the captain and his men were swept through the courtyard of the citadel in bloody scraps. The staff of one of the Sdisian sorcerers was emitting a gray light.

Once again there was a rumbling, though not as loud as before, and all that remained of the necromancer and the Nabatorian standing closest to him was a wet spot. The Walker was invoking her Gift, and the Ember was standing next to her, pressing her palm into the Lady's back.

"The Gates! Close the Gates, screw a damn toad!" cried out Luk, who had finally come to his senses.

From the direction of the village he could see a few hundred cavalry galloping at full tilt toward the Gates. Alongside the Nabatorians, keeping pace with the horses, ran bony creatures that resembled skeletons.

Morts!

Rek ran to an enormous horn, breathed deeply, gathering the air in his lungs, and then blew it. A low booming sound spread over the Towers, sounding the alarm and raising the entire garrison to its feet. Men ran in from every quarter with no idea of what was happening. Many of them were without weapons.

The Wings of the Gates finally shivered and slowly began to close.

Too slowly.

Beneath the walls the battle raged on. The six Nabatorian warriors, under the auspices of the remaining necromancer, were holding out until the arrival of the main force. A lowering portcullis rumbled, and then another. Then there was a roar, and a warning cry rang through the fortress courtyard: "The sorcerer blew up the portcullis!"

Things were looking bleak if the Walker didn't do something soon.

As if in response to Luk's entreaty, the air shimmered and thickened over the Lady and the Ember, transforming into a massive many-faceted spear of ice. It deployed, aimed for the Sdisian. . . . Then the woman who was sitting on the caravan seat thrust up one of her hands as if annoyed at the distraction from her contemplation of the combat.

Crash!

For a moment it seemed to Luk that he had died and found himself in the drum of the northerners' god, Ug. There was a ringing in his ears, and all around him hung a thick cloud of dust. Bewildered at first, the guard realized that he had fallen.

He shook his head dazedly and then got up onto his hands and knees. There was a roaring in his ears, and blood was pouring down his face. Spitting out grit, he staggered to his feet and rushed toward where the Walker had been standing.

Enormous stones, which had been set into the walls by the Sculptor, had been plucked out and scattered for hundreds of yards. One of the boulders had fallen on the barracks of the second company, reducing it to rubble. Another, launched as if from a catapult, had crashed through the facade of the Tower of Rain. A third had smashed down onto the road, crushing three heedless Morts and five Nabatorians along with their horses.

The section of the wall on which the magic blow had fallen was severely damaged. It was as if a giant hammer had struck it. But the Walker was alive. Forgetting about his usual shyness around those who possessed the Gift, Luk rushed over to the woman. And then he shuddered. He had never seen such wounds during his time as a guard, and he strived to look only at the woman's face. Only now did he appreciate the fact that she was no more than nineteen years old, and that she had sky blue eyes.

She smiled and, very quietly but astonishingly clearly, said, "Tell my sisters that Rubeola has returned."

A Damned!

"Are you sure, my lady?" babbled Luk, who was suffocating from terror.

The Walker did not answer. Her eyes faded, and for some reason the guard had the strongest urge to cry.

A succession of magical blows battered against the Gates. They remained intact but stopped closing. The forward detachment of Nabatorians had held out long enough to ensure that the cavalry and Morts swept into the courtyard.

A massacre ensued. Over and over the Sdisian's staff flared dully.

The Damned just sat on the caravan seat and watched in a bored manner as an endless blue-black ribbon of soldiers flowed into the fallen citadel.

1

The day had started out warm, and now the cows, lazily chewing their cud, were sheltering from the midday heat in the shadow of a large oak. A yearling calf, tormented by gadflies, dragged himself to the river and slipped in, thereby ridding himself of the feisty insects. His dappled mother was trying to warn her son away from the water with a plaintive moo, but he was far too occupied with the water and ignored her summons.

Pork sighed disappointedly and set aside his homemade reed pipe. What kind of music could he make when there was such a racket? The damned cow just wouldn't quiet down. He should drag the calf out of the river, but he was feeling lazy. There was no point. He'd just wander back in again.

The day seemed infinitely long. His jug of milk was half empty, but his bread remained untouched. He had no desire to eat. Or work, for that matter. While the village boys fished for trout and played at being knights, why did he have to keep an eye on the cattle? But the children had no desire to include the overgrown village idiot in their games. Pork didn't know why, and as a result he was horribly offended, not understanding the reason everyone always laughed at him and twirled their fingers around their foreheads.

Yawning, he was about to nap for another hour, since the shade of the bushes he was stretched out under wouldn't go away for a while yet, when he noticed four riders appear on the road in the distance. They crossed the river unhurriedly, making their way along the sturdy wooden bridge constructed by the villagers, and, passing by the standing stone (standing stones are set at all crossroads. According to legend, they keep evil from finding its way into people's homes), headed off toward the village.

Pushing out his lower lip so that saliva dripped down onto his shirt, Pork watched the strangers avidly.

People wishing to visit Dog Green were always few and far between. The village was located in the foothills of the Boxwood Mountains in the middle of the densely thicketed Forest Region. People rarely came here.

The riders did not resemble the Viceroy's tax collectors in the slightest. The tax collectors wore gorgeous black-and-white uniforms, which Pork really wished he could try on, but these men were wearing simple leather jackets and linen shirts.

"And there's no herald with a trumpet," muttered the half-wit under his breath. "Nope, nope, nope—

the Viceroy's soldiers dress far better." True, these men had swords as well. Sharp ones. Much sharper than his father's knife, which Pork had cut himself on. Oh, that had hurt so much! And one of them even had a crossbow. Probably a real one, too. That would leave quite a hole. If Pork had such a crossbow, no one would laugh at him. Nope. The girls would love him. Yes, they would. And the horses these fellows had were much better than the villagers'. Horses like that could trample you right down, and not even a smudge would be left behind. They were knights' horses. When Pork left the village, he too would become a knight. He'd rescue virgins. But these fellows weren't knights. Where were the multicolored coats of arms, the plumes and the chain mail? Every knight should have them, but they didn't. If they were knights, they were doing it wrong. Yes, they were. But maybe they were bandits? No, they didn't look like that either. Even the dimmest five-year-old whose parents wouldn't let him go off into the forest hunting for mushrooms knew that bandits didn't travel the road so boldly—otherwise the soldiers of the Viceroy would hang them from the nearest aspen tree. And of course, bandits wouldn't have such splendid horses. Plus, all bandits were wicked, cowardly, filthy men with rusty knives in their teeth. These fellows were not like that. Anyway, what would bandits have to do with the village? The locals around here grew nothing valuable. Except perhaps old Roza's turnips, which the daring little people, as his father called them, try to steal.

Pork imagined how a horde of unwashed little men with overgrown beards, hatchets gripped in their teeth, grunting, would scale the wicker fence and, looking around fearfully, dig up the turnips from the vegetable patch of that wicked old grandmother. And she would stand on the porch, shaking her walking stick and giving them the tongue-lashing of their lives, calling down curses on their ugly heads. And then she would throw her stick at them, the old viper. She threw it at Pork once, when he broke her fence. What a bump on the head that was. His father simply told him that it was time for him to wise up. But that didn't happen. Just as before, everyone laughed at him, called him a half-wit, and didn't let him play with them. Well, what of it—he didn't really want to, truthfully.

One of the riders noticed the cowherd and said something to his companions. They left the road and made their way toward him over the field.

At first Pork was terrified. He wanted to take to his heels, but running away—that meant leaving the cows unattended. And of course, they'd scatter. He'd have to search for them again. And Choir would wander into the ravine again, and he'd get stuck there unable to get her out. He'd catch hell from his father. There was nothing for it; he'd get either the nettles or the whip. He wouldn't be able to sit on his fanny for a week. So there was no sense in running. And anyway, it's a long way to the forest. And those armed bulls were on horseback. They could catch him and give him a good drubbing. And besides, he still didn't know why they were coming. But his father wouldn't pat him on the head if he lost the cows. And so, making the choice between the clear threat and shadowy danger, Pork decided to stay put and see what would happen.

The riders came up to him, drawing in their reins.

"Are you from the village, friend?" asked the oldest of the four. Lean and tall with a pointed face and deep-set, clever eyes, the man regarded Pork without malice. Cordially and just a bit mockingly.

No one had ever called Pork "friend" before. The cowherd liked the way it sounded.

"Uh-huh."

"You're from Dog Green?"

"Yeah."

"Is it far?"

"No. Not very, sir. It's just beyond that hill. As soon as you get to the top, you'll see it."

"We've finally made it," said another of the men, sighing with obvious relief. His face was pitted by smallpox. "It's well hidden, eh, Whip?"

"Did you doubt the words of Mols, Bamut?" chuckled the one who had called Pork a friend.

A third rider, the youngest one, answered that question with a grunt. Pork disliked him right away.

He was sullen and wicked. A man like that would have no problem boxing you on the ears. And then he'd laugh.

"Is there an inn in the village?"

"In the middle of nowhere? What kind of inn would they have not ten leagues from the mountains?" snapped the youth, who had blue eyes.

"We have an inn," replied the cowherd, offended. "It's right by the road after you go through the village. It's quite large. With a red chimney. They have tasty meat pies. And shaf. My father gave me some to try once. But why have you come here? And are your swords real? Will you let me hold one? And your horses, they are Rudessian stock, right? Are they yours? They are like knights' horses. I'll soon be a knight, too. They're fast, aren't they? You aren't knights, by any chance, are you?"

"Hold on, hold on!" laughed the lean rider cheerfully. "Not all at once. You're in quite a hurry there, friend. Let's start at the beginning, I beg you. Are those cows yours?"

"No. I look after them. Yeah."

"Do you enjoy it?"

The cowherd pouted and looked at the man, offended.

He was mocking him. But he had called him his friend. He thought they were friends.

The man laughed once more. The other three riders remained silent and didn't even smile. They seemed completely uninterested in the conversation.

"And how many households are there in the village?"

"A lot." Pork showed all the fingers on his hands. "Six times as many."

"And you're literate. You can count," the man said respectfully.

"No," sniveled the half-wit. "My father showed me. I can't count on my own."

"Tell me, friend, do you have any new people in the village?"

"Are you talking about the Viceroy's people?"

"Well, maybe. Tell me about them."

"They came here at the beginning of spring. They were handsome. Important. And they had horses. Now we're just waiting until the end of fall. There haven't been any others. It's just us. Only the loggers come."

"The loggers?" asked the man with the pock-marked face.

"Yeah," sad Pork, nodding hastily, pleased that he could carry on such an important conversation. "They chop down our trees and then float them down the river to Al'sgara. They say they make really great boats from our trees. Oh, yeah! The best of all boats. They float. Yes."

"And what about these loggers?"

"I don't really know, sir. They come here in the summer. They live in mud huts beyond Strawberry Stream. They're mean. Once they beat me up and ruined my new shirt. Then I caught it again from my father, because of the shirt. Yeah. But they leave in the fall. They don't want to stay here for the winter. They say that the roads get blocked with snow. You can't get out until the end of spring."

"I told you, it's a swamp," spat the young one.

"No. The mountains aren't far from here. And they say that there are the Gates of Six Towers, though I've never seen them. And to get to the swamp, you have to go through the forest for several days. There's a bog there, you know. You go there, you'll fall right in."

"It's unlikely our friend would be found in the company of loggers," said the short man who looked like a ferret and had kept silent so far.

"I'd have to agree with you. But tell me, friend, do you know everyone in the village?"

Pork screwed up his eyes in suspicion. These men were strange. They'd asked him about the mean loggers, and then again about the village. And about the Viceroy's soldiers.

"Don't be afraid." The lean man tried to appease him with a smile. "We're just looking for our friend. He's about this old." He pointed to the man afflicted with pox. "He has light hair, gray eyes; he rarely smiles and can shoot better than anyone from the saddle. Do you know such a man?"

"Gnut shoots better than anyone from the saddle, but he has black hair and one of his eyes isn't even there at all."

"He has a woman with him, too. She's tall and

beautiful. She has long blond hair and dark blue eyes. So, what do you think? Are there any people like that in your village?"

"There might be," said the cowherd reluctantly. "I don't really have the time to remember. I've got to herd the cows. Or Father will cuss me."

"I hope this will jog your memory." The rider threw Pork a coin.

Pork caught it and his jaw dropped. The silly bear had thrown him a whole sol! Now he could buy himself sweets and eat them where no one could see. Pork wouldn't share them with anyone. That'd show them, calling him an idiot! The cowherd bit into the coin and, quickly, so they wouldn't be able to take it away, hid it in his bag.

"You described them really well. That's Pars and his wife, Ann. I recognized them right away."

The men exchanged looks.

"Where can we find them?"

"Oh, that's really easy. He lives just outside the village, not far from the blacksmith's shop. You'll see his house right away. It has little ponies with wings etched on the gates. They're pretty. I want some. If you go through the whole village, you'll see it."

"Has he been living here for a long time?"

"I can't remember." The half-wit scrunched up his brow, strenuously trying to recall. "A long time."

"Take it easy, friend," said the lean rider.

The strangers turned their horses. When they got to the road Pork's shout carried to them.

"Hey, misters! It's just that Pars can't shoot from the saddle. He's a carpenter!"

"Did you need to coddle him so, Whip?" petulantly asked the rider that Pork had dubbed young. "Why did you need to have that conversation with a half-wit? We could have asked anyone we met in the village."

"It's so kind of you to try to teach me. Anyone else we met wouldn't be an idiot. You couldn't have bribed them for a sol. You don't know villagers. They won't budge if they've decided they don't like your face, and then there's nothing you can do."

"We could tickle them with our knives."

"Well, then you would be the idiot, Shen," sneered Whip. "Four against how many? This is not the outlying towns of Al'sgara with our timid peasants. The locals here wouldn't jump at the sight of your blade and fawn over you. These places are savage. Every man can stand for himself. There's enough axes and clubs around here that you won't know what hit you. No little knife would save you."

"Well, then we could just check every home ourselves. We'd find him somewhere."

"Oh yes, very simple. Sixty households. How much time do you think we'd need to get that done?"

"An hour? Maybe two?"

"Exactly. And if we encounter some kind soul

who runs off and warns him about our arrival? And he decides he has nothing to say to us? What then? Do you want to go to Mols and offer excuses?"

This last argument completely drained the young man of his desire to quarrel. He petulantly pursed his lips and fell silent.

In the meantime the riders had crested the hill and caught sight of Dog Green. The village was situated along both banks of a narrow river. The idiot had led them astray—there were far more than sixty houses. To the right of the road was a small grave-yard, and just a bit farther on, a clear-cut area. On the farther shore there was a field, upon which encroached the gloomy wall of impenetrable forest. The village, lost on the edge of the province, had been carved out in a circle from the forests, low hills, and numerous ravines.

Whip's team had taken a long time to get here from Al'sgara. These last few days they had been forced to sleep beneath the open sky. For leagues around there was not a single inn. They had completely left behind tolerable food, wine, and women. All they had for company were mosquitoes and gadflies. Thank Melot that they hadn't encountered any forest spirits or goves (a species of lower demon) in the wilderness. They had kept to the road. True, even though no evil creatures had crawled out of the depths of the forest, wild animals had.

"Damn, but that blessed idiot didn't say which

shore we should search for our carpenter," said Bamut, the one who was ravaged by smallpox.

"We'll find him. The task's almost done. We've reached the end." Whip urged his horse forward.

His companions followed him without hesitation. They rode past the graveyard, which didn't even have a fence around it. They passed by a well, where two peasant women were cursing at each other, arguing over who would draw water first. And then they were in the western part of the village.

They were being eyed warily. Rarely were outsiders seen here, especially ones on horseback. But no one questioned them.

The riders found the inn quickly. The building stood out from the rest. It was large with a red chimney and ornamental doors. The innkeeper, having caught sight of potential lodgers, practically choked on his shaf. His eyes went so wide that Whip began to fear that he had suffered a stroke.

Whip had no doubt there would be spare rooms.

"We rarely have visitors here," hurriedly muttered the innkeeper as he pocketed the soren (a large gold coin) he'd received from the shortest of his guests. "Come in, please. Usually people just ride straight through to El'nichi Ford. We're out of the way here. Do you wish to eat something? We can get everything ready quickly, in no time at all."

"How do you even make a living? If you have so few guests, I mean?"

"There hasn't been anyone since midspring. We only survive thanks to the loggers. They come to drink shaf and wine. But only in the evenings. Right now there's no one here. There will be nothing to bother you. Come in, come in. Thank Melot, who sent you to my modest hearth!"

"Is there a blacksmith in your village? My horse has a limp," said Whip casually.

"Of course. Old Morgen. Go down the road, good sir. Then take a right, ride through the square until you get to the edge of the village. Right by the woods. You can't miss it."

Shen and Bamut exchanged significant glances and once again climbed into their saddles. Whip and the short one, who answered to the name of Midge, followed their example.

"Prepare rooms and supper for us," the eldest of the four said over his shoulder. "We'll be back soon."

The innkeeper hastened to assure the benevolent gentleman that everything would be done to the best of his ability, and then he ran off to execute the order. It didn't even enter his head to wonder why all four were going to the blacksmith when only one of their horses was lame.

"According to the half-wit, he's not far from the blacksmith."

"If he wasn't having us on," remarked Shen.

Whip chuckled. The kid was hoping that the fool had led them astray. That would indeed be an excellent confirmation that his commander had made a mistake.

In his dreams.

Whip didn't really understand why Mols had found it necessary to break up their tried and true threesome with a fourth. Shen was far too green to even be able to think. He acted first, and only afterward did he perceive the consequences. He was foolish. It wouldn't be long before he died as a result.

"If he was having us on, I'll go back and toss him in the river," replied Whip, trying not to show his annoyance. "Everywhere you go, you'll find an idiot who's willing to sell out the people closest to him."

They slowly rode along the street, attentively looking around. From under a fence a dirty, shaggy hound shot out with a high-pitched yipping. It didn't dare run after the horses, but it hurled invective at the riders until they had disappeared from its sight.

"Looks like we found it." Midge nodded toward the gates. "There are the ponies."

In point of fact, thin-legged horses with swan's wings were carved on the wooden doors. It was the house they were searching for. It was large, bright, and built out of pine logs.

"Well, you see there, Shen," said Whip with a smile. "Seems you should trust people sometimes. Including idiots."

The young man just twisted up his lips in response.

"Bamut, stay here. Keep an eye on the horses," ordered the leader of the team.

"Damn, but what if he slips out through the back?"

"You have such a bad opinion of our friend."

"Time changes people. Hey! Damn! Leave the crossbow!"

This last was directed at Shen, who was reaching for the weapon that was hanging off his saddle.

"Why should I?" he asked uncomprehendingly.

"Do as you're told," said Whip, in support of his comrade. "We came here to have a chat. Just a little chat. That thing could ruin everything."

"You're not afraid, are you, boys?"

"It's none of your business what we're afraid of and what we're not." Midge edged into the conversation. "It's your job to keep your mouth shut."

Shen had been getting on the shorter man's nerves for a while now. It was highly probable that sooner or later they would have a serious dustup and after the fight one of them would never get up again. Whip would put his money on Midge. He was experienced, cruel, and cunning, and he knew his business well. Only Mols knew how many souls that diminutive assassin had sent to Melot's bosom.

"Both of you shut up!" yelled Whip, seeing that the young man was not holding the crossbow as casually as before. "You can sort out this stupid quarrel when we get back to the city, if you still wish. But right now we have a common cause. There's no time for getting into a knife fight. I'm telling you right now, if you grapple with each other, you'll be booted out of the guild faster than Mols can think of your names. Do I make myself clear, you blockheads?"

"Yes," said Midge, taking his hand from his knife. "I got carried away."

"I understand," agreed Shen easily, handing over the crossbow to Bamut.

"Then let's do what we came here for. I'll be the one to talk. No sudden moves. Shen, that means you."

"Yeah, I get it! I get it. Why are you talking to me like I'm a child?"

"Because chopping cabbage with a sword is one thing, but talking shop with a gardener is something completely different."

Having said this, Whip opened the gate and walked into the yard, immediately catching sight of the man he was looking for.

Naked to the waist, the man was chopping firewood. Shen had heard about him from his associates, but he turned out to be completely different than he'd imagined. He'd thought he would be sturdy and strong, with large pectorals and massive fists. The man who was known as Gray in Al'sgara did not correspond to the image created in Shen's imagination at all. The man was not burly. And he didn't seem to be a hulking giant capable of decapitating a five-year-old bull with one swipe. There was nothing threatening about him. He was lank and wiry. He didn't have a single bit of excess fat, nor of bulging muscle, on him.

Shen had known people like this before. They didn't use force so much as the energy stored in the bands of sinew in their arms. A tough fellow. And probably as durable as a hundred Blazogs (a race of swamp dwellers). The heavy axe was practically flying through the air.

Just then the man stopped chopping and saw his guests. He narrowed his gray eyes and with a casual motion changed his grip on the axe. This gesture did not go unnoticed by the riders. Shen stiffened and slowed his pace. Midge quickly glanced to the side. Only Whip remained calm. He smiled; only his alert eyes spoke to the fact that the leader was drawn as tight as a loaded crossbow. He continued until he was five yards from the master of the house and then Mols's messenger stopped.

"Hello, Gray."

The man stayed defiantly silent for a moment, and then he replied, "Hello, Whip."

"How are things going?"

The carpenter grimaced angrily.

"Not bad. Until today."

Whip preferred not to notice the grimace on their host's lips.

"You've settled down really well. The wilderness,

the forest, the river, no city noise. And your house is excellent."

"I can't complain," came the dry answer. "What brings you here?"

"Business, of course. Can we talk?"

"That's strange. I thought that was exactly what we were doing."

"You won't invite us in?"

"It's messy in there," he replied sullenly.

Whip chuckled. "Six years have gone by, and you haven't changed a bit. You still hate having company."

"Seven, to be exact. Hey there, Midge."

"Hi, Ness. I didn't think I'd ever see you again. You disappeared quite cunningly."

Their host shrugged his shoulders.

"Seeing as you found me, not quite as cunningly as I'd hoped. I suppose that Bamut is waiting outside the gates?"

"You know him. The man has no love for house calls. Mols sends his regards."

"Good old Mols," drawled the carpenter. "It's hard to escape from him."

The master of the house took a step to the right and forward, going around the split wood, and Midge echoed his movement, taking a step backward. Unlike Shen, the diminutive assassin preferred to keep a distance between himself and their unsociable host. For the first time since the beginning of their conversation, Ness smiled knowingly. Then he planted his axe in the stump and dragged his fingers through his flaxen hair.

The tension lessened slightly.

Just then a tall young woman appeared on the porch. Her light, almost-white hair was held back in a tight braid, and she was wearing a long black skirt and a linen tunic. When she saw the strangers, her dark blue eyes flashed with rage, and her thin lips pressed into a straight line. A shadow ran across her face and Whip involuntarily reached for his pouch. He had a talisman blessed by a priest of Melot in there. He knew that the amulet would be of no help against her, but the foolish superstition proved stronger than his reason. Only at the very last moment did he restrain himself and remove his hand.

Now he had to keep an eye on both the man and the woman.

"Good day, Layen."

She ignored the greeting. She looked at her husband. He looked back at her in return. It seemed as if they were speaking with their eyes. Layen turned around and went back inside. Just before she closed the door, she cast the unwanted guests one last warning glance.

Midge let out a relieved breath. He'd been holding his breath the entire time the woman was on the porch.

"Didn't you used to work as a threesome?" Ness asked Whip.

"That we did," said the leader wryly, showing just

how pleased he was with the circumstances that had foisted a fourth upon him.

"All right, tell me why you've come," said their host, pulling on his shirt.

"Mols sends his regards."

"There's no way I'd believe that he sent you all this way just for the sake of a greeting."

Whip frowned.

"Not just for that. He sent me to tell you that they are offering five thousand sorens for your head. And just as much for Layen."

The carpenter remained unmoved. "Are you really here to aggravate me and tell me that Mols is that hard up?"

"No, he simply wanted to warn you. In remembrance of your old friendship."

"That's very kind of him. How did he find me?"

"How should I know? A little birdie whispered it in his ear. I'm told what to do—nothing more. The reward was offered about two weeks ago. There was a rumor that you were alive. It's pretty clear that they want to make a trophy out of you. And you must agree that it will be easy to find idiots willing to do anything for that kind of money."

"Quite so. If there's one thing in this world of ours that will never change, it's idiots. Midge, relax and get your hand off your knife."

"Sorry; habit," he apologized hastily, and as evidence of his peaceful intentions even stepped back toward the gates.

"So you understand that these whispers of so much money have not gone unnoticed. Your life is at risk."

"What else did my old friend wish to convey?"

"Not much else. It was Joch Threefingers who named the price."

Fire flashed in his gray eyes. And then it instantly faded.

"Well. Thank you for the news. Give Mols my thanks."

"Actually, he'd much prefer that you gave it to him personally."

"I've not been missing Al'sgara so much that I would return."

"It's dangerous here—all the rats know you. Don't flee. We're staying at the inn. We'll be there for five or six days. If you change your mind, let us know."

"An honorary escort?"

"Something like that. Take it easy."

Without saying a further word, Whip walked to the gates. Midge was the last to exit. True to form, he left walking backward.

2

I wasn't about to show them out. That would have been too great an honor. I stayed on the porch, watching as the runt closed the gate behind him. That fellow is truly repulsive. In the good old days in Al'sgara I'd had a face-off with him. At the time, it was Midge who had to step aside. But that doesn't mean that he recognized my right to take the best contracts. Far from it. It was nothing more than a temporary, forced retreat. And now, despite all the years that have passed, I could expect trouble from him at any moment. I will not turn my back on him.

The unexpected arrival of my former business associates had made quite an impression on me. The Damned take them! Until now I had thought us impossible to find. Five years of moving from place to place and all of it in vain!

We hadn't lingered anywhere for long, and we didn't allow ourselves to become acquainted with anyone, let alone befriend them. We held ourselves stiller than the water under the grass. Layen and I knew that regardless of the fact that we were long dead to all, they would keep looking for us. Especially in the first two years.

We successfully avoided the roundups. At that

time the Guards, the Viceroy's soldiers, and the Walkers' people were searching for a man and a woman. Twice they all but caught us, and twice we escaped by the skin of our teeth. Then, when the worst was over, we kept being cautious. Thus another three years passed. Subsequently, believing that everyone had forgotten about us, I brought Layen to the very outskirts of the Empire. To the south. Beyond the Blazgian swamps. To the forest.

We had spent two tranquil and happy years in this village. Neither my wife nor myself was especially overjoyed to live in such a godforsaken place, but we needed to bide our time, wait it out a little longer, and then head to the sea and try to find passage on a boat of some kind. To sail off somewhere even farther away.

And now, just when I had begun counting the days until our departure, the past, from which we had so long and successfully run, was insensitive enough to just show up at our door. It passes all understanding how they could have found us after we'd run like jackrabbits, twisting our trail so the hounds wouldn't catch us.

It's laughable!

That which the spies of the Walkers could not accomplish, that old buzzard Mols had pulled off with ease. How? How, the Abyss take me, had he found us out?

The door swung open and Layen sat down next

to me. We were silent for a time. We just listened as Whip's associates climbed up onto their horses and rode away from the house.

"What do you think?" I asked my wife.

"They speak the truth—you can't run from the past; sooner or later it will catch up with you. We have maybe a week, but no more. Then it will be too risky to stay here."

"It's too bad we'll have to leave all this. It's a good house."

And I really did think it was too bad. It's funny. All the time I was dreaming about leaving this hellhole, but now the time has come and I am loath to just abandon it. After all, I'd built this house with my own hands.

"These past few years have turned you into a real homebody, my dear," she said, grinning. "You weren't like this before."

"You were different, too," I said, copying her grin. "The time has come to get back on the road."

"Mols could be lying. He's wanted to send Threefingers off to the Blessed Gardens for a long time. And here we are at hand, fortunately for him. There's nothing we can do but remove the client. And that's exactly what Mols is counting on. Whip didn't tell you that he was waiting for your thanks personally for nothing."

"We'll have to get rid of Joch, that's true. But will that really help us? If those who are searching for us are lying in wait, it won't do any good. They won't let us live in peace."

Layen frowned and rested her head on my shoulder. My sun understood who I was talking about, who might still be searching for us. The very same people who were searching for us when we faked our deaths and left Al'sgara behind forever seven years ago. . . .

It was already the second day that the snow had been falling. Massive white flakes dropped continuously from the low gray sky. They settled on the bridges, on the squares, on the trees, on the watchtowers, on the market stalls, on the red tiled roofs, on the spires of Melot's temple, and on the hoods of the people walking by. Al'sgara the Green, as the capital of the southern province of the Empire was called, had been transformed into Al'sgara the White.

The children were overjoyed at the fresh snow. For everyone else it was just an inconvenience. It was the start of spring, but the snow was pouring down just as if it was the Feast of the Moon (an important religious holiday celebrated in the middle of winter). Such truly awful weather!

I cursed inwardly and rubbed my gloved hands together. My fingers were beginning to go numb. Cold ruled supreme in the attic where I had been loitering for the past three hours. Admittedly, there was nothing surprising about this. The glass was missing from the window and an icy wind was blowing through the attic. Yet another inconvenience was added to this—darkness. The meager light streaming in from the evening street was no help at all. But I didn't dare light a candle. Of course, the chance that some passerby would see the flame was not all that great, but it wouldn't do to risk it.

Damn it! This damn cold! I began rubbing my hands against each other more strenuously, but the tips of my fingers still refused to get warm. It's a good thing that this really wasn't the middle of cruel winter. Otherwise I would have already dropped dead.

I cautiously looked out onto the street. And cursed again. It would be fully dark in half an hour but the target was still nowhere to be seen. She was an hour late. The bell on the Overgate Tower of Hightown (the oldest part of Al'sgara; it was built on the Cliff, as that part of the city used to be called, around which the rest of the city subsequently expanded) rang twice. It was nine o'clock. Damn it. Where is she? Where? I realized I was getting nervous.

It's no wonder. The purse Layen and I had scored for this was rather large. Fifteen thousand sorens in denominations of five-hundred-soren gold Imperials—an insane amount. That kind of money had never been offered for just one person's head. Not even for a Viceroy. Such a contract was worth all the possible consequences. We decided to risk it.

True, we'd have to take care of today's business and disappear forever, but with that kind of money (which, incidentally, had been paid up front), we wouldn't have a care in the world.

When I had told Layen about the proposal, received from an unknown client, she did not bother trying to dissuade me from the risky venture. She realized that I'd already taken the bait. She heard me out without speaking and then stood up just as silently and left the room, gently closing the door behind her. She returned after an hour. I do not know where she was that whole time. By her reddened eyes I could see that she had been crying but it would not do to ask her about it. She hated it when someone witnessed any weakness in her. So I pretended that I didn't notice anything.

Layen sat down at the table, took me by the hand, and nodded. My sun was still with me. And that meant that we could take on the job. Without her participation the contract wouldn't be worth a Blazog's empty eggshell. They'd drag me out feet-first.

The view from the attic was dreadful. I couldn't see much, only a small space just in front of the exit from the square and what was located directly below the window. I knew that I would have to shoot from this extremely awkward position. I'd barely be able to see the target.

Anyone who had even the slightest understanding of archery would say that constructing a "nest" in such a place was absurd. That's precisely why I chose this spot. When the chaos starts, all the attention of the security will turn to the bell tower and the house of the wealthy nobleman standing opposite it—you could arrange a truly excellent ambush there. And it would be very convenient. But it wasn't worth sitting in such an ambush because you could only leave it in one direction, and that led to the cemetery. And in my opinion, I'm still too young to be sent there.

Ness?

Layen had been silent for more than an hour and her voice resounding in my head caused me to flinch.

I'm here, I answered her mentally.

The target isn't. I'm worried. If she doesn't arrive within the next fifteen minutes I think we should leave.

I see.

I frowned in vexation. She was right. The chance of missing the shot in the dark was far too great. And I couldn't miss. It needed to be a clean shot. A single shot. There simply wouldn't be time for a second.

Warmth ran along my spine in a tender stream and I relaxed my tense muscles. I exhaled gratefully and leaned against the wall. My mate, who was located at the far end of the street, knew when to comfort me.

Layen possessed the Gift, although she was neither an Ember nor a Walker. She had the ability to speak over a distance with anyone. But this was not the limit of her abilities, even though no one knew about most of Weasel's other talents besides me.

How she had been able to kindle her "spark" without the help of the Walkers—this was something I did not understand. I did not want to ask about her past, and she never initiated such conversations. It is possible that it was too dark, and that it would do no good for me to crawl into her soul. I swear with everything I am, that it didn't matter to me who she had been before. So I simply told myself that it was an established fact—Layen has the Gift and that's that. I knew that I loved her and that I could trust her. We were not just friends and partners, but also family. No one but Mols had any idea about the latter, but he never asked about it as he wasn't one to pry into other people's private business.

She's here! I see her. Get ready.

I calmly took off my warm gloves and tucked them into my belt. I put on the ones I used for shooting. Then I picked up my one-hundred-and-eighty-pound (the draw weight of the bowstring) bow. Resting the bottom limb to the ground, I leaned on the upper limb and, holding my breath, forced the string into place. I had shot this monstrosity over a week ago and easily managed to pierce an oak plank from a distance of two hundred yards. It's too bad that I'd have to leave it behind. But after the assassination it would be utter stupidity to walk about on the street with it.

I'm ready.

They're coming down the street. Quickly. They'll be near you in a minute.

Got it.

On my signal.

I nodded and then immediately realized that Layen couldn't see me.

She's got six with her. Two Embers and four of the Viceroy's Guards. Two have crossbows.

I'm more worried about the Embers.

A warm wave once again rushed through me.

Don't worry. I'll take care of them.

I chuckled. Layen had the most difficult job—she had to overwhelm the sorceresses, to take away the protection they afforded the target. Not for long. Just for three, perhaps even four seconds. Just enough time for me to take the shot.

Suddenly the falling snowflakes swirled. A moment later their speed and direction changed. The northwest wind had replaced the north wind. This was not good.

The wind changed. Layen was also keeping track of the changing conditions. *Northwest. Gusts. A quarter of a finger.*

A quarter of a finger. That's even worse. I'd need to aim slightly off and pray to Melot that when I shot, the fickle elements did not act up. It's a good thing the bow wasn't weak and that the arrow was heavy.

I see. I'm aware. Thanks.

Twenty seconds. They're near the treasurer's house. Walking toward you.

I tried to even out my breathing. Exhale, inhale. This is a normal shot. Nothing more. I've been shooting with a bow for as long as I can remember. I spent the war in Sandon. And in war everything is far more complicated. At least here no one would run at me with a sword. I just needed to sight, aim, and do what we had been paid for.

Grabbing the arrow that had a white arrowhead made of some material I was unfamiliar with, I quickly examined the fletching. Was it crooked?

The client's man had given me the arrow along with the compensation. When Layen saw it she refused to pick it up. All she said was that such devices were created to kill the foundation of the Gift in people, to extinguish their spark and to destroy the very soul of the mage. I'd felt uneasy about this "present" from the beginning. But using the arrow was a nonnegotiable term of the contract. I had to clench my teeth and accept it. But I had no idea how it would behave in flight.

We'll meet in Haven (a neighborhood of Al'sgara next to the sea), *where we agreed. If I don't come after an hour, leave without me.*

You know very well that I won't go anywhere without you!

We were intending to leave the city, but not in the way the client had planned. There was far too great a chance that he or she would decide to kill off the people who had done the dirty work. Layen had come up with her own plan and was now prepared to put it into motion. Only she and I knew where we were going after the task. For everyone else, Gray and Weasel would just disappear. They would die.

I rested the arrow on the bowstring and did not take my eyes away from the snow-covered street. Twilight. The idiot lamplighters are late again. Damn it! I need light right now!

The wind's still moving to the northwest. Half a finger. After a minute it will change to the north.

I'll keep that in mind.

Good luck. There they are!

And then I saw them. A group of people walking quickly toward Sacrum Square. In the front were two Guardsmen, followed by a woman. Then two more people behind her. The procession was tailed by a pair of soldiers.

The tip of the arrow suddenly gleamed with a purple light. I almost dropped it.

Layen! The arrow is glowing!

Don't worry. It senses the spark of the target. One hundred and five yards.

Don't worry? If they got it into their heads to look over in my direction I could forget about luck.

Which one of them? The first one?

Ninety-five yards. No. The second to the left.

Are you sure?

Yes. Listen to me. The one in the sable coat. Ninety. As soon as I say. . . .

I watched the small female form in the sable coat. They were approaching the minimum distance but I didn't shoot. It was a bad angle. After a moment the second woman obstructed my view of the victim.

Ninety-five . . . one hundred . . . one hundred and five . . .

She was walking farther and farther away from me. Another twenty seconds and the nearby house would block my view.

To the north. A quarter of a finger. A wagon is coming toward you. It will hide the target in eight seconds. Wait. One hundred and ten.

I watched her back as it withdrew. But I fully trusted Layen's instincts. There was the wagon. A moment and it was gone.

One hundred and fifteen. . . . Now!

Years of training took hold. I acted without thinking. I raised the bow up, drew explosively (a shot from a powerful bow generally has to be made without a long pause while holding the string taut and aiming. Because of the great force of the tension the shot proceeds like a so-called explosion since both hands jerk away from each other) and shot.

Twang!

I immediately jumped back from the window to the wall, having noticed that the arrow darting toward its target was leaving behind a purple trail.

Layen acted simultaneously with me. Of course, I didn't feel anything but I knew that the protection of the unsuspecting Embers had been crushed.

Thwack!

For a moment the street was illuminated with the purple light. The arrow had found its target.

Boom! Boom! Boom!

The din from outside made it clear that the Embers had recovered and were striking out at random. Layen was quiet, fearing that now the sorceresses might be able to hear our silent communication. I hoped with all my heart that my sun had already fled.

I dropped the bow and, slipping off my gloves as I ran, fled from the attic. I descended to the second floor by way of a rickety ladder. I opened a door and entered the room I had rented out earlier, where I changed quickly into an apprentice baker's smock that was lying on top of a loaf of fresh bread. I did not neglect to rub my clothes and hands with flour.

As I walked, I bit off a chunk of bread and, chewing, opened the window that led out onto the backyard. Having measured off the distance, I leaped onto the shed. From there I dropped down into a snowbank. I stood up and looked around.

The yard was empty. I ran up to the low fence, easily hopped over it, and passed through a breezeway that emerged into a narrow alley. And then, without any undue haste, I strolled away. I could hear shouts, muffled by the distance, coming from Rukovits.

From my spot all I could see was the looming bell tower. Or more precisely, what remained of it. The

Embers had gone berserk and, without pausing to think, were focusing their magics along the upper floors of the nearest buildings, hoping to wound the assassin.

Well then. It's a good thing I made my nest in a less noticeable spot, otherwise I would have been flattened. By the time they understood the what and the how, Layen and I would be far away, and our alleged corpses would be found burnt to a crisp in the old hideout of Jola and Ktatak. I hope my friends will forgive us for burning up one of their storehouses.

I left the scene with brisk strides.

"I'll get ready," Layen sighed, and stood up from the steps.

I shook my head, banishing the recollections. Seven years have gone by, but I remember it as if it were yesterday.

"Yes. You're right. We'd best ditch the village by tomorrow evening. I won't be able to pick up the money."

"I'll fetch it. But I'll do it tomorrow."

"Alone? Are you sure you'll manage?"

"Quite sure. Will we tell Whip?"

Whip was not a bad man, but it would not do to stay too close to him.

"No."

I frowned. I really didn't like the idea of her going

into the forest alone. But only she could get at the money. That was the truth.

"And if he figures it out and decides to keep us company?"

I considered the alternatives and declared, "It would be better for him if he didn't find out."

Layen smiled tightly and went back inside the house.

3

Ga-Nor leaned toward his captain's ear and softly whispered, "I don't like this."

The shaggy-haired Da-Tur said nothing in reply. Ta-Ana answered for him, "The whole time we've been cooling our heels here, not a single one of those six men has budged. They sure sleep soundly!"

The Children of the Snow Leopard (one of the clans of the northern part of the Empire) were crouched on a low rocky ledge. Below them a small fire was burning, around which lay their adversaries, bundled up in tattered blankets. The cautious highlanders usually set a watch, but this time they hadn't. And this fact did not sit well with the squad's tracker. One might have thought that Ga-Nor had overlooked an ambush, but the captain of the redheaded soldiers would sooner chop off his own hand than believe that his blood brother could have missed a warning sign.

The uncertainty was throwing him off balance. Da-Tur thought yet again that their reconnaissance mission was cursed. The northerners who served at the Gates of the Six Towers knew the gorges and trails of the Boxwood Mountains like the backs of their own hands. They were the best scouts in the Empire. No enemy patrol could possibly slip through the mountain passes unobserved while the Children of the Snow Leopard watched over them.

When Da-Tur's ten had left the Gates of Six Towers, they hadn't thought they would encounter any trouble. Everything had been quiet as the squad descended into the valley beyond the primary ridge. But every settlement, every square inch of land had been swarming with Nabatorian soldiers. And then Ta-Ana had noticed the white robe of a Sdisian in their midst. The scouts returned back the way they had come without hesitation. They had to report what they had seen to the commander of the Gates as soon as possible.

On the return trip, in one of the gloomy ravines, they had been attacked by a mountain gove. They had acted foolishly. They should have bypassed the old watchtower that had been abandoned by the Empire's soldiers back during the War of the Necromancers (fought over five hundred years before the events described here, after the Dark Revolt of the Damned. After the war the Empire gave up the lands that lay beyond the Gates of Six Towers and, having retreated across the mountain range, began a war with the Highborn for the forests of Uloron and Sandon). But the northerners were in a hurry, so they decided to cut their journey short and they did not take the detour. And so it was that they chanced upon the ravenous creature, which had just emerged from its summer hibernation. Only three of them survived: Da-Tur, Ga-Nor, and Ta-Ana. Seven Children of the Snow Leopard remained forever in that narrow gorge.

Ga-Nor, a tall, tanned man with red mustaches, raised himself up on his elbows and looked below. He contracted his bushy eyebrows. It really was strange that the highlanders hadn't bothered to set up a watch.

Nothing. No movement at all. There was no sound except for a distant measured droning—a mountain river thundering through the shallows. There was no cause for alarm. If this was an ambush, it was very skillfully done. But skillful ambushes were beneath the dignity of the impatient highlanders. In any case, the Chus, as they called themselves, could not lie still for so long unless they were dead.

Suddenly Da-Tur understood.

"I swear by the hide of an ice demon! They're dead!" he said, stunned.

"Let's get out of here," whispered Ta-Ana, marveling at herself. She had never been afraid of corpses, but everything that was happening right now seemed strange. "We shouldn't disturb their souls."

Ga-Nor nodded grimly and backed up the archer. "Dawn is still a long ways off. We can cover a lot of ground."

Da-Tur stood up quietly, walked along the rocky ledge for about ten yards, getting as far away from the fire as possible, and then jumped down below. His comrades followed him. Glancing backward, they tried to hurry away.

A green glow suddenly flared up on the western side of the twin-peaked mountain. It turned into a ball of fire, which soared up into the sky in a steep arc, paused for a moment at its highest point, and then fell toward the spot where the carcasses of the Chus were lying. It burst soundlessly when it hit the ground, scattering emerald flames in every direction.

"A Sdisian sorcerer!"

This was an ambush, and it was made just for them. The White, the one Ta-Ana had spotted among the Nabatorians, had probably noticed the interlopers and decided to intercept them. Why risk letting the garrison at the Towers be forewarned?

"Let's go! Quickly!"

Da-Tur could feel it in his gut as danger flooded into the ravine. He really hoped that the trap that had been set had not yet snapped shut and that there was a chance they could escape the necromancer's grasping fingers.

"Look out! Behind you!" shouted the archer, who was standing on the ledge.

The captain of the squad turned around and recoiled. He swore loudly. The corpses scattered around the bonfire were standing up. Ga-Nor pulled his sword from his back. These creatures were surprisingly agile. The northerners barely had time to prepare for the fight.

Two set upon Da-Tur, and yet another one engaged the red-mustachioed Ga-Nor, but the last four headed straight for Ta-Ana at a brisk trot. The woman let loose an arrow into the face of one of the magical creations, but it had no effect.

The deformed faces shining in the moonlight, the bared teeth and the eyes burning with green fire would terrify anyone. Da-Tur pierced the chest of one of the Chus but it made no impression on his opponent. Ga-Nor, who had dispatched his adversary, ran to his aid.

"Cut off its head!" barked the tracker, deftly striking at the nearest corpse's legs.

The captain spun about, split the skull of the Sdisian's servant in half, and lunged forward to help the woman. After a minute everything was over.

The two men were panting heavily. Ta-Ana pulled an arrow from a stilled corpse with trembling hands. Da-Tur grabbed the small archer by the scruff of her neck and lifted her from her knees to her feet.

"To Ug with your damned arrow! We've got to

try to get out of this ravine and lose ourselves in the mountains."

They were racing along a stream, ghosting across the wet stones, their feet barely touching the ground. The ravine had turned into a narrow canyon, and the canyon walls shut out the sky. The moon was obstructed by clouds, and they had to run under the light of the stars. In the darkness all that could be heard was the heavy breathing of the scouts, the murmur of the stream, and the ever-increasing rumble of an unnamed river. After an eternity Da-Tur ordered a halt. Ga-Nor dropped down right where he stood and pressed his ear to the ground.

"No one," the tracker breathed out finally, rising up from the stones. "They're driving us into a trap, brother. There's no escaping it."

He was right. Only a mongoose could scale such steep cliffs. If they cut off the entrance and exited to the canyon, they would not escape.

"If we could get to the river," Ta-Ana put in hopefully, "we could get away by the water."

"We'll get there," said Da-Tur, his eyes glinting resolutely.

The current along the shore was strong, and they emerged from the water with difficulty. Only people ready to commit suicide or the Children of the Snow Leopard would dare swim in the dark through such a swift, icy mountain river. The former would crack their skulls against the shoals, but the latter pulled through. The soldiers had swum for more than half an hour and, thanks to the swiftness of the current, had left the danger far behind.

They collapsed upon the river stones, catching their breath. However, Ta-Ana immediately pulled herself up into a squat and pushed her hair out of her face. Then she attached a new, dry string to her yew bow, opened up a large wallet made of leather, and unfolded the oiled paper where she kept her arrows. The archer understood that without her bow things would go poorly for her and her comrades.

Ga-Nor had swallowed water while they were swimming and was now coughing it up.

The wind drove away the clouds, the moon emerged anew, and the northerners beheld the bleached and majestic ruins of an ancient city. People had abandoned the mountain capital of this former Imperial province when the War of the Necromancers began. Since then more than five hundred years had passed. No one had ever returned to live in Gerka, the City of a Thousand Columns, as travelers called it. The centuries had transformed this former pearl of the highlands into a dead kingdom of cold wind. It came here every evening from the snowcapped heights and mournfully wailed through the ruins of the ancient buildings. This place was known as a ghost town. The highlanders detoured around its borders and did not rest for the night if there was a distance of less than a league between them and its white walls.

But the northerners weren't superstitious. The way through Gerka was five times shorter than any other. At the southernmost tip of the city a trail commenced, and that trail led to a pass, and from there it was no distance at all to the Gates.

They passed through a tall arch that had once been the main gate, and came out onto a wide street. Wherever they looked there were crumbling houses and hundreds of marble columns stretching toward the sky. The moonlight sparkled on them, enlivening them, making them seem as dazzlingly beautiful as they had been in those years when life teemed here. The silver-blue light gleamed in the gaps of the empty street, the old buildings cast dark shadows, and faint bluish wisps of incipient fog crept along the time-ravaged pavement.

Gerka stared impassively at the outsiders from the gloomy ruins of her buildings. She had no care for who came to her or why. She only sang her song with the wind. The wind was her eternal friend, but people always left and betrayed her. She had no desire to take vengeance on them for their treachery; she only desired one thing—to be left in peace. So the once great city let the three warriors from the far north pass through her without inflicting any harm on them.

Just as she would let those who followed after the redhaired warriors pass through.

The trail skirted the edge of a precipice. To the left of it was a basalt wall. To the right—a chasm. The scouts had been climbing for more than an hour already, and the valley that held the City of a Thousand Columns was far below. Da-Tur kept casting his eyes up at the faint stars. Dawn was not far off. By the time it arrived they needed to be at the pass, or better yet, beyond it.

Inhospitable, biting, icy wind; snow on the path. The pass was just a stone's throw away. The night had robbed them of all their strength, and they were tired, but they continued to move forward doggedly. Ga-Nor repeatedly stopped and looked back. He didn't really believe that they'd succeeded in deceiving the necromancer.

Ahead of them, a figure appeared on the path. Against the background of the rapidly brightening sky and the white stain of the snow only his silhouette was visible—tall, compact, wide-shouldered. He was walking from the direction of the pass. He was not hurrying, but ambling, as if he were out for a stroll.

Ta-Ana was in the lead. She took aim.

"May a snow gove take me! Who is that?" said the archer nervously, biting her lips.

"I don't know," replied Da-Tur tensely. "No one

but the servants of the White could be here. In the leg."

The woman smiled wolfishly and pulled back her bowstring. The stranger was almost upon them. Ga-Nor strained his sight and saw that the entire body of the man was covered in scaled armor.

"Don't shoot! It's a Fish!" he shouted at the exact same moment that Ta-Ana let loose her arrow.

An earsplitting crash rang out.

The stranger burst like an overripe melon. A warm shock of stinking air threw Ga-Nor, who had not been holding on to anything, into the chasm. Ta-Ana was also unlucky. As soon as the thing exploded hundreds of sharp metal scales flew from it in every direction. At least ten of them sliced through the woman, killing her on the spot.

Da-Tur had been standing by the wall, and it was only because of this that he did not fall below. One of the scales grazed his head, another left a deep cut along his forearm. The air stank of burnt flesh, hair, and something else. Something strange. Something repulsive.

On shaky legs the northerner walked over to Ta-Ana and fell to his knees beside her. He felt sick; blood was flowing down his arm. His head felt like it was splitting. Chunks of flesh that had very recently belonged to that deadly creature were scattered all around.

It was already light out, but still he was kneeling over the body of the woman. Finally he woke from his stupor, ripped his clan scarf from his neck, and wrapped it around the wound on his arm. He planted his sword into the ground, rested his weight upon it, jumped to his feet with a jerk, and . . . came face-to-face with three Morts.

They were ghastly, bony creatures, with long arms and legs, slender necks, and lustrous skulls. Sleek ebony skin stretched tightly over their protruding bones. Their amber eyes seemed to flash above the dark pits where their severed noses should be. They wore no armor at all. They held skeem-swords in their hands. They were the necromancer's body-guards, come to fetch their trophy.

Da-Tur roared and raised his blade, planning to sell his life dearly. The path was so narrow that his enemies could only come at him one at a time. This gave him a chance, if not to live, then to draw it out for as long as possible.

The redhead dealt with the first of his opponents quickly, despite its skill, by seizing the moment and simply tossing it into the chasm. Then he sprang forward, swinging his sword in a backward arc, forcing his enemies to retreat.

From somewhere below an all-too-familiar ball of green light came flying upward. It burst apart behind his back. The sorcerer was below, in the valley, by the exit from Gerka, and it would take him a long time to reach the Son of the Snow Leopard. By that time Da-Tur would have already won or lost.

A Mort lunged for his neck with his blades crossed

like scissors, but Da-Tur dropped down and impaled the creature through its chest. He kicked at the body, freeing his blade and . . . choking on his own blood, fell onto his side.

At first he did not understand what had happened. He tried to get up but he couldn't. For some reason his legs weren't obeying him. Ta-Ana was standing over him. Her eyes were blazing with green fire.

When they had stumbled upon the Fish, Ga-Nor was the one standing closest to the edge. This circumstance actually saved him. As the explosion unfolded, the northerner was tumbling down below and so managed to escape being shredded by the steel scales.

He didn't fall very far. His journey into the chasm was cut short by a most welcome white cedar. The dense, tenacious boughs of the atrophied little tree, which had driven its roots right into the cliff, took the force of the falling human body unto themselves and snapped. But they saved the Son of the Snow Leopard. Two yards below the cedar there was a narrow ledge. It was there that Ga-Nor's fall came to an end. A fall from such a height onto a hard surface should have broken Ga-Nor's bones, but thanks to the tree he only lost consciousness.

When the tracker regained consciousness, he let out a low groan. He opened his eyes and lay there, trying to figure out where he was. The sun was at its zenith. Quite a bit of time had passed since their encounter with the Fish. The memory of the sorcerer's creature caused him to cautiously move his arms and legs to check if they were still whole. Everything was in working order.

It didn't take him long to figure out where he had fallen. Ga-Nor gave sincere thanks to Ug for his survival. If not for this ledge, beaten into the cliff by wind and rain, the northerner would have fallen and fallen. And from this height the City of a Thousand Columns seemed no larger than his palm.

Ga-Nor examined the cliff closely and came to a disappointing conclusion. There were, of course, plenty of cracks, but he wouldn't be able to stick his fingers in them. Just a bit higher was the cedar with its broken branches. If he could grab it with his belt, he might be able to reach it. But would the roots be able to take his weight? Unlikely. And even if he did manage to climb up there, what then? He still wouldn't be able to get to the trail.

There was nowhere to go from this bird's ledge. Going up was impossible, and you'd only go down if you wanted to end your own life. So he'd meet death alone with the mountain wind, the sky, and hunger.

The tracker tried not to think about what might have happened to his comrades. Ta-Ana had been standing closer than any of them to the Fish; it's unlikely she managed to survive. Da-Tur, even if he'd remained whole, would most likely assume his kinsman had perished. If so, his blood brother was probably already beyond the pass and on his way to the Gates of Six Towers.

During the fall, Ga-Nor had lost his sword and all he had left was his dagger. If he had two of them, the northerner would not hesitate to climb the wall with them. He'd performed similar feats before, and once he'd even climbed up the sheer wall of the Tower of Rain on a bet. But there was no point in dreaming of getting to the top with just one dagger. It'd be easier to sprout wings.

The entire day passed by in fruitless efforts to find a way out of this trap. Ga-Nor paced his little platform from edge to edge but it was all in vain. Curses and prayers were no help.

Toward evening, when there was not more than an hour left until sunset, the tracker was leaning against the wall, picking up stones lying around him and chucking them into the chasm. Realizing the hopelessness of his situation, he was numbly counting the remaining days Ug had given him. He figured that he'd suffer quite a bit before he died of starvation. It was a chilling prospect.

His emotions got the better of him and the northerner began to swear. Loudly. And as he expected, nothing happened. Then he felt a shower of dust and small pebbles come down on his head and the nape of his neck. Ga-Nor leapt to his feet, fearing a potential rockslide. But nothing of the sort happened. The northerner gazed upward tensely and waited.

Finally, pebbles showered down on him again, and then a few slightly larger stones. All the signs pointed to the fact that someone was walking up there. At this point the Son of the Snow Leopard couldn't care less whether it was friend or foe. Forty was too young an age to die like a winter squirrel caught in a snare. It would be far better to die by an enemy's blade and have a little vacation with Ug than to turn into a pale ghost.

"Hey!" he yelled with all his strength. "Hey! I'm here! Down here!"

At first no one answered. But then he saw a person looking down at him from above. Drawn by his cries, the stranger had lain down on the edge of the trail, peering down into the precipice. Ga-Nor wanted to shout yet again, this time from joy, but then he examined the stranger more closely and the shout stuck in his throat. He knew that face. Neither dirt nor blood could change it. The sharp jaw, the shaggy red hair, the scar on his brow. Da-Tur. But his upper lip was twisted into an evil grimace, baring his straight white teeth, and his eyes . . . his eyes were green.

The creature who had been his blood brother stared at him unflinchingly. Without taking his gaze from the corpse, the northerner reached for his dagger and this served as a signal. The corpse, bristling with the enchantment of the Sdisian, pounced on Ga-Nor. Splaying his arms and legs like a spider he fell to the spot where the soldier had just been.

The sound the body made as it met the ledge caused the Son of the Snow Leopard, who was long accustomed to both death and blood, to shiver violently. It seemed like the crunch of the bones could be heard even in the Golden Mark. Despite the broken ribs protruding through both flesh and clothes, the shattered arms and the right leg that was sticking out of its socket at an unnatural angle, the dead man tried to get up.

Ga-Nor did not hesitate. Pulling out his dagger he slipped behind the creation of the Sdisian sorcerer and grabbed hold of its bloodstained red mane, pulling the head of the dead man back and cutting open its neck with one swift motion. The weapon made a vile sound as it scraped across the creature's vertebrae. The tracker stopped only when the green light faded from Da-Tur's eyes.

Breathing heavily, he took his prize—a broad dagger—from the twice-dead body and with his foot he pushed the corpse over the precipice. Ga-Nor was not going to risk having that thing next to him. The Son of the Snow Leopard did not feel any regret over his actions. Da-Tur was long dead, his soul in Ug's halls, and the thing that remained in this world was only a shell subject to the Sdisian's whims.

The sun had almost reached the mountain peak and long shadows were covering the valley below. Ga-Nor quickly began his climb.

It was all much simpler than he had expected; the northerner easily found holds with the help of the daggers. He saw a crack, drove the dagger into it, pulled himself up by one arm, planted the second knife just a bit higher, and pulled himself up again. Over and over again. The Son of the Snow Leopard had no fear of heights and he was slowly but surely coming closer to the edge that would be his salvation. When no more than two yards remained until he reached it, the tracker paused and allowed himself a short rest. The top part of the cliff was far more difficult than all that had come before. The cracks were smaller. And the wind had picked up, too, threatening to blow him into the chasm.

Ga-Nor reached the very top just as darkness fell. Recalling Da-Tur's fate he cautiously raised his head over the edge. Allowing his eyes to get accustomed to the darkness, he studied the area thoroughly. No one there. Wheezing in relief, he rolled over the edge and immediately sprung to his feet, menacingly clutching a dagger in each hand.

There were neither corpses nor Sdisian sorcerers. It was empty. Quiet. Ta-Ana's body was nowhere to be found. That caused his hackles to rise. The tracker peered intently into the darkness, prepared to do battle, but no one attacked him. Whatever had become of the archer, she wasn't here.

Ga-Nor saw Da-Tur's sword lying right there on the trail. He picked it up and set off at a brisk pace for the pass, looking around constantly. The Son of the Snow Leopard had not yet given up hope of reaching the Towers and warning the commander. Perhaps it was not too late.

Before the War of the Necromancers the lands of the Empire stretched into Nabator itself and did not end at the Boxwood Mountains. All of what was now called the Borderlands had been part of the Empire. Cities and villages grew up in the valleys through which the trade routes wended their way. But everyday life shattered when the Damned appeared. From that point onward, these lands were abandoned by the Empire. Their dark fame spread too wide. Only the highlanders dared to live in the cheerless, cold valleys.

The people left, but the cities like Gerka remained. Eight of the Spires, watchtowers built by the Sculptor himself, were also abandoned. Only the ninth, dubbed the Alert Tower, was still used by the armies of the Empire. The ancient books tell that the Sculptor carved out these towers at the same time he created the legendary Gates. Soaring upward of sixty yards in height, constructed of black stone, with a multitude of arrow loops, they had stood for a thousand years.

From the outside you would never be able to tell that the last Spire in use had experienced many wars over the years. It looked exactly as it had the day its construction was finished. It seemed fragile and lovely, as if the Sculptor had not been a human, but a Je'arre. Some people said that the legendary master took a flow of mountain air into his hands and fashioned it into this shape of celestial beauty. And then he turned that air into stone.

In the stories told to us by our elders, it was said that until the War of the Necromancers, the watchmen in the towers could easily converse with their colleagues who were located in the other eight Spires. Perhaps there was an element of truth in these stories, but at the present time they seemed like fairy tales.

There were similar whispers that there was a vault under the tower, sealed nowadays, where the Paths of Petals slumber. Through them, a soldier could instantly travel to the Spire that required his assistance. But this too became legend long ago. The Walkers can no longer control the Petals.

The Sculptor built the Alert Tower not far from the road that led to two passes. Ga-Nor reached it at midday. From a distance, the tracker could see that there were dozens of vultures circling over the cliffs beyond which the Alert Tower was located. The Son of the Snow Leopard stopped and frowned. To an attentive man, such a congregation of scavengers spoke volumes.

The reality confirmed his worst fears. A gallows had been constructed in front of the Spire, and three dead men in the uniform of Imperial soldiers were dangling from it. All the rest were scattered below the walls; they hadn't even found the time to bury them. Replete with the meat of the fresh corpses, the vultures were shrieking nastily at one another, fighting over the tastiest morsels.

The tower had new masters.

Nabatorians.

Ga-Nor hid behind some rocks and studied his enemies. What had happened was beyond his comprehension. Apparently a detachment of enemy troops had slipped through the pass and slaughtered the watchmen. The last part didn't really surprise Ga-Nor. In former times, two hundred of the most select soldiers had served here, but recently the commander of the Gates had been sending about twenty. And sometimes not even that many.

The long years of peace had given them the impression of security. And as usual, it was a false impression.

And now it had come to a head. The watchmen had been caught unawares. They hadn't even managed to raise the alarm. Twenty soldiers had no chance whatsoever against a hundred well-trained black-haired warriors.

The Nabatorians were making themselves at home and had already begun to settle into the Spire. That could only mean one thing—they weren't expecting any danger from the direction of the Gates. What had happened to the fortress?

Ga-Nor stopped losing himself in speculation when cavalry appeared on the southern road. The northerner began to count, but he gave up at six hundred. A large squadron of pikemen and crossbowmen passed by next. Apparently, an entire army was gathering beneath the walls of the citadel. Ga-Nor wondered what the King of Nabator was expecting. The Gates were not so easy to take.

Throughout the day, companies of soldiers kept passing along the route. Ga-Nor also saw a group of six Sdisian sorcerers and dozens of their acolytes. A score of Fish slowly lumbered by, and nearly eight hundred Morts ran past swiftly. Two hundred creatures, equipped with enormous, powerful bows, floated past him, hovering over the ground. He recognized them as Burnt Souls. Judging from everything he had seen, the perpetual enemy of the Empire, the Kingdom of Nabator, had signed a treaty with Sdis and amassed a considerable force.

The tracker could not figure out what to do next. It would be sheer idiocy to remain where he was. They'd see him sooner or later. Fleeing into the mountains and waiting for it all to be over was unbefitting a Son of the Clan of the Snow Leopard. Should he try to make for the Gates? That was the most insane course of action he could think of. There was no way he could break through the enemy lines.

He put off the decision for the time being and remained where he was, having decided that it was best to take things slowly.

Toward nightfall he began scowling. The weather had turned cold and severe, and leaden clouds had enveloped the valley in a thick veil. And then the clouds burst, and the driving rain chased the enemy soldiers into the tower. The birds feasting on the corpses took to the air with indignant squawks. Stumbling and slipping in the greasy mud, a hundred corpses under the supervision of five Whites marched by, awkwardly keeping pace with the sergeant's drums. Then the road was empty.

The northerner was beginning to think that under the cover of the inclement weather it might be worth the risk to try to sneak into the town by the Gates at the very least. There he could see what was happening and then decide what to do next.

At that moment two men exited the tower. Wrapping their cloaks around themselves, they picked up some shovels and headed in the direction of the hidden northerner. All he could do was try to refrain from bringing attention to himself. It shouldn't really be all that difficult. It's not particularly easy to catch sight of someone who's lying up to his ears in mud.

The men halted about ten paces away from the Son of the Snow Leopard and began digging a pit.

"Damn that sergeant! He's inside warming his ass up, and what about us?"

"We're on the outs, like always!" agreed the second man. "I'd like to choke the life out of that bastard."

"Oh yeah, you'll choke him!" grumbled the first. "He'll outlive us all, the rascal. He should be the one trudging about in the rain, digging a grave. I didn't sign up for this!"

He huffed, angrily cast his shovel to the ground, grumbling curses, and walked over toward the place where Ga-Nor was hiding. Standing over him, the man began to untie his trouser strings. The Son of the Snow Leopard, realizing that he would soon be inundated not just by the rain, but by a much more unpleasant stream, rose up to his full, not insignificant height.

The Nabatorian thought that a demon had risen from the earth and he pissed his half-undone trousers with fear. The northerner swung his sword blindly and then leaped over the body as it fell into the mud and rushed toward his second adversary.

When it was all over he cast a quick glance at the tower. Grabbing the first body by the feet, he dragged it behind the cover of the rocks. Then he hid the second corpse. All this took about a minute. Sooner or later someone would come out into the rain to see how the gravediggers' work was going. It would be a good idea to be as far away as possible at that moment.

He'd killed the second Nabatorian with a blow to the temple from his sword hilt. It would be thoughtless to soil the man's clothes with blood, especially when they would fit so well. The redheaded warrior exchanged his clothes for the other's quickly, and then he concealed his face beneath the hood of the cloak. He folded up his kilt and clan scarf and took them with him.

Four dozen horses were standing beneath an enclosed canopy attached to the side of the Alert Tower. Three of them were still saddled. He took one of the animals by the reins and led it out onto the road.

The foul weather had driven off the Nabatorian patrols to such an extent that no one bothered to stop a solitary rider. After an hour the northerner spied the small town spread out before the Gates and he grunted in surprise. He'd expected to stumble across ashes and ruin, as well as the enemy army. But the town seemed untouched, as if thousands of humans and nonhumans had never been there.

The tracker slowed his horse to a walk. Where had the enemy army disappeared to? It couldn't have just vanished into thin air, unless, of course, that was something the Walkers could do.

He was riding slowly down the town's only street when three riders appeared from beyond a turn and made their way toward him. He remained calm. The soldiers rode by him slowly, disinterestedly glancing at the emblem of one of the Nabatorian companies sewn into his cloak, and went on their way without saying a word.

That worked out quite well.

All at once, the citadel emerged from the shroud

of rain. Four of the six towers were in ruins and the Wings were flung wide open. Until this moment Ga-Nor hadn't really entertained the notion that the Gates could really have fallen. He could not imagine how this happened. Who was to blame for such a blunder? Who was responsible for the fact that the enemy had entered the lands of the Empire?

"Hey, you!"

He pulled at the bridle and turned around. Two men with crossbows were standing in the road.

"Are you from the tower?"

Ga-Nor couldn't deny that, so he nodded.

"With a message for the commander?"

He nodded again. One of the Nabatorian soldiers frowned.

"Why so shy, friend?"

"Would you feel like chatting after bumping along for an hour in the rain?"

Ga-Nor tried to soften out his hard "r," which would give him away as a native of the north.

"Well, all right. On with you."

He thanked Ug that the war dogs hadn't bothered to peek under his cloak. There's no way he could explain away his red hair. Redheads are a rarity in Nabator, where almost everyone is swarthy and black-haired.

It would be smart to turn back while he still could. The mountains were vast; he could easily hide himself there. But it would be even better to head west. Sooner or later he'd reach the Golden Mark, and from there he could reach the Empire by sea. But . . . There they were, the Wings. Five more minutes and he'd already be home.

Ga-Nor came to a decision.

At the turn they tried to stop him but he hollered, dug his heels into the horse's sides, and, not paying any heed to the outraged cries behind him, galloped through the inner courtyard. He trampled an idiot who didn't have time to jump aside, hacked away at a fumbling halberdier with his sword, and then passed through the gate of the Viceroy into the lands of the Empire.

Horns sounded behind his back.

4

Vzzzzzick . . . Vzzzzzick . . . Vzzzzzick . . .

The whetstone scraped repulsively along the knife's edge. Whip watched Midge's daily ritual incredulously. He thought there was no point in such activity, and that the stunted assassin was merely expending time and energy for nothing.

"Aren't you bored of that yet?"

"Why? You think it's sharp enough?"

"Sharp enough?" said Whip indignantly. "That's all you've been doing since we left Al'sgara. Soon you'll be able to carve stone like butter."

"Is that really a bad thing? And anyway, you're exaggerating like always. You can't even shave with it. Here, look."

As proof, Midge tested the knife on a lock of his own hair, which was instantly shortened by an inch.

"Oh," said the man, looking at his reflection in the knife with dismay. "It seems it really is sharp enough."

Shen came in from the street. Midge caught sight of him and picked up his whetstone once more. Glaring wickedly at Mols's young protégé, Midge once again began sharpening his knife, which still emitted that repulsive sound, much to Whip's dismay.

"Where'd you lose Bamut?"

"He's following our friend, while Midge here screws around."

"It's curious that you left him. You get bored, little boy?" replied the runt. Whip scowled.

These two just wouldn't leave each other be. He tried not to pair them up, but what else could he do? Put them on opposite ends of the village? Ah, thanks, Mols! You did me a bad turn, make no mistake!

"Enough!" growled Whip, running out of patience. "I told you yesterday—if you wish to draw each other's blood, you have to wait until after the mission."

"Well, we kind of carried out the mission yesterday," said Shen through clenched teeth, not taking his eyes off Midge.

"It's for me to decide if we've carried it out or not. Midge, get up off your ass and go find Bamut. Consider it the start of your shift. And you, sit down and eat."

"You took a dislike to me from the start. Is that not so?" said Shen as he sat down on the bench.

Whip waited until his shaf had been brought to him, took a sip, and only then did he answer.

"All right then, lad. I'll be honest with you. You're unnecessary to our well-worn threesome. Like a fifth wheel on a wagon. I don't know what pit Mols dragged you out of. And what's worse—I don't know what your deal is. I don't know if we can count on you, and I don't know what to expect from you."

"So you should test me," said the blue-eyed man.

"How can I? For right now, as long as we can't verify that you're good at your job, I, Midge, and even Bamut, good soul that he is, will think you're a burden."

Shen scowled and then laughed shortly.

"Say what you like! If you think I'm happy to be in your company, you are sadly mistaken. Gallivanting around the periphery of the Empire, being food for mosquitoes and rubbing shoulders with sullen old fools is not as much fun as you think!"

Whip did not take offense at the word "fools."

"My, my, aren't you scholarly. The words you know. 'Periphery'!"

Shen, realizing he'd blundered, sniffed loudly and

began digging into his food. The leader of the team watched him mockingly. This was not the first time the kid had let his tongue slip. Every once in a while he peppered his speech with words or phrases that sounded strange to the ears of a native of the underworld. The lad played his part well, but it was clear he didn't have enough experience. However, Mols surely had to have a reason for sending him with them.

"Don't mess with Midge. That's my advice to you. My friendly advice. And don't make such a face; you're still too much of a pup to tangle with the likes of him. Midge will chew you up and spit you out. Leave him alone, I'm telling you."

"Yeah, sure, that runt will give it to me good!" replied Shen, spearing a piece of pork sausage. "He means nothing to me. I'd rather you talked to me about how much longer we're going to be hanging about here."

"We only got here yesterday and you're already homesick?"

"Imagine that. . . . So, how long?"

"Right now time is working against our friend. He's not an idiot; he's bound to realize that if we could find him, others could, too. A day, maybe two and he and his woman will go into hiding."

"And?"

"Like I already said, Gray is an intelligent man. He understands that concealing himself will be hard.

When there's such a price on your head, they'll even follow you down into the Abyss. He could put off the day of his death by running away to the edges of the Inhabitable Lands. He could creep into the swamps of the Blazogs, or into the aeries of the Je'arre, or the forests of the Highborn, but sooner or later he'll get caught. You don't just find ten thousand sorens lying about on the road. The hunters will find them, mark my words. There's only one real option—to get them to leave you alone you have to kill the client."

"So you think Joch is doomed?"

"Well, I think he has very little chance of seeing the next Feast of the Name."

"That's too bad. They say that he disperses money on all the city holidays. Al'sgara will lose much with his death."

"So will the Viceroy. His hand appreciates the money, too. He's everything to everyone. I've never seen another whose ass can fit so well on three different stools. The Emperor, the Walkers, and his own private interests. Ha! Sometimes I think being the Viceroy isn't too shabby."

"Mmm-hmm. It's a lucrative business. And not boring. All you have to do is be aware, write decrees, report to the capital, and dance with the ambassadors of Nabator and the Golden Mark. That, and rake the money in."

"You got the gist of it," grunted Whip. A glimmer

of respect slipped into his voice. "By the way, have you been in the guild long? I've never heard anything about you before."

"And who told you I was from the guild?" asked Shen, grinning suddenly.

Whip squinted at him.

"Mols said that you would come with us . . ."

"But perhaps he said something about why I'd been attached to you?"

No. He had said nothing of the sort. He'd simply ordered Whip to take the young man with him and not to ask any questions.

"I owed him a favor, so he asked me to put you through your paces."

"Uh-huh."

It couldn't be that simple. Why would Mols suddenly send a completely unknown man with them for no discernible reason? Simply to put him through his paces? Whip was not an idiot, and he didn't believe in such nonsense. Shen understood that but he did not bother trying to reassure the leader.

"I don't know if you should talk about this with your friends."

"I shouldn't. They have very little love for you anyway. Does that mean that you're not one of us?"

"If you think I'm going to start running around the village with a garrote or with throwing stars then you will have to be disappointed. Anyway, why would you need my help? To get your hands on the reward for Gray and his wife?"

"No. Mols didn't give such orders."

"What does Mols have to do with it? With ten thousand sorens you can spit on the guild. Begin a new life, yeah? Have you really never thought about risking it?"

Whip didn't say anything but by the way he tensed his fists, Shen knew that he had hit the mark.

"It's not important what I thought about or what I didn't. What's important is what I will do in the end. I won't mess with Gray and Layen without orders from Mols."

"Are they so dangerous?"

"That's not the only reason. I never go against the orders I've received. No matter how much money is at stake. You don't understand."

Shen shrugged his shoulders, indicating that for such a sum he personally would immediately forget about such scruples.

"As far as Gray goes," continued the leader, "he really is quite dangerous. Do you know his history?"

"No. Only what you've talked about amongst yourselves."

"He arrived in Al'sgara about ten years ago. From somewhere to the southeast. Supposedly before that he had been shooting the Highborn in Sandon. He was very familiar with the bow, and not just with that. He rose very quickly. He began getting the most difficult and high-paying contracts. Certain people in the guild, especially those who ply our trade, didn't like this. They were found one day in a cesspit. Dead.

Midge, by the way, was also among those who were dissatisfied, but he quit while he was ahead. His friends didn't. By and large, after that incident, no one bothered Ness. And then Mols took the lad under his wing. I worked with Gray once. I can say that he is entirely worthy of respect. He's the best shot that I know of."

"Why did he go off to such a backwater after so many successes?"

"No one knows for sure. Except perhaps Mols. I can only guess."

"I'd be very interested in hearing your guess."

Whip closely studied Shen's countenance. Was he mocking him? But the young man didn't bat an eye.

"It's time to go, to track down Bamut," said the leader, getting up from the bench. "You coming?"

"Yes. You'll tell me your guess?"

"Why should you care?"

"I should know what to expect from him. Mols didn't say anything."

"Hmmm . . ." Once again Whip looked searchingly at his companion. "Until Joch put the price on Gray's head, I thought that he and Layen were dead. Seven years ago two burnt-up bodies were found in their hideout. Everyone, including myself, thought that some clever lads had managed to do Ness in after all. But now . . . now I'm beginning to think that he did everything right. At the time when our friend supposedly died, a very notorious assassination was carried out. The target was destroyed by an arrow. It was a masterful shot. Perfect. The archer was located in such a spot that he could have only made that shot if his hand was guided by Melot himself. I know only one archer like that, and that's Ness."

"So Gray hit his target, duped everyone, grabbed his wife, and disappeared?"

"That's about it. By the way, he and his wife work together."

"Am I wrong or did it seem to me that you were more afraid of her than of your miraculous archer?"

Whip frowned petulantly. Midge was right. Sometimes this lad annoyed him to no end.

"She could boil your brain faster than you could pull your knife from its sheath."

"All women can do that." Shen laughed.

"I'm serious. She's the only one in our line of work who has the Gift. Everyone thinks that Layen can only talk without opening her mouth, but when I worked with Gray I saw her blow up this one man's head."

"How's that work? Is she a Walker or something?" asked his companion.

"No."

"An Ember?"

"Why are you bugging me? No one knows. She has the Gift and that's that. What difference does it make what kind? That's enough talking. They're waiting for us."

They stepped out onto the street and headed toward Ness's house. Shen was thinking quietly to himself and Whip was beginning to wish that he'd held his tongue.

"So who was the target?"

The leader looked at his companion uncomprehendingly.

"Who did Ness swat down that he had to flee so quickly?"

"A Walker," said the assassin dryly and, ignoring the dropped jaw and the look of utter shock on the face of his subordinate, he walked on.

Pork shuffled along through the forest, delightedly gnawing on a piece of honeyed gingerbread. The pockets of his torn trousers were bursting with sweets. The half-wit had bought the treats with the money that had been given to him by that kind gentleman. The one who rode on a knight's horse but wasn't a knight. But he was nice. And his horse was nice, too. And his sword. Also, he was Pork's friend. Uh-huh. They were the best of friends. Pork would do whatever Uncle wanted. He'd even treat him to a bit of gingerbread. One he had nibbled on a bit. Or not! Maybe even a whole one! Then the village children wouldn't say that he was greedy and stupid. Lies! All lies! They were always mocking. So he wasn't going to give them any of his tasty treats. Never! Why should he share with those wolves anyway? All it'd get him was a dirty shirt and mud flinging again. And they won't let him play knights.

So when Pork ran away from home and became a knight, he'd show them all. They'll be jealous!

Now he was walking to his favorite glade. There, next to the swift river, he could eat up in peace and quiet, unafraid that someone would notice. Or even worse, start badgering him. Pork, let me try it. Just a piece, hey, Pork? There's a good lad!

Oh! The clingy leeches!

In a fit of pique the half-wit kicked at a mushroom near his foot. Its cap flew into the air, slammed against a tree trunk, and burst apart into many pieces.

"Whoo-hoo!" said Pork rapturously.

He never would have guessed that mushrooms could fly and smash apart so well. This was so much better than old Roza's turnips. The fool twisted his head around, searching through the grass for the prominent red caps, but there weren't any nearby. Huffing in frustration, he walked out into the glade, but then he immediately retreated under the cover of the trees.

He petulantly puffed out his lips. What crap! His favorite spot was already taken! Ann, the wife of the carpenter, was standing next to the old oak. What was she doing here? He'd just have to eat another piece of gingerbread, and then go out there and tell her that this was his glade. So go away!

While Pork was chewing the gingerbread, he got another idea in his head. What if Ann suddenly stopped drilling holes into that silly tree with her eyes, and decided to take a swim in the river? Why not? It's hot right now, she might want to. And he'd sit here all quiet and he'd watch. He'd see her naked. Pork had seen naked girls once before; they were bathing in the Black Pool on the night of the summer solstice. Of course, the village lads had noticed the half-wit skulking in the bushes and had beat him up. They nearly broke all his bones.

Then Pork nearly choked on his gingerbread. The trunk of the oak split in two as if it had been struck by the axes of a hundred spiteful loggers. All the cowherd's attention was fixed upon the tree, which is why he didn't notice right away that there were men exiting the forest on the opposite side of the glade.

Old Morgen the blacksmith greeted me affably. He invited me into his house and sat me at his table. I did not want to offend him so we calmly discussed the weather, the future of the crops, and our neighbors. Finally it was time to get down to business.

"That's what I owe you for my tools." I put six sols on the table.

"There's no hurry. I can wait," said the blacksmith in his booming voice.

"There's no such thing as too much money," I disagreed. "Anyway, I heard that you sent the matchmaker to your son. You're going to have to count every penny now."

"You speak the truth," Morgen said, grinning expansively. "Why have you begun to pay off your debts? You aren't planning to leave us, are you?"

"I must. On business."

"It's good to have business." The blacksmith grunted. "It's far better than wearing out your trousers. When do you return?"

I smiled wryly.

"That's why I came to you. We won't be returning. I don't want to sell my home. And anyway, I don't have enough time to do it. They say that your boy Ren has nowhere to take a wife. You only started building a month ago. It's too long to wait. Take our house. Have them live there. Either permanently or until you finish your own cottage."

Such a generous offer bewildered him. He grunted, settled back in his chair, and thoughtfully contracted his brows.

"This is unexpected. Melot as my witness, this is quite unexpected. You really are a strange man, Pars. To give your property away just like that."

"I'm generous." For all my efforts to the contrary, my smile still came out slightly bitter. "If it's got to be given away anyway, it should at least go into good hands. So, will you take it or not?"

"Of course I'll take it. I'd be a fool if I didn't. It's just awkward to take it for nothing. People will talk."

"People always talk. Let them."

"Let me at least pay you a part of the money. So you won't be living in poverty."

I did not have time to reply. A burning summons exploded in my mind.

Help me!

The mental picture that Layen sent me showed me the glade where we'd hidden the money received for the assassination of the Walker. Without so much as a good-bye, I tore out of the home of the rather startled blacksmith and set off to help her. As I ran I kept trying to call out to her. To no avail. For the first time I could remember, Layen was silent. In light of what she had shown me, it was safe to assume the worst. I'd already cursed myself five times that I had allowed her to do this by herself.

The only weapon I had was a throwing axe. It was useful on a hunt, and perhaps even for assassination, but it would not work against a bunch of well-armed opponents.

I flew through the brush growing alongside the river and immediately saw what was happening in the glade. About twenty steps away from me a short lance was stuck in the ground. Next to it was the body of a man. There was another corpse not far from the forest edge. Layen was lying still on the opposite edge of the glade.

Three men were standing above her. They were laughing and joking, and apparently they were not at all concerned about the death of their comrades. One of them had just lowered his trousers.

A whirling sphere flew through the air and then

my throwing axe hit the back of the would-be rapist's head with a vile thud. He flapped his arms and, gushing blood, fell to the ground. I rushed out into the glade toward the two survivors.

One of them began to lift his crossbow, the second reached for his sword. This did not frighten me. I merely grinned and sped up. Just as the scum pressed the trigger I flipped. The crossbow bolt zipped by me without causing any harm. I landed on my hands, slowing down as I rolled over my head onto my back. I leaped to my feet near the spear. I grabbed it as I ran and I cast it at the swordsman. The spear caught him in the stomach, hurling him backward and pinning him to a tree. The bounty hunter screamed in pain and started grabbing at the bloodstained shaft with his hands.

My remaining adversary was clenching a bolt in his teeth and frantically trying to load his crossbow again. I didn't give him the chance. I landed near him, fell to my knees, and ducked under the weapon when he tried to smash it into my head. Twisting my fist, I hit him hard in the hamstring. He shrieked, lost his balance, and fell.

I rolled away from him and ended up next to the corpse that had my axe sticking out of its head. I pulled out the weapon and rushed back over to my adversary, who was beginning to stand. I put all my strength into kicking him in the face, breaking his nose. And then I laid into him with two swift, strong strokes, breaking open his skull. By this time the one run through by the spear had stopped struggling and let out a final gasp.

It was all over.

I rushed over to my wife. I was relieved to see that she was alive—she was just unconscious. A large bump had formed on her left temple. The skin was badly cut and blood was dripping down her cheek.

Behind me a bowstring twanged loudly, a bolt whistled, a cry was heard. Bamut flew out of the underbrush with his discharged crossbow. Whip and the kid, whose name I hadn't bothered to find out, appeared behind him.

"They found you quite quickly," shouted Whip.

For all his friendliness he did not take his eyes off my utak (a Blazgian throwing axe) for a second. As for me, I cast my eyes to the side, without losing them from my sight, and saw the man that Bamut had taken down. One of these guys, hungry for easy money, had hidden himself during the fight. When I was distracted by Layen he decided to try his luck and take the prize. Well. He'd almost succeeded.

I'm losing my grip.

"Damn, what would you have done if we hadn't shown up?"

"I'd have managed," I replied sullenly.

By this time Bamut had dexterously reloaded his weapon and cocked it in the bend of his elbow. I didn't like the way he was looking at me. It looked like he wanted to make some easy money himself, by the way he glanced quickly at his leader, searching for approval. Whip just gave a barely discernible shake of the head to the unvoiced question. Bamut smiled, shrugged his shoulders, and slung the weapon back over his shoulder. And then, no longer paying any attention to the rest of us, he began going through the pockets of the dead men.

The tension lessened slightly, but we were all trying not to make any sudden moves. As before, I stood between Layen and Mols's people. I wasn't persuaded of their peaceful intentions, not at all.

"What's wrong with her?" Whip asked cautiously.

I didn't answer; I just narrowed my eyes in suspicion. I had to figure out what this threesome had in mind.

"If we wanted you dead, you'd already be dead."

I smirked disdainfully and remained silent.

"Layen needs help," Whip insisted.

"How did you find us?"

"We followed you."

"More like chased you," the young one corrected his leader.

He was avidly studying the corpse pinned to the tree.

"You handled him really well."

"So you decided to take on the role of bodyguards?" I asked, and after a slight hesitation I tucked the axe into my belt. "Is that really in your job description?"

"Well, it seems we changed it just in time. I don't

recognize their mugs." Whip idly nudged one of the bodies with his toe. "They're not ours. Stray birds. How's Layen?"

"Alive."

"Can I take a look at her?" asked the young man suddenly, and then he flinched at my savage glare. "She needs help now."

"I can help her myself," I snapped.

None of these men were going to come anywhere near my wife.

"I'm a Healer."

"Since when does the guild take on Healers?"

"I'm not part of the guild. Whip can attest to that."

Whip hesitated, but then he nodded. Was he lying or not?

Bamut had to ask, "Whip, what's Shen talking about?"

Whip winced and changed the subject. "What about the stiffs?"

"Two of them have their faces burnt off," replied Bamut. "I didn't know that Layen could do that. You can't tell who they are. Damn. . . . Is he really a little Healer? Do you think Mols could send us off with an apothecary next time?" Bamut chuckled heartily, but no one else found his joke amusing.

"So can I take a look?" asked Shen.

"Okay," I said, moving reluctantly to the side. "But you watch yourself . . ."

"Don't threaten me!" he said, his eyes gleaming angrily.

I stood so that I could keep an eye on both the Healer and Bamut at the same time.

Frightened screams came from the forest. Midge appeared. I'd been anxious about where that bastard was hiding himself. He was dragging Pork, who was balking and shrieking, by the scruff of the neck. What was he doing here?

Next to the tiny assassin the half-wit looked like a giant. But this didn't bother Midge in the slightest.

"The stupid swine shat himself."

"Where did you find him?"

"In the brush, of course. He was peeping. But perhaps he was with these lads. There's seven horses not far from here. Should I kill him?"

When he heard these last words, Pork howled. Choking on his sobs and entreaties, he crawled toward Whip on his knees. All I could make out was "not my fault I thought naked auntie and then those wicked . . ." Then, "I'm no-o-o-othing! I he-e-erd co-o-ows! I'll give you gingerbrea-ea-ead!"

"Calm down, friend. And keep your gingerbread. No one's going to kill you."

Layen groaned and I immediately forgot about the half-wit and rushed to her. I growled and Shen prudently moved aside.

My sun opened her eyes.

"Shhh. They're dead. I got here in time."

What are they doing here?

They followed me. I wasn't really in a state of mind to worry about a tail.

I'm too weak. I can only deal with one of them right now.

I saw the magical storm gathering in her dark blue eyes and said quickly, *Stop! There's no point. It seems that for today we can go our separate ways peacefully.* "How do you feel?"

"My head is splitting," she said, carefully prodding at the bump on her temple. She frowned.

"Can you walk?"

"There's no need," said Whip as he walked toward us. "Midge went for the horses. Is there a path to the village?"

"There is. Beyond that copse."

"We'll get you there. I had a word with the halfwit. He claims that there were more attackers than the corpses we have here. He doesn't know how to count, but judging from the horses there were seven. And one had wings like a bird."

"Yes. A Je'arre, damn him!" cursed Layen as she got to her feet with my help. "I didn't expect him. He crept up on me from behind. It's a good thing he didn't kill me."

"I wonder where he could be?" said Shen, transferring his attention to the surrounding trees.

Bamut got his crossbow at the ready.

"Calm down. You won't catch him now. The little birdie vanished. Hey, friend! Stop crying. Go on then. Yes, yes. You! Go blow your nose at your cows!"

Pork didn't need to be told twice. He hopped up and, forgetting about his gingerbread, which was scattered all over the grass, he fled into the forest. There you go. Now he'd go spread gossip about what had happened here around the entire village.

"Oho! What's this?"

Shen peered into the belly of the cleft oak and then fished a pack out of it.

"It's heavy."

Without saying a word, I reached out my hand for his discovery. The lad was taken aback at my impudence, and he was about to object, but then he saw the threat in my eyes and gave it back.

"Is that yours?" inquired Whip.

"It's ours," I replied in an even voice.

They didn't ask any more questions.

5

Rek died quietly. Luk missed the moment when it happened. He had fallen into an uneasy slumber and when he woke up the wounded man was already in the Blessed Gardens. His friend's dumb luck had finally come to an end, but before then he'd managed the impossible—he and Luk had escaped from the Gates. He'd had to carry Rek on his back for part of the way; the man had lost too much blood. Then the guard had gone into the forest—the road was dangerous and they needed to wait a couple of days until everything quieted down. A deserted silver mine was located in the foothills not far from the citadel. There were scores of them in the area. In former times, silver for Imperial sols had been extracted here, but the veins had run dry and so the place had fallen into disrepair. Luk doubted he could find a better place for a temporary shelter. It was unlikely that the Nabatorian soldiers would bother to check a mine that had been abandoned more than eighty years ago.

Now he needed to go up. He fumbled for his axe and picked up his lantern but didn't light it. He made his way by touch until the low ceiling forced him to crawl on his knees. Only then did Luk decide to expend the oil. The light that came from the lantern was meager, and he couldn't even make out what was one and a half piss-poor yards in front of him. He crawled on all fours along the damp ground, cursing his own caution. He shouldn't have gone in so far. He could very well have stopped by the entrance. No one would search for them here. When he was finally able to stand up to his full height, the guard breathed a sigh of relief. Walking was easier now. After some time he felt a weak gust of wind on his face and he knew that the exit was only a stone's throw away. Passing by the fork that led to the lower mines, he scrambled over a pile of processed material and saw a weak light in the distance.

Doubts began to torment him once again. Suddenly the world outside seemed dangerous. Hastily dampening down his lantern, he walked forward slowly, constantly stopping and straining his ears. At one point he seemed to hear footsteps, and he practically jumped out of his own trousers, but there wasn't a single sound in the mines other than his own labored breathing.

When he was about twenty yards away from the exit, Luk heard a gentle rustle and once again became frightened. But then he realized that it was only the rain. The guard smiled in relief and hung the lantern on a brace, the one from which he'd taken it when he'd gone below.

The rain was unexpectedly intense. Night was falling. The world was enveloped in a web of gray shadows. The wet earth smelled strongly of leaves and something rotten. Opposite the mine shaft, no farther than ten yards away, a thin man dressed in rags was standing with his back to the former guard of the Gates. The rain, which had thoroughly drenched his tatters of clothing and sparse hair, did not seem to bother this strange person in the slightest.

Holding his breath, Luk examined the stranger. The famished-looking man held himself stiffly and didn't have any weapons on him. He didn't seem dangerous. Although, the Damned also seemed like peaceful little lambs until the time came. The memory of Rubeola made Luk tighten his grip on his axe. Melot only knew what to expect from the stranger.

"Screw a toad," muttered the soldier, and then he spat angrily. "He's standing right in my way. Why couldn't he enjoy the rain in a different place?"

Luk was starting to get very angry. Both at the stranger and at himself. His own caution, or more precisely his cowardice, infuriated him beyond belief. He had an axe. He was at least twice as strong. But he was still standing in the same spot as three minutes ago. Spitting once more on the rocky ground, the guard came to a decision. He stepped out into the rain and, gathering a bit more air into his lungs, he shouted, "Hey, you!"

The man turned around and Luk's mouth instantly went dry. He saw the pale, so pale it seemed blue, face of the stranger; he saw the sunken-in nose, the black lips caked with blood, and the eyes burning with an emerald fire.

After his frantic flight, Ga-Nor pulled in the reins and jumped from his horse. Sooner or later the horse would get tired. The road was dangerous, and pursuit would certainly be sent from the Gates. The tracker was under no illusion what would happen then. One against many—he wouldn't be spared. So he had to leave the road as soon as possible and disappear in the forests of the foothills. And then afterward perhaps he would head home, to the north.

The horse, its ears lowered, stood meekly in the driving rain. He pitied the animal, but there was nothing he could do. Ga-Nor took out his dagger, pricked the horse in its rump, shouted loudly, and quickly jumped to the side. The animal whinnied from pain and galloped away at full speed. The Son of the Snow Leopard watched it leave and then began the arduous climb up the rain-washed slope of a small hill. Above him grew a thick spruce forest—an excellent place for someone who wanted to disappear. Clenching his teeth stubbornly, the northerner continued crawling up the slippery slope.

Finally he reached the trees. When he was hidden beneath their bristly boughs, he stopped to take a breath. The road lay below him, but despite the rain and the imminent twilight, he could see it quite well from his hiding place—a narrow ribbon that curled between the low hills not far from a swift river, which was now brown from the driving rain.

About five minutes later a group of pursuers shot out from around a bend—a score of angry Nabatorians, whipping their horses into a lather. They rushed past, not even glancing toward the spot where the tracker had hidden himself. Ga-Nor hoped that the sons of snow maggots would not find his horse anytime soon, but when they did, just let them try and guess where he decided to get off to go on foot.

After waiting several minutes, the Son of the Snow Leopard crawled away from the edge. He stood there, carefully examining the spot where he'd been lying. The thick carpet of soggy needles looked trampled. That was bad, but there was no help for it. He couldn't wipe away all traces of himself even if he tried.

Ga-Nor flung the hood of his stolen cloak over his head and trotted along the route he'd chosen. He didn't think that he should try to go very far into the mountains; it would slow his progress too much. It would be better to walk along the ridge under the cover of the forest. Very soon the foothills would turn into rolling hills and then into flatlands. There he could turn to the west and try to reach the frontier garrison if, of course, it had not yet fallen to the advance troops of the enemy. The tracker wanted to hope that the well-fed, idle southern army would be able to hold back the wave of dark blue (referring to Nabator's colors) locusts that would soon come swarming over them.

It got dark quickly. The rain didn't let up for a minute. As he passed through the branches of the drowsy trees, so heavy with water that they brushed against the ground, it seemed to the tracker that the forest was conducting an unhurried argument with the sky. Suddenly the experienced ear of the tracker caught the distinct sounds of a battle winding through the disarming murmuring of the trees.

Someone yelled, "Well, come at me, you bastard!

Come on!" Someone else croaked brokenly in reply and then bellowed. Ga-Nor unsheathed his sword and resolutely headed toward the sounds. He would not leave danger at his back. Furthermore, someone needed help and that someone could very well turn out to be an ally.

The sounds of the scuffle were closer. The invective ceased, and in return the groans became more bloodthirsty. The Son of the Snow Leopard pushed aside a fir bough that was blocking his view and saw a rocky hillside with the dark square entrance of an abandoned mine carved into it. A bit farther on stood a barracks, ravaged by time, on whose roof a young tree had already managed to take root. The path along which the ore had been transported was overgrown with young spruce trees, so the only clearing was the one right in front of the mine itself. Mounds of rubble, extracted from the depths of the earth, rusted braces, water-filled carts, roof support beams rotted down to nothing. Amid all this desolation a fight was going on.

Ga-Nor instantly recognized the stout man regardless of the fact that his face was dirty from spending the last twenty-four hours in the mine. He had no doubt whatsoever—it was Luk, a guard from the garrison of the Towers. A lover of dice, and in his debt.

He was standing in the empty doorway to the barracks, clearly in jeopardy as he swung his axe at his lunging opponents. One of the walking dead had already been taken care of. It was resting right by the entrance to the mines with a fractured skull. But there were four others who were avidly trying to feast upon the meat they hungered for. Luckily, the soldier had chosen a good defensive position so the dead men kept getting in one another's way—otherwise they would have long since reached him. As the northerner watched, Luk cut a chunk out of the shoulder of one of the corpses with his axe and kicked it in the stomach, pushing it away. He couldn't continue like this for much longer. The guard was starting to get tired.

Ga-Nor slipped out from underneath the cover of the trees and rushed to help.

He couldn't imagine a worse situation. The creature that Luk had originally taken for a living man had turned out to be a walking corpse. The soldier had never come across anything like this before. Sure, he'd heard all kinds of tales, but he'd never seen it for himself. Necromancy was banned in the Empire. This wasn't Sdis, where sorcerers practiced black magic and controlled the dead.

It all seemed unreal. Luk didn't want to believe his eyes but he had to. And quickly.

The creature lunged at him without any warning. Regardless of how frightened he was, Luk knew his business and killed the man-eater with the first strike, cutting off its head with a single well-placed blow. Before the soldier had time to come to his senses and curse as he always did, two more attacked him.

The first corpse had been hanging over the entrance to the mines the entire time. Melot knew what he was doing there, but he jumped and nearly landed on Luk's back. The man was only saved by the fact that he'd decided to take a closer look at his kill and had stepped forward. A second corpse emerged from the darkness of the mine to help the first. The soldier had just heard his footsteps when he burst out of hiding. The former guardian of the Gates gave thanks that fate had so providently kept them apart in the mines. If he had encountered the monster in the darkness underground who knew how it would have ended.

Luk managed to hold back the first assault, but then two more unwelcome guests emerged from the barracks. They cornered him. He had to turn tail and stand in the doors so that the bastards would come at him one at a time. While he had so far managed to hold the charging creatures off, it was becoming harder and harder with every second. His arms felt like they were filled with lead, and the astonishingly nimble dead men were not tiring at all.

Moans, green eyes burning with fire, gnashing teeth, pale skin, caked blood.

He groaned in despair, hacked into the shoulder of one of his enemies, kicked him in the stomach, almost cut off the arm of another, and then sunk his axe into the face of a third.

"Cut off their heads! Their heads!" somebody shouted.

Two of the corpses immediately turned their attention to the new arrival. Luk was far from relieved. He could see that the man, his apparent savior, was wearing the cloak of the Nabatorian cavalry. But this was something he could try to understand later. Right now, the stranger was not coming after him. And he was also fighting for his life.

The two corpses who ran away allowed Luk to go on the counterattack. He sprang to the left and then forward, spun around, and with all his strength swung a blow at the skull of one of the corpses jumping at his heels. But his aim was off and he tore through the corpse's collarbone and sternum, the momentum of his swing forcing the axe to hit the ground. He wrenched it up, twirled it around, and brought it down on the head of a corpse that was trying to sneak up behind him. He spun the axe again, raining down a hail of blows on the first zombie, which was already rising up from the ground. Its shattered skull burst apart repulsively and the corpse, enlivened by the magic of a necromancer, jerked, and then went limp.

"It worked! Screw a toad!" spat the winner victoriously.

Only now did the soldier recall his savior. The man had just finished dealing with his own troubles and was wiping off his blade.

Luk had not been mistaken. This man really did

seem to be a Nabatorian. It was impossible to tell what he looked like because of the hood riding low over his face. The man finished wiping his sword, nudged the headless corpse with his foot, and began walking toward the soldier. Luk waved his axe threateningly.

"Have you gone mad?" asked the stranger.

"Listen," said Luk, breathless from the battle. "I'm grateful to you for your help but our paths diverge here. You go that way, I go the other way, and we forget about meeting each other."

"Did you lose the last of your brains from terror?" the stranger asked warmly, and then he took off his hood.

Luk stood stock-still and gaped. He recognized that visage. The lean face with high cheekbones, the hawkish nose, the red mustache, and the hair of the same color pulled back into short, thick braids. It was Ga-Nor, Son of the Snow Leopard, who had been lost in the mountains with Da-Tur's squad. The very northerner to whom Luk lost money playing dice.

"I don't believe it," stammered the soldier.

"You mean that I returned from the other world and decided to get my debt from you?" said Ga-Nor, smiling wearily.

"If you're a dead man, you're a lot worse than these bastards. At least they didn't ask me for money."

"Indeed. Though they'd have been quite happy to suck out your heart."

The soldier shuddered at the prospect.

"How did you get here?"

Ga-Nor didn't reply; he turned his head back in the direction from which he'd come, listening intently to the patter of the rain. Luk did the same but unlike the northerner he didn't hear anything suspicious and so he dared to ask a question. "What is it?"

"Shut up," snapped the Son of the Snow Leopard.

In the twilight his face sharpened, heavy shadows gathered under his eyes, and he himself began to resemble a corpse. Luk shivered involuntarily. A minute went by, another began. The rain came down even harder, even though this seemed completely impossible. The tracker didn't have any rain gear, and he'd been soaked through for a long time, but still he peered into the darkness and scented the air. Luk tried this as well, but he only smelled the stench emanating from the dead bodies.

"Come on, what's the matter?"

"We're leaving."

"What?"

"We're leaving. Quickly."

"But . . ."

The Son of the Snow Leopard glared at him angrily.

"I'm not going to bargain with you. Either you come with me or you stay here to greet your guests."

Luk only needed a second to realize what kind of guests he was talking about. The ones with the glowing green eyes.

"I'm coming with you," he said quickly, and looked around in alarm, expecting dark figures to leap out of the dense forest at any moment.

"I'll be walking quickly. We need to shake them. Watch your feet. Keep up."

Luk nodded frantically and, glancing back one last time, hurried after the northerner.

Regardless of the wet firewood, they managed to make a fire without too much difficulty. The flames crackled and threw up sparks, and the thick smoke wafted up through a hole in the ceiling. And that, right now, was the most important thing. Luk was as frozen as a dog and this was the first opportunity he'd had to warm up and dry out his clothes.

They'd run through the forest for half the night. They walked down a slope, only to climb up the next, and then they walked along the ridge of the next hill and descended another slope. Then for a long time they plodded their way upstream against the current of an icy river. Luk slipped on the wet stones three times and fell, cursing, into the water, and three times the strong arms of the northerner pulled him out by the scruff of his neck and set him back on his feet.

The Son of the Snow Leopard surpassed even the unrivaled, now deceased captain of the Tower of Ice. Even that man had never driven his subordinates through an obstacle course like this one. Luk was exhausted, his legs hurt something fierce, his breathing was labored, his axe seemed unspeakably heavy, he wanted to collapse and shove it all up his toad's ass, or better yet, up the ass of the northerner's little god, but he didn't. His fear urged him on. And so the exhausted soldier doggedly trotted behind Ga-Nor.

The man hardly spoke at all, constantly changing directions, slipping between tree trunks and streams, circling around copses, every now and then pausing to listen, smell the air, and then continue on. At one point it seemed to Luk that they were going in circles. Finally, just when the soldier had decided he couldn't care less if a corpse wanted to suck his heart out or not, they arrived.

In a grove of old sycamores, in the midst of tall blackberry bushes, stood a hunter's cabin. It was ancient, covered in moss and shelf fungus, with a partially fallen roof, broken windows, and an insecure door. Inside it smelled of rotten wood, humidity, and the droppings of wild animals. The floor creaked awfully and the tiny stove was being used as a nest by mice. It was obvious that no one had been here for a long time.

Luk did not know if Ga-Nor already knew about this refuge or if he stumbled upon it by accident. But, contrary to his habit, he wouldn't ask any questions, because he thought that spending the night here was far better than out in the rain.

The tracker still wouldn't say a single word. He

silently kindled the fire using a pile of sodden wood that was lying in the corner. Then he closed his eyes and apparently went to sleep. The soldier considered doing the same, but with all his questions he couldn't manage it. He stood up quietly and tried to push the door closed.

There was no latch. So the guard fashioned a makeshift one out of the trunk of a young tree. It was still unsound. The rotten planks of the door could not even withstand two good blows. Luk understood this but for some reason he felt much calmer with a closed door. At any rate, if they tried to break in here then he would at least be forewarned and not find out about it when their enemies were already standing over them.

All that remained were the windows. He studied them quickly. They were small. Luk wouldn't be able to crawl through them, but for someone thin enough it would be easy. There were no decent boards, no nails, and no hammer here. The only thing he could do was hope that all their enemies were big and fat.

"What happened at the Gates?"

The sound of Ga-Nor's voice ringing out caused Luk to flinch.

"Screw a toad! You'll drive me to my death!"

"Then you'll rest with Ug."

"You can rest with Ug all you like, but I intend to live," grumbled Luk as he checked his drying clothes and sat down by the fire. "Do you have anything to eat? I haven't eaten in over twenty-four hours."

The northerner rummaged in the bag that he'd taken from the saddle of the Nabatorian horse. He extracted sugar, an onion, a small hunk of cheese, and a quarter of rye bread from it.

"I trust you're capable of eating and talking at the same time?" asked Ga-Nor as he sliced the onion with his dagger.

His companion nodded and told his story as he ate. The Son of the Snow Leopard listened attentively. Everything was far worse than he thought. The Damned were involved in this business! Rubeola's name used to terrify him as a child. And it probably wasn't just her. How many of them were there? Six or eight? The Damned would be far more trouble than all the others. If, of course, Luk wasn't lying, as was his habit. But he was clearly not lying.

Nabator had been wanting to conquer the south of the Empire for centuries. And now that long-awaited event was coming to pass.

"Surely someone else must have escaped."

"Maybe," replied Luk listlessly. A blind man could see that he didn't really believe it. "Rek and I managed to get out because we ran from the walls along the southern stairwell. It's not far from there to the fifth portal. I just don't think that anyone followed us. A swarm of Nabatorians fell on them. And Morts, too. We barely got through."

"Did the Walker really die?"

"Yeah," said the soldier mournfully. "The Damned hit the wall so hard that . . ."

He didn't finish, and he didn't really need to. A heavy silence fell. Both men watched the flames of the fire and thought their own thoughts.

Luk considered himself lucky. Ga-Nor was an excellent tracker and not a bad swordsman. The chances of living were far better with him than if he were alone. If the northerner hadn't come to his rescue, he would already be dead.

"Ga-Nor? What now?"

The Son of the Snow Leopard answered reluctantly, "We will have to get through on our own. Going to El'nichi Ford makes no sense. I'm sure they've already taken it. I think that Nabator will head for Okni and Gash-Shaku. That would deprive Al'sgara of support. And it will give them the opportunity to gather up their forces to strike at the heart of the Empire. As soon as we leave the foothills, we need to head west."

"I need to go to Al'sgara," Luk declared suddenly. "The Walker begged me to report about the Damned."

"I'm sure they already know."

"And if not?"

"Then they'll know in a day or two. At any rate, you'll be too late."

"I promised."

Ga-Nor looked at the obstinately pursed lips of his companion with astonishment. He hadn't expected it—that a gambler would keep his word.

"If you won't go with me, I'll go by myself."

"There's forest all around. And beyond that the Blazgian Swamp begins. You'll die."

"If we keep going west, we'll get to Dog Green. There's a road there that goes to Al'sgara."

"Do you really think that the Nabatorians haven't blocked it off?" scoffed the northerner.

"It's worth the risk. Are you coming with me?"

"Let's talk about it tomorrow. Right now I need to sleep. I'm very tired."

"I'll keep watch," Luk offered at once, immensely cheered up. The northerner didn't refuse him; he promised to think about it. That was a mercy. It would be much worse if he refused to budge and said no. It was as easy to change the minds of that stubborn tribe as it was to get a Je'arre to sell his silk cheaply.

The soldier picked up his axe and sat down by the door, laying his weapon next to him.

"Wake me up toward morning. I'll relieve you." The tracker pressed his back against the wall and closed his eyes.

"Sure. Ga-Nor?"

"Yes?"

"Where did those corpses come from? Shouldn't they be with their necromancer?"

"They should. But they can run away."

"How?"

"With their legs."

"And what about the ones chasing us? They aren't

going to come here and surprise us in the early hours of the morning?"

The Son of the Snow Leopard snorted crossly, but he still answered, "Only if they know how to track. But they are far too stupid for that. They shouldn't find us. If they do, wake me. And now shut up and let me sleep."

Luk nodded but his companion didn't see it. He was asleep.

The soldier shifted about, trying to get comfortable. He glanced at the door. He took a deep breath, yawning widely. Listening to the patter of the rain falling on the roof, he watched as the flames died down.

Ga-Nor awoke and heard peaceful snoring. Without opening his eyes, the northerner cursed. Luk had fallen asleep without waking him up, of course. An infuriating blunder that could have cost them their lives. But this time they had been spared. No one had tried to infiltrate their asylum during the night, and that meant that they had managed to get the creatures off their trail.

That was good.

Judging by the sun striking him in the eyes, the weather had changed. That, and it was probably late morning. He'd slept deeply. But that was not surprising—the strain of the last few days necessitated a proper rest. Maybe Luk was right not to wake him. He needed to gather his strength.

He recalled last night's conversation. Luk's proposition was sound. It was unlikely that the Nabatorians would be tempted by that little village. Beyond that, there was no point skulking about in the forest on an empty stomach. He had little food, and without a crossbow he couldn't survive by hunting. That, and there wouldn't be time for it. But in Dog Green he could stock up on food and at least one of his troubles would be lessened.

The sun was beating down on his eyes. He knew he should get up, but he didn't feel like it. The warm light was an unexpectedly pleasant sensation. Suddenly a shadow of some kind ran across the sun; the rays stopped falling on his face for a second and then returned again. It was just for a moment, and it could have meant nothing at all, but the northerner's complacent mood disappeared instantly. He quickly opened his eyes and squinted against the light.

Through the window opposite where he was lying, he could see the crowns of the sycamores and a swatch of clear blue sky. Which meant, as he had supposed, that the fleeting shadow had not been a cloud.

He kept perfectly still and did not take his tense gaze from the window. He cautiously dragged in air through his nostrils. The scent was so slight that even the keen nose of the northerner did not smell it immediately. But when he detected it, Ga-Nor's blood ran cold. They were in a heap of trouble now. Ug take him if he was mistaken!

The air smelled of almonds.

He only knew of one creature that gave off such a smell. And right now it was not on the side of soldiers of the Empire. If it hadn't been for the shadow, Ga-Nor never would have sensed the danger. The intelligent creature had placed itself downwind and the forest was not silent. The birds were chirping with all their might, not at all bothered by the presence of an intruder.

What now? Would the enemy wait until they left the hut? How long would its patience last? Could it see him right now?

The northerner glanced at Luk. He was sleeping with his mouth open. The soldier was lying opposite the second window and he didn't even suspect that his scalp was at risk of becoming a trophy.

Ug, help me! What bad timing!

Trying to make as few movements as possible, Ga-Nor groped for the bread that remained after last night's meal. He ripped off a piece with his fingers and rolled it up into a ball. He took careful aim and then flicked his makeshift projectile at Luk's forehead. Luk opened his eyes.

When he saw the northerner's troubled face, Luk clearly wanted to ask what was going on. Ga-Nor quickly held up his fingers in warning, begging him to keep silent. Thank Ug! He understood. Using his fingers, the Son of the Snow Leopard tried to explain that they were in danger. And that too was understood. Now for the most difficult part—they had to back away from the window so that they weren't visible from outside. They needed to do it quickly, and if possible simultaneously. He didn't know which window their adversary was watching from.

Unfortunately, the soldier did not understand the complicated clan sign language of the Children of the Snow Leopard, but he did know the customary army hand signals. The redhead tried his best to explain to him what he had to do.

"On the count of three," mouthed the tracker. "One . . . two . . . three!"

Ga-Nor shot up into the air. There was a whistle, followed by a dull thud. The tracker crashed to the floor, went into a roll, and landed right underneath the window. He quickly looked around.

Luk was alive. Right then he was pressed against the door but his chubby, good-natured face had turned the color of sour milk. A yard-and-a-half-long shaft was sticking out of the wall right where the soldier had just been leaning. It was thick. With violet-red plumage.

"Damn it!" swore the northerner.

"What is it?" gasped Luk, who was scared nearly to death, vividly imagining how he would have been nailed to the wall by that thing.

"Away from the door! Move!"

If there was one thing Luk did not lack, it was

quick wits. He didn't bother asking stupid questions and did what he was ordered. Holding his axe fast in his hand, he rolled to the side and crawled on his stomach to a less dangerous spot between the wall and the stone stove. It was a blind spot for the bowman.

The next arrow punched right through the flimsy door panels, coming out of it two handbreadths. If the guard had stayed put, he'd already be dead.

"Luk? You alive?"

"Seems like," said the soldier, touching himself with trembling hands. "What is it?"

"A Burnt Soul."

"A real one?"

He instantly realized the stupidity of that question. This wasn't one of his old sergeant's boozy tales.

"Where did it come from?"

"Ask me something easier," grumbled Ga-Nor. What had brought the creature to the forest was another question entirely. "Sit still, keep your head down."

"No problem!"

Luk realized that they had been backed into a corner. It was keeping an eye on the hut so that they couldn't get out. If they stuck their noses outside, they'd get hit by an arrow.

For the time being, Ga-Nor was out of the eye line of the Burnt Soul, but it could easily change its position. Trying not to raise his head and clinging to the wall, the northerner quickly crawled over to a corner where he couldn't be reached.

Luk tensely watched the Son of the Snow Leopard from the opposite end of the hut. The tracker crouched down and, catching the troubled look of his companion, smiled joylessly. He understood what a mess they were in.

"How long do we have until he gets tired of waiting?" asked the guard.

Ga-Nor noted that the soldier was not panicking and that he had his weapon in hand.

Good for him.

"It all depends on how long he's been here and what he wants."

"Scalps. I don't know about you, but my hair is dear to me."

"You barely have any left."

Luk smiled sourly.

"And yet. What do you plan to do?"

"I plan on thinking."

How could he kill a Burnt Soul without a crossbow? If they tried to run past him, he'd pick them off like fattened hens. Going out the door was suicide, as was the window. And the roof.

Burnt Souls were excellent archers. It was possible that the humans and the Nirits of Bragun-Zan shot more accurately than the inhabitants of the Great Waste, but in terms of strength the Burnt Souls had no equal. The longbows of these creatures rivaled the most formidable crossbows. One of their arrows could easily pierce most of the armor made by the blacksmiths of this world.

The Imperial forces had come up against the warriors of the Burnt Souls a few times since the War of the Necromancers. Most often these confrontations did not end favorably for the humans. The dreaded bowmen had not been seen in the lands of the Empire for a long time, but they were well remembered. And if even the smallest parts of the stories about them were true, dispatching the archer would be far from easy.

"Will he come in here?"

"I don't know," replied Ga-Nor after a little thought. "If he's an idiot then he might. Take a look at the roof. If he climbs up to the smoke hole, he'll pick us off like rabbits."

"You go take a look." Luk picked up his axe with a decisive air. "Screw a toad, but I don't plan to waste away here."

Before the Son of the Snow Leopard had time to ask what the soldier was up to, he began to chop away at the floor. The axe rose and fell, breaking the old floorboards. After only a few minutes a hole appeared in the floor, which would be wide enough to crawl through without too much difficulty.

While he was working, the man was out of breath and sweating but his good-natured face looked utterly pleased.

"My father was a hunter. These log houses are always built on stilts. The floor is raised a yard, if not two, above the ground. When they spend the winter, they keep produce down there. We can't get to the trapdoor; it's under the window. That's why I'm doing this."

"And what then? Are you suggesting that we crawl under the floor?" The northerner's expression was skeptical.

"No. I'm suggesting that you do that." Seeing how the red eyebrows lifted upward, Luk rushed to explain. "It's unlikely that I could kill off that beast, but you can."

"How will I get out of the ground? Dig a tunnel?"

"I'm telling you, the hut is built on stilts. Planks are fastened between the floor and the ground. They're all rotten. It won't take much strength."

"And while I'm crawling around down there you're just going to sit it out up here?"

Luk shrugged. "I could crawl around with you down there. That's not a problem for me. But sneaking up on a Burnt Soul—no way. You know he'd hear me coming a league off. I've never gone scouting through the Boxwood Mountains, you know."

Ga-Nor pondered it. A way out was being offered to him. The risk, of course, was great, but they either had to risk something or wait here until they died of hunger. Or until help came for the Burnt Soul. Morts, for example. Then it would be far too late to do anything. And the soldier was right. There was no way he could do this. He walked through the forest like a wild boar, making so much noise that even a deaf man could hear him. He would do more harm than good. Ga-Nor would have to do this himself.

"All right, we'll do it your way."

He crept along the wall to the window and then to the stove. Then he had to pass through an area that was in the line of fire. Luk, realizing what was about to happen, moved over. Ga-Nor took a leap and again he anticipated the arrow that struck the floor by a fraction of a second.

"Persistent brute," said the Son of the Snow Leopard through clenched teeth.

"Screw a toad, at least he missed you."

The northerner snorted in agreement and, without further delay, slid down into the hole. The storage pit was not very deep; it came up to about waist-high.

"Wait here. In case I call out for you."

"Can I do anything to help?"

"Pray for me if you have nothing else to do," suggested Ga-Nor, and then he disappeared under the floor.

Twilight reigned here, and it smelled strongly of mold, dampness, and earth. He quickly oriented himself and chose a path to the wall that stood opposite the door. The Burnt Soul was unlikely to be keeping watch there. Why would he, when he assumed that the only exits were through the door or the windows?

With all the will in the world he couldn't straighten

up here, so he had to crawl on all fours. Fortunately, he didn't have far to crawl. The Son of the Snow Leopard stopped at the boards that were fastened to the stilts. They extended down from the walls of the cabin and covered the gap between the ground and the floor. Just as Luk had suggested, parts of the boards were rotten and other parts were nailed haphazardly so that they fit loosely against each other.

Ga-Nor listened closely and didn't hear anything suspicious. Birds were chirping, insects were buzzing, wind was sweeping through the crowns of the lofty sycamores. The tracker put his eye to a chink between the boards and carefully checked the area. Most of his view was obscured by the blackberry bushes that had grown into a living hedge weighed down by large, dark purple berries. All he could do was hope that his enemy was on the opposite side of the cabin.

Ga-Nor took out his knife, wedged the blade in between the boards, and, using the weapon like a lever, began to clear a path for himself. As he worked, the northerner tried not to put too much force into it; he moved smoothly so that, Ug grant it so, the lumber would not creak. He was successful. The wood gave way easily and after a few minutes of patient effort, the Son of the Snow Leopard climbed out from under the cabin.

Without raising his head, he crawled like a snake on his stomach toward the blackberry bushes. Ignoring the thorns, he struggled through the hedge and crawled through the moss to the nearest sycamore. It took him nearly fifteen minutes to cover a paltry ten yards. But Ga-Nor could rival even the High-born when it came to the art of merging with a tree to make a single whole. Not a single twig snapped, not even the most fragile bush swayed at his passing, and the birds remained undisturbed.

Once he'd hidden himself in a hollow between the massive roots of the tree, the northerner breathed a sigh of relief. The hardest part was behind him. What came next should be easier. He had the advantage—his enemy did not know that someone had escaped from the cabin. He just had to use it.

True, his crawl through the blackberry bushes had taken its toll. His entire body, including his face, was covered in shallow, bleeding scratches. But he could deal with this aggravating trifle later. A Burnt Soul was not a Mort; its sense of smell was not as strong and so it wouldn't catch the scent of his blood.

Keeping low to the ground, Ga-Nor ran from the bushes in brief dashes from tree to tree. He didn't turn back until he'd run about eight hundred yards into the forest.

If not for Luk, he would have kept going. It would be quite a while before his disappearance was discovered. He could cover his tracks so well that not even one of the Damned could find him. But he had to return. Ug would not approve of a Son of the Snow Leopard abandoning his comrade. The reckoning after death would be terrible. Wallowing in the icy abyss of Oblivion was far more terrifying than any Burnt Soul.

Changing direction from the north to the east, he ran for another four hundred yards or so. To an outside observer it would seem that the northerner was meandering throughout the forest without rhyme or reason. But in reality, Ga-Nor was outflanking the ensconced archer in a steep arc, planning to come upon him from behind. It took over an hour of these meanderings for him to quietly draw near the front of the cabin unobserved by his adversary.

The cabin was no more than fifteen yards away. He could already see the closed door with the arrow sticking out of it. But the Burnt Soul was absent, even though all his suppositions led him to believe that it was somewhere nearby, judging by where the shot had come from.

Had it changed position?

This was bad. The creature was sitting under cover and there were many trees and bushes around the cabin. Where could it be hiding? The northerner had hoped to calculate the places from which the Burnt Soul could have taken an easy shot through the window. The first spot was the very place where the Son of the Snow Leopard was lying; the second was thirty paces from him behind a sycamore. But it seemed that there was no one there. Obviously he couldn't be hiding in the first spot either, or else Ga-Nor would already have departed for Ug's judgment.

"Where have you gotten to, you filthy little toad?" he whispered through clenched teeth.

Time passed but he still couldn't find his adversary. There was every indication that for some reason he'd up and left. Ga-Nor did not even begin to pay attention to that idiotic thought. He was far too cautious for that. He was going to wait for as long as he needed to.

A large spotted woodpecker flew over the bushes and caught his attention. The bird alighted on the trunk of a nearby sycamore and then instantly took wing, as if something had frightened it. The tracker peered avidly into the thick brush growing beneath the tree. He'd examined it earlier but he hadn't noticed any signs of danger and had been content to ignore it in his search for other hiding places where the Burnt Soul could have secreted itself.

There was nothing suspicious. Just the bushes. Very little to frighten a bird.

Again, endless minutes of waiting passed by. Ga-Nor did not take his eyes off the bushes. Then the wind changed. His nose was immediately assaulted by the scent of almonds.

The northerner nearly cursed. The beast was hiding all of twenty paces from him. He was so blind that if it were not for the bird, he would never have noticed his enemy. Thank Ug that when his eyes betrayed him, he still had his nose.

He began to crawl backward and to the side.

When the distance was shortened to ten paces he saw the Burnt Soul. A head, an upper body, and two arms. Instead of hips and legs these creatures had a short, scaly serpent's tail. It wasn't clear what purpose it served, since the brutes moved through the air as if by magic, hovering over the ground. But not very high. It was rumored that they could rise up to the height of a grown man.

The creature's skull seemed misshapen. A too high and heavy brow, a sunken face, delicate cheekbones. Sparse hair, into which the red-and-purple feathers of some unknown bird were braided. Yellow, shriveled skin, a small lower jaw; the face of an old man. It had no nose or ears. In their place were black holes. Its long arms, as thin as a skeleton's, looked deceptively weak but they could easily bend a horseshoe. A dirty gray-green tunic was thrown over the desiccated, angular body. A quiver with a bundle of arrows was on its back. Another three arrows were planted in the ground. The bow grasped in the creature's hands was so large that Ga-Nor began to have some misgivings. You'd use a bow like that to hunt Snow Trolls, not humans.

The archer was completely focused on the cabin. The Burnt Soul didn't bother to look around and had no clue that a human had been hiding near it all this time. Ga-Nor unsheathed his sword. He took a step toward his enemy. He froze. Another step. He froze again. Now more than ever he resembled a large, redheaded snow leopard. A cat stalking its un-witting prey.

The Burnt Soul shifted and the northerner stopped stalking him and rushed forward. The beast heard him, yelped, turned, and raised its bow. It was far more nimble than he had thought it would be.

At the last moment, Ga-Nor leaped aside and the arrow flew past his ear with an aggravated buzz. He brandished his sword and swept downward, driving it into the creature's face. The sword sheared through skin, flesh, bone, and brain, destroying the head of his opponent. Its back arched and it flew upward a good two yards; then it fell back to the ground, crashing into the bushes. Ga-Nor did not stop at this and struck the already dead Burnt Soul with three more tremendous blows. In the tracker's opinion, the creature deserved it.

The Son of the Snow Leopard returned to the cabin and drummed on the door.

"Luk, get out here!"

The door creaked open and the soldier gingerly stepped out of the cabin.

"Screw a toad! I was thinking he'd done you."

"It was I who 'did' him."

"You're covered in blood."

"It's from the blackberry bushes. The beast almost shot me."

"Was it alone?"

"Yes. Let's get out of here."

"I want to see it."

"Why?"

"I've never seen a Burnt Soul."

Ga-Nor shrugged his shoulders indifferently and indicated the spot where the body lay. He went into the cabin and quickly packed his things into his bag. When he got outside, he could see Luk circling the carcass. The redhead walked over to the guard and also looked at the corpse. The tracker couldn't really see why it was so interesting.

"You got to kill several of ours, you viper," spat Luk, pointing to three human scalps attached to the Burnt Soul's quiver.

"Good riddance," Ga-Nor responded gloomily.

The soldier pulled a red-and-purple feather from the hair of the slain creature. The feather had miraculously escaped being covered in blood.

"I'll take this to remember. Do you know the legend of how the Burnt Souls came to be?"

"No," said the northerner as he tried to draw the captured bow. It was useless. You needed to be a real leviathan to do that. The northerner wistfully dropped the useless weapon to the ground.

"In ancient times, the race of the Burnt Souls was exactly the same as the Je'arre. They lived together in the south, beyond the Great Waste. It was only afterward that the winged (one of the names given to the Je'arre in the Empire) flew to the north. According to the legends of our feathered friends, the tribe of the Burnt Souls, which was called something else before, violated the covenants of their god and he punished the heretics. He took their wings away, cast them from the sky, and burned their souls. The beasts grow up, live, die, and then nothing awaits them. They have no chance at all of finding themselves in either the Blessed Gardens or in the Abyss. Only the void and oblivion. And that's who these Burnt Souls are."

"Even without wings they fly perfectly well. Get yourself together, storyteller. We need to leave."

"Where are we going now?"

"Where you wanted to go. To Dog Green. And then we'll see."

Without responding, Luk smoothed out the feather and tucked it into the inside pocket of his old jacket.

6

The Nabatorians entered the village early in the morning.

The first riders appeared on the road that led to the Gates. Sixty cavalry galloped down the central street and gathered next to the inn, which they quickly turned into something resembling an army headquarters. They threw the four lodgers out on their ears, but the foursome acted intelligently and did not rebel or offer resistance of any kind. The innkeeper, pale from terror, shoved the gold coins into his pockets with trembling hands and, faltering, mumbled about how happy he was to have such welcome guests. The remaining soldiers were quickly quartered in the nearby houses. They did not cause any harm to the villagers and they were remarkably civil. They didn't murder, they didn't rob, they didn't rape the women, and they paid for all services without fail. It was obvious that they would be there for a long time, and there was no sense in plundering and filching that which had become their own anyway.

Toward dinnertime, a squadron of infantry appeared on the road. Eighty men, maybe a hundred— the villagers didn't count. They too conducted themselves well, obeying the commander of the cavalry in everything and quickly dispersing among the cottages. Half of the warriors were armed with axes and they began to cut down trees. The commander was planning to build a small outpost and barracks along the road.

The loggers were conscripted to help the soldiers, but they proved to be too proud and foolish to work for outsiders. They brandished their axes instead. On the officer's orders, three of the ringleaders of the riot were hung and a further two were drowned in the river as a warning. These executions had a sobering effect on the remaining loggers, and no further problems arose with the wood-fellers—they industriously felled timber for the future stronghold.

The logs were transported to the standing stone with the help of horses. It was there that the commander of the Nabatorians intended to raise a fort that would seal off the road to the Gates of Six Towers.

One day a soldier found a bottle of moonshine hidden by the locals. He got plastered and began hassling the thatcher's wife. The thatcher would not stand for it and punched the attacker right in the face. The soldier grabbed his sword, and the peasant, his pitchfork. The patrol arrived and disarmed the men, and the commander passed out a heavy sentence on them—they would both be hanged. The soldier, for not carrying out his orders; the thatcher, for daring to raise a hand against a soldier of Nabator.

Almost all the inhabitants of the village were rounded up for the execution. The men frowned and clenched their fists but they didn't do anything stupid; their women restrained them. Many of the women cried, fearing that soon retribution would befall all the villagers. However, their fear was not justified. None of those assembled were harmed. Standing by the gallows, the captain read off a declaration written by the Nabatorian King to his new subjects, which stated that the villages and cities occupied by the glorious army of the allied forces of Nabator and Sdis would rest under the auspices of His Majesty until the end of time. All who lent support to the army and took the oath of fealty to His Majesty would be granted permission to live in peace, to work and not pay taxes over the course of the next ten years. It also promised that the punishment for offering resistance to the valiant army of the Nabatorian King, for aiding the enemy soldiers of the Empire, or for any other transgressions against the crown would be death.

The execution took place. There were no further deaths.

"It won't work. Not today, anyway. There are patrols. And sentries on the outskirts. We'll have to stay." Layen had come to this distressing conclusion.

She had just returned from outside and was telling me the latest news. I was listening while I secured an arrowhead to a narrow shaft. A few other provisions were spread out on the table. Next to them were eight already completed arrows. Near at hand was an unstrung bow. As distinct from the straight longbow (a bow that is composed of a single piece of material, usually wood) that I had used on our last job, this was not as big and long-range. It was a composite bow (a bow made of three materials: wood laths, horn, and sinew. Since it is a recurve bow, the tips of the limbs curve away from the archer when the bow is strung), smaller than the other. But in capable hands, it was at least as dangerous a weapon as its big brother. And without undue modesty, I can attest that my own hands are sufficiently capable.

"We'll try to leave at night."

"That's unwise. These first days they will be on the alert. But when they realize that the peasants aren't going to run off, they'll stop guarding the borders of the village. We need to wait."

"Layen, we can't wait. It's a miracle you're alive after yesterday."

"I was careless. A mistake I won't repeat." She angrily flipped her braid over her shoulder. "Are you afraid of our new guests?"

"Somewhat," I replied reluctantly. "I'm more afraid of what that little captain said. An alliance between Nabator and Sdis. Do you realize now how they managed to capture the Gates?"

"I'm not an idiot," she said, smiling crookedly. "Necromancers. And the Damned that have stood behind them for the past five hundred years."

"It's unclear what they want here."

"The Empire used to be their country. They decided to pay it a visit."

"Sarcasm doesn't suit you." The latest arrow was ready and I set it next to the others. I searched for a new arrowhead and chose a broad serrated one. "You, my lady, may be in danger."

"I scarcely think that the former Walkers will come here searching blindly."

"And I think that a week ago no one would have thought they would decide to come into the Empire at all. I don't know what the Damned want in our country. But it's dangerous here now. We must stick to our original plan and head for Al'sgara. Joch has a debt to pay."

"What's that matter? A war is coming."

"Giiyans always need money. The assassins won't stop coming until we take care of the client."

Layen shook her head. She understood my point, but she still questioned it.

"You're as stubborn as a herd of thickheaded donkeys, Gray. We won't be able to handle it."

"And you put too much hope in the mercy of Melot, Weasel. As a general rule, trouble falls on one's head unexpectedly."

I could see that she wanted to growl at me, but she curbed her temper. Over the course of the years spent living together, she had come to realize that my reaction to that would be to dig my heels in and do as I wished. So she curbed her outburst and smiled soothingly.

"Let's wait until evening, dear."

"Let's," I agreed easily. "But nothing will change. We're lucky we live on the outskirts. Otherwise we'd have to let some of these scum into our house."

I took the news that the Gates had fallen and that enemy forces had encroached upon the Empire calmly. Of course, at first I hadn't believed it. But I saw the Nabatorians with my own eyes and that meant they had somehow managed to pass through the Boxwood Mountains. That could only be done through the Gates, and it was unlikely that the garrison of the citadel had let their enemies pass through out of the kindness of their hearts.

As a matter of fact, I didn't care at all who ruled. Whether it was the Emperor or the Damned, it was all one and the same to me as long as they did not harm me or my sun. If they let us live in peace then everything would be as it should. And all the rest, their private squabbles and jockeying for position— it was absurd. Who needed it? Other than storytellers whose only dream was to turn the reckless deeds of the latest dead "hero" into the next mawkish legend?

"Well, look who it is," sighed Layen, glancing at the window. "All you have to do is think about rubbish and there it is."

I saw that Mols's foursome were entering the yard.

Weasel narrowed her eyes dangerously.

"Should I send them off?"

"No," I replied to her quickly. "Let's see what they want this time."

Bamut and Midge were standing at the gate, while Whip and Shen walked up to the porch. We met them on the threshold.

Seeing us, Whip asked complacently, "How's your health, Layen?"

"Since when are you so solicitous?"

"Since Mols asked me to conduct you safe and sound to Al'sgara. I'm making money on you."

She laughed grimly. "An honest answer. I didn't expect that from you."

He shrugged his shoulders serenely. "We came here on business. The Nabatorians took away the inn for their 'perpetual use' and asked us to leave while we were still whole."

"I marvel at their kindness. If we were in their place, we'd string up the outsiders. From far off you look like spies."

"Melot spared us from the Gaunt Widow. We decided not to wait around until they recalled us. Their commander, regardless of his youth, is a brute."

"And they took all our damn horses away, the bastards!" Bamut said with a malicious grimace.

I tossed my utak up into the air and caught it by the handle. Toss. Catch.

"What do you want from us? We can't give you back your horses."

"Can we lodge here?"

Layen and I didn't even exchange glances.

I don't trust them.

Neither do I, Ness. But they could turn out to be useful if we decide to leave.

It'll be simpler without them. With them we'll have to grow eyes in the backs of our heads.

It will be easier to get out of the village with them. Then we can try to get rid of them.

She had a practical way of thinking. She never hastened to abandon useful things. A smart woman.

We can't try to get rid of them. Either we do it or we don't. Are you sure you can deal with all of them, dear?

Yes.

All right, we'll do as you say. But first let's try to escape without their help. "I don't see any weapons on you," I said, glaring at our uninvited guests.

"They told us to surrender them. Bamut got in a spot of trouble for his concealed crossbow."

"Good. You can stay that way. You can use the southern half of the house. The entrance is in the backyard. I hope you won't cause us any trouble."

I attached threatening overtones to the last words.

"There won't be any trouble," Whip hastened to assure me. "Do you intend to stay here long?"

"We're toying with that question," I replied ambiguously.

"Just a thought for reflection. Today a Nabatorian patrol tried to stop two riders who were heading for your village from the direction of Al'sgara. From the conversation I heard, they put up quite the fight. They had to be shot down with crossbows, but they still managed to take down four soldiers. They were serious lads."

"Are you telling us this for the good of our souls?"

"Just that daring fools are being drawn to Dog Green recently. We all need to get cracking. Even the Nabatorians will let someone slip through sooner or later. Or they'll go after the villagers. I don't trust their benevolence."

"We'll think about it."

"As you will. Think on it. We'll wait a day or two and then we're out of here."

"But what about your money?" asked Layen mockingly. "Would you really leave us here?"

"Money is good, of course, but life is far more precious. I lose my appetite near Nabatorians. And if our troops come suddenly then there will be such a stew that getting out of the cauldron might be difficult."

"Only time will tell how it all turns out," replied Layen. "Dinner is not for a while. Since you're staying here you can fill the water barrels out by the shed."

"So now I'm hired out to work around the household?" said Midge indignantly.

"Consider it payment for your lodging. Oh, and by the way, give me the knife."

"What knife?" he snarled immediately.

She smiled. "I would never believe that the Nabatorians could take it away from you. If you want to live here then you have to do it under my rule. And I say no concealed knives."

Midge frowned, about to start an argument. Whip scowled darkly at him. The diminutive assassin cast a dissatisfied glance at his commander but submitted to the unspoken order. He pulled his weapon of choice from under his jacket. He dropped it at my feet.

I picked it up.

"You'll get it back when you leave. Don't forget about the water. He who works, eats."

Pork did not agree with the people around him. He thought that the arrival of the Nabatorians was a mighty fine thing and terribly interesting. Until now the village idiot had never seen so many armed men in one place.

He reckoned half of them were knights. Yeah. Also, he'd never seen anyone hanged before. And that had been very informative and entertaining. A thwack, and they began to so amusingly twitch their legs and croak. Then their tongues popped out and turned dark blue like a dewberry. Pork loved dewberries. They were sweet, just very prickly. It hurt. He should offer a prayer to Melot so that he would drive away all the thorns from the bushes and then Pork could gobble up the yummy little berries to his heart's content.

And also, those hanged men, or rather just the soldier, had wet his trousers when he was already dead. He was probably scared of going to Melot and the Blessed Gardens. What an idiot. Yeah.

It was too bad, of course, about the thatcher. He never bothered Pork. . . . But then it was stupid that the people in the village said that the Nabatorians were despicable. They're not despicable at all. They showed the loggers right away who was boss now. They gave it to them good, and they quickly became quiet as mice. Now they were chopping away at the forest so hard that chips were flying. They probably don't want to be hanged. To turn blue and have their tongues pop out. And they don't want to be drowned in the river. The soldiers are kind. And their commander is kind. And smart. Direct, like Pork himself. Yes. He'd instantly realized that the loggers were evil when Pork complained that they had ripped his shirt. And the commander had laughed and said he would punish them. Later. Somehow. He really wanted to watch them be punished. That's far more fun than watching cows graze. Yeah.

The Nabatorians were not evil. And those who said so were idiots. Pork would go and tell his friend the commander what the people thought of him.

In the beginning he hadn't hoped that the soldiers would become his friends. They seemed frightful and horribly mean. They pushed him about when he started telling tales about knights, but then they realized that he was very, very smart, and they began to talk to him. They were pleased to joke with him and they laughed so very, very much. They were happy to see him and they always asked when Pork would become a knight. They even promised to give him the biggest real sword and to teach him how to use it. Until then they told him to practice with a stick. He chopped down a whole sapling, imagined that it was a sword, and went off to rout old Roza's turnips. You wouldn't believe how she railed at him! She nearly threw her cane at him. And when he told her that the commander himself had given him permission she began to curse him, calling him a stupid idiot. Just who that old hag was calling an idiot, Pork wanted to know. But tonight he was going to tell Captain Nai all about the repulsive old crone. Let him know all about her. And then he'd hang the old slut together with the loggers. So that it wouldn't be boring. And Pork would watch and laugh at the evildoers.

The cowherd suddenly remembered that it would be very difficult to hang the loggers now. He had seen them being chopped up into little pieces with his own eyes. It was the day before yesterday. Pork, as always, had been grazing the damned, lazy cows in the same old place not far from the standing stone. Or more accurately, the cows had been grazing themselves and he had been watching them build the wooden fort. It was a real fortress, even though half the stockade hadn't been set yet. But they had already managed to build a tower, and an actual archer was sitting on it watching the road! He could shoot anyone he wanted. And he'd hit them, too. They were brave, these archers. And really good shots. Almost as good as Gnut from the village, just not one-eyed.

So anyways, there were the loggers and a few soldiers with them, building the fort, and just who do you think popped out onto the road from Al'sgara? Imperial soldiers. About forty of them. They were all on horses, screaming, waving their weapons around. They started hacking away at anyone they could get their hands on. Pork was actually horrified—they were cutting down both the loggers and the soldiers! They didn't even bother to sort out who was good and who was evil. They needed to kill the loggers! But they could befriend the Nabatorians. They could meet in the evenings, chat about weapons and virgins, drink the innkeeper's shaf. His shaf was so tasty! Every day now the Nabatorians treated Pork to it and then they laughed when his legs gave out. But he didn't have any hard feelings against them. No. He understood that it was all in good fun. Plus, they were going to give him a sword soon. It wouldn't do to get in a fight with them.

But the wicked Imperial soldiers didn't get away alive. The commander of the village rode to the rescue with his soldiers. And every soldier had an archer with him. They jumped down from the horses, and how they started to fire! Hoo-wee! And the one who was still sitting in the tower helped. Wow, how they rained down arrows on them all! They killed so many. Uh-huh. And those they couldn't, the riders cut down. As they should. Serves them right. And the villagers considered them friends. What idiots, right?

Pork watched as the Nabatorians inspected the bodies of the dead men. They took their horses, weapons, money, their beautiful boots. That was the most interesting of all. He wanted to do that, too. Except that no one called him over to the dead men. So all the spoils fell to others.

And then Pork recalled the other dead men. The ones in the forest glade. The ones killed by the fearsome carpenter. They probably still had all sorts of money and other pretty things. He could keep them for himself or trade them in for tasty food. Oh, yeah. And Pars, who looked so kindly on the outside, had killed those strange men just as fast as the Nabatorians had killed the swift troop of Imperial soldiers. It was good that Pork never thought to tell anyone what had happened. Then others would have taken everything away from the dead men and kept it for themselves, and Pork would be left holding the bag. What a smart boy he was after all!

The half-wit had a goal. He decided to lay hold of the belongings of the dead men and so, leaving the cows in Melot's care (after he diligently prayed to him), he headed for the forest. He had to walk far, through the entire village. Pork was afraid that his father would see him and then he'd really be in trouble. But he was lucky. No one stopped him.

In the forest, Pork began to have doubts.

What if someone else had found the wonderful dead men and robbed them? What then? He'd be going there for nothing. He wouldn't have any of those useful things or tasty treats. And what if the dead men had gone off somewhere?

The closer he came, the more terrified he became. The stories that the miller's son told him last summer came back to him. All about how dead men can come to life, how they crawl out of graveyards and gobble up anyone who dares to walk past them at night. And even if you didn't walk, but ran instead, they'd just chase you down and then gobble you up.

During one especially chilling story, L'on had sneaked up on Pork, grabbed him by the shoulder, and barked. The half-wit soiled his trousers from fear and stuttered for a week. And everyone had laughed and called him Rotten Turnip.

His nose was hit by the foul odor of decay and the idiot realized that the dead men hadn't gone anywhere. He saw the glade, the bodies that had been fairly devoured by the vultures and ravens, and an outsider, who was attentively inspecting the corpses. The fetid air and the thousands of flies fighting over the carrion didn't seem to bother him at all.

Pork nearly started crying from disappointment. He was too late! Now that man would take everything! All the money and everything else. He'd lost his sweets and his wealth! The vile bastard!

The man was standing with his back to Pork. He was tall. Broad in the shoulders. There was something strange about the black staff he held in his hands, but the half-wit couldn't figure out what it was. The man was dressed in a long, white hooded robe, cinched at the waist by a wide black belt, on which hung a formidable curved sword.

Oh, yes, it would be bad to argue with him. He had a weapon. He'd be sure to use it to cut off your head if you asked him to share his spoils.

Frustrated, Pork whined softly, smearing tears across his dirty cheeks with his fists.

The stranger had excellent hearing. He instantly

turned sharply and peered at the bushes where the cowherd was hiding. His rival's face was concealed by the hood and all Pork could see was a dark opening. When the cowherd saw the darkness under the hood, he felt pierced to the bone by the man's gaze, and he experienced a fresh onslaught of terror. He pressed himself into the ground and held his breath, hoping that the stranger wouldn't see him.

But he didn't think of turning away. He just stood there and watched. Pork's heart felt like it was about to burst out of his chest from terror. He regretted that he'd come here at all. He'd rather be herding cows. Better them than these treasures. He'd lived without them so far, and he could live another hundred years without them. Right now the half-wit wanted only one thing—for the creepy man to leave.

He slowly began to crawl backward, and instantly the man in white began walking quickly in his direction. Now Pork could see that the head of his staff was carved out of a piece of black stone in the shape of a skull. The cowherd froze, horror-struck.

"Come out," ordered his rival, as he stopped in front of the bush. "I won't cause you any harm."

Pork didn't dare disobey. Squeaking from fear, trying not to look at the man who was talking to him, he wormed his way out into the glade. For a fraction of a second the man regarded him, and then he removed his hood from his head.

He didn't seem horrifying and ominous anymore.

He was a bit older than Pork. He was tanned, with black hair and high cheekbones, refined features, handsome brown eyes, and a neatly trimmed beard.

The stranger was looking at the half-wit with curiosity but without any ill will.

"Are you from the village?"

Pork nodded hurriedly, trying to show how nice he was.

"Do you know what happened here?"

Another nod. He wasn't about to lie.

"Who killed them?"

"Pars the carpenter."

"And did he kill these two as well?" The man pointed at the two bodies nearest him.

The cowherd wrinkled his brow, trying to remember. Then he shook his head no.

"No, no. Those two were already dead when Pars came running to help his wife."

"His wife? Was it she who burned their heads?"

"I don't know," said Pork truthfully. "I didn't see."

"Interesting," muttered the stranger as he pensively stroked his staff with his fingers. "Do you know where this woman lives?"

"Yeah. Here. Not too far."

"Will you show me the way?"

Pork nodded in agreement and then hiccupped in surprise. It seemed to the half-wit that the skull on the staff was grinning at him.

———

We couldn't leave Dog Green the day that Mols's foursome waltzed into my home. The Nabatorians, for all their amiability, vigilantly guarded the ways out of the village. The nocturnal attempt undertaken by Layen and me to escape into the forest nearly ended in disaster. Two ambushes, plus the frequency of patrols, plus the watchers on the towers and the fields lit with bonfires put a wrench in our plans. We had to return. We ran into Whip in the yard. He was not in the least surprised by the return of his hosts, armed and geared up for travel. He only chuckled meaningfully, took a bite out of his turnip, and, without saying a word, headed for the section of the house allocated to our guests, all the while whistling a soft tune.

Throughout the following days I was sullen and mean. And only Layen, who had long since gotten used to such fits of petulancy, could calm me. I felt like a wolf ready to snap at anyone who got in his way. Idleness threw me off balance. Beyond all that, I had a sense of impending disaster and it made me feel like an animal caught in a snare.

Whip tried not to get under our feet too much. The others also conducted themselves more quietly than the water under the grass. Even Shen and Midge stopped squabbling, though that was all they did the first evening. Now they had concluded a sort of temporary truce—they were ignoring each other's presence. Our guests saw us twice each day, at lunch and at dinner. We all kept our silence, quickly ate the proffered food, and then retired. And Midge, despite his grumbling, took it upon himself to fill the huge barrel by the shed with water from the well. But no one really objected to his taking the initiative.

A week after the arrival of the Nabatorians, Whip decided to have a little talk with us. "We're leaving in a couple of days."

At that moment I was morosely dragging my spoon through my soup and I asked mockingly, "You planning on prepping in the meantime?"

"Yes. I need to clarify the patrol routes and the shift changes."

"I can tell you that right now."

"Then what's stopping you?"

"The desire to live a long and happy life."

"I see," he muttered and then fell into thought for a long time. Eventually, and for some reason looking at Midge while he did so, he asked, "There's no chance?"

"Well, there's always a chance." My tone was still derisive. "But you won't get out quietly. That I guarantee. But fighting your way through isn't very sensible. Not right now, at any rate."

"Why can't you just go through the forest?" wondered Shen.

"And what then? The only road to Al'sgara is here. It's forest for leagues around. And beyond that there are swamps. The Blazogs have tried to dam it, but you can't get through. The only feasible path is the highway. And they are watching it."

"And yet we'll risk it. Staying here any longer is too dangerous."

"As you wish," I said, shrugging my shoulders apathetically.

"Are you afraid?" Shen asked tauntingly. Whip hissed at him in warning, but the Healer didn't bat an eye.

Contrary to the expectations of all those present, I did not get angry and just said lazily, "I'll tell you what, kid. On the day I fall for such an idiotic trick, you can demand a hundred sorens from me. If, of course, you don't lose courage."

Midge brayed with delight that his antagonist had been so readily handled. He slapped his hand on the table. But before Shen had time to come up with a scathing rejoinder, he was interrupted.

"Damn. . . . We have a guest!" warned Bamut, who had been sitting by the window all this time, carving a silly little man from a wooden block.

Seeing who was entering the courtyard, Layen's face went whiter than the stranger's cloak and she swore obscenely.

"Nobody move. Be calm," I said, picking up a hatchet from under the table.

"He's alone," marveled Midge.

"Midge, stay quiet! I have no desire to scrape your intestines off my ceiling. Whip, put a muzzle on him. And on that milksop, too."

Shen didn't get offended at the term "milksop"; more than that, it seemed that he didn't even hear it. He was just as pale as my sun. Midge changed his tune slightly and asked in a plaintive tone, "Will somebody tell me who this guy is?"

"Just stay quiet, okay?" Even the perpetually composed Bamut was starting to get nervous. "We can leave out the back."

"What's the point? He'll still sniff us out," said Whip with hopeless anguish. "The bastard pinned us down! We've really stepped in it now! What does he want here?"

"We're about to find out." Layen flicked away a strand of blond hair that had fallen in her eyes and went out to meet the necromancer.

They watched each other for a second. Layen hoped that she looked sufficiently frightened.

The necromancer was young. No more than twenty-five. But judging by his staff, he was a master of the Fourth Sphere (after they have graduated from the Sdisian magical academy, competent mages enter into the Spheres of Mastery. The highest Sphere is the Eighth). For such an age, that was exceedingly high. *That means that the boy is talented, obviously.* Layen tried to choose her actions wisely, knowing that the most important thing was that she not overact her role. *And he's undoubtedly intelligent. He could cause us a lot of problems. How unfortunate that he came! What if this sorcerer is also a Seeker* (bearers of the Gift who are able to detect the spark in other people)? *Did he catch the scent of my Gift?*

She bowed quickly, hiding her eyes so that the White would not read anything in them. Quickly, swallowing her words, she began to chatter, "What brings such a fine gentleman to our home? Do you wish to place an order? Please don't worry, good sir, everything will be made to your specifications, whatever you like. Just ask anyone, they'll tell you the best carpenter in the village lives here. Why, just last year, at the fair, the one they put on at El'nichi Ford, there—"

"Be silent," the visitor interrupted her calmly. He'd obviously lost all interest in her. Now he was looking around the yard searchingly. "I was told that Ann and Pars the carpenter live here."

Layen's heart beat painfully.

"You were shown the right path, good sir," she replied obsequiously, privately wishing that she could disembowel the damned chatterbox who led him here. "That's us."

"I want to see them. Urgently."

"I'm Ann. My husband's in the house."

Tenacious brown eyes searched her face. Thick, black eyebrows crawled upward in surprise. Suddenly the necromancer chuckled. "Either you've been deceiving me, or you're smarter than you seem."

Layen tried to maintain her subservient countenance. She decided not to look at the Sdisian any longer. She was afraid her eyes would give her away.

"Lead me inside!" he said sharply, not waiting for an answer.

"Please, please," she said in a rush. "I invite you in, good sir. We always welcome guests to our table."

The necromancer entered the house and saw the five men. He snorted.

"You have quite a lot of husbands."

"I'm her husband," I responded calmly as I got up from the table. "And these are our kinsmen. Come in, have a seat."

"Guests do bless a home, after all." The Sdisian shifted the curved sword hanging from his belt and sat down at the table. "You, carpenter, sit down as well. Don't wait on me. Do you know what I am?"

"I do."

"And your kinsmen?" He pronounced the final word with a smirk.

"They know."

"That's good. That means they won't do anything stupid and they'll save me from the effort of destroying your hut. Mistress, I seem to recall you promising to feed me. I'm hungry from the road."

A few minutes later a bowl of hearty chicken soup, a slice of black bread, butter, an onion, a jug of sour cream, and a mug of cold mint shaf appeared before him.

The sorcerer ignored the others and began to eat. Everyone was silent. Bamut continued to carve his ridiculous little man as if nothing were amiss, but he was betrayed by the sweat on his brow and a certain nervousness in his movements. I could see he was agitated; the hand holding the paring knife was shaking slightly, and every once in a while he gouged into the wood a little deeper than he should. Shen and Midge were sitting by the stove. The first had put on a bored countenance and looked like he was trying to see the sky through the ceiling. The second, having finally realized who it was that had come to visit them, laced his fingers together and began muttering under his breath—whether prayers against evil magic or curses, I do not know.

I chewed my bread listlessly. My wife and I exchanged glances and she indicated I should be quiet. Layen didn't know whether or not the necromancer could hear our mental conversations, and she did not want to find out.

"You're quite a good cook," said the unwelcome guest as he pushed the empty plate away from himself. "Sit."

She hesitated; then she walked over to the table and sat down opposite the sorcerer. Next to me.

"I heard that in the forest, not all that far from here, someone was killed. Do you know anything about that?"

"No, kind sir."

The necromancer smiled and nodded. It was hard to tell if he believed her or not.

"Some very strange murders they were," he said.

"Two corpses left among the others. You would think the poor souls had stuck their heads in a furnace. But of course, you haven't heard anything about that, either, have you?"

"We rarely go into the forest. Melot be praised, we haven't seen any corpses. And there's been no talk of them in the village," I replied.

"I was not talking to you!" His brown eyes flashed angrily. "So, Ann? Do you know anything about these poor men?"

"No, kind sir."

"Don't lie to me," he warned her.

"I'm telling the truth," said Layen.

All of a sudden I remembered Pork. He'd seen us. We should have drowned that gossiping idiot in the river while we had the chance! What possessed us to let the tattletale live?

"Look at me." That same deceptive blandness could still be heard in the sorcerer's voice. "In the eyes."

She harnessed her willpower and did as he asked. The necromancer looked at her for a long time. Intolerably long. I tensed my muscles, ready to turn the table over on this wretch if I had to.

Suddenly the Sdisian started laughing.

"You have a talent, girl." It was almost ridiculous to hear the word "girl" from a man far younger than she. I saw that my sun was biting back a caustic retort that was just begging to slip through her lips. "You lie skillfully. Or are you not lying?"

"I have no reason to lie. Why would I dare deceive you?"

"Oh, yes! That would indeed be very . . . imprudent of you. Lying won't do you any good. You should know that. And you know what? I believe you. What would such a good housewife like yourself be doing in a forest glade with the deceased?"

The necromancer was obviously mocking her. He knew. He knew that she had been there, or he had sensed the remnants of her magic. Was such a thing really possible?

But for some reason he continued his game.

Whip casually tucked his legs underneath him so he'd be in a better position to jump on the sorcerer's back. I comprehended what he was doing, but unlike him I relaxed and put my hands on my knees, closer to my utak.

"Where do your kinsmen come from?"

"From Al'sgara," Shen said softly.

The White broke forth into a happy smile as if he and the Healer had turned out to be compatriots.

"A fine city. Beautiful, so they say. My brothers and I plan to take a look at it in due time. A very interesting place. Many from Al'sgara possess the Gift. Do you have it, Ann?"

"No, kind sir. I'm not from that city."

"Too bad." Then he kept talking, as if reasoning with himself. "You don't seem like a Walker. Perhaps an Ember? But I don't feel your heat. What are you? A prodigy? If so, how did the Seekers miss such power?"

"I don't understand what you're talking about, kind sir."

"Perhaps you don't understand." He didn't bother to argue. "And perhaps you do. Alas, I can't really tell. It's heartbreaking, you know? So we'll just have to continue this conversation later. In the presence of another . . . person. I'm going to tell him all about you today. You should be flattered by the honor."

He stood up from the table, walked over to the door, and turned around.

"I will return with new questions, and it would be best for all of you if you prepared answers that will satisfy me. I'd be upset if I had to destroy a family circle so dear to my heart. The one I'm waiting for will arrive soon. And in the meantime, I've arranged some reliable protection for you so you won't feel the need to run away in fear. See you soon, Ann."

The sorcerer walked through the gate at an unhurried pace. He closed the latch securely behind himself. The five Morts who were waiting there for him shifted.

"Guard the house," said the necromancer offhandedly. "Keep an eye on the humans. No one is allowed to leave. If they try, bring them back. But don't maim them. And don't even lay a finger on the woman. I need her intact."

Ann seemed intelligent and not at all timid. The

Sdisian admired that in people. She had lied, of course, when she said she hadn't been in the forest. The beating of her heart gave her away. But when he'd mentioned the Gift, it was as if she didn't have a clue. There was no indication she was lying. It was a pity he wouldn't be able to sense her power unless she invoked it.

It's possible he could deal with this himself, of course. He could easily torture her if it came to that. But he was fearful of making a mistake. If Ann died, and her ability with her, the Superiors (the title of sorcerers of the Eighth Sphere) would not be pleased. So he had to ask for help. The sorcerer didn't like it, but he had no other choice. The command was crystal clear—if a person possessing the spark is found, they must be reported immediately.

Using the end of his staff, the Sdisian traced an undulating line in the dirt, which had been baked hard by the intense heat. He finished off his design with a triangle; then he spoke a short summoning incantation. A Herald wove itself from the meager shadows, spat angrily, received its instructions, and melted away. It knew whom to search for and what it had to convey.

Now all he had to do was wait.

7

Ga-Nor was a decent teacher. Over the past few days, Luk had learned more about the forest than he had in his entire life. Whenever a chance presented itself, the northerner trained his companion in the principles of tracking. Luk gained the skills slowly, but his progress was clear. At least the soldier had stopped trampling through dry bushes and leaving tracks in wet soil. He tried to walk on the edge of the trail so that he wouldn't shred the cobwebs strung over it, and he walked in the Son of the Snow Leopard's footsteps. He breathed far more quietly, spoke in a low tone, listened to the forest, and kept his eyes open. But the most important thing he learned was not to get in Ga-Nor's way.

After several days of such training, Ga-Nor found that he didn't have to keep an eye on his companion as much as before. The distance they traveled in a day's march increased exponentially.

After their encounter with the Burnt Soul, no one else pursued the humans. It seemed that their enemies had finally lost track of the fugitives. But Ga-Nor played it safe and pushed them onward as if the entire Sextet (one of the titles given to the Damned) were at their heels.

At first they made their way through the forested

foothills, which quickly gave way to rolling hills. After three days, they entered a wooded plain with many lakes, rivers, and streams in its low places. Impassible, thorny underbrush and thick fir copses blocked their path through the dark ravines and gloomy sycamore groves.

The companions moved westward rapidly. They avoided roads. In the beginning, when the terrain was rough, they traveled parallel to the road, but when they began moving away from it, Luk lost all sense of where they were and how far they had gone. He had no idea how the northerner determined their route. He tried to orient himself with the help of the sun, but that didn't work. The soldier didn't believe that the detours and spirals they wound through the forest every day would bring them to Dog Green. Once Luk dared to voice his concerns about the validity of their route, but all he got for his pains was a meaningful snort. Ga-Nor wasn't going to explain anything to him.

The guardsman heaved a sigh. The endless, exhausting daily marches had him losing faith that they would get to where they needed to be. A village is not a city. The chance that they would pass right by it, not noticing it amongst all the beech, spruce, and oak groves, was great. And if they got lost, they could wander through the forest until the end of their lives. Or maybe stumble into Sandon (the vast forested territories to the east of the Empire. The Kingdom of the Highborn). And of course the Highborn would be beyond thrilled to greet the intruders. But then again, the tracker seemed to be heading in the wrong direction.

Stupidly, Luk decided to ask Ga-Nor which direction they were traveling.

"East."

"What do you mean east? Are you sure?"

"I'm sure," he replied serenely.

"But we need to go west, screw a toad!"

"But right now we're going east," said the northerner absentmindedly.

He stopped and crouched down, gingerly probing the ground with his fingers.

"What do you mean we're going east? Why east?"

"Don't panic! We're going the right way. We just needed to make a detour. There was a really bad spot. We had to retrace our steps. Go more to the east."

"Retrace our steps . . ." whined Luk petulantly. "And what about that route displeased you? It was just fine."

"I told you, it was a really bad spot. A gove's lair. Didn't you smell it?"

"Well . . . yes. I smelled something strange. I thought it was some kind of herb blooming."

"An herb . . . I have no idea what you would do without me. An herb! That's what a forest demon smells like during its molt. So I decided not to meddle with it. It isn't worth the trouble to get mixed up in that. Far better to lose a day of traveling."

"Well, if there was a gove, then it's understandable," said Luk, forgetting his outrage. "But will you tell me when we're going to get there? All we do is walk. I'm sick of all these trees. I want to get to the city. Have some shaf. If we keep going like this, I'm going to die."

"Shaf!" scoffed the woodsman. "Right now, brother, the Nabatorians are gulping down your shaf."

"But that doesn't mean I can't dream of it."

"Drink some water from a stream and shut your trap." Ga-Nor stopped feeling the ground and stood up.

"That's all you know, isn't it? 'Shut your trap,' 'quiet,' 'don't shout.'"

"Don't shout."

"Who's going to hear us out here?"

"You clod, how many times do I have to repeat myself?" whispered the Son of the Snow Leopard. "The forest adores silence. Your shrieks can be heard for leagues. Speak in a whisper; I'm not deaf."

Luk sniffed aggrievedly, but he lowered his voice. "You still haven't told me when we're going to get to that damned village."

"Soon. We're basically already there."

"There's no habitation anywhere near here."

"Look under your feet. Do you see the tracks?"

"No."

"The marks are old. They've already faded, and the earth doesn't stick to my fingers. They're twelve to fifteen days old."

Ga-Nor passed his hand over a part of the footpath. To Luk's eyes the spot looked no different than any other.

"Tracks still don't mean anything."

"Of course they mean something. And here, they mean a peasant's bast shoes. Someone from the village was hunting. I'd advise against walking over there. There's a trap."

"Where?" The soldier stopped dead in his tracks.

"About five paces away from you. Straight on."

"What do you mean? There's nothing there, screw a toad!"

The ground looked like any other ground. If there really was a trap there, it was perfectly camouflaged.

"You never really see anything," said the Son of the Snow Leopard irately. "But that doesn't mean it's not there. Walk behind me. Follow in my footsteps."

He stepped off the footpath and walked around the dangerous spot.

"Why did they put it there?"

"How should I know? Maybe for the gove. Maybe for animals. Anyhow, we have no more than four hours to go."

"And then we'll get to relax!" This was the only thing Luk now dreamed of.

"If all is well. But no, we have to go farther. To Al'sgara. West of here is not like the north. We won't encounter any civilization along the road. It's just forest and the Blazgian swamps. And we'll have to slog through them for another two weeks, if not more."

The soldier groaned loudly, hoping the sound would express the full extent of his despair and frustration.

When it was past midday, and the shadows made by the trees were starting to lengthen, the travelers emerged onto the shore of a river.

Ga-Nor sat down on the ground and untied his bootlaces. Luk took off his shoes entirely. He walked over to the sun-warmed rocks and, blinking contentedly like a cat that had drunk its fill of cream, he lowered his feet into the cold water.

"You'll get a chill," the Son of the Snow Leopard warned him.

"I'm seasoned," objected the soldier, and then he sneezed loudly.

Gnawing on a blade of grass, Ga-Nor chuckled knowingly.

"It's not much farther. We'll walk with the current. There, beyond that bend, that's where the open forest begins. If we get through that, we'll wind up in the village."

"What do you mean? Have you been here?"

"No."

"Then how do you know?"

The tracker shrugged.

"Fine. I'll take your word for it. You don't argue with northerners when it comes to instinct. Whew! I was starting to think we'd never get there. I've just realized how much I hate the forest." He got up out of the water and began fumbling with his foot bindings. "Happiness is close at hand."

"You're rejoicing too early. We still don't know what's going on there."

"What do the Nabatorians want with this backwater? Okni and Gash-Shaku, that's where they'll attack. If they go creeping into Al'sgara, they'll be leaving the Steps of the Hangman open and they'll get hit from behind. No. They will take the south first, besiege the pass, shut off all the retreats to the north, and only then will they turn around and take the Green City. That's what I would do. I'd block the Steps first, and then have my fun."

"You're such a strategist. . . . The Nabatorians want everything. It's possible that they passed by the village; it's true that it isn't really of strategic interest to them. But it's also possible they didn't. I don't want to argue. We'll see in an hour."

"Well I'm quite willing to argue," said Luk, narrowing his eyes craftily. "I bet a soren against what I owe you that we won't see any Nabatorians."

"You're hoping to win back your debt?" The Son of the Snow Leopard chuckled and twirled his mustache.

"You got it."

"It's a deal. If everything is as you say, I will gladly forget about what you owe me."

The soldier chuckled contentedly, thinking that victory was already in his pocket.

As Luk walked along the woodland trail, he wondered if there would be an inn in such a backwater. He seemed to recall that the lads from the third squadron had stopped by at an inn in Dog Green when they had to accompany the commander to Al'sgara one time. So he could expect shaf, edible roast meat, hot water for a bath, and a nice long rest on a decent bed. The two of them even had a whole soren, which had been sewn into the guard's boot. He'd been saving it for a rainy day. It was a good thing he hadn't had time to lose it at dice. Very soon this coin would give him and Ga-Nor the chance to feel like normal people once more. He wondered if the tracker had any money.

This question hadn't bothered Luk before. There'd been no point. He glanced quickly at the northerner walking in front of him.

It was unlikely he had anything at all. The scouts didn't carry money when they went on their forays through the Borderlands. Who would they trade with there? The highlanders? So if the redhead had any savings, they had been left behind at the fortress and had probably migrated to some Nabatorian's pocket by now. May they all rot.

"Luk, keep up," commanded Ga-Nor without turning around.

"I'm practically running already, screw a toad," said the former guard indignantly. "And I have to drag my axe along, too."

The tracker didn't reply. Squatting down on his haunches, he began studying the ground. Luk, already long accustomed to his unhurried ways, waited patiently.

The thought crossed the soldier's mind that the citizens of the Empire were unjust to the northerners. Especially the citizens of the central and southern provinces. They considered the Children of the Snow Leopard barbarians. Savages. Stupid, temperamental, crude people.

Dressed in wool and leather, parading about in kilts, constantly rattling their sabers—most people thought they were only fit to die for the glory of the Empire. Terrible lone wolves who gorged themselves on raw meat. Red-haired berserkers who painted their faces red and inked dreadful tattoos on their backs. And what's more, they idolized the strange and incomprehensible war god Ug. It had yet to be determined if he was an enemy of the all-merciful Melot.

The most foolish rumors about them abounded: that they devoured the flesh of sickly infants born into their clans; that they took their own granddaughters to wife; that they bathed in melted snow, liberally seasoned with the hot blood of their enemies—these were just a few of the things said about the Children of the Snow Leopard when they were out of earshot.

Before, Luk had considered many of these rumors to be the truth. Of course, he didn't believe in such nonsense as blood baths. But at the same time he was in agreement that all northerners were rude, unpolished, and impenetrably stupid. The guard didn't even change his mind after he came to serve at the Gates of Six Towers and saw the Children of the Snow Leopard for the first time. The brief interactions he had with them only served to drive home the truthfulness of most of the rumors. They'd growled at him a couple of times, and almost struck him in the face. Luk didn't try to chat with the barbarians all that much after that, and truthfully, it wasn't that hard to avoid them. The garrison guards spent all their time circling the walls and gatehouse, or puffing their way through drills under the supervision of the sergeants, while the northerners went off on reconnaissance. They ran around the Borderlands, retraced their steps, rested, ate their fill, and again left for the mountains.

Traveling with Ga-Nor forced him to reassess his opinion of the northerners. The soldier could not call his companion a savage. It was possible that he would seem like one to the majority of the inhabitants of the enlightened Empire, but not to Luk. The tracker was not stupid, rude, or quick-tempered. Just the opposite. Experienced, intelligent, prudent, and dispassionate, he was able to size up any situation and he never made hurried decisions.

"There's quite a few tracks. Even hoof prints.

They come here often," noted the Son of the Snow Leopard, narrowing his eyes.

Suddenly stepping away from the path, he sniffed the air.

"You smell that?"

A gove? A Burnt Soul? The walking dead? The thoughts flew by in a vortex in Luk's head. After the events at the Gates of Six Towers he expected anything at all.

"No. What's there?"

"Get your axe ready. Cover my back. Follow me, but keep looking around. If you see something, tell me, but don't shout it out loud."

The path fell behind them. The companions walked through the dense underbrush, holding the river to their left the entire time. It was hidden from their eyes by dense thickets, but Luk could hear it murmuring over the sandbar. They came out into a forest clearing where the grass was up to their waists. Ga-Nor again began to scent the air and listen intently.

"What?" asked the guard, trying not to breathe too loudly. Right now the northerner was his sole support and hope. "What kind of crap is it this time, screw a toad?"

"We'll see soon. Stop leering at me, I'm not a whore! Didn't I tell you to keep looking around? We're in no less danger in high grass than we are among the trees. An entire army could hide here."

Luk gulped fearfully and squeezed the shaft of his

axe with damp palms. The clearing suddenly seemed dangerous to him.

Contrary to the guard's expectations, no one rushed to jump out of the grassy overgrowth. They passed through the clearing without any misadventures. They entered an oak grove. And it was only then that Luk smelled what Ga-Nor's sensitive nostrils had picked up a long time ago—the scent of rotting corpses.

The corpses smelled awful. Even if Pork decided not to bathe for an entire year (which, of course, his father would never allow him to do), he would not reek so badly. The village idiot, who had returned to the glade for the third time, wasn't feeling very well. His head was spinning and his belly was churning from the smell. He'd already been sick twice, the last time right on his shirt.

This was bad, so very, very bad. Now he had to wash it, or there was no way he could go home. He'd have his backside tanned so hard that he wouldn't be able to sit for a month. His father wouldn't see that he was friends with the kind, glorious Nabatorians and that man who turned out to be a real magician. After Pork asked, he even gave him these dead bodies. And now they were his. He could do whatever he wanted with them. Ha!

And everything that belonged to these dead men

was also now his. None of the Nabatorians could take it away from him. And if they did, Pork would go to his friend the magician, tell on them, and he'd turn the pissants into something moldy. He'd let them all know that Pork had been wronged! What friends he had, oh my!

Thousands of flies were circling over the rotting bodies and buzzing obnoxiously. They kept trying to fly into his mouth. The idiot spat and swatted at them, but this helped little. The heat was making him sweat, and the sweat, as well as his soiled shirt, only served to attract the vile insects. But Pork kept doing what he'd come here to do.

He was already the proud owner of two pairs of boots that stank pretty strongly of carrion (one pair fit perfectly and instantly found itself a more worthy master); one gold chain; three purses with a bit of small change; a knife with a pretty handle made of stag horn; a sharp, very sharp sword; and all sorts of other things. In the course of a single hour, Pork had become a truly wealthy man.

His dream had almost come true—he'd buy all sorts of things and then he'd be taken into the knighthood. Just try and let them stop him! And if they didn't take him, he'd go into magic. And then what? He'd wear a curved sword and carry a staff, too. Why not? It turns out people are far more frightened of necromancers than knights. You see, all the villagers only spoke about Pork's best friend in whispers, and only during the daylight hours.

Chickenshits! Even Captain Nai, the bravest Naba-torian in the village, spoke very respectfully to the magician and didn't argue with him.

Except, Pork was a bit jealous of Pars the carpen-ter. What if he was a closer friend to the necromancer than himself? Just look, the magician went to his house, stayed there for a while, and then left behind five Morts. They were bone-dry, like little skeletons, and they had skeem-swords. And their faces were noseless, and their eyes were yellow, so very yellow, like the eyes of old Roza's cat. Last month, Pork had decided to check if the tub of lard knew how to swim, and he captured the cat, but he couldn't get it to the river. The old woman's house pet fought for dear life and scratched his arms up. He had to drop it. Right into a puddle.

But those Morts were beyond hideous, really! When Pork saw them he nearly died of fright. They were standing without moving a muscle. They just swiveled their eyes all around and didn't let anyone near Pars's house. True, no one really went there. People were afraid to walk along that street. . . . How contrary this corpse is! He doesn't want to give up his boots, not no how.

Pork kicked the body out of spite, causing hun-dreds of flies to shoot up into the air.

The nasty boot didn't want to slide off the foot of the nasty dead man.

He tried and tried. He puffed, pulled, yanked—it wasn't happening. But the boots were really nice.

Leather, embroidered with gold thread near the eyelets. If you wore such boots, all the virgins would be yours. You wouldn't even have to persuade them. You'd just have to get there in the nick of time and climb off your horse. So what if they smell—that's nothing. That's not at all terrible, you know. The pigsty reeks, too. He washes that every week. He could wash the boots too. And clean them. And then go charm the virgins.

He dawdled there for a long time. He had a whole heap of goods. He needed to go back to the herd before Choir ran off. But he couldn't leave boots like these. Someone would definitely come by and snatch them up. And a good thing if it was only them. There was more wealth than the heavens here. They'd filch it before he had time to blink. He couldn't take it with him. How could he drag all this away? In what? And he couldn't lift it all, either. It was too heavy. He needed to hide it. Maybe in the trunk of the cleft tree; perhaps the fools wouldn't look there. Or in the bushes. He just had to get these damned boots off.

Pork turned around so his back was to the dead man, grabbed the boot again, and pulled. The bushes on the edge of the glade suddenly rustled and two men appeared in front of the frightened cowherd. The first was tall, redheaded, and old. With a sword and a funny skirt. The second was chubby with a face overgrown with bristles. He had an axe.

"A logger," muttered Pork.

He also realized that the strangers had come at a

really bad time. Just when all his riches were heaped in a single pile. Of course, they had to come for them now.

"Mine!" screeched the cowherd as he vacillated between the pile of stuff and the boots that were still attached to the corpse.

Then, realizing that there was no way he could deal with the men, he ran away from both them and his pile, shrieking with resentment and fear.

"Who was that, screw a toad?" asked Luk through the arm of his shirt, which was pressed up against his nose and mouth.

The carrion stank so badly that he was afraid he would pass out.

"It's obviously not a living corpse. Usually they run toward you, not away," Ga-Nor replied sarcastically.

"Melot only knows. He looked like a—"

"A looter. It's a pity he ran away."

"Why?"

"Because we could have asked him some questions. And also because he might get it into his head to lead someone here. We're leaving. Move!"

Luk raised no objection. He regarded it as the greatest fortune that he was allowed to quit the putrid glade where the dead (definitely dead, thank Melot!) bodies were lying.

Ga-Nor set off at a run. The guard was panting

but he did not lag behind. They kept up that tempo for about ten minutes. Finally, the northerner stopped, hopped into the underbrush, and disappeared. Luk nervously stayed where he was.

"Am I going to have to wait long for you?" The disgruntled face of the tracker appeared from out of the thicket.

"How was I supposed to know that I should go in there too?" the soldier said as he crawled under cover.

"Look."

"Where?"

The Son of the Snow Leopard shifted a branch.

"There."

Beyond the edge of the thicket stretched a small field, and beyond he could clearly see the village laid out along the shores of the river. Luk was so overjoyed at this sight that he didn't immediately notice the search tower where the figure of an archer, just barely visible from such a distance, stood, nor did he notice the patrol of three soldiers walking through the houses.

"Now you owe me two sorens."

Luk mentioned his toad in a dispirited way. The money was a trifle. To the Abyss with it! The Nabatorians were far worse than losing a bet. Were they really fated to make their way through the forests and swamps all the way to Al'sgara?

"I'd rather die here," he groaned.

"Hold off on dying. Wait."

"We can't think of something just sitting here."

"I'm not asking you to think. I'm asking you to wait. We need to stay for a while and watch. It's too early to leave. We'll wait until nightfall, and then we'll see."

"There's no way we can slip through the village unnoticed."

"Nonsense!" spat Ga-Nor. "Just look at them. What are they guarding, and what do they have to fear? Especially from this direction. If it wanted to, a Snow Troll could slip into that village, to say nothing of a man. Look now! They seem to have caught wind of us."

Luk watched as ten riders galloped across the field from the village. One of the horses had two riders. The first was a Nabatorian soldier, but the second, judging by his bright shirt, was the very same lad they had frightened away from the glade. At the edge of the forest the soldiers drew in their reins, jumped down from the horses, left one of their own behind to watch over them, and disappeared into the trees.

"Won't they find us?" Luk shifted in the grass and, just in case, hugged his axe even closer.

"Don't worry. Those dolts couldn't find a mammoth locked in a cage in broad daylight. Besides, we're not at all where we should be, according to them. They'll search a bit then settle down. They won't go far into the forest."

"Perhaps they're persistent."

"Did you see their gait? Cavalry. What do they

know about the forest? They'll just leap about and bellow at the top of their lungs. They'd get lost in their grandmother's vegetable patch. Are you looking for a fight?"

"I've had enough fights today. I'll be happy just so long as they don't find us. But what if they know how to read tracks?"

Ga-Nor's face twisted up contemptuously, clearly indicating that he hadn't expected such an unpardonably stupid idea from Luk.

"One of them might keep at it like a stubborn fool. We're just lying here. We can't see what they're doing. What if someone suddenly comes up from behind?" asked Luk.

The northerner gave this conjecture the thought it deserved and then sighed deeply.

"All right. For the sake of your nerves I'll go and check. You have an unsettling habit of making people doubt their own strengths."

"I've been cautious since childhood," Luk justified himself.

"Rest here. And, for the love of Ug, keep your head down until I return."

He disappeared into the tall grass. Luk waited for him, sweating from nervousness. The northerner returned after about twenty minutes, just not from the direction the guard expected.

"Well, what of it?"

"I told you—they're only good for braiding their horses' tails, not for roaming about forests. They poked around and didn't find anyone. Then they gave that lad a few good smacks about the head for dragging them there for nothing."

In point of fact, the men returned from the forest just then. They greeted their horses, mounted them, and turned back the way they had come at a much slower pace.

"Thank Ug it was boneheaded cavalrymen that came searching for us, and not a scouting party. They would have examined every blade of grass before they left. But those guys—idiots!"

All was quiet and peaceful in the village. The cavalry had disappeared behind the houses, the archer was slowly roasting in his tower, and the patrols were sauntering along the outskirts of the village. Ga-Nor left and returned three more times.

"So, are we setting out when it's dark?"

"I'm setting out. You are going to wait here for me."

He was right. On a nighttime excursion Luk would be more hindrance than help. So the guard didn't even think to object. It was hard enough to keep up with the northerner. And it was beyond his skill to do it quietly, leaving as little trace as possible.

"Bring me something to eat, will you? My belly's full of spiderwebs."

"You ate this morning."

"So in your opinion, a crust of bread and a bit of cheese rind is food? I can suffer through the night, but I'll drop dead of hunger without some scraps by morning."

"And where am I going to get it for you? Should I stroll into the inn and buy some? Or waltz over to the Nabatorians and beg some off of them?"

"I'm just saying that if the possibility should arise to . . . um . . . borrow something edible, I would be really happy. I would pray for the health and life of your family until the end of time."

"I don't have a family."

"Oh." Luk, realizing he'd made an awkward blunder, frowned but then suddenly hit upon the answer. "Well, then I'll just pray for you, and also I'll—"

"Be quiet, you windbag," the Son of the Snow Leopard cut him off genially. "You're messing up my count."

"What are you counting?" The soldier tore himself away from his contemplation of the pastoral landscape of the village and its surroundings and finally turned toward the northerner.

"The Nabatorians. I need to know how many patrols are here."

"There are three men on the tower. One is always on the lookout, while two others, I think, sit on the floor. Probably playing dice. It's a smart arrangement. If someone attacks, they'll think the archer is alone up until the last moment. You can't see them.

They change shift every two hours. There are four patrols. Three men in each. The time between the first and the second, and the third and the fourth, is about ten minutes. It's almost twenty between the second and the third. They rarely look around. The third patrol once paused for a half an hour. The darkness knows what they were doing. Just hung around not moving. It's always the same men. The sentries walk around the borders of Dog Green. It's the usual arrangement for an occupied village. I can't say anything about the actual number of Nabatori- ans. We're at the farthest end of the village. Judging by the houses and all those fields, not too many people live here. I might be able to get a better idea from a different vantage point."

While Luk was talking, Ga-Nor was looking at him in shock, his eyes narrowed. The northerner hadn't expected such attention to detail from his companion.

"What are you looking at?" asked the soldier gruffly. "I haven't grown horns yet."

"How did you notice of all of that?"

"What do you think I am? A complete idiot? Un- able to do anything besides play dice? I spent many years serving in the garrison of the Towers. You never trained with the men posted on the Wings. We drilled constantly. We had to be familiar with the faces of everyone in the area. Who drives what. Who visits whom. How to sniff out contraband. You scouts think we're all just trash, but we—"

"You left the Gates open," the tracker finished mercilessly.

Luk wanted to say something nasty in return, but at the last moment he just waved his hand at his companion, turned his back to him, and did not speak to him until evening.

Night fell warm and clear. The moon had not yet appeared, but due to the thousands of stars strewn across the sky, there was enough light. Luk was lying in a secluded forest hideout, and the bushes industriously hid him from outside eyes.

Ga-Nor had left more than an hour ago, and the soldier was getting nervous. The shirt on his back was soaked with sweat. Plus, his stomach was aching from anxiety. In his solitude, he'd managed to think through all the alternatives that would account for the tracker's extended absence ten times. The worst of them was that the Son of the Snow Leopard had been killed. That would mean that staying in his hideout was dangerous. If the Nabatorians began searching in earnest, they'd let out the dogs. Or someone worse. Then it wouldn't matter if he hid or not—they'd find him all the same.

Dread seized his throat, squeezing it so that it became hard to breathe. Luk almost made a break for it, but he willed himself to stay put, closed his eyes, and began slowly counting to ten.

Don't even think of fleeing. He couldn't allow

himself that kind of cowardice. Abandoning the northerner would be low. He'd done too much for him.

He looked at the sleeping village once again. Not a soul. No movement. No light shining from the houses. Here, just as in any other village, they were early to bed, early to rise. Summer was the time for work. They had no love for idlers. Luk recalled a saying of his grandfather, "If you sleep in during the summer, you'll go hungry in the winter."

The loud shriek of a nocturnal bird made him flinch, and all extraneous thoughts flew out of his head. Luk hated the forest with all his heart. He didn't understand it, and he was afraid of it. The constant rustling in the crowns of the trees. The odd screeching, so reminiscent of the wailing of a child. Every now and then, the trees took on the forms of dreadful monsters. Burning eyes looked out at him from the roots of an oak tree. There were ominous shadows everywhere. The soldier didn't know where he would rather spend the night if fate gave him a choice—in the forest or in a graveyard. After a moment's consideration, Luk chose the graveyard. At least there he knew what it was he had to fear.

The guard made out the figure of a man only when it was less than five yards away. He grabbed his axe and jumped into a fighting pose, intending to sell his life dearly.

"Calm down."

"Screw a toad! You're alive!"

"Follow me. But be quiet," whispered the northerner. A bag was hanging over his shoulder. "I found a safe place."

It took quite a long time to get to this "safe place." When Ga-Nor led Luk out of the forest the village houses were within easy reach.

Luk glanced at his companion in bewilderment.

"You mean to tell me that it's less dangerous here than in the woods?"

"Not here. At the mill."

"It doesn't look abandoned," said the soldier skeptically, studying the building next to the river.

"I didn't say that."

Luk wanted to object that it was idiotic to hang about where the locals might see them, but the Son of the Snow Leopard was already standing by the waterwheel.

"What, they don't lock the doors?"

"Who's going to steal? Everyone knows everyone else. And the Nabatorians wouldn't steal from themselves. They need bread, too. Get in."

The northerner shut the door firmly behind them. He struck a fire and lit the wick of a lantern standing on the floor. Then he closed the metal shutter so that the night watch wouldn't accidentally see the light.

"You already took a look around?" It hadn't escaped Luk's notice that the tracker was already well acquainted with the layout of the building.

"Yes. See that staircase? Go up."

The staircase wound its way past enormous gears and millstones. The second floor was full of machinery. It smelled appealingly of grain and flour.

The Son of the Snow Leopard picked up a ladder that was resting on the floor, leaned it against the wall, and checked it for stability.

"Go on."

There was a wooden trapdoor in the ceiling that led to the attic.

"They'll find us here," the guard predicted gloomily.

"They won't. I checked. It's been two months since anyone's poked their head in here. It's far safer here than in the forest. As safe as Ug's bosom. And besides, most of the village is laid out before our eyes from this spot. Climb."

Luk still had his doubts, but all the same he climbed up the rungs and pushed at the heavy hatch. He crawled through and took his axe from the northerner.

The attic smelled of dust and discarded objects, and slightly of bird dung.

"Tell me, won't the miller miss his lantern in the morning?"

"It's not the miller's. Some farmer might be missing it though," said the tracker, chuckling into his red mustache.

He took the ladder away and put it back in its

place. Then he jumped up smoothly, grabbed the edge of the hatch, and pulled himself up into the attic.

Ga-Nor lowered the trapdoor in place. It slammed shut, raising a cloud of dust into the air.

"We should put something on top of it. So that no one can climb up. Come on, help me."

In one of the corners there was a pile of broken, rusted hoes, pitchforks, scythes, and other scraps of iron. The kinds of things you would find in an attic. Even a small, cracked millstone was lying there. It had to weigh at least three hundred pounds. The damned miller couldn't bear to throw his trash away, and so with the usual peasant frugality, he'd stored it. Perhaps it would come in handy someday.

The two of them dragged the millstone over and put it on top of the hatch.

"There. Now we can sleep soundly. Take a load off," said the northerner as he spread out his hands.

Only now did Luk take a proper look around. The planks on the floor and on the slanted walls were rough. Unsanded. You could get a splinter from them easy as pie. Fly-speckled cobwebs had accumulated in the corners of the attic. Opposite him, against the background of the already brightening sky, gleamed the large rectangle of a window. It didn't have a frame, or even any glass. It was simply a hole cut in the wall. In winter this place was sure to be full of snow.

Luk approached the window and sat on his haunches. Below him was the river, and in front, the village. Just as good as an observation tower. The view wasn't any worse.

"Come morning only a blind man wouldn't notice us."

"Well, you could bare your ass for them. Then they'd be able to see you a league away. Get away from the window, you ninny."

"What do you want to see from here?"

"Anything I can. Here. Take this."

Ga-Nor tossed the bag to his friend. It held a smoked mutton leg, the heel of an onion with five green offshoots, just as many apples, a small pot of honey, and a turnip.

"Oh!" the guard cried in delight, and his belly rumbled in welcome. "And who was nice enough to share with you?"

"A barn and the nearby vegetable patches. I couldn't get any bread."

"You mean you pinched it." Luk grunted approvingly, cutting into the meat with his knife. "That's as it should be. Asking or buying would be dangerous. What if the locals reported it to the soldiers? Best to keep on the way we've been going. Very sneaky. Take what they put down and carry it off."

"Very sneaky," grumbled the Son of the Snow Leopard. "I almost gave my soul back to Ug. Besides the patrols, there was an ambush I didn't notice. Very well hidden. I stumbled right into them. They were just as astonished as I was."

"Did you get them all?"

"I did. But I was sweating as I dragged the bodies to the river and erased my tracks. They'll be missed come morning. They'll start combing the surrounding forest. It's getting serious now."

"They could also search the village."

"Unlikely. The Nabatorians are thick on the ground here. While I was running around the gardens and fields, I tried to count them. They're in nearly every house. On the eastern side, by the road, there's a barracks. And a bit farther on something like a fort or a stronghold. They're even working on it at night. They're entrenching themselves. Our foolish troops are sitting around catching flies, and they're going to be swimming in blood soon."

As Luk listened to the tale of his companion's adventures, he didn't neglect to eat. He became warm and comfortable from the food. He began nodding off.

The soldier had just about succumbed to sleep when a terrified dog howled in the village. A second one joined in. Then a third. Then more and more.

Luk sprung to his feet. Creeping horrors ran up his spine. For some reason the howling seemed sinister.

"What are they howling for?"

"I don't know. Sleep," said the tracker without opening his eyes.

"They're not doing it just for the fun of it. Listen to them!"

The bleak howls of the pack of dogs ascended to

the heavens, echoed off the clouds and swept through the river valley, disrupting the predawn quiet. It seemed like the earth itself was groaning and trembling from the sound. The guard wanted to cover his ears with his hands. Just so he didn't have to hear *that*.

"Our elders say that when a single dog howls, it's sick. But when they all do disaster awaits," said Ga-Nor after a brief pause.

"What are you trying to tell me?"

"Just what I said." The Son of the Snow Leopard rolled over onto his other side. "Sleep. It'll be morning soon."

Then, as if by an invisible command, the howling ceased.

The tracker had been snoring for a long time, but there was no way Luk could sleep. The howls of the dogs were still ringing in his ears.

8

The krylgzan twitched his large, damp nose from side to side and shivered. He caught a scarcely perceptible scent weaving its way through the smells of early morning, fresh grass, and blooming strawberries. It was so desirable and enticing. The wind ripped through it, changing it into a phantom, and if he didn't rush in pursuit of it, all traces would fade away.

Not hesitating, the beast unfolded his wings and flew upward in search of his elusive prey. Awoken after his five-year slumber, the krylgzan wanted to eat. He flew over the forest, amassing the venom in his jaws. As he flew over a large, marshy lake, he flushed out a fawn, but he didn't let himself get sidetracked by it. The prey that the creature planned to take was far more worthy.

He had to travel more than eight leagues before he reached his goal. First the intensely sweet, deliriously tantalizing, pleasantly hot smell of fresh meat struck his nose. And then he saw eight tiny specks moving in a line down a forest road.

There were six quadrupeds, warm and trembling—horses. And six bipeds, tender and sweet—humans. But the last two were strange, with an unpleasant smell. He'd never encountered the like. At any other time the krylgzan would have exhibited caution before attacking them, but his hunger was far too great. Besides, how could these land-dwellers harm him?

The krylgzan was so focused on his choice of victims that he did not immediately see the village beyond the forest. But when he did, even the beast's wings quivered with anticipation. So much meat! He hadn't known there was so much food in these lands. It was a good thing that he'd left his old nest and flown here. Of course, the flight had taken all his strength, and he'd have to sleep for a long time, but he was about to eat his fill. First he'd eat the riders and then he might drag some of the human cubs from the large wooden nest on the shores of the river.

The beast selected his first victim. He would grab it before the others had time to come to their senses and understand what was attacking them. And then he'd spit his venom and kill the horse. And perhaps, if he was lucky, another rider as well.

The krylgzan folded his wings and plunged through the air like a stone. The black specks grew larger by leaps and bounds. While he was falling, something buzzed past him. Unfortunately for him, he ignored it, and the second shot was more accurate. A painful sting struck him in the chest. The pain spread.

The beast shrieked, spread his wings, causing him to slow down, and displayed his dreadful talons, threatening to rip his tormentor to shreds and—another four arrows found their target. The krylgzan, out of his mind from pain, spat venom without aiming. A wing exploded with pain, and it became hard to hold himself up in the air. With difficulty, he changed the direction of his flight, thinking of only one thing—flying away from here as quickly as possible. But when he passed over the tops of the spruces, they hit him again, this time in the eye, and the beast slammed into a tree trunk, breaking his wings. He fell to the ground and collapsed into a heap, convulsing fitfully.

Tia drew up her reins, a disinterested expression on her face, which hadn't so much as twitched during the unexpected attack. Quite unlike her fellow travelers. Those idiots, stuffed into the black armor of the Nabatorian King's Guard, had soiled their trousers the instant they were called upon to deal with something more dangerous than swords or spears. And they were supposed to protect her? The girl was sure that Tal'ki had been joking when she advised her to take an escort with her. Her Shay-za'n were far more useful than the guardsmen.

"Don't bother, Sha-kho," she said in a soft voice. "Don't waste arrows on carrion. It'll die anyway."

The ancient Shay-za'n with the six violet feathers in his hair put his serrated arrow back in his quiver.

"As you say, my lady." His soft voice sounded like the rustling of leaves. "It was circling above us. It may have wanted meat, but my brother and I killed it."

"You did well. I'm pleased with you."

This small praise was enough to cause both the old and the young Shay-za'n to rise up a yard and a half from the ground.

She slipped gracefully from the saddle.

"Lady," said a gray, whiskered veteran. "That monster is still dangerous. I wouldn't advise—"

"Did I ask you for your advice?" she asked coldly.

The captain choked and bit his tongue. His inferiors pretended they had heard nothing. The battle-hardened soldiers may not have outright feared the girl, but they were wary of her. They'd heard all sorts of stories about her callous nature.

At first glance, Tia looked no more than nineteen. She was of average height, lithe, with an excellent figure and a beautiful face. Her slanted, brown eyes, her perfectly straight nose, and her plump lips suggested ancient blood. Her black hair, which was twisted into two complicated braids, and her golden skin were the inheritance passed on to her by her mother, a southerner.

Her split skirt was dusty from the long road, and she wore suede boots with pointed heels, a man's white shirt with a sharp collar, and a lady's vest of a warm color that matched her skin.

She wore no adornment but a necklace made of tiny brown shells. She carried no weapons of any kind. There was nothing at all threatening about this girl. But the five Nabatorians and the two who were usually called Burnt Souls in the Empire obeyed her without question.

The krylgzan finally stopped wheezing, snapping its jaws and spitting its yellow, foamy saliva, and died.

"Check yourselves," she said, not raising her voice. "If there's any venom on your clothing or weapons, discard them. Sha-kho, follow me."

Accompanied by the taciturn Shay-za'n, she walked over to the corpse. The krylgzan aroused her curiosity. These creatures lived far to the south, where the Boxwood Mountains turned into the impassable Cloudy Peaks. At the very edge of the earth. These beasts frequented the lands of the Empire even more rarely than they did those of Nabator and Sdis. This made the encounter all the more wondrous.

Trying not to step in the drops of poison, Tia walked around the body. She thought that Tal'ki would sell her soul for the beast's poisonous fangs. She grinned balefully—she would not lift a finger to extract the priceless treasure from the jaws of the monster. She had no need of it. And she wasn't about to bend over for Tal'ki's sake. If the old crone wants it, let her come here herself and mess about with the corpse.

Of late, her mood had left much to be desired, and with good cause. When the Herald had appeared before her, she was many leagues away, traveling toward Leigh in Rovan's company. Leigh had gotten mired in the Isthmuses of Lina and was in urgent need of help. The Herald had overturned all her plans, and she had to turn back quickly. The mad round-the-clock dash, constantly changing horses, the bad food, and the stupidity of her companions were driving her out of her mind.

When she had returned to the Towers, Mitifa was still hanging about, doggedly digging through the library of the Walkers. The stupid bitch had gotten it into her head that she could unravel the secrets of the Paths of Petals. It would be lovely to be able to travel great distances in an instant. It would solve a mass of logistical problems in a single stroke, but Mitifa was getting nowhere. She didn't have enough brains to find the key to the Sculptor's creation or to Sorita's (a Mother of the Walkers. She died during the Dark Revolt, battling against the Damned) final incantation. Only Ginora could have wrestled with such a problem, but her bones had been lying in the Marshes of Erlika for a long time now. However, Mitifa did not realize that her efforts were doomed to failure. She fell greedily upon the old archives, and she'd been gnawing on them for more than a week with no results. Tia hated that fool with all her soul. Of course, if sworn to tell the truth, she would say she had no love for any of her associates. And she didn't trust any of them. It was really only Tal'ki who deserved to have her advice listened to and even sometimes, under rare circumstances, followed. But the girl did not harbor any delusions about the Healer. As soon as she got the chance, the old hag would be the first to sell Tia off piece by piece.

Regardless of the wearisome journey, there were a few good things that had come from the Herald's appearance. First, she got out from under Rovan's intrusive regard, but more important, Leigh's. That pair couldn't hinder her now. Second, if the man who found the carrier of the Gift was not mistaken, and if she was able to get the spark under her control, her strength would increase. And that would be very good. Forever playing second string was becoming tiresome.

Tia leisurely walked back to her horse and mounted it. Her companions wisely kept their peace.

The small procession once again set off down the road.

Her bodyguards kept looking at the sky, but the girl did not bother to explain to them that a second krylgzan was unlikely to appear in these parts for another hundred years. Definitely no sooner than that. Right now, all she wanted was to be away from these people. She ached to rid herself of her dusty clothes, redolent of sweat, crawl into a hot herbal bath, and sit there until the end of time. And she wouldn't say no to a pretty little servant girl washing her back, either.

The forest fell away to the sides and the road, briskly running past wildly colorful bushes, descended a hill toward a bridge. Not far from the standing stone, the road forked. One fork climbed a low hill, while the second swerved sharply to the west, cut across the valley, and once again plunged into the forest. Toward Al'sgara. Not far from this road, construction was fast under way. They'd already managed to erect one tower and the western wall of a fort, a large barracks, and two observation towers. There was also construction going on near the hill. They were raising the foundation of the future command post and fortifying the road on either side. At the crest of the hill was another tower.

The group encountered a checkpoint patrol—five riders armed with swords and light bows.

"What fate brings you to this hellhole?" one of the patrolmen greeted Gry.

No one paid attention to Tia. Sha-to and his brother were far more interesting. Most Nabatorians still hadn't gotten used to that race.

"Who's the commander?" demanded Gry.

"Captain Nai," said the patrolman, instantly pulling himself together in his saddle.

"Take us to him," said Tia with a smile.

The astonished soldier peered at the King's Guardsman, but he was unperturbed. The rider proved himself a clever man and luckily did not ask why he should follow the commands of some girl.

"Yes, my lady."

Tia squinted her eyes against the intense morning sunlight. Her mood was improving. The long journey had come to an end, even if Dog Green wasn't all that impressive. True, the girl hadn't really expected otherwise. It was a village, like any other village. There were thousands like it in the world. She only hoped she'd be able to find a bath.

A strong, solid gallows stood just outside the little village. It consisted of two columns, a crossbar, and five reeking corpses. Tia frowned. What a nasty habit, leaving such filth around. Once they'd executed them, they should have buried them before they started to stink. This was exactly like Rovan's attitude toward execution, and she hated him for it. That maggot, for all his luck and usefulness to the cause, had suffered from a virulent depravity from a very young age—an irrepressible urge to surround himself with dead bodies. He tortured people with cause and without, and afterward he enthusiastically added their heads to the little decorative stockade that surrounded his tent so he could inhale the perfume of their decomposition in the weeks that followed. Tia hated Rovan. She did not understand how such a brute could be born from the same mother as Retar.

"Take those corpses down," she said in a low voice. "Right now."

"But, my lady, we should stay with you," Gry tried to object.

"Nothing is going to happen to me. However . . ." She thought for a second and then came to a decision. "You can stay."

A soldier riding ahead of them overheard this conversation and nearly fell from his saddle. Was this a joke? Were the warriors of His Majesty's Black Guard really going to become gravediggers on the whim of some wench?

Stopping at the inn, Tia nimbly slid from her saddle and stretched. She thought that if Mitifa really did succeed in animating the Paths of Petals, she would be the first to thank her. Traveling in such a manner would be far easier than by horse.

After the long stint in the saddle she felt like an old woman, and only a bath could save her.

Melot be damned if she was not ready to kill for one.

Tossing her reins to Gry, the girl walked into the inn. The common room was bright, spacious, and clean. And it smelled good. Tia felt cheered. The chances of getting a bed without bedbugs had risen sharply.

A tall, bulky village boy was sitting on the floor next to the potbellied wine barrels. Judging by his face, he was a half-wit. Once he saw Tia, he forgot all about his shaf and gaped at her in shock as if he'd never seen a woman before. Ignoring the lustful gaze of the nitwit, she walked over to a table where five officers were sitting. As she walked she commanded the innkeeper, who had appeared in front of her, "A room. Your best. And a hot bath."

"But my lady!" he said, startled. "There are no spare rooms."

"Gentlemen, which one of you is Captain Nai?" she asked the officers calmly.

"I don't know why you're looking for me, but I am entirely at your service, gorgeous," said a young, black-mustachioed man with a charming smile. "And my friends would be all too happy to make your acquaintance and give you your bath."

One of the men laughed gleefully, another whistled admiringly, evaluating the beauty of the nameless girl.

"Where have you been hiding from us all this time?" asked a stout, balding man, laughing. Judging by the ribbons on his sleeve, he was the commander of the archers.

"Can't you see, she's not a local. She doesn't look like the village maids," said another soldier, and then he took a sip of his shaf.

"You're right. Nai, let me be the first to get acquainted with this beautiful stranger."

The officer stood and grabbed Tia by the waist.

"Come on then."

She mockingly raised her eyebrows and smiled thinly.

"Remove your hand."

"Oho!" chuckled Nai. "What an uppity lass!"

"I like that even more." The hands on the girl's waist squeezed even tighter. "Arrogant whores are such a rarity."

If Alenari were in Tia's place, she would kill the bumpkin for such unbridled behavior. Mitifa would have ripped off his arms without thinking twice. Tal'ki would chat with him amicably, and then she would come up with some perfect punishment. However, it's unlikely the officer would hit on the old hag. He amused Tia so greatly that she decided not to punish him. She'd let Gry, who at that very moment was walking into the inn, do it.

The captain, who had been entrusted to safeguard the lady against any kind of trespass, instantly grasped the situation. His fist, vested in a glove with metal bars across the knuckles, slammed into the face of the impudent man and threw him backward. The officers began yelling indignantly; they jumped up and seized their weapons, and only then did they take the time to examine the new arrival. A stunned silence enveloped them. Even the officer with the broken jaw stopped swearing.

"Thank you, Gry." Tia thought it fitting to show the man some gratitude.

She reached out her hand and her bodyguard immediately gave her a document. The girl never scorned using such documents. Now and again a few official signatures and seals worked far more effectively than any magic. The girl passed the document to Nai.

Frowning blackly, he opened the leather case, dropped it on the table without looking at it, and spread out the paper. He read it and his face instantly paled. When his ability to speak returned to him, he said, trying not to look her in the eyes, "Forgive me, my lady, for this misunderstanding. We all offer you our apologies for such improper behavior toward you and are prepared to accept the punishment we deserve."

"Hmmm . . ." She wrinkled her charming little nose. "I like that you know how to acknowledge your mistakes. That's a good quality. Just refrain from making the same mistake in the future. Try to find me a room and a bath. I also think that Gry and his men would not say no to a decent meal."

"Yes, my lady. I would be happy if you would take my rooms. Allow me to accompany you."

"I'll allow it," she agreed graciously.

"Innkeeper! A hot bath! Now!" bellowed the captain and, gesturing that she should follow him, rushed up the wide oak staircase that led to the second floor.

"Where is the necromancer?" Tia asked casually when the Nabatorian opened the door for her.

"Somewhere in the village. Or near the fort."

"I want to see him. Right away."

"I'll search for him personally, my lady."

"As soon as you find him, send him to me. Don't delay."

After saying these words she entered the room, dropped her vest onto a chair, and stretched languidly.

Just as Luk had assumed, in the morning the miller and his sons came and started working at the mill. They set the stones spinning, began bringing in sacks of grain and leaving with sacks of prepared flour. At first the soldier was nervous but after a short while he realized that the locals had no business up in the attic. He relaxed and even slept for another hour. Then he had a substantial breakfast, and Ga-Nor told him that they had noticed the absence of the men he'd killed and concealed in the river. They were checking adjacent houses and combing through the nearby forest.

"It's a good thing we came here. I wasn't sure they wouldn't find us. Oho! Take a look at our new visitors!"

Luk brushed the crumbs from his palms and, trying to keep his head down, looked out the window.

A group of riders were descending down the hill on the road. In the middle of the soldiers was a woman, and right behind her followed two creatures that the guard easily recognized as Burnt Souls.

"Screw a toad! We need to get out of here," he moaned in fear.

"Don't fall apart from panic," snapped the Son of the Snow Leopard. "If we flee, they'll hunt us down like rabbits."

"And if they find us, they'll besiege us like wolves."

"Oh, who needs you? No one even knows you exist. And they're better off for it. Stay where you are. Don't move."

"Well, now we're up the creek with no paddle, my dear friend," said Luk, a bit too calmly. "We can't get rid of that bastard so easily."

Far away on the field, right by the forest where Ga-Nor had come across the Nabatorian ambush, stood a man dressed in white.

The Sdisian checked the spot three times and did not find a single sign of struggle. The three idiots had disappeared without a trace. The grass was lying flat, but that always happens when three healthy men sit in one place for several hours.

The necromancer was not too concerned about the missing soldiers. Even if another twenty soldiers had gone missing this morning, he usually would have ignored it completely. But today the boredom of inaction had made him a bit touchy, and this was at least a diversion. That was what made it worth investigating.

The men had been missed early in the morning when their relief arrived at the ambush and did not find their comrades in the usual place. They immediately informed Captain Nai about the incident, and he sent fifty men out to search for them. As one would expect, nothing came of it. The search parties hunted through the village and even poked around the forest, but they didn't find any trace. It was as if the ground had swallowed the three of them whole. Where could the idiots have gone? There was forest all around; you could never scramble your way through it. They'd never approached the road, that's for sure. The patrols didn't see anyone.

It didn't look like murder; there were no tracks for two dozen yards around. There should be something left behind. Trampled grass, blood, a body, something at least! Unless of course someone fell on them from the sky, grabbed them by the back of the neck and carried them off. The sorcerer didn't believe in such things. There weren't any creatures in these lands that could do such a thing. He still hadn't solved the riddle after half an hour's search. Of course, he could use his magic and check if there was an echo of their souls, which always appeared after people's deaths. But the incantations would require such an expenditure of strength that . . . these missing sheep simply weren't worth it. Giving up all hope of finding a rational explanation for the strange and entirely unexpected disappearance, the necromancer pursed his lips in disappointment and, leaning on his staff, headed back toward the village.

A rider was galloping over the field toward him at full tilt. The Sdisian squinted and recognized Captain Nai.

"There you are! I've been looking all over for you!" cried the Nabatorian as he reined in his horse.

"And what do you require of me on this fine day?"

"A . . . lady . . . is waiting for you."

"Really?" He instantly realized who he was talking about. Praise be to the dark gods. His Herald had been taken seriously. And that meant that the tedious waiting had come to an end. He wondered which of the Overlords had answered his summons. At any rate, regardless of who it was, he would now find out if Ann had the Gift or if it was all for nothing. "Has she been waiting long?"

"About half an hour, I'd say. She's in my room. She said that you should go to her immediately."

"Give me your horse."

"Of course."

The sorcerer did not hesitate to leap into the saddle.

"Well? Have you calmed down? He didn't find anything," said Ga-Nor when the necromancer disappeared among the houses. "You always get so panicky."

"Look who's talking. Screw a toad, but you're no less frightened than I am."

The northerner snorted into his mustache.

"I'd really like to know where that Sdisian was rushing off to," he said instead of replying.

"Well, at least he wasn't rushing off for your soul."

"Who knows. Who knows. I'm beginning to think it would have been better if we'd slogged our way through the forest to Al'sgara like you suggested at first. Dog Green can go to the Abyss! It's not enough that there are Nabatorians here, but a real live necromancer has to show up as well! I don't like it. The dogs weren't howling for nothing. I can smell it—trouble is brewing."

And again the Son of the Snow Leopard fell silent, but by his eyes it was clear that he shared the fears of his companion.

———

The sorcerer stopped by the door, obviously nervous. He tugged at his robes, trying to make the folds fall neatly. Then he smoothed out the links of his belt and adjusted his saber. It wouldn't do to appear before the Overlord looking unkempt. He was about to knock on the door, but he was forestalled.

"Enter, Elect, enter. Don't stand on the threshold."

There was mockery in the woman's voice. The necromancer pushed the door open, took two steps in, got to one knee, and fixed his gaze onto the floor. His left hand was on his staff. His right was held over his heart. It was the ritual obeisance of an Elect before an Overlord.

"If you'd be so kind, drop the niceties and close the door. It's cold."

He was startled, but he did exactly as he was asked, keeping his eyes on the floor the entire time. When he was done he raised his eyes and then instantly shifted them back to the toes of his own boots.

Tia gave a quiet snicker. "I asked you to leave convention at the door. Look. I permit it."

She was sitting in a bronze bathtub with her back to him. Two dark braids were entwined around her head and held in place with diamond bobby pins. Bronzed skin, narrow shoulders, elegant neck. Everything else was concealed by soapy foam.

He couldn't see her face, but he didn't need to. The sorcerer knew who was before him. One of the Overlords, Lady Tia. The Flames of Sunset, as the races of the Great Waste called her.

It was she who bore the alias Typhoid in the Empire.

"Speak."

"I found a woman. She may have the Gift."

"*May*? A bad word. If I've had to travel so far just for *may*, I will be quite irritated." Steely overtones slipped into her voice. "Continue."

"As soon as I entered the village, I felt the echoes of the use of the Gift."

"Very interesting. And you didn't think this might be a mistake?"

"I did, my lady. And before I sent the Herald to you, I tried to check for myself. She is not a Walker. Perhaps she is a prodigy, although I couldn't feel anything from her. Either I am mistaken or she is very discreet."

"Or we're dealing with a real natural if an Elect cannot read her. Is she still in the village?"

Tia had not glanced at her companion a single time over the course of this conversation.

"Yes. I put her under house arrest."

"Then why is the peasant still somewhere else? Bring her. Let's have a look at your find."

"She'll be before you within half an hour."

The Damned waved her hand, allowing the sorcerer to leave, closed her eyes, and blissfully stretched out in the bathtub.

9

———

Some bastard stole the lantern from the yard last night. And those damn dogs were howling before dawn," said Bamut, as he carved another little man out of wood.

Shen, his hands resting on his chest, was lying on a hard bench with his folded shirt under his head. He was dozing, but as soon as his companion was done talking, he said, without raising his eyelids, "Mark my words. They won't be howling after the necromancer returns. Neither will we."

"Nonsense. He hasn't been here in a week. He's long since forgotten about us."

"Don't be an idiot," said Whip morosely. "If he'd forgotten about us those noseless freaks standing guard by the gates would have disappeared. The sorcerer sniffed out Layen from a league away, and he's not backing off anytime soon."

"He's only interested in her soul. The White won't bother us."

"Fool," declared the commander with relish.

"Why a fool?" asked Bamut, not at all offended.

"You expect good from a necromancer. That's why. He'll take the woman away and drag us along for company."

"Damn. . . . I should have wasted Gray in the

forest. I threw away such an opportunity. We could already be back in Al'sgara."

Midge, who was listening in on the conversation, had something that looked like agreement written all over his face.

"Mols would have whacked you himself afterward."

"Mols, Mols. I'm fed up with working for him. Damn. . . . This is so stupid! Don't we have our own brains?" This time no one encouraged him. Bamut grumbled to himself for a little while and then asked, "Am I to understand that we can't get past the Morts? Even with Gray and his woman?"

"That took you a whole week to get, did it? I talked to Ness the same day the necromancer came here. We could overwhelm the Morts. But the necromancer would find out about it."

Bamut finally shut up. Shen went back to his dozing. Whip and Midge started to play dice. Only when it was time for lunch did they walk over to the part of the house where Ness and Layen lived.

Seeing provisions and weapons strewn out over the table instead of the food they'd become accustomed to over the past several days, Shen asked breathlessly, "What's all this?"

"We're leaving," replied Ness grudgingly, stuffing his axe into his belt.

"Right now?" Whip blurted out.

"Yes."

"Have you lost your minds?"

"No one asked you." Layen was frantically stuffing things into a pack. "You can stay here 'til hell freezes over. The house is entirely at your disposal."

"Tell me what's going on," said Whip darkly. "Ness, at first you were playing it safe, and now you're fleeing in the light of day! Do you think the Morts and the sorcerer will simply let you leave?"

"I know only one thing," snarled Gray, taking a quiver with arrows out from under the table. "If we don't leave now, we are never leaving. And the necromancer and those creatures of his will seem like child's play to us."

"And who is it that's going to come down on our heads?"

"I don't know."

"Perfect!" Shen snorted angrily.

"Where did you get this information?" asked Whip, scowling.

"Layen sensed it."

The leader scratched his chin. It was a serious claim. Ness's girl didn't panic so easily. He needed very little time to come to a decision.

"We'll go with you."

"Have you lost your wits? We're going to stick our necks out because of something she saw in a dream?" Bamut demanded of his leader, flabbergasted. "Damn. . . . I'm not taking a step away from here."

"It's you who's lost his wits!" disdainfully spat Midge, who also saw to the heart of things quickly.

"It's not just about her seeing things. Have you forgotten those animals howling under our window last night? I'm with you, Whip."

"Shen?"

He stretched languidly and shrugged. "I suppose I'll keep you company," drawled the Healer.

"We're too late!" Layen did not say the words; she moaned them as her face turned white.

The necromancer was entering the yard.

I wanted to smack myself about the head for my own stupidity. I had sensed that we needed to flee earlier, at the very moment the Sdisian first dropped by to see us. I sensed it. But because of my own caution and stupidity I sat in my lair to the bitter end. What was I waiting for? I didn't even know myself. And this was the result. I just sat here, the Damned take me!

There's no way we could escape now.

"Don't panic." I heard my voice as if someone else were talking. "Take everything off the table! Now!"

Thank Melot, this wasn't the first time my former pals had found themselves in a tricky situation. They did not bother to contest my right to command them. They asked no questions and got down to business. Quickly and precisely.

"Layen, go into the other room."

I won't let him take me so easily!

And I won't let him have you either!

I tossed Midge his knife. He caught it deftly and slipped it into the top of his boot. I hope the little rat will be able to use it if we get pinned down.

I quickly glanced around at my troops. They had skillfully positioned themselves around the room—they were Giiyans, after all. They occupied all the most favorable spots. Midge sat by the door, and Whip was next to the stove. Shen was not far from the oven fork. And Bamut was standing by the window.

Steps rang out on the porch and then the necromancer entered. I disliked his face before, but today I wanted to punch it.

"Where is she?"

The Sdisian took no notice of Whip's men. Not a very smart move, if you ask me. Especially if Midge is looming behind your back. If I found myself in such a situation, I'd be trying to grow eyes out the back of my head.

"Who?" I played the fool.

"Your wife. I'd advise against concealing her."

"What's she to you, sir? We haven't done anything."

"You have nothing to fear, carpenter. We simply want to talk to her."

"And if she doesn't want that?" I asked, somewhat rudely.

"Do you wish me to tear your house down around you?"

He was too sure of himself and he didn't consider

us a danger. Those who possess magic very often put ordinary people on the same level as animals. Big mistake. The lad clearly didn't know that sometimes animals are dangerous to people. Especially rats. They bite when you're least expecting it. Stealthily. Suddenly. Just like my friend Midge loves to do.

And just like he was doing right now. Obeying an almost unnoticeable sign from Whip, he went into action. For all my dislike of Midge, I was ready to kiss him. Regardless of what a brute he was, you could see he was a master from a league off.

It was so quick that I missed the moment when his knife migrated from his bootleg to his hand. The next second the Sdisian's throat was slit open from ear to ear.

It turns out that killing a necromancer isn't a speck more difficult than dispatching some fat merchant to the Blessed Gardens. For a moment it was as if a stupor fell over all of us. And then the usual frenzy of battle set in. I hurled my axe at a Mort who appeared on the threshold. I hit him, but unfortunately I did not kill him.

Whip, who had armed himself with the heavy wooden bench, smashed it into the wounded creature's face with all his strength, causing him to fly backward out the door. He slammed the door shut before the four remaining Morts had time to get to us.

No more than five seconds had passed since we'd attacked the White.

"Layen!" I bellowed.

My sun was already next to me. She handed me my bow and quiver, and then she rushed to help Midge. He was sitting on top of the still living sorcerer and repeatedly stabbing him with his knife. The white silk robe had turned red. The face and hands of the Giiyan were covered in the other man's blood but this did not disconcert him at all. Better to be befouled than to give the necromancer the chance to speak an incantation.

Layen took the staff that the necromancer had dropped on the floor, thrust the sharp end of it into the body of her enemy, and twisted it. The sorcerer shuddered and finally died.

"Ready!" Midge quickly liberated the saber from the corpse. He tossed his prize to Whip, who completely forgot about the bench once he had his hands on the blade.

"Bamut, in the other room, under the bed," I said. "There's a crossbow and the bolts are . . ."

I didn't even have time to finish speaking before he was rushing for the weapon.

One of the Morts decided to come in through the window without stopping to think. There he encountered Shen and the oven fork. He struck at the Mort's face, nearly got hit by the creature's skeem, jumped backward, and jabbed it in the gut. That time he was successful. The time had come for me to do a little work. The first arrow sliced clean through the neck of the most persistent of these warriors of the Waste. The second hit his comrade in the face. Everything was suddenly quiet.

Bamut returned. His pockmarked face was shining with happiness. And really, how could it be otherwise? He'd finally been reunited with his closest friend—the crossbow. Whip's henchman was quite a good shot with that thing, so I was sure we'd work well together when it came time to shoot. Just as long as we had enough arrows and bolts. I had five regular arrows, another two were serrated, and five more with narrow heads that could pierce armor. It really wasn't enough, but there was nothing I could do about that. All my reserves were in the shed, but we couldn't make it there now.

"That's how you take down sorcerers." Midge's ratlike face was covered in blood. "He's deader than dead."

"You're mistaken." Layen turned toward the assassin, and he shrank back in shock. He was right to be afraid. My sun's eyes were blazing with blue flame. She was harnessing her spark. "They're trying to revive him."

"Who?" blurted Shen.

"The one I'm afraid of. Hold the door. I need time." She picked up the Sdisian's staff with two hands and the top suddenly flashed, began to change shape, to dwindle. The skull transformed from a man's to a woman's and opened its gaping mouth.

Tia immediately sensed that somewhere nearby a person had died, but she didn't give it any special consideration. How should she know who it might be? Peasants have been dropping like flies since the dawn of time. Some from hunger, some from illness, some from drunkenness. It's hardly surprising, with the life they led. So when her inherent, feminine curiosity finally got the better of her laziness, it was almost too late.

She immediately felt the silvery filaments of the necromancer's soul, vibrating like a string. It was about to flow away into the Abyss.

There was no time to be astonished or to guess what had happened. Without a moment's hesitation, the Damned seized the filaments, trying not to let them leave this world. She succeeded. Now she had to return them to his body and attach them to the dead shell in time. She still had uses for the sorcerer.

Typhoid began slowly and carefully drawing the silver strings back, simultaneously weaving a complex incantation that would allow her to relinquish her hold without fear of losing the soul.

She almost succeeded. When all that remained were a few short tugs on his soul, the Damned was rudely interrupted. The blow to her hold was so strong and sudden that, not expecting anything of the kind, Tia momentarily lost control of her own magic. Just for a brief minute her grip weakened and the essence of the Elect, captured with such difficulty, flowed like water through her fingers. And then it was gone.

Roaring with rage and frustration, Typhoid leaped from the bathtub.

"It's done!" sighed Layen.

She faltered and I grasped her by the elbow to keep her from falling over.

"He very nearly stood up! With that slit throat! Did you see that?" Bamut's hands were visibly shaking and his voice was hoarse.

"We saw," replied Shen gloomily. All his mockery and spite had melted away in an instant. His face was serious and even the oven fork in his hands no longer seemed comical. "What else can we expect from your hobgoblin?"

"Anything at all. Now he knows about us. I can't hold out against him for long."

"Shouldn't we get to the forest?" asked Midge, wiping off his face with the white tablecloth taken from the table.

"We're going to try," I replied, calculating our line of retreat. The best bet was probably to go along our street to the bridge and then past the mill. The forest was very close there. It wouldn't be hard to get lost in it. The main problem was getting out of the village.

"Stop gossiping!" The voice of Whip, who was standing by the window, brought me back to earth. The Morts were rallying.

I reached for my quiver but Layen tossed her head wrathfully.

"Don't waste your arrows. Let me. We'll make a break for the forest. Whip! Heads up!"

He didn't need to be asked twice. He quickly ducked to the side. My sun spun the staff over her head, pointed it at the door, and cried out in a guttural voice, "Rragon-rro!"

The skull howled deafeningly. Bamut, forgetting about his crossbow, fell facedown onto the floor. The house shook so hard that for a moment my vision darkened.

"Ha!" exclaimed Luk, who was lying near the window, as he grabbed Ga-Nor by the sleeve of his shirt. "Ha!"

Even from so far away, it was obvious that something out of the ordinary was happening on the other side of the village. The roof of one of the houses flew a good twenty yards up into the air and then crashed down in the neighboring vegetable patch. Then the view was obscured by a cloud of dust rising up to the sky.

————

The sudden burst of power caused Tia to swear in surprise. She even stopped getting dressed. She just froze on the spot. Wet and half-naked.

What was happening right now seemed impossible. Oh, that necromancer! It's too bad they'd killed him; otherwise she would have done it herself. How could that ignoramus not have noticed how powerful a prodigy that peasant woman was!

The nameless woman was strong. The Damned had not expected to find such a vivid spark in this wilderness. Judging from the magical echo, this peasant could hold her own with many of the Walkers. In addition, the fool had an uncommon mastery over her own talent, because very few people could take control of someone else's staff and weave their Gift around magic of a different persuasion. But this one dexterously toyed with the power of Death. A real talent. A woman like that needed to be nourished and cherished. Or killed, so she could capture that spark for herself.

Typhoid took the pins out of her hair, causing both her braids to slap down onto her wet back. She tossed the costly trifles onto the floor without so much as a look, and quickly pulled on her skirt. Of course, she could attack from here, but that would be the same as shooting blindly. She'd either miss her mark or kill the woman outright. No. She would catch this bitch alive and question her properly. She must have had a teacher. Without the proper knowledge and preparation, it was impossible to overwhelm a khilss (a staff of a necromancer. This magical artifact is the result of a succession of complex magical rituals and is a half-dead, half-living object. Its magic can only be aroused if its master unites his soul with the staff and imbues it with a portion of his Gift and vital force. The head of the staff takes on the form of the skull of whoever is master of the khilss at a given moment). And when she knew everything, she'd take that power for herself.

It crossed Typhoid's mind that it might not be a childlike girl-prodigy standing against her, but a Walker from the Council.

No. What nonsense. The Mother (the leader of the Walkers. She is selected by a majority vote of the Council of Walkers, thirty-three of the strongest mages in the Empire) would never send one of her daughters on a suicide mission. Besides, if the girl were a Walker, she never would have exposed herself like this. But all the same, she should exercise caution and look before she leaped.

The Damned snapped her fingers and the room darkened for a moment. The shadows condensed and twisted into the shape of a black raven. It cawed hoarsely and flew out the window, breaking the glass.

Putting on her shirt as she went and cursing at the stiffness of her boots, Tia ran out the door.

I had seen Layen's Gift in action more than once or twice. But even in my most daring dreams I never imagined she was capable of this.

The roof of our house flew up to the sky with a roar and a crash. The solid pine logs, from which the walls were constructed, flew apart in all directions like kindling. My eyes stung from the cloud of dust enshrouding us and, frankly speaking, it was not easy to breathe. Also, I feared that while we couldn't see any farther than our own noses, the Morts would seize the moment and hack us into tiny chunks. But my fears were for naught; no one rushed in to attack us. Midge was swearing and blaspheming so loudly that, should Melot catch wind of his clamoring, Whip's companion would never see the inside of the Blessed Gardens. Bamut was trying to support his comrade in the high art of swearing, but by the fifth word he began coughing and couldn't continue.

Eventually the dust began to settle. I stood right by Layen, protecting her from any possible dangers. My chance companions, on the other hand, tried to move as far away from her as possible. Idiots! Did they really not have enough brains to realize that we wouldn't make it a hundred yards down the street without her magical protection?

Despite the lull, I did not take my arrow away from the bowstring. Who knew what might jump out at us? It's thoughtless, at the very least, to be absently picking your nose when trouble threatens. You might just get your hand cut off while you're pulling out your finger. Layen wasn't counting crows either. The staff was unambiguously pointed at the spot where the door used to be. I have to say, the necromancer's bauble unnerved me. No, there was nothing calming about a hissing skull, obviously displeased with the sudden change in its master.

Layen noticed my anxious gaze and said soothingly, *I have a hold on it.*

Hold tight, I advised just in case. *I wouldn't be surprised if that thing bites.*

Believe me, that's the very least it's capable of. She chuckled.

Then humor me and don't take your eyes off it. Drop it if it starts to lash out. I turned to Whip's team and yelled, "Let's move!"

We headed out into the yard and rejoiced at the sight of the Morts, who had been ripped to shreds by Layen's spell. The warriors of the Waste were no more solid than the walls of my house. One of the Sdisian's servants had survived more or less intact, but he'd been crushed by a beam. And even he looked as if he'd been chewed up.

The house was gone, as was the hedge. While my companions coughed, spat, wiped their eyes and cursed, I peeked out into the street and let out a dazed whistle. Pine planking and logs were strewn about the entire neighborhood. The cottages of our closest neighbors had also suffered greatly from the blast. There were no people in sight. They were hiding under their beds and in their cellars. You wouldn't be able to drag them out for a week. Well, that was to the good; there'd be less hassle with no one crawling around underfoot. I pulled my axe from the body of the Mort I'd slain.

"Is everything all right?" asked Layen as she walked up to me.

"Yes. It's just not every day that you see the roof of your house learn to fly." My smile came out crooked. "As it turns out, I know very little about your talents."

"Fortunately, I didn't have the need to demonstrate them before," she replied a bit too casually. "Let's go. The khilss sucks out magic. I don't have enough for long."

I didn't immediately realize that she was speaking about the necromancer's staff. I think it's likely that if you gave that thing free rein, it would suck out not just your magic, but your soul as well.

"We'll talk later," I agreed.

My troops looked like they'd spent the better part of the past year crawling around a badger's tunnel. They were as filthy as Blazogs in a swamp. And as enraged as Nirits after an offense to their queen. Midge was cursing a blue streak, not even pausing for breath. Whip was still coughing and looking in all directions with streaming eyes. Bamut was the only one who was not wasting any time. He held his crossbow at the ready, and was intently watching the street on the chance that someone might want to come and find out what had happened here.

Shen sneezed loudly, dropped the oven fork, and walked over the body of a Mort. He picked its skeem up off the ground. Well, I hope the kid knows some other way to make a living besides healing. Midge, who had probably exhausted his supply of words and phrases, stopped swearing.

"Damn it. . . . Are we sticking around here for long?" snapped Bamut nervously.

He got there just before me. I wanted to ask the same thing.

"Don't yell," wheezed Whip, and he spat. "We're leaving now."

"No, did you see that! Did you?" Luk was choking on his own words from agitation. "Wow! What could blow a house to bits like that?"

"I don't know." Ga-Nor was dismally watching the dust settle.

Nabatorians were scurrying about on the far side of the river.

"I'd bet my eyeteeth that this is the work of the necromancer's hands," the guard continued. "Someone displeased him and so he went into a rage. All Sdisians are deranged, they rub shoulders with the dead, screw a toad! Oh, I just know the bastard's not going to calm down. He's going to go through the village, smashing everything in his path. He'll even get to us eventually."

The northerner stretched so strenuously that his joints cracked and, springing lightly to his feet, he began to pack their things into the bag.

"What are you doing?" asked the guard, taken aback.

"Can you really not see? The Nabatorians are running around like lice on a flaming head; there's no way they'll get us now. I'm not joking. If we leave quickly, the patrols won't pay any attention to us. We're leaving by the forest."

"Sure, and we'll turn into old men by the time we get through that thicket to Al'sgara," Luk replied bleakly. He was not at all tempted by the impending journey. "Perhaps there is another way."

"Of course there is. It's right over there. Over the bridge and then to the Sdisian's house for dinner. He'll be glad to meet you," said the Son of the Snow Leopard sarcastically. "Don't think about what's in store for us. If we're lucky enough to break through, we can try to go out onto the main highway and continue our journey like normal people."

Hearing the words "normal people" from the gloomy northerner with the overgrown ginger beard and the bedraggled clothes would have, at any other time, caused Luk to go into fits of laughter. But right now there was nothing to laugh about. Besides, he didn't look any better than his comrade. He looked like a scarecrow. But to scare people instead of crows. A city guard would take them for beggars or highwaymen.

"All right, let's do it your way," said the guard, reaching for his axe.

"I'm glad we agree." Ga-Nor grunted approvingly. "Just, you're being too hasty. It's too early to move yet. The archers won't just let us go."

"Where are they?"

"There's two of them about a hundred yards from here. They're coming toward the mill. Don't look! They'll see you. It's still too soon."

The soldier breathed a sigh of disappointment and rested his axe over his knees. He closed his eyes and tried to calm his furiously beating heart.

Tia was forced to pause in the middle of the inn's staircase because just at that moment the raven called her. Her vision momentarily darkened, a greasy lump stuck in her throat, her ears began ringing, and her eyes were struck by a glaring light. The Damned needed several seconds to orient herself and to apprehend what she was seeing. The first moments of looking at the outside world through the bird's eyes were always difficult.

She was hovering between earth and sky. To her left flashed the dark blue ribbon of the river, reflecting the bright sun and the dark wall of the forest. Tia sent a mental command and changed the direction of its flight. Farther away from the market gardens and outskirts, closer to the center. People were scurrying about below. She wasn't very high up, so

Typhoid could make out the Nabatorians clearly. A cart laden with firewood was slowly making its way down a dusty street. A foursome of cavalry flew by it at a full gallop.

"Well, where are you hiding?" whispered the Damned. "Show yourself."

She had to trust that her luck would continue to accompany her. Typhoid again changed the direction of flight. She drifted toward the river, closer to the eastern part of Dog Green. The raven flew over a water mill, a bridge; it dashed by roofs, alleys, gardens, vegetable patches, and then she saw the gutted house and the people. Five armed men and a woman with a khilss.

She didn't think the girl would be so young. To have such blazing potential at such an age! No, she did not resemble a Walker at all. Her strength was palpable, but there was no trace of the characteristic weaves of the Imperial mages. She had clearly not been taught in the Rainbow Valley (the magical school of the Walkers is located in the Rainbow Valley). Through the raven, the Damned reached out to the bearer of the Gift, trying to surreptitiously test the extent of her powers. The fool, of course, wouldn't be able to feel a thing; it was beyond the limits of her capabilities.

But then the woman turned her head sharply. Squinting for a moment, she looked at the bird and then pointed it out to a blond man standing next to her. Before Typhoid had the chance to lead her helper away, the man cast up his bow.

Her ears burned with a sharp pain, the world went dark, and the enraged Damned once again found herself in the inn.

Impaled by the arrow, the bird crashed to the street like a stone. I didn't really know why Layen had made such a fuss about it, but I did what she asked without any unnecessary questions.

"Getting a little practice in?" asked Shen venomously.

I scowled at him. Sooner or later the kid would get what was coming to him. He'd come up against some nice man who'd be all too happy to cut out his tongue.

"No, he knocked it down for your supper," Midge teased him.

"You eat it yourself!" snapped the Healer.

"Shut your traps!" yelled Layen. The idiotic bickering was starting to irritate her. "Let's make time!"

Just then the body of the raven dissolved into thin air, leaving behind only the arrow, which I quickly returned to my quiver. Midge exclaimed loudly at the strange disappearance of my trophy.

"The bird was his eyes." My sun was trying to calm the hissing staff. "Now he knows where we are."

"Can I give some advice?" Whip was looking at me questioningly.

I shrugged my shoulders. If he had something to say, let him say it.

"We need to get off the street. Right now any mutt can see us, and any minute now the Nabatorians will come and—"

As if in answer to his fears, four riders galloped out onto the street.

Before Bamut and I had the chance to aim, Layen leaped in front of us. The loathsome wail rang out again, and a magical concussion struck the soldiers. Until today I never would have thought that people, not to mention horses, had the ability to fly; it turned out they did, even if they couldn't do it quite as well as most birds. I got the impression that an enormous club struck the group of riders and heaved them up into the sky as if they weighed less than flecks of dust. If any of them chanced to live through that blow, I didn't envy them. Landing on the unforgiving earth isn't really good for your health. I was ready to bet all the money Layen had in her pack that those lads wouldn't be able to pick up their bones.

Midge, having seen what became of their enemies, once again began a catalog of all the curses he knew. For the third time that day. I didn't know what his words conveyed more—fear or admiration. And then there was Whip, who tossed his head as if thunderstruck, and said approvingly, if far too loudly, "They flew beautifully, the bastards."

"They sure know how when they want to," Bamut added. Then he giggled nervously.

The bloodcurdling wail rang out so suddenly that Luk, who was not expecting anything of the kind, nearly jumped out of his own skin. It seemed to him that he was hearing the warbling of a kirlee (a spirit, most commonly encountered in ancient ruins. According to popular belief, those who hear its song will soon die). The soldier pressed close to the window. Something black fell out of the sky on the opposite shore of the river and hit the ground with a dull, repulsive thud.

"Wow!" was all that Ga-Nor had to say.

The deformed, bloody thing had been a living man not all that long ago. Judging by the fragments of clothing, it was a Nabatorian soldier. Before the guard had a chance to say anything, the sky sent down yet another victim. A cart, loaded to the brim with sacks of flour, was hit by the terrible blow of a horse's heavy body and was smashed to pieces. Flour dust whirled up into the air.

The people working at the mill darted away in all directions, shrieking in horror. The archers who were standing not far off, on the other hand, rushed to the site of the incident.

"Hide!" The tracker sprung back from their vantage point and the soldier followed his lead.

They listened in as the Nabatorians chattered loudly and fearfully.

"I told you that the White was deranged. First he

went and destroyed a house, and now he's attacking his own. You mark my words, before an hour has passed, he'll upend the whole town."

"I can hardly wait. It will be much easier to disappear in the chaos."

"Fleeing an addled sorcerer isn't that simple," objected Luk. "He can send this little mill and us in it to Morassia with a wave of his hand. Oh! We're done for!"

When the Nabatorians beheld Tia, sloppily dressed and pale with rage, they jumped up from their tables.

"Nai," wheezed the Damned. "Get all your men to the eastern half of the village immediately. Seal off the streets. Detain everyone. At the slightest resistance—kill them. But leave the women alone. Take them alive. Alive! I hope that's clear? Go!"

"All my men are at the building site, my lady! I need ti—"

"I don't care how you do it," Typhoid interrupted him.

The captain and his men rushed to carry out her orders without further dispute.

"My lady, is it something serious?"

"Bring your men, Gry. I have pressing business."

She tore out of the inn at a run and looked around. "Sha-kho!"

The Shay-za'n floated over to her and stared at

her without blinking, the phosphorescent pits of its violet eyes intense. The Damned showed him the street by drawing a map to it right in the air.

"Go to this place with your brother and apprehend the people there. Don't you dare harm the woman!"

His feather-crowned head lowered in an affirmative bow. Both Burnt Souls floated off in obedience to her command. Tia watched them go and then turned back to the guards waiting for her.

Whip's advice that we get off the street as quickly as possible was sound and Layen decided to take it. She jabbed the staff at the nearest gates, and they flew apart into splinters. Our companions had already become accustomed to such things, so they weren't surprised. Midge, for example, didn't even swear.

Our neighbors were cowering in their homes, so no one came out to meet us. A watchdog, who had long ago sniffed out that something bad was going on in the neighborhood, was in no hurry to crawl out of its doghouse and greet uninvited guests with barking. All the better. We had no time to fight off dogs.

The path we took resembled an obstacle course. We stole through yards and vegetable patches, climbed over fences, walked along the roofs of sheds and henhouses. When a barrier seemed insurmountable, or when it would require too much effort,

Layen used her Gift, punching wide swaths through the peasants' buildings. No one dashed out to stop us. The terrified inhabitants did not stick their noses outside. There were also no Nabatorians to be seen at the moment, and that suited me just fine.

Whip and Shen were walking in front, Layen was right behind them, followed by Bamut and me, and Midge was manning the rear. I must confess, having the runt at my back for so long was making me nervous. Over and over the image of the necromancer's slit throat rose before my eyes. I wasn't sure if he would guard my back or take me out. I calmed myself only with the thought that as long as Midge and I were on the same team, he wouldn't think of settling old scores.

We walked briskly, lingering as little as possible, and I began to hope that we would succeed in escaping this predicament. The only thing that really worried me was Layen. Regardless of the fact that her eyes continued to glow with the feverish fires of magic, she was clearly weakening. Her skin had become deadly pale, her cheekbones had sharpened, her hair was dull and wet with sweat, clinging to her temples. The refractory staff of the sorcerer was draining her life force.

"Isn't it about time to get rid of that?" I asked my wife when we were cutting across old Roza's turnip patch.

"Not yet," she replied reluctantly, barely moving her lips. "We still need the khilss."

"I really hope you know what you're doing," I grumbled petulantly.

"Just stand by me."

I nodded. Of course I would.

From somewhere to the right, beyond the fences, we heard shouts. They were looking for us. For the time being they didn't have enough brains to check the yards and were prowling about the streets, but that wouldn't last for long. Even if the soldiers were that stupid, the officers were not. They would definitely begin to comb the yards, and if they had enough men, they'd simply cordon off the village. Time was working against us. Speed was the most important thing. If we managed to break free while the Nabatorians were running around open-mouthed and wide-eyed, everything would work out just fine. We had to go with the flow, in a figurative sense, but I wasn't sure we'd ever reach the shore. We might just all sink to the bottom together.

Speaking of which, we were nearly to the river. Right then we were not very far from the bridge. All that remained was to run around a barn, make it through the gate that led to the neighboring yard, and from there out onto the street. It was risky, of course, but there was no other way.

Near the barn, Whip stepped in a cow pie, swore crossly, then drew up even with Shen and continued walking beside him. Old Roza began calling curses down upon us from behind her closed door. We were trampling her vegetable patch. The flimsy gate was boarded over in such a way that it was obvious the hag was trying to protect her yard from the half-wit, Pork, who lived next door. As I heard it, he was a big fan of creeping over here where no one wanted him.

"Whip, let me," said Layen.

But he didn't obey. With a single kick of his foot, he ripped the gate from its hinges and then fell with a split skull from the blow of a Nabatorian soldier. Shen leaped back and to the left, my sun cried out and I fired quickly. Another two soldiers replaced the dead one. And then the entire world collapsed into the pandemonium of battle.

I heard Bamut's crossbow twanging dryly near my ear. I ripped my axe from my belt and threw it at the last assailant. But then four more surrounded us, appearing as if they'd risen up from the ground. Shen and Midge came to grips with them; the sound of steel on steel rang out. While they were trying to get rid of their opponents, Layen jabbed the staff into the face of the soldier nearest to her. The skull instantly bit off half his face. The man, forsaking all else on this earth, crumpled to the ground, wailing and spurting blood, pressing both hands to the terrible wound.

The last unoccupied Nabatorian tried to get around me on the right, but when he caught sight of the bloodthirsty khilss in my wife's hands, he froze. That's what killed him. Bamut wasted no time and plunged his dagger into his stomach.

"Shen, look out!" shouted Layen.

The Healer, who had expertly repelled the attack, retreated to the line of "magical defense."

The little skull wailed and the enemy was blasted away together with the gates, which were reduced to splinters. Midge had already taken care of his own troubles and was dispatching the soldier whose face had been bitten off.

"The darkness take me! What were they doing here?" asked Bamut as he stared at Whip's body bitterly.

"They were waiting for us," Shen replied, breathing heavily.

"Don't talk nonsense." I pulled my axe from a corpse, wiped the blade on its clothes, and put it back in my belt. "Look at that pair, they're practically in their underwear, even if they are well armed. They're spread out among the houses. They have to live somewhere while the barracks are under construction. We just chanced upon them."

"It was Whip who chanced upon them. Why did he go forward? Layen told him. . . . How many years has he managed to get off scot-free, but here, some young pup takes him down. The fool . . ."

With ashen lips, Bamut whispered a hasty prayer. It really was too bad about Whip. He wasn't the worst man, and he knew how to keep these jackals of his under control. But now I could only guess when they'd snap.

"You can't bring him back. Bamut, reload your

weapon," said Layen as she crossed the yard with swift steps.

A drunken face peered out of the house. It was Pork's papa, as I live and breathe.

"Heeey, now . . . whas you doin, eh?"

"Beat it!" commanded Midge, and the man vanished like the wind.

There was no one on the street. We quickly crossed it and, pressing close to the fencing, rushed toward the river. On the other side, by the mill, people were bustling about.

"There's archers over there!" Shen shouted to me in warning.

"I'll attend to them," volunteered Layen.

Over the past several minutes she had grown even more haggard and pale. Her skin seemed transparent and waxy, formidable dark blue circles had appeared under her eyes, and her hair looked like it was melting away. I could take care of these clods before they had time to aim properly. There's no need to play with Death, when you can do it all with conventional weapons. The archers, who had their backs turned to us, did not present the most difficult of targets.

I barely aimed. The wind was blowing away from me, my target was standing still so I did not need to offset my aim, and even an infant could work out the trajectory. And a distance of a hundred and fifty yards was no distance at all for this bow. At the very moment when the first arrow hit its target dead on, its sister was already flying away from my bowstring.

"They really got them!" was all that Ga-Nor said when the Nabatorians were shot down.

"Where did they shoot from?"

"From the other bank. No, to the left!"

Only now could the northerner's companion make out the shapes of four men and a woman. One of the newcomers, a towheaded man, was frozen in the middle of the street. His weapon was still raised and his right hand was drawn back toward his ear. He'd just finished shooting and was apparently admiring his handiwork. Well, he had a reason to be proud. He'd killed the two archers in the space of a breath.

"I would really like to know who those people are."

"What does it matter, if they save us the trouble?" said Ga-Nor, shrugging.

"They could be our allies. Let's make ourselves known to them!"

"You see two corpses, and just like that you lose the last of your brains," the tracker commented warmly. "Where's your caution? Think with your head. I doubt if we show ourselves to them that we'll be greeted with open arms."

"I didn't really think of that." Luk was rattled.

"Why is it that you dare to call my people numb-skulls?"

"I never called you that!" objected the guard indignantly; then he changed the subject. "Let's get a better look at what they decide to do next."

This girl was the most beautiful in the world. Yes. Far more beautiful than the village maidens, who, when they see her, will burst with envy and chew on their own braids. There had never been such a maid in Dog Green. Even his best friend, Captain Nai, obeyed her. And the magician was also her friend.

Really soon, Pork would become a knight and then the maid would love him. And he would save her from all sorts of bandits and dragons. Just so she wouldn't get bored. And if anyone spoke meanly to the beauty, he would teach him a lesson and force him to ask forgiveness from his lady love on bended knee.

The half-wit would force those who refused to eat dirt. Or even better, he'd rat them out to Captain Nai, and the scoundrels would be hanged.

Right now the "lady love" of the village cowherd was rushing somewhere, surrounded by five soldiers. Pork wanted to go with them but he was struck by the evil scowl of the silver-haired captain and realized he didn't mean him well. So he shuffled along behind them, trying not to lose sight of his love.

"Hey, and how's that for a wonder?" I heard the dazed voice of Midge.

The runt was looking at something behind my back. I turned sharply.

Two beings were floating toward us along the empty street from the center of the village. Sure, sure. I didn't believe it myself at first. They really were floating. Without any wings at all, they were soaring toward us about the height of a human man above the ground. They didn't have any legs, by the way. Just some kind of pathetic little snake tail. All told, I had never seen anything like it, and that was probably a good thing. I don't want to have anything to do with such creatures. Especially when they were holding bows so large that the strongest man in the world could not draw them.

"Behind the house!" I commanded and, not checking whether my companions had obeyed or not, I reached for my quiver.

The newcomers, as if on cue, raised their bows. They did it so quickly that I barely had time to hop backward toward the fence. I ducked low to the ground, and the arrows slammed loudly into the slats. I swore, rushed toward shelter in a crouch, and at the last moment executed a little twirling jump that even a drunken flea would envy.

"Are you okay?" bellowed Shen.

I ignored his question as I carefully leaned forward around the corner of the house, and then I quickly staggered back. An arrow thudded into the ground. Not an arrow really, more like a spear. It could easily break a horse's back in two.

The things kept up a steady bombardment, make no mistake. We couldn't even stick our noses out, let alone find a way to get over the bridge. They'd turn us into porcupines soon enough.

"What are they, the Abyss take me?" squealed Midge.

He wasn't really expecting an answer. Neither was I. So I was quite shocked when Shen responded, "Shay-za'ns."

"What?" Midge did not understand.

"Burnt Souls," explained the Healer. "That's them."

Just great! I'd never really planned on encountering them in this life; it was like running into creatures from bedtime stories. I didn't think the inhabitants of the Great Waste would come so far to the north.

"Layen, do something!" implored Bamut.

"I can't do anything when I can't see them."

But she couldn't see them, because then those bastards would have us in their sights. If you so much as stuck your head out of cover, you'd get an arrow in the eye.

"We need to distract them!"

Shen's idea wasn't all that original. Why didn't I think of that?

"You're such a clever fellow!" I snorted contemptuously. "Why don't you tell us the secret of how we do that?"

At my words, he immediately snapped back, "Run along the street. Just when they're about to fill you full of holes, your woman can whip up some terrible spell."

I had the strongest urge to push the little bastard away from the wall and into the opening between the houses. I'd be happy to let the Burnt Souls shoot him.

It's the only way out. Layen's voice resounded in my head.

Are you serious?

I can feel him *approaching. We have to take a risk or it won't matter at all. Will you help me?*

I didn't waver for a second.

"What do you need me to do?"

"It seems that our friends got themselves into trouble," said Ga-Nor meditatively.

Luk nodded quickly in agreement and then, realizing that the northerner was not looking at him but at the window, he swallowed convulsively. The soldier was shuddering fearfully because of the Burnt Souls. Those creatures were even worse than the walking dead, and they weren't nearly as easy to dispose of.

"Hey! You aren't about to go and help them out, are you?" It had suddenly occurred to the soldier that his friend was about to rush to the aid of the people who'd gotten themselves in hot water.

The Son of the Snow Leopard looked Luk in the eyes and reluctantly shook his head.

"No. Of course not. That would be suicide."

"Damn. . . . If we stay here, we'll be overrun by a whole pack of Nabatorians. We don't have enough bolts and arrows for that."

He was right. All too soon our enemies would turn up to help the Burnt Souls. We could forget about reaching the forest then. We wouldn't even make it to the local cemetery.

"I can cast three or four more spells," whispered Layen. "There's almost no time left."

"Are you ready?" I asked her.

"Yes. On the count of three. One! Two!—"

"What are you going to do?" asked Shen suspiciously.

"Three!" she finished.

I had complete faith in her and her abilities, so I didn't hesitate for a second and rushed out from the protection of the walls into open space. A spell slipped from the head of the staff and struck the gravel near my feet. A dusty shield shivered in the air, which trapped the arrows of the Burnt Souls. If Layen had been a moment late, I would have been a goner.

The magical shield protected me from the arrows so I weaved like a rabbit, dashing around the street, trying to make it so that the archers didn't lose sight of me for a second. While the Burnt Souls were distracted by me, Layen had time to cast another spell.

Tia saw the woman the moment she stepped out from behind the corner of the house and raised the khilss. The Shay-za'ns were raining down arrows at a blond man who was darting about the street, instead of sending an arrow at her legs. The aura of the Arms of Dust was shimmering around the man. The fools! Did they really not notice that all their efforts were in vain? There was no way the arrows could pierce that shield.

The bitch was smart. When she bound her, she'd have to ask who taught her such a spell. It was Death magic; the Walkers knew nothing of it. Who could her teacher have been? Not taking her eyes off the woman, the Damned began to weave a spell of binding. It was supposed to cut the woman off from her Gift and bind her arms and legs.

She sensed the explosion of power at the very moment when her spell was ready to leave her fingers. The air crackled with magic, dark blue sparks scintillated in the Damned's hair and disappeared, and then there was a bang so loud that she bit her tongue in surprise.

In the place where the Shay-za'ns had been standing there was now a tight-knit, blue-black tornado of sand. Sha-to and his brother had been spun about and ripped into thousands of tiny pieces.

Fool! Idiot! Amateur! Upstart! Why would she use such a powerful spell and waste so much of her strength just to kill two? It was like wielding a hammer to kill fleas! She really didn't have any sense! The thoughtless, incompetent bitch!

Typhoid frowned darkly, and in the next instant the curse fled from her fingers.

Luk yelped fearfully at the thunderclap that roared out of the clear sky and then rubbed his eyes, not believing what he was seeing. Nothing changed. The magenta whirlwind continued to rage between the houses.

"Here comes the necromancer!" predicted the guard.

"You're wrong." Ga-Nor was more observant than his comrade. "It was that peasant woman."

"A Damned!" gasped Luk.

"Or a Walker. Either way, it's nothing to do with us. Get ready."

"What, right now?" he asked in a stunned voice, but he obediently stood up.

"You can wait until they destroy the mill." It was unclear if the tracker was seriously suggesting that, or if he was joking. "But I've recently grown quite fond of the forest."

"Me too, screw a toad!" said Luk hurriedly, as if he was afraid he'd be left behind.

They rolled the millstone away from the trapdoor

and jumped down. No one stopped them or even noticed them. The mill was running but it was empty. All the locals had run away as soon as things had become dangerous.

Without looking back, totally unconcerned with the events unfolding behind them, the scout and the guard negotiated the open space of a fallow field covered in tall grass and found their way into the welcoming arms of the forest.

When the whirlwind dissipated, I saw a girl, surrounded by five Nabatorians in black armor, moving toward us with resolute steps. Dealing with those warriors in close quarters was out of the question. They had shields, swords, and heavy armor. They'd chop us into pieces if we didn't pick them off first.

Then the staff roared nastily and triumphantly. Layen shrieked shrilly and threw it away from her as if she'd been burned. But it didn't help. Her arms, from the tips of her fingers to her shoulders, were covered in a purple nimbus.

With a cry of despair and pain, my sun fell to the ground. The nimbus was now only covering her wrists and it had taken on a shape that closely resembled shackles. I rushed over to help her, but she cried out to me, "Keep away! It's not a *him*! It's *her*!"

I've never had any complaints about my intuition, and I realized right away that the trouble was coming from the Nabatorians' companion. The purple magic was the work of her hands. Without thought, I tore an arrow from my quiver, stretched the bow-string, and shot. Two of the men in black shifted their triangular shields, protecting the girl from harm. I cursed.

Out of the corner of my eye, I could see that Midge and Bamut weren't even thinking of helping. They flew past me and ran for the forest with all their might.

Tia had not thought it would be so easy to bind the bitch. Up until the very moment when the curse struck her through the khilss, the fool did not suspect what was about to happen. She didn't put up any opposition. Either she didn't have enough strength, or she hadn't gotten around to learning about it. The curse, worked through the staff she'd cast away from her, held her firmly. But the Damned didn't even consider relaxing her grip. In the first place, she did not for a second forget that the girl-prodigy in front of her had a very powerful natural spark. Secondly, Typhoid was still expecting a trick. She was having difficulty dismissing the idea that this was all some trap of the Walkers. Only when the magical chains appeared on the thin wrists of the blue-eyed peasant woman did Tia breathe a sigh of relief.

It worked! Now the girl was in her grasp!

The two guards walking in front of the Damned

interlocked their shields. An arrow struck them with a dull thud. Typhoid flinched in surprise. All her thoughts were so focused on her opponent that she completely forgot to consider other perils. If not for her bodyguards, that which Tia had avoided with so much success these past few centuries might have happened. The unknown archer was far from shy, and he'd almost succeeded in exploiting the situation to his advantage.

Tia was about to take care of the impudent fellow, but then a young man ran to the staff, which was lying on the ground.

When Midge and Bamut ran off, I completely forgot about the Healer. I dismissed him, thinking that he was likely to be as useful as milk from a male goat. So when Shen appeared out of nowhere and jumped into the street and raised up the staff Layen had cast aside, I lost the power of speech.

Just as it had done earlier, the skull melted and took on a new form. The lad, as white as chalk, quickly pointed the staff toward the woman who had attacked Layen and, carefully enunciating the sounds, shouted the very same phrase I had already heard from my sun.

"Rragon-rro!"

The skull emitted an entirely human howl of pain, and our foes were struck by an incandescent white lance of light.

The boy's behavior was strange. What did he hope to achieve by grabbing the khilss? She couldn't even feel the smallest hint of the spark in the boy.

But when the staff read its new master and changed its shape, Tia didn't have enough time to be astonished. She instantly shifted part of her power to a shield, thrown up to meet the other's spell. In the next second, bright light surrounded her.

Pain surged through every part of her body, forcing her to curl into a ball and let out a hoarse, animalistic bellow of torment.

The ground shuddered intensely under our feet. Multicolored spots floated before my eyes.

Shen was standing in the same spot, but the necromancer's staff no longer existed. It had broken apart, dissolved into black flakes, which were instantly taken up by a light breeze and playfully carried along the street. Layen was no longer screaming. The purple light on her wrists had gone out and she was trying to stand. I rushed over to her, grabbed her, and set her on her feet. She was trembling intensely, her teeth were clicking, and an unhealthy flush covered her cheeks. She was repeating one word over and over.

"Healer . . . Healer . . ."

"Can you walk?"

For a moment my sun looked at me, not grasping what I wanted from her; then she nodded. She walked several steps on shaky legs and nearly fell.

"I'll help!" Shen appeared at her side and supported her.

The lad was streaming with sweat. Blood was dripping from his nose. His light blue eyes were bloodshot. But he was still standing firmly, and his strength was undiminished. I handed Layen to him.

"To the forest! Come on!"

He easily lifted her over his shoulder and carried her toward the bridge.

Three of the five Nabatorians were dead. One was screaming continuously. Another was shifting about listlessly. The spell had hit them straight on and even the ground around them was pitted.

The girl had caught the worst of it. Her hair was burnt off. All that remained of her face after the miraculous fire was a mass of bloodstained flesh. Her left forearm was missing, and she was clenching the stump with her right hand, trying to stop the flow of blood. And still, despite her appalling wounds, the woman was trying to get to her feet.

I didn't give her the chance and ruthlessly shot at the viper, planting three arrows in her. The first hit her on the right side of her chest and caused her to fall back to the ground. The second struck her side. The third, her neck. I don't know who she was, but she died just like regular people do.

Pork, who'd been crouching all this time behind

an outdoor well, began to wail mournfully. I paid him no heed as I turned and ran to catch up with Shen and Layen, who were already on the other side of the river.

Captain Gry was brought back to consciousness by the endless screams of Lye.

"There now, buck up, my boy," whispered the captain of the guards through split lips. "There now."

The wounded man didn't heed him and continued to wail.

Overcoming the pain, Gry scrambled to his knees and groaned. His right arm was burned like he'd stuck it into a brazier full of hot coals. The blood flowing down from under his helmet got into his eyes, but he could still see well enough to make out the wound. He could forget about ever carrying a sword again. His thumb and index fingers were missing.

Gry tore a piece of what had once been clothes from the bloody thing lying next to him and improvised a field dressing for the wound. Lye finally stopped screaming. He was dead. The Nabatorian looked around, continuously wiping blood off his face. It was all over. He was the only one who survived the Walker's attack. His comrades and his lady were dead.

The lady was dead.

He couldn't believe it. It was beyond his comprehension. Gry had never thought that those who were called the Damned by the inhabitants of this country could die. But she lay before him, broken and bloody. And the three arrows that bristled out of her body were a silent reproach to him.

He'd failed. He couldn't protect her. He had betrayed the honor entrusted to him. He had disgraced his family.

On the very edge of his consciousness, which was blazing with pain, the Nabatorian noticed that someone was moving nearby. The hearty fellow with the face of an idiot, the one who had followed them from the inn, got up to his feet. He walked over to the Nabatorian and said with an intonation so well known to him, "You executed your duties poorly, Gry."

The wounded man flinched, raised his head, and groaned in fear when he saw the lad's eyes. They were absolutely white. Sightless. A sepulchral flame seemed to burn in them. And that lightly mocking and familiar tone of voice. Only one person dared to speak to the King's Guard that way.

"It . . . it isn't possible," whispered Gry. "I don't believe it . . . my lady . . ."

Tia's gaze did not bode well.

10

The first time we came to a halt, Shen punched Midge in the face for running off and taking Bamut with him. To my surprise, the runt did not hit back. It seemed that for the time being he had decided to stay out of any scuffles, since he didn't have the upper hand. And Layen and I were not too fond of the degenerate.

Midge and Bamut behaved as meek as lambs and little by little the atmosphere stopped being so tense. Offenses took a backseat to survival. We were all stuck with one another, so we had to pretend that nothing had really happened.

Toward nightfall on the fourth day, we stopped for the night in a sycamore grove. We'd covered a lot of ground over the course of the day, and we could allow ourselves to rest until morning with a clear conscience.

"Are you sure it's safe here?" Midge asked me.

"Judge for yourself. We've been struggling through the wilderness at a trot for four days. We'll head out for the road tomorrow. We're going the right direction. If there was a pursuit, it's turned back long ago. Otherwise they would have picked up our trail. I doubt a small fire would do much harm. Besides, eating partridges raw isn't very good for you. Personally, I prefer my birds cooked."

Midge listened sullenly, nodded to show that he was in agreement with the arguments I set forth, and he then poked Bamut in the side. He stood up, groaning discontentedly, and the two of them left to gather kindling for the fire. I followed them with my eyes until they disappeared behind the trees. Layen was dozing, leaning against a tree with her legs tucked under her. The journey had exhausted her. She still hadn't recovered her strength after what had happened in the village.

I took my jacket off and carefully, so as not to wake her, covered my wife with it.

"Keep an eye out," I asked of Shen in a whisper.

The Healer was plucking the partridge I'd shot and he nodded without looking up from his work. Neither I nor Layen nor he had spoken about what happened in Dog Green. We assiduously avoided that topic, sheltering behind the lack of time. In part, that was the truth. The debilitating foot marches always ended with a halt for the night, where everyone had a hurried bite to eat and fell into exhausted sleep until morning. Sometimes we didn't even have the strength to post a watch. Then we were traveling again, and we couldn't talk. I did not want Midge and Bamut to overhear us.

Our "runaways" knew nothing about Shen's strange talents. Perhaps that was for the best. The lad was evidently not at all eager to share his secret with those around him.

I grabbed my bow and walked off in the direction in which my "good friends" had headed not too long ago. I didn't trust that pair before, and after their flight, there was no way. Without Whip to look after them, Midge had become a worrisome problem, a thorn in my side, especially since Bamut obeyed him unconditionally. Layen and I were lucky that Shen was on the outs with them. But the Healer also required a careful eye, since he could not only heal but also cast incandescent fire. Any fool could see that the lad was quite dangerous and that he might have his own reasons for sending us to our eternal rest without any encouragement from my brothers in arms. I wanted to get rid of them all, but I wasn't sure I could do it without real damage to my own hide.

Besides spying on our wood gatherers, I needed to walk a circuit around our camp for the night. There is little joy in getting cozy near a gove's lair or a den of shpaguks. And waking up in their stomachs isn't any fun, either.

Besides all that, I was worried about the last bit of ground we'd covered. I've been naturally suspicious since childhood. But recently my suspicious nature has been responding very sensitively to any oddity. As soon as we hit the forest, I sensed that someone was shadowing us. However, "sensing" will only get you so far. If we were being followed, they were doing it skillfully. Yesterday afternoon I'd fallen behind my companions and set up a small ambush. The sensation of being shadowed instantly disappeared. Either I really had imagined it all, or the unknown dodger had become more careful.

I didn't tell anyone about my suspicions. Not even Layen. They didn't need to be bothered for nothing.

The sky was still light, but here between the powerful trunks of the enormous sycamores, thick twilight reigned. The forest seemed gloomy and vacant as it prepared for sleep. There were no paths, not even animal trails. I had to walk randomly and to watch under my feet so that I did not tread on dry branches or trip over the black braids of the roots protruding from the ground.

Without false modesty, I can say that I know how to walk in a forest. I acquired the experience in my youth, when I'd been forced to wander around Sandon for a time. Even now that forest has no love for outsiders, and at that time humans were strictly forbidden from entering the kingdom of the Highborn. There was no peace treaty between the Empire and that race, and so anyone who entered that wilderness had to put all his hope in his own cunning and experience.

After some time, I could hear the disgruntled grumbling of Bamut. "It's so dark, it's as if my eyes have been plucked out!"

"If you keep horsing around out here, you're going to have to feel your way back by touch," replied

Midge. Immediately after these words, the sound of a branch snapping rang out.

"Come on, you, damn. . . . You just try and teach me how to gather wood."

"You need to move more quickly. We'll lose our way in an hour or so. I've heard of men wandering through the pines and dying of hunger, and all the while, there was the path. Right next to them."

"It's only like that when there's magic, damn it," drawled Bamut petulantly. Another branch snapped.

"And who told you there isn't any here? This spot looks like it's cursed. I wouldn't be surprised if something nasty happened to us."

Bamut laughed nervously and, judging by the rustling of the leaves, began to hurry up. Trying not to make a sound, I crept closer and watched them from behind a tree. They'd stopped a bit farther off. There was kindling nearer to the camp, but for some reason they decided to wander farther into the thicket.

"Hey, tell me this, you, damn. . . . Why should we be out here doing everything while they're resting?"

"Shut up."

"No! Why am I always on the bottom? I'm sick to death of it."

"Are you suggesting we bleed them dry?" asked Midge sneeringly.

"Yeah. I think about those ten thousand sorens all the time."

"Don't you even think about that! It's not worth it!"

"But what could be better than money?"

"Well, for example, a proper grave."

"Ha!"

"I realize that it's not as nice as sorens, but you're more likely to get that than Joch's reward."

"Damn. . . . What do you mean?"

"What are you? Completely stupid?" Midge suddenly bristled. "You're constantly forgetting about Layen. Were you sleeping when she turned half that village into rubble?"

Bamut got down on his knees and began collecting kindling. For a short while the crossbowman grumbled angrily, trying to think up a suitable reply.

"Good steel will stop any lousy magic if you go about it right. Wasn't it you who slit the necromancer's throat?"

"Of course it was me. The sorcerer didn't know our worth. But Layen knows what you and I are capable of. I don't want to go near her, even when she's asleep. There's also Gray. He's quite good at setting people's souls free when he's backed against a wall. It's too risky."

"There are three of us and two of them."

"Those two could stand against five. Besides, do you really think Shen is on our side?"

"Yes."

"Why would you think that?"

"I talked to him."

"When?"

"I managed it when we stopped yesterday."

"Well, now. I'm not very sure of him."

"Damn. . . . It doesn't mean a thing that you don't like the lad. Whip got along with him just fine."

"And where is Whip? He's rotting with a crushed skull in some dung pit. Melot forgive me for such words. I tell you again; I don't trust Shen. Besides, it makes a lot of difference if you divide ten thousand between two or three people."

"So you've decided to do this after all?" Bamut was clearly thrilled.

"Deciding does not mean acting. We'll wait for the right moment. If one presents itself. But right now it's too early to make a move. Gray is guiding us. If we pick him off, we'll never get out of this forest."

"And what if your moment doesn't happen before we get to Al'sgara?"

"Then you'll have to forget about the money. Let's go. It's almost dark."

Midge and Bamut picked up the gathered firewood and walked off in the direction of camp.

Well, well, well.

My suspicions about those alley cats were completely justified.

I restrained myself from going after them. In spite of the perils of coexistence, the lads could come in handy. Spare hands are never really spare in the wilderness. But if we should happen to chance upon a gove, I'd send the three of them down its gullet without any remorse.

While Layen was beside me, there was no point in worrying overmuch that they would send us to the Blessed Gardens. I don't think they'll strike until we get out onto the highway. We'll just have to get rid of them when we leave the forest.

I began to make my way toward the footpath we'd walked along all day. It was located about three hundred yards to the right of where Midge and Bamut had been hanging about. The sky had taken on a deep violet color and the first stars were shining forth. The Serpent was perfectly visible, and the Blue Flame on its tail was shining brightly, pointing to the south. I took my bearings and moved on.

I hate walking through the nighttime forest. It's not a business for humans. Even though I'd known experienced trackers in my youth who could move through the darkness of the dense wilderness as if they were walking down a city street, I did not possess such skills. I had to practically push my eyes out of their sockets so I wouldn't crash into some tree trunk. It didn't help very much. The moon, as luck would have it, was still not out.

I stopped and, holding my bow at the ready, stood behind a tree. My eyes were of no use whatsoever so I had to listen, hoping to catch a suspicious rustle. But the minutes dragged on and nothing happened. Everything was the same as usual in a nighttime forest. The wind sighed through the treetops, and somewhere a roused bird gave a shriek.

Well then. I'd have to hope that there really wasn't anyone chasing us. I crossed the path, once again delved into the thicket, and made my way back to where I'd found Midge and Bamut. Ahead of me the warm light of the fire twinkled. I smelled roast fowl and my stomach rumbled urgently. I was already dreaming of my share of partridge when a twig crunched softly to my left, very close by.

My arrow sped off into the darkness before I had a chance to think about what I was doing. The sound that followed a moment later let me know that I had missed and hit a tree. I shouted loudly, alerting those sitting by the fire about the danger, and sent a second arrow at the rustling, which was moving away from me. I had no idea if it hit or not.

Damn it! I was nearly taken unawares! If the person lying in wait had not stumbled over that miraculous twig, who knows how it all would have played out.

"What happened?" Layen ran up to me first.

Midge and Shen hurried after her with burning branches instead of torches. Bamut was armed with his crossbow.

"There was someone here," I said, not taking my eyes off the direction where my arrow had fled.

"Who?" asked Shen, scowling.

"How should I know? You have a light. Check the ground. Maybe some tracks were left behind. Over there. And over there."

We found the first arrow fairly quickly; it was lodged in a sycamore. Not far from it we found the broken twig that had saved my life.

"That means nothing." The Healer didn't believe me. "It could have been like that for a year."

"I suppose I just heard it crack in my head," I responded sourly.

"I shouldn't wonder," he snapped. "There's too little light to see anything."

A glowing ball of turquoise light appeared in Layen's hands. It was bright enough to light up the forest around us for a distance of two yards. I noticed that when my sun cast the spell, Midge winced. Excellent. That would make him be careful and not act recklessly.

"Is that enough?" she asked, holding out the glowing ball to Shen.

The Healer took it in his palm without flinching. Then he looked at me questioningly.

"I shot twice."

"Where?"

Once they'd received the direction they began to search.

"Here it is!" Bamut shouted back to us after a minute.

We hurried over to him and saw that he was twirling an arrow in his hands. Midge took it and raised it up to his eyes.

"You nicked someone after all. There's blood on

it." The small assassin cautiously tasted the bloody arrowhead with the tip of his tongue. "Human."

"You don't say? Have you tried any other kinds?" asked Shen spitefully.

"Screw you!" roared Midge instantly.

"Cut it out," ordered Layen. "Whether it's human or not, one thing is clear—there really was something here. I think we need to post a watch at night. Otherwise we might not wake up the next day."

Her suggestion was met with an approving silence.

I finally got a chance to speak with Layen in private during our halt the following day. The important conversation had been delayed by five days, but there was nothing I could do about that now. She had answered all my mental appeals with obstinate silence.

While the threesome imposed on us by Mols were taking off their boots and sprawling out to rest under the tall golden pines, we walked away to a small glade teeming with raspberries. Before we could get to a good place to speak without witnesses we had to scramble through the brush. Along the way, my wife took the opportunity to gather an entire handful of the large, fragrant berries and now, leaning against a tree trunk warmed by the sun, she was chewing on them thoughtfully.

After her communion with the necromancer's

staff, she was still pale, but the sickly, anemic gleam had disappeared from her skin and her hair was no longer lackluster. Enough of her weakness had disappeared that I couldn't help but rejoice.

"How are you?"

"Huh?" Distracted by her weighty thoughts, she looked at me for a moment without comprehending what I was talking about. "Better. Much better. Thank you. What do you think? Who's following us?"

"I'd like to know that myself. He's been following us since the first day."

"I can't say that this worries me all that much, dear."

"You're right. He could have attacked us a while ago, if he'd wanted to. The first three nights all of us slept like logs. The man's had a heap of chances."

"You noticed how experienced he is. Those idiots didn't even look at the tracks, but did you see them?"

"Well . . ." I paused. "Let's just say that, from what he left behind, you could say he's not an ordinary man. There were almost no prints on the ground. It's not the first time he's worked in the forest. And he fled from my arrows with ease, while I would have shot down almost any other. He knows the forest well. But if I'm honest, he concerns me far less than what happened in the village. You don't want to speak mentally, but maybe now that we're alone you can explain everything that happened to me."

Layen smiled understandingly and dropped another berry into her mouth. Her expression became surpassingly melancholy.

"You really don't understand anything, do you?"

"What don't I understand?"

"Ness," she said sweetly. "I 'don't want' to speak with you in mental whispers only because I can't. It's not that I don't want to. You note the difference?"

My expression was undoubtedly quite foolish, and my sun sighed in disappointment.

"Hmmm . . . Those who use the Gift call this an attenuation of the spark. The sorcerer's khilss required all my capabilities. It almost drank me dry. The staff constantly requires vital and magical power. It feeds on them; otherwise it will decline to obey. And then that woman came—"

"Who was she?" I interrupted.

Layen looked at me searchingly and ate another berry without replying. She wiped her hands, stained red from the juice. She imperceptibly shook her shoulders.

"She was very strong. So strong, in fact, that I assume that she is one of the Damned."

I didn't realize immediately that this wasn't a joke.

"A Damned? That's ridiculous! She wouldn't have died so easily!"

"Who said it was easy?" Her piercing gaze sent a shudder traveling through me. "I can only call it a miracle that we were able to face her at all. She didn't take us seriously, and we caught her off guard."

For some reason it was beyond my comprehension that one of the Damned could have crossed our path. While they frighten you with such tales in your childhood, you stop believing in them after you grow up.

"You think this is nonsense?"

"Just a bit," I replied unwillingly. "You have to admit, it's very hard to believe that not a few days ago, I sent one of the Sextet to the Abyss with my own hand."

"As you will, dear. I can't make you believe. If it's easier for you, you can just consider her a very strong sorceress and that's all. Without any names. But she was strong, that's the truth. In case you didn't notice, I lost good and proper when I came up against her."

"On the plus side Shen managed quite well," I said, changing the subject of the conversation.

Layen twisted her mouth as if I'd presented her with a cup of vinegar.

"I'll say. He definitely managed."

"What is our mutual friend?"

"A Healer."

"I know that."

"Don't confuse the concepts. He's not a doctor, he's a Healer. More a shaman than anything else."

"Why? Is there a difference?"

"A vast difference. Healing is one of the rarer aspects of the Gift."

What an idea!

"Hmm. In other words, the lad is similar to you?"

"Yes and no. He has a spark, but it differs from mine. And from the sparks of the Walkers. And from the Embers. And from the necromancers. I can't say that it's very strong in him; if anything it's the opposite. It doesn't shine very brightly, so he doesn't have very much potential just yet."

"Not great? He dealt with that minx effortlessly. Thwack! And that's that!"

"That was nothing more than chance," she replied tranquilly. "Healers are very rare in our world. One out of ten thousand who possess the Gift carry such a talent within themselves. You can count people like him on the fingers of one hand. Plus, he's a man! As far as I can recall, the Sculptor was the only man who possessed such talents. All the other Healers are women."

"I don't understand how the ability to heal people with magic would aid building."

"Everyone with the Gift can heal with magic. Even the necromancers. But no one has the ability to do it quite like the Healers. Their Gift is focused specifically on healing. So much so that they can return the dead to life. The flip side of necromancy, if you will. The result is not an empty, vicious shell, but a real living person. And the abilities of the Sculptor surpass our understanding. That's why no mage today can duplicate his creations, or even come close. The Gates of Six Towers, the academy of the Walkers in the Rainbow Valley, the eight Spires, the palace of the Emperor, the Tombs of the Fallen, not to mention the Paths of Petals."

"Umm . . ." I paused, taking in the list. "Why have I never heard anything about Healers?"

"I told you, people with that kind of spark are born very rarely. And they don't go running around the cities and villages hoping to heal as many people as possible. The last Healer was a Mother of the Walkers. Five generations ago. Since then, no one has been born with such a Gift."

I preferred not to ask how Layen knew all of this.

"But let's return to my question," I reminded her. "What does healing have to do with injuring someone?"

"Every spark has its reverse side."

"Those words mean nothing to me."

She narrowed her dark blue eyes thoughtfully.

"The idea is the same in regular healing. Say you take a tisane of bloodroot for a cough. If you drink too much, instead of curing of your illness, you get the complete opposite result instead. Your lungs will collapse and you'll drown in your own blood. It's the same here. Who ever said that a doctor can't kill?"

"Well, if he's a quack," I said, chuckling.

"Not necessarily from ineptitude, dear. You must admit that an experienced doctor knows the human body so well that, should the desire take him, he could easily send anyone he liked to the Blessed Gardens. It's exactly like that with the magic of the Healers. To stop the heart? To burst the blood vessels? To send pestilence? If he can repair a broken spine, then why wouldn't he be able to break it? It's a unique battle magic that has nothing in common with the customary canons of the academies of the Walkers and Sdis. Not Life and not Death. Beyond that. Completely different. If a person turned a Gift like that to evil, he could cause such calamity that he'd be remembered for centuries. You don't need to go very far for an example. Leprosy, one of the Damned, is a Healer."

"Hey! According to legend, half the south died because of a disease she sent."

"That's exactly right. I think you can imagine now what an experienced Healer is capable of. No," she said, guessing what I wanted to ask. "Shen can't do that. Yet. I told you that his Gift is not yet developed. Like I said, it was nothing more than an accident. The boy was lucky that he could overpower the khilss. It was even more lucky that when Shen passed his Gift through it, his spark was not burned out. When Life encounters Death they usually kill each other. But Shen's magic is different. When it tangled with the necromancer's magic, it behaved in an inconceivable way. I've never heard of anything like it. A purifying, scalding light. I don't think he knew what he was doing. Even the Damned didn't suspect anything. She erected a shield so strong that most Walkers wouldn't be able to break through it. But the shield did not save her because of what resulted from the intermingling of the spark of the Healer and the magic of Death. Frankly, I'm not sure if there's even a way to combat such a spell."

"Is it really possible that neither you nor that girl nor the necromancer sensed who our Healer is?"

"It is. We didn't sense it. Not every bearer of the Gift is able to sense another's spark. And if it's skillfully hidden . . . The White didn't have the experience to catch me out. But about the Gift of a Healer. The temperature of his spark differs radically from the majority of sparks you come in contact with. You can only sense a Healer when he is exhibiting his abilities. Not before then. So that's why neither I nor the Damned nor the Sdisian suspected anything about the talents of Mols's friend until the very last moment."

"Speaking of . . ." I hesitated, but then I said it anyway. "Of the Damned. If you're right and it was . . . Which one was it?"

"Hmmm," she pondered, pulling her knees up under her chin and circling her arms around them.

I waited patiently.

"Initially there were more than twenty rebels in the Council of the Towers, but only eight of them survived the Dark Revolt and those are the ones known as the Damned. Delirium and Cholera died during the War of the Necromancers. Six were left. Two of them are men. That leaves four women. Only two of them fully match the characteristics we saw. So it was either Rubeola or Typhoid we came up against."

I shivered. But I still couldn't believe that we had seen one of those who had fomented the Dark Revolt and triggered the War of the Necromancers.

"What would a Damned want with a place like Dog Green?"

"The answer is obvious, my dear. Me. Or rather, my Gift. Of course, one might think that she came there out of pure curiosity or with the hope of enticing me to her side, but I don't really believe that. A few of the strongest mages have the ability to fuse others' sparks to their own Gift and become stronger."

I saw that this subject was disagreeable to her and refrained from pursuing it. I turned the conversation to something else. "So why did Mols send a Healer to us?"

"Are you positive that he knows about Shen's Gift?"

"No," I replied after a brief reflection. "But if that's so, then I really don't know what would cause him to send a common Healer with Giiyans."

"What or who?" Layen's expression turned cunning.

"Are you insinuating that it was Joch?"

"I don't know. When do you think we'll get to the road?"

I estimated the distance we'd traveled.

"The day after tomorrow, if we keep the same pace and nothing happens."

"You know that as soon as we get to the road they will become too dangerous for us. I can't vouch for Midge."

"And I can't vouch for any of them. I happened to overhear a conversation between our firewood collectors last night."

I briefly recounted Midge and Bamut's conversation.

"Maybe we should try to get rid of them today?" I suggested.

"It will be tricky," Layen said reluctantly. "I'm not sure that I can fight against even one of them. Plus, who knows what Shen will throw at us if we pin him to the wall."

"But I'm not asking you to brawl. Your Gift is far more useful than your knife."

She looked at me for a second in surprise and then sighed heavily. "I thought you understood."

She was silent for the longest time after that. Then she whispered quietly, "I cannot use my Gift."

I thought I had misheard her.

"You . . . What?"

"I *can't* use my Gift!" she screamed, losing control of herself, and then she buried her face in her hands.

For a short time I watched, stunned, as she sobbed soundlessly, and then I gathered her into my arms.

"Shh, hush. It's all right," I tried to console her. It helped a bit. The sobbing turned into quiet hiccups.

"I can't . . . I lost . . . I can't . . . That's why I didn't reply to your mental calls. I simply didn't hear them. I was planning on telling you today. I started but then you asked about the Damned and I couldn't go on.

"I told you already about the attenuation of the spark. The sorcerer's khilss drained me. Then the Damned's spell bound what remained of my magic. My spark has faded so much that I can't invoke my Gift."

"But you created that little ball of light yesterday for Shen."

"It needed doing, even if it required the last of the power I'd regained. Midge had to see it."

"So your Gift hasn't left you forever?"

"Of course not. My spark hasn't gone out. But quite some time will be needed to restore it."

"How long?"

"I've never had anything like this happen to me, so I can only guess. Two weeks. Perhaps a month."

I had to bite my lip to keep from swearing. I hadn't thought everything was this bad. We didn't have two weeks to rest; we didn't even have two days. Without my sun's magic backing me, I would be hard-pressed to deal with our three intrusive companions.

With an outraged shriek, a dappled bird flew out

of the thick brush about fifteen yards away from us. Right away I was on my feet, ready to shoot. Layen jumped up as well.

"Something spooked it," she said.

There were no suspicious movements or sounds. If someone was hiding there, he was being extremely quiet. We stood there for several minutes, tensely listening to the sounds of the forest.

"It's useless," said Layen. "If there was someone there, he's long since made himself scarce."

"Or he's still hiding," I said, disagreeing with her. "He could have heard us."

"I don't think so. It's far enough away."

"Some people have excellent hearing," I objected again and cast up my bow.

Twang!

The arrow flew to the place from which the bird had just flown. I waited another minute and then I took my axe in my right hand and a long dagger in my left, and went to scout it out, not all that hopeful that I'd managed to wound someone.

Just as I assumed, the arrow had hit the ground. I put it back in my quiver and examined the ground. The grass all around was undisturbed, but one of the branches of a raspberry bush was broken. A few ripe berries had fallen to the ground.

This could mean much.

Or it could mean nothing.

———

"Oh, Al'sgara!" sighed Bamut dreamily as he pillowed his arms under his head and stretched out on the leaves. "Damn. . . . Who would have known I'd miss it this much!"

"Long walks are good for your health." Layen pensively poked at a coal of the dying fire with a branch. An entire flock of sparks rushed up into the night sky.

"Anything but that for me! I think I have the spirit of the Green City in my blood."

"Thinking is bad for you, my friend," said my sun softly. "As you well know, too many thoughts can lead to a whole heap of troubles. Pass me some water, please."

Bamut sat up and stretched so that his joints popped. He did anything that was not part of his work at a leisurely pace. I could see how his laziness was enraging my wife.

"Take mine." Midge threw her his flask. "A century will pass by before he gets moving."

"Don't bad-mouth me," Bamut huffed as he stretched out again. "There's no rush."

I stepped out of the gloom where I'd been standing this whole time.

"Is everything all right?" Midge asked after clearing his throat. My appearance had caught him unawares.

"So it seems," I answered him vaguely. "It's quiet for the second day. It seems like they decided to leave us alone after all."

"Glory be to Melot," said Shen as he tossed a log onto the fading fire. "Spending every watch just waiting for something—"

"The longer you wait, the safer you'll be." Layen took a sip from Midge's flask and frowned. "Ugh! Where did you get this water?"

"From a stream." The runt was clearly not expecting such a question.

"You found a bad stream. It's bitter."

She spat and dumped out the flask.

"Hey! Hey!" Midge cried out. "What are you doing?"

"Don't whine," I advised him. "Is there nowhere to get water? Every day there's two or three springs on our path. You won't die."

Still spitting, Layen tossed the empty flask to its owner.

"I'd have given permission, if only she'd asked," he said grumpily as he twisted the lid back on. "We'll get there tomorrow, right, Ness?"

"Who said?" I asked dryly.

"Well, that's the way it looks. We've been walking in a straight line recently. We're headed west. In the evenings the sun beats down right into my face, especially when we're tromping through a field. If you count the days, we should already be there."

You smart little toad. We should get rid of you. Today. This night. When everyone would be asleep. We no longer required your company.

"Should have doesn't count in the forest."

"I think that a child could find the road now." I really didn't like Midge's smile.

"What's that supposed to mean?" I said.

"I'm simply happy. I'll be home soon." He was still smiling boldly.

Layen and I exchanged furtive glances.

So then. What follows from everything we just heard? Even a child could find the road? Is that to say that he no longer requires a guide? Are they sure that they can get out of the woods themselves? Apparently. The idiots don't know that there is a swamp in front of us, and we need to turn to the north. They believe they can get out of this scrape themselves. So of course our designation has changed—from dangerous companions to dangerous trophies for which quite a lot of money has been promised. Have they decided to do away with us? Yes, only we'll do it sooner, boys.

We had to terminate Shen first. I couldn't care less whether he was a Healer or not. Even if people like our Healer were born once in a hundred or even a thousand years, he was the most dangerous of the three.

"When I return to Al'sgara, I'm going to live it up." Bamut sat up again. "Damn it. . . . I'll buy myself a little house. On the outskirts. By the seashore. Or even better, a nice inn closer to the pier. And what are you going to do with your share, Midge?"

"Me?" The runt was lovingly picking the petals

off a small, unattractive flower. "It's too early to think about that. When I get it, then I'll decide. So-rens always find a way to be spent."

"You need to think about it in advance."

"How are you planning on getting rich, boys?" I tried to enter the conversation casually, but inside I was cringing. "You expecting an inheritance?"

"Something like that." Midge finished tearing off the petals and tossed what remained of the flower at me. "Here. Feast your eyes on that."

Bamut suddenly guffawed.

"What is this?" I ignored the laughter.

"Greater Valerian. The key to ten thousand so-rens. You still don't understand? The root of that little flower could make even a horse fall asleep."

"I never would have thought that you were so at home with forest herbs," I said, drawing out the words.

"Unlike some upstarts, rcal Giiyans undergo lengthy schooling." Midge wasn't smiling anymore. "Don't! It'll be worse for you."

I couldn't reach for my bow. Bamut's crossbow was unambiguously leveled at my chest.

"What should I make of this?" I asked coldly as I slanted my eyes to the right. To my surprise, Layen was sleeping.

"The water in the flask was bitter!" The realization stunned me.

They had outplayed us.

"Excellent!" Midge approved of my guess. "So it was. I don't rely on it very much, but luck loves me. When the witch awakes—"

"She'll boil your brains."

"So we believed as well. I heard that she can't do anything. Your woman is no more dangerous than a mosquito."

That means it was him hiding in the bushes. They spied on us, the Abyss take me!

"If she hadn't swallowed that junk we would have just whacked her over the head." Bamut edged into the conversation.

"Mols won't be happy." I was regretting like never before that Whip wasn't here.

"With that much money I can spit on both Mols and the guild, Gray."

"Then I don't understand why you're chatting with me."

"We don't intend to kill you. What would we do with your heads in the forest? They'll rot ten times over before we get them to the city. Threefingers might not believe us then. So we'll bring Joch live goods. And whole. We won't even beat you if you yield."

"I'm simply thrilled," I said and dropped sharply to my right side, simultaneously throwing my hatchet with my right hand.

The crossbow gave a loud crack and the released bolt passed over my head. Bamut hadn't expected something like that from me, and he had fumbled and missed the shot. However, hitting your target when you have a Blazgian utak lodged in your forehead is not very easy.

One down!

Midge roared, leaped up into the air, and crashed into me with all his weight before I had a chance to get to my feet. The blow threw me over onto my back. At the last moment I intercepted his hand, which was holding a knife ready to pierce my hide. The blade froze an inch from my face. Midge was pressing down with all his strength in one direction, and I was pressing up in the other. With my free hand I scratched at his face, trying to get to his eyes.

"Do you need any help?" Shen's voice rang out lazily.

"Of course! Yes! Idiot!" snarled Midge.

The knife came half an inch closer to my face. Suddenly my opponent shuddered and went limp. Shen was standing over him with a bloodstained skeem. Noticing my bemused expression, he smiled nonchalantly.

"I always disliked him."

I pushed the corpse off me and stood up. "So what next?"

"Nothing. We may as well get along. I hope to hell that we'll get to Al'sgara together."

"And then?"

He looked at me for a very long time; then he put away his skeem and said quietly, "Let's try to wake Layen."

The forest thinned out. The impassable thickets and mighty trees disappeared; little paths emerged; and a multitude of clear springs tumbled out of the earth and flowed into a small lake, which was hidden from curious eyes behind a wall of thick spruce trees. The ground became boggy in places; the black flies and mosquitoes increased. They didn't leave us be until the weather soured and it began to rain. It became damp, muggy, and nasty. All signs pointed to the fact that the Great Blazgian Swamp lay not far from here. We struck north in the hopes of sooner or later emerging onto the road that traversed the boundaries of the swamp and the forest.

Layen was constantly spitting out bitter saliva and recalling Midge and Bamut with "kind" words. If she had her way, she would have happily killed the scoundrels a second time. We didn't bother to bury them. I doubted this would offend Mols. The guild never defends those who go against its will. So the bodies remained there where they lay. Forest creatures need to eat too.

The Healer walked ahead and when he began to go astray I corrected his course. For obvious reasons we were not going to risk having Shen at our backs. Even after yesterday's assistance, it wouldn't do to trust him. But I did understand that all my precautions were just a drop in the ocean. Physically, I could wrap the kid around my finger, but I was powerless against his magic. And not just me, but Layen as well. Shen had definitely heard yesterday's conversation with Midge and so he knew that my sun had temporarily lost her Gift.

The unprotected back of the Healer was always in front of my eyes, but the temptation to stab it with something sharp didn't arise. The lad had one goal, and he voiced it more than once—to get to Al'sgara. From this I deduced that prior to the moment when the walls of the Green City appeared, his only interest in us would be as traveling companions. And killing everyone to your left and right is something only lunatics and scoundrels do. I dared to hope that after all my years of work I hadn't become as vile a brute as Midge or Bamut.

By noon we were soaked to the skin from the endless rain. I feared for my bowstrings, although they were hidden away in a metal box at the very bottom of the pack in which we had our money. The fletching of my arrows should also be kept dry, but there was nothing I could do about that. It's a good thing that we were walking under the trees, as some of the drops settled on the branches and leaves instead of on us.

"It's going to be extremely difficult to light a fire this evening," said Shen. The hood of his jacket was pulled close over his face so that I could only see his stubbly chin.

"We should be out on the road by this evening."

"That's good news."

"Shen, I've been meaning to ask you for a while now, who taught you?" asked Layen as she pulled up even with the Healer.

"What are you on about?" His voice was full of contrived incomprehension.

"Who quickened your spark and helped you master the Gift?"

"And who taught you?" he asked defiantly.

"No one," she answered immediately. "I didn't need a teacher."

"As if I'd believe that," he grumbled from under his hood. "In Dog Green you showed yourself in all your glory. That kind of skill would be challenging without a proper mentor. I may not have those abilities yet but I, like you, am familiar with the fundamentals. None of the Walkers would be able to master a khilss."

"You yourself sent a spell through the staff."

"Don't confuse an ordinary spark with a Healer's. Besides, you saw how well that turned out. I hadn't reckoned on that outcome."

"I don't doubt that for a minute."

"And yet." Shen would not let it go. "Who was your mentor that you would so easily flirt with Death? It definitely wasn't one of those who live in the Rainbow Valley. They can't teach such things."

"Are you really so sure of this, little boy?"

Against all odds, he didn't take offense at "little boy." He only laughed mirthlessly.

"I'm sure. Otherwise you'd be with the Walkers. They'd never neglect such talent, and they'd be even less likely to leave it unsupervised. Tell me, why didn't you kill that necromancer right away, as soon as he came to see us? I don't doubt that you could have handled him readily."

"Don't overestimate my powers."

"I'd rather that than underestimate them." The Healer was still agitated. "I just can't help but wonder how the Seekers missed you. And how many years you were under the noses of the Imperial mages and escaped their notice."

"And we're once again back where we started, Shen. If you're not hiding, that means the Walkers know about you, and you and them together—that's unacceptable to us right now. Or are you just as clever as I am, and you've been lurking all this time?"

"Nothing's easier than hiding the spark of a Healer from others. They don't sense it until I use my Gift."

"Oh, yes! I can attest to that myself. So that means you're hiding, right, Shen? You're self-taught?"

"Something along those lines."

"Even if it's not so, we'll really never find out, isn't that true?"

"If you won't talk about yourself, neither will I. In my opinion, it's all pretty straightforward. Let's abandon this subject. I for one am not planning on discussing anything."

"As you wish. I can say one thing—your potential is hardly developed. You flare up and fizzle out right away. Do you know how to do much of anything at all?"

"Look after yourself, Layen. Yourself. I'll deal with my problems on my own."

After this conversation, silence reigned for a long time in our little group.

"Do you think this is wise?" said Luk, his voice full of doubt.

Ga-Nor, who looked like a soaked ginger dog because of the rain, tossed his head without turning toward his companion. The guard didn't know how to take this gesture and so he set about to refresh his companion's memory.

"They killed two men last night."

"Perhaps they wouldn't share. All sorts of things can happen."

"All sorts?" said Luk, horrified. "Those people just cut down their own comrades, screw a toad! And you expect them to be civil to us?"

"Damned rain. The tracks disappear so quickly." The Son of the Snow Leopard tugged at his mustache angrily, and then responded to his companion's indignation, "I'm not planning on facing them. Nor offering my hand in friendship. We're traveling the same path, that's all. We're following in their tracks and not making a sound. That's all we need to do. I think that even you can manage that."

"They have an archer. Have you forgotten?"

"Like I'd forget." Ga-Nor tapped the bandage on his left shoulder. "Make no mistake, the man's good."

"It's too bad they didn't cut him down, too. I'd feel much calmer if I knew I wasn't going to get shot at. We're not going to walk too quickly, right?"

"We're keeping our normal pace."

"We're going to catch up to them!"

"The tracks tell me that everything is all right."

"Didn't you just say that the rain was eating away at them?"

"Don't fret."

"Don't fret. Don't run. Don't hop. Don't skip. Don't sleep. Walk faster. Walk slower. Quite frankly, sometimes I regret that that man didn't drill a hole in you."

The tracker chortled gleefully in response to these words, but when he cast his eyes down to the ground he instantly became serious.

"Be silent!" hissed the northerner. He examined the meadow pensively.

"What?" asked Luk with bated breath as he began to look all around.

An arrow with white fletching cut through the veil of rain and landed in the ground by Ga-Nor's left foot. The archer was at the other end of the meadow, hood thrown back, yellow hair stuck to his forehead, gray eyes, and the tip of an arrow resting upon the bowstring of a powerful curved bow, steadily aimed at the Son of the Snow Leopard.

"We're really in it now, screw a toad!" groaned Luk. "I told you we were walking too quickly."

Ga-Nor frowned. If the archer had wanted to, he could have finished them off a while ago. Without any warning. But he was hanging back. That meant he didn't really want to take their lives. There was hope that they could come to an arrangement.

"And here come the rest," muttered the soldier when a young man, no older than twenty, and a woman with a pack over her shoulder came out from behind the trees. The woman was the same one from the village who had reduced the Burnt Souls to nothing more than wet spots on the ground. Luk wasn't sure if she was a Walker or an Ember.

"Who are you?" The gray eyes of the archer were like ice.

"Ga-Nor from the clan of the Snow Leopard. Tracker for the reconnaissance squad of the Gates of Six Towers."

"Luk, guard of the first squadron of the Tower of Ice. Of the Gates of Six Towers."

The boy standing next to the woman whistled.

"What brings you so far from the Boxwood Mountains? Have you lost your way?"

"Need compelled us."

"I am sure the need was great."

Luk liked the youngster less and less.

"Yes. It's called the Nabatorian army and Sdisian sorcerers."

"How long ago did you leave?"

"We left when they stormed the fortress. We are making our way home through the forest."

"And why are you following us?"

"We share the same path. It's not our fault that you are headed to the same place we are."

"And just where do you think we're going?" asked the youth, squinting suspiciously.

"To Al'sgara, of course."

"Is that right?"

"Take it easy, Shen." The woman reined in the youth. "We're not sure you're here by chance."

"If you don't want to travel together, then don't," the tracker replied in a surly manner. "We're not looking for your company. You go on ahead. We've nothing to quarrel over. To each his own."

"You've been tromping along behind us since the village, haven't you?"

Luk really wanted to lie, but, judging by the expression on the archer's face, he had no love for fairy tales.

"Yes. We left a bit earlier, but then we let you go on ahead."

"So it was you who was walking around our campfire at night?" The gray-eyed one had noticed Ga-Nor's bloody bandage.

"Precisely. You're a good shot."

"And you're a good runner." He gave back as good as he got, but his face was no longer quite as dark. "You're a lucky man."

"Ug preserves the skillful," said the tracker serenely. "May I know your name?"

"Gray," replied the man after a short pause, and then he lowered his bow. "Drop your weapons and you can walk in front. So I can keep an eye on you. And no tricks."

11

Tal'ki often insisted that mirrors love to lie, even if you ask them to tell the truth. When commanded to show fact, they always answer with a laugh and a distortion of reality. They wheedle, play tricks, dodge, and they lie and lie and lie.

"Never trust mirrors, honey. And never turn your back on them. They'll burn you," the old crone had said, smiling kindly and sipping on her cold shaf.

Tia had never believed her—a mirror always reflected reality. But all that changed today. For the first time it deceived her, and the Damned stared at her reflection with hatred; it had suddenly become alien to her.

She wanted to howl. To scream. To kill everyone within easy reach: the stupid locals, the frightened

Nabatorians. But most of all, she wanted to kill those whose fault it was that she was now like this: that slut of a girl, the insignificant little whelp who turned out to have the Gift of a Healer, and that archer. The last one especially. She'd rip the flesh from his bones and force him to eat his own eyes.

A fat, wide-shouldered thug with chubby, drooping lips, a flat, dull face, and white, inhuman eyes looked at Typhoid from the false reflected world. And she couldn't stand it. She snarled like a she-wolf at bay and with all her strength swung a heavy fist at the abhorrent face. It shattered and showered the floor with sharp, oblong shards that threatened to cut her bare feet. The face disappeared and . . . remained.

Here. With her. Hers. Forever.

The knuckles of its right hand were burning; blood was trickling onto the floorboards. Tia ignored this and tried with all her might to calm the rage seething in her chest. Only now did she truly understand Alenari, who always smashed these liars wherever she found them.

It is intolerable to know that you are no longer yourself. Alenari had been lucky. She may have lost her face, but she kept her body. Tia couldn't even claim that. In one moment the Damned had lost all that she had, all that she had rightfully taken pride in. Eternal youth and beauty, fallen into the Abyss. Her true form was destroyed, and only her spirit remained, trapped within the soul and body of a fool, to whom she was bound. Tia's spirit stood behind the left shoulder of the boy and, keeping a tight hold on the reins of control, examined the odious degenerate.

The body that Typhoid was linked to, like a dog on a chain, was mortal. A horribly short amount of time had been allotted to it. Sooner or later it would get old, die, and what then? The Healer wouldn't be nearby the second time.

The boy's unpredictable soul lashed out, rebelling at the pain in its hand, and for a moment Tia released the reins. Before she had the chance to wrest back control over the other's body, the cowherd whined, saw his bloody fist, and yelled, "Let goooo!"

The ghastly whiteness fled from his eyes and they once again became blue and watery.

Cursing, Typhoid "embraced" him from behind by the neck, trying to suppress her aversion, and began whispering soothingly. Pork's pupils dilated, turned white, and the whiteness flowed outward, consuming the iris and melding with the sclera, transforming them into appalling cataracts. At the same time Typhoid cut off the soul, which was surprisingly strong, from control of the vessel.

She succeeded, but it was hard work. Every attempt to overwhelm the foreign vessel required an incredible exertion on her part. And if she had to execute a more complicated movement, like walking or running, the Damned thought she might be ripped away from this safe haven and spat out into the Abyss. All her power was focused on control. Using a different side of her magic was out of the question. Typhoid could only produce the simplest of spells. Without her own skin, she couldn't feel the depths of her Gift.

The Damned still didn't understand how this had happened. The boy, who had used the khilss to create the most unbelievable incantation, had almost been the last thing she saw in this life. The incredibly complicated, threefold weave of her shield had been burnt to a crisp, dissolving the ethereal fibers. In the fraction of a second before the all-consuming light engulfed Typhoid, she cast up the only thing that came to her head—the Mirror of Darkness. The spell should have saved her, even though she would have paid for it with disfigurement. Given time, she would have been able to cure that. But then the archer played his part, coming in at the worst possible time! Tia had been so blinded by pain that not only could she not kill the yellow-haired bastard, but she couldn't even stop his arrows. The last one finished her off. Her body could no longer keep hold of her soul, and Typhoid died.

It was a complete mystery what happened after that. She saw darkness and light, the tremulous embers of the living all around her, and the bright orange palpitation of the ether in the firmament. She tried to claw after her lost shell, but she had neither teeth nor nails. The Damned would have been dragged into the Abyss if the bright light of the

Healer's magic hadn't seeped into the negative side of the world. It snatched up the silvery filaments of her soul and scorched them, stripping away her innate strength, mercilessly freezing her talent and wits, and murdering the very substance of her Gift itself. It flung her left and right; bathed her in an icy spring; flung her under scorching rays; squeezed, stretched, twisted, turned her inside out, and spat her straight into one of the surrounding embers of life. The sharp thorns of the Healer's magic impaled the Damned, tied her to a foreign soul, anchored her there, and forced her to hover over the back of a stranger.

She didn't hesitate for a second. Realizing that this was her only chance to push the peasant's soul aside, she decisively took the body under her own control. And then she shuddered.

Light, life, the world struck her through another's eyes. The skin sensed the warmth of the sun, the tenderness of the wind. Air entered the lungs, and Tia, opening an alien mouth, wailed like a newborn. Pain tormented her and she had to let go of the reins; she had to give the man his rightful body back for a moment so she would not lose her mind from the strange, unbearable, foreign sensations. Only then, when she was able to think sanely, did she see herself lying in the street—dead, covered in blood, and broken. She wailed in grief and self-pity, wishing that all this were nothing more than a dream. A nightmare that had caught her up in its web. But no one could hear the Damned except for Pork.

Now, after several days had gone by, she was beginning to believe that all of that had really happened to her. A cruel joke of fate. Tia's spirit was firmly tied to a foreign soul. And there was no way to disrupt this connection—otherwise the last thread between her self and this world would disappear. Even more bitter was the fact that she existed but was visible to no one except for Pork. She was fated to hover over the man's back without a body, as a shadowy spirit. Until the moment he died, at any rate. The Damned tried not to think about what would happen after that. Her spirit would be free, but it was unlikely that it would escape the Abyss's attention.

And in the meantime there was no way to escape this trap. It was a dead end.

"Go sit on the bed," Typhoid whispered in Pork's ear. He flinched but, not having the strength to resist her, obeyed.

She kept watch so that the fool's bare feet did not tread on the mirror fragments, but on the way the cowherd once again lashed out, trying to throw off her mastery. The Damned, who was already well versed in the ways of her charge, was ready for this. She pulled at the reins and got him under control, hissing from the intangible pain that was inflicted on her by the Healer's weave, and then she stumbled, tipped a chair over, and swore crossly. The other's body was still unfamiliar, too massive, and far less agile than the one to which she had become accustomed over the centuries. Tia had to exert a lot of effort to cope with the recalcitrant man.

The abhorrent vessel was driving her mad. It was uncomfortable, clumsy, poorly controlled, and it smelled awful. Saliva was always dripping from its mouth to its chest. But she had already started working on the appearance of her disobedient puppet. Step by step, little by little, she changed the face, intertwined the muscles, filling them with power. She needed a tough vessel; she had no wish to ride a moronic gelding. Another two, three weeks and his own mother wouldn't know this blimp. Typhoid would completely rebuild this body underneath her as she saw fit. The only thing she couldn't do anything about was the chalky color of his eyes.

The Healer's magic had incinerated much of what she had. Her spark was not blazing, but smoldering, and she had to waste all her resources on watching over Pork. She couldn't even think about any other displays of her Gift. Right now Typhoid could hardly light a candle, let alone raze the village to the ground. In one moment Typhoid had lost not only her body but also her powerful Gift. That which remained was only a pathetic grain of sand compared to her former might.

She had become weak and defenseless. Any of her brothers or sisters could now dispatch her effortlessly. Even Mitifa, the most unskilled of the Octet.

"What should I do?" she whispered, and Pork, who was sitting rigidly on the bed and staring dully at a single spot, flinched in fear and looked over his shoulder.

Suddenly a warm wave surged up her spine. Typhoid frowned, not wanting to answer. It was Tal'ki. She was the only one of the Octet who radiated warmth. Alenari's summons could be distinguished by cold shivers; Rovan's by an unpleasant burning; Leigh's by demanding jabs; Mitifa's by impossibly timid, objectionable caresses. Ginora and Retar had died so long ago that she had forgotten what sensations they produced. But they hadn't been pleasant either. Only Tal'ki's summons never vexed the Damned. The warmth emanating from the Healer always felt pleasant. At times Tia wondered how the rest of the Octet perceived her during such conversations. But she had never once bothered to satisfy her curiosity.

Typhoid felt the summons once more and hesitated. Could she put her trust in Tal'ki? What would she do when she learned what happened? How would she proceed? There had never been much peace among the Octet. And when two of them died after the Dark Revolt, the squabbling over precedence only increased. Rovan and Mitifa would gladly annihilate her. She had never been on friendly terms with Alenari either.

Pork also felt the warmth and he shivered in delight. It ran pleasantly up his spine, embraced his shoulders, and crept up the nape of his neck. Then the Damned came to a decision. She forced the cowherd to leap up from the plaintively squeaking bed, rush over to the table, grab an earthenware jug full of water, and heave it at the wall.

Fragments of pottery flew in all directions. The water, instead of falling to the floor, flowed down the wall and took on the form of a large oval that shimmered like quicksilver. This substance absorbed magic into itself, and after several seconds of tedious waiting, it showed the one who had sent the summons.

Tal'ki, known in the Empire as Leprosy, was sitting in a stuffed rocking chair. A fluffy white cat was dozing on her lap, which was covered with a wool blanket. The old woman's round, good-natured face was intent because she was the one that was holding onto the weaves of both sides of the Silver Window. When she saw a stranger, the Healer frowned and her faded blue eyes narrowed.

"It's me. Tia," Typhoid said quickly. She feared that the one who had called her would disrupt the spell or even worse, attack. She didn't even have a ghost of a chance of withstanding the strongest of the Sextet.

Pork's voice sounded hoarse. Tal'ki stared at him for a moment and then smiled amiably.

"I simply don't believe my eyes, my dear."

"You have to believe, Sister. It really is me."

Leprosy answered with her habitual smile. But her eyes were not smiling.

"What is your name?" the old woman asked abruptly.

"Tia."

"Forgive me, I meant your full name."

"Tia al'Lankarra."

Her interrogator kept smiling.

"Typhoid. Murderer of Sorita," Pork obediently repeated that which was whispered in his ear.

The same expectant smile.

"The Flames of Sunset! Blade of the South! Daughter of Night! Rider of Hurricanes! The Abyss take you! Which of my names do you wish to hear?"

"I'm satisfied with those you have named, child. The names weren't the point. It's just that you've always been impatient and rude to your elders. Yes. It's you. Though I really don't understand how this is possible."

"I'd like to know myself."

"What happened?"

Typhoid shared her recollections with Leprosy, having decided that things couldn't get any worse.

She was listened to in silence.

"Interesting," Tal'ki finally said thoughtfully, and she scratched her cat behind its ears. "I would even say it's very interesting, my sweet one. Such a . . . strange resolution of a spell. It's a curious puzzle. I will try to reproduce the boy's weave. Such an unexpected result calls for careful scrutiny. What does your friend have on his hand?"

Only now did Tia recall that Pork's broken knuckles had been bleeding all this time.

"It's nothing. He cut himself."

"You shouldn't shed his blood over nothing. You only have one body, girl. Treat it gently."

Seething internally that the old woman had fixated on such a trifle, Tia complied with her request and allowed the cowherd to bandage the scrape.

"Can you help me?" she asked with bated breath.

"I don't know. I don't know." Her withered hand continued to stroke the cat. "Not right this instant, at any rate. I need time."

"How long?"

"An hour. A day. A year. A century. An eternity. Time is so relative, my dear. You'll just have to wait."

"You're a Healer!"

"So what? I've only heard of what happened to you once before, when I was still a young girl and I had just come to the Rainbow Valley. I've no desire to run afoul of such a manifestation of a Healer's Gift. Patience, my darling. Patience. It's possible I can help you. But not right away. I'll have to work on it properly."

"And what should I do while you 'work on it'? Can't you see, my abilities are far from what they were."

"You put it mildly, girl. You don't have any abilities. That with which you keep that boy under control does not count. Hush now! Don't frown and huff at an old woman. What my heart thinks, my tongue speaks." Tal'ki giggled. "The Healer's weave took a lot out of you."

"It took everything!"

"You're mistaken. If that were so, you'd be dead. A person strong enough in his Gift won't die when his body is destroyed. His true essence can continue existing for some time afterward."

"I didn't know that."

"I don't doubt that. None of you, besides Mitifa I suppose, know things like that. You set aside your books, my dear one. But every now and then you can find something very interesting in books. What happened to you is just like I said. Your true essence, your spirit, which now hovers before me, stayed behind. We won't guess what would have happened to it without the magic of the Healer. Perhaps you might have intuitively settled in someone else's body, but perhaps you would no longer exist. The manuscripts from the time of the Sculptor tell us that accomplishing something like this without the proper experience is difficult."

Typhoid did not doubt for a second that if Tal'ki were in her place, she'd figure it out.

"But you're in luck. The weave of our talented boy fettered your soul to the soul of the man who is chatting so sweetly with me on your behalf. You are connected by one chain, and you can control him. Even alter him, as I see. But that's all you can do, isn't it? You can't arouse your spark."

"I knew that without you."

"Don't be rude." Tal'ki smiled coldly. "If you're bored, I won't continue."

"Pardon me."

"Your spark doesn't blaze because you don't have the proper vessel. Yes, your spirit is strong, but without the required, shall we say, *fervor*, you can do nothing. To use your real Gift, even at a quarter of its strength, you need a vessel."

"I can't move into another body. I don't have the ability. Plus, you yourself just said that I'm shackled to the soul of this idiot."

"So I did. And I wouldn't recommend breaking the chain. It's not that easy to return from the Abyss."

Typhoid did not like Tal'ki's smile.

"Then I don't understand."

"Dead bodies."

"What?"

"Dead bodies, my dear girl. They don't have souls. The house is empty and a new tenant may as well inhabit it. For a short while, naturally. The chain will let you pull off such a stunt if that young man is nearby."

"I'm not going to crawl into the body of a corpse!"

"Then forget about the possibility of using your Gift."

"I simply could not accomplish such a thing!"

"It's not that difficult. Memorize the design of this weave. It's pretty much the same as for control of kukses. And it takes about as much strength as a mouse's spit."

Tal'ki drew a flaming pattern in the air with her finger.

"Did you memorize it? Excellent. And now another two little designs, my sweet. The first will make it so that you don't have to whisper in the boy's ear. You can control him as if it were your own body. And the second will make it so that the Healer's weave no longer inflicts pain on your spirit. I think they'll both let you feel like you are far more free than before. Memorize them."

Two more patterns appeared in the air.

"Will I have control over the corpse and this body at the same time?"

"No. You won't need to control the corpse. You'll become it. And the strength that will emerge in you will allow you, in some measure, to restrain this charming little boy as well. Just don't forget, please, that the dead bodies should be fresh. And you can reside in their shells for no more than three days. After that not even the power of your spark will be able to keep the body from decaying. I advise you to leave before that happens or else you might remain there forever. And don't forget to control your ward. He shouldn't go more than twenty yards away from you. You wouldn't want to be pulled out like a dog on a leash, would you?"

"I think I can cope with this."

"Well, that's good. I'll attend to your problem right away. Frankly speaking, I'm quite interested in it. It's not every day that something like this happens.

Even if it's just a diversion for a sick old woman. One more thing, my dear. I'm awfully interested in that talented girl and the boy Healer."

"I'll kill them!" wheezed Tia, trembling from the hatred that rushed through her.

"Don't you even think about doing something so stupid!" Tal'ki snapped. All her goodwill suddenly disappeared. "The girl, who so easily mastered the khilss and who knows the weaves of Death, which only Elects of the Sixth Sphere and up are capable of, is essential. We need to know who taught her! We must!"

"She's of no use to me!"

"But she's of use to *me*," snapped Leprosy. "And you're not in any condition to be acting precipitously."

"And the little boy? Give him to me, Tal'ki."

"He's a Healer, my dear. Don't you understand how valuable he is? Or has the thirst for revenge entirely blinded your reason? Killing him would be very . . . inopportune. That sort of Gift . . ." She smiled at her own thoughts. "Plus, if you want to fully return to yourself, he might be needed. It's possible that only with the help of his spark will I be able to break the chain and transfer your soul back. If the lad did it once he might do it again. The young man could be a fallback, in case your spirit does not surrender to my Gift."

"I can't come back. My body is dead."

"There's plenty of that stuff around," said the

Healer dismissively. "Of course, it would be better if the vessel already carried someone's spark within it. To that end, our talented little girl could come in handy. Of course, only after she's answered all my questions. Right now you have only one task—to find both of them and bring them to me. Alive."

"I understand. I'm not a fool."

"Can you find them?"

"I think so. There's only one road here. To Al'sgara. I'll try to overtake them."

"Lovely, my dear. By the way, I wanted to tell you something. I found two girls with the Gift. Both Walkers. One isn't against helping us. The other is still giving me cheek."

"Are you sure of the first?"

"Oh yes. She's a very driven child. She reminds me of Alenari when she was young, my sweet."

Tia wrinkled her nose.

"Well, you're going to have to hurry if you want to catch our friends." Tal'ki smiled. "Remember, I need them alive."

In the next instant the Silver Window went dark, and the freed water spilled to the floor. Typhoid swore, and Pork, obeying her command, kicked out with all his strength at the capsized chair, which was blameless.

The old hag dared to admonish her!

The Damned was furious that she would have to submit to Leprosy, or else the hag wouldn't lift a finger to help her. The boy and girl could hardly have gone far. If she needed to overturn the entire Empire, she would find them and drag them back to Tal'ki in chains. All but the archer. She didn't have to give him to anyone.

12

Despite my fears, our new companions did not seem to be planning any trouble. They behaved meekly, just like the acolytes of Melot during a long fast. Of course, the Son of the Snow Leopard took being parted from his beloved blade quite poorly. The poor fellow was practically twitching with indignation.

Well, to the Abyss with him.

It would be downright folly to allow the redhead his sword. I'd seen how the northern people handled sharp objects. Before you have a chance to say a word, you're kissing your head good-bye. It must be said that even without a weapon, the redhead was a dangerous opponent. I hadn't forgotten how easily he eluded my arrows nor how he prowled in the forest.

His figure and gait gave him away as a seasoned campaigner. If he didn't like our orders, then dealing with him would be no easier than handling an enraged snow leopard. I had no idea what to do with the redhead when we stopped for the night. We'd have to tie him up to get any sleep. It wouldn't do to forget that all northerners are quiet and peaceful until the time comes. And when it does, they'd as soon hit you over the head as say hello. You can only stop them with a crossbow. Sometimes not even then.

And then there was Ga-Nor's friend, a man of a completely different disposition. Nothing ominous there. At first he was as quiet as a mouse, but as soon as he realized that no one was planning to kill him, he livened up right away and came out of his shell so much that for the past two hours he'd been chatting away nonstop, happy to have found himself an appreciative audience in Layen.

My sun listened to his story of the fall of the Gates of Six Towers and their subsequent meanderings through the forest with interest. When I heard him mention the Damned, I also pricked up my ears. If the man was lying, he did it well. But, judging from his description, Rubeola did not at all resemble the girl who attacked us in the village. Layen caught my gaze and with just her lips whispered, "Typhoid."

So that's who confronted us. Well then, the murderer of Sorita, if it really was her, had received a most unpleasant death as payment for all her crimes.

In the meantime, Luk continued to hold forth. Shen was not paying the slightest attention. He brought up the rear, sullen and somber. It was not at all to the Healer's liking that I chose to accept the strangers into our group. As usual, I spat on his opinion and his discontent.

There was an opening in the trees ahead of us. We descended a low pitched hill covered in spruce trees and then we were at the road.

"We made it!" Luk exclaimed triumphantly. "We made it, screw a toad!"

He had this habit of interjecting his toad whether it was appropriate or not. Odd.

"Why are you so happy? We still have a long way to march." Ga-Nor did not share his comrade's enthusiasm.

"But along a road, not through the forest!"

"Uh-huh. That's what I meant."

"What are you talking about? Someone might pass by and give us a lift."

"Exactly." Taking advantage of the halt, Shen was shaking a pebble out of his boot. "A Nabatorian patrol, for example. I'm sure they'd be happy to give you a lift to the nearest cemetery."

"I don't think we need to worry about Nabator," disagreed Layen. "They're not yet interested in taking Al'sgara."

"I wonder why that is?" I interjected. "The city is much closer than Okni or Gash-Shaku."

"I really don't know. But for now they're leaving Al'sgara alone. So the road there should be free. But it's going to be a while before we find horses. 'Til we get to Bald Hollow, at least."

"How far do we have to go?" Ga-Nor approached

her too quickly, but his hands were in sight and I wasn't about to get twitchy over a trifle. "How many days?"

"As many as we need," I replied. "The sooner we set off, the faster we'll get there. So let's not delay uselessly."

The rain had stopped a while ago, but the road was studded with puddles and there was so much mud that we had to walk on the shoulder, where it was a bit cleaner. The thick spruce forest continued to stretch on to our right, but it soon dropped away to the left, giving way to the cheerless landscape of a swamp. Moss and flimsy saplings are not at all pleasing to the eye. I wanted to pass through this part of our journey as quickly as possible. I didn't feel like feeding the mosquitoes, and there were more terrible things that could emerge from the swamp to feed on us. People say all sorts of things about these places and most of them are bad. I'm not inclined to believe in nonsense, because I know that the Blazogs are far from monsters, but besides this fairly peaceful race, there really are dangerous creatures living here as well. The sole good thing about our environs was that in the summer vast numbers of birds nested in the swampy lakes, and I held on to the hope that we might not have to go without dinner. To that end, I put a fresh string on my bow so I would be ready to shoot at any moment.

Ga-Nor didn't look backward once the entire time

we were walking. The pace the northerner set was astonishing. It was like he wasn't tired at all, but was ready to walk across the entire Empire. Luk was humming a tune I didn't recognize and after a while Layen began to accompany him. I snorted. The song got stuck in my head. If the Healer joined in, we'd make a pretty band of traveling musicians.

Fkhut! Shloop!

Shen, who was bringing up the rear, gave a strangled cry.

I deftly hopped forward, while simultaneously spinning around. The Healer was lying in the road, floundering in a gray slime which only by some miracle hadn't hit him in the face.

"Hold still, you fool!" I yelled, but he didn't heed me. He kept struggling and spewing curses. The muck he was covered in was beginning to harden.

"What is that?" Luk instantly forgot about his ditty. Without a second's pause I gave him back his axe, which definitely convinced him that the Healer was in a lot of trouble.

"Layen, give the northerner his sword," I said, not taking my eyes off the gloomy wall of the forest.

Right now it was better to give them their weapons. They might be needed very soon.

The gray slime clinging to Shen finally hardened and he was completely immobilized.

"What's attacking us, screw a toad?" Panicked notes slipped into Luk's voice.

"A shpaguk." Ga-Nor took his sword from its sheath and stepped aside.

"A male," I clarified. "That means that the female might be nearby. Don't all stand together. Disperse. So it can't reach all of us at once."

"So what can't reach us?" Now the soldier was looking into the forest as well.

"Its saliva."

"What should we do about him?" Layen nodded at the Healer.

"Let him lie there. We don't have time for him right now."

Fkhut!

A clump flew out of the trees and would have hit Luk directly if he hadn't jumped to the side with all the grace of a blind boar.

Shloop!

The soldier lost his footing and fell face-first into a puddle. But he immediately hopped to his feet, spitting and swearing fiercely.

Fkhut!

This time it was Layen who had to move aside, and the shpaguk missed again.

Shloop!

I finally marked where it was spitting from and randomly shot off an arrow in that direction. Of course, it didn't connect, but the threat forced our opponent to go from spitting to attacking. It jumped out onto the road from the upper branches of a spruce tree, landing dangerously close to Shen, and croaked deafeningly.

It was short, about waist high, and as round as a saucer, with eight furry legs that ended in serrated claws. Thick green fuzz blanketed the creature's entire body, and its two pairs of small, black eyes looked like precious stones. It clicked its formidable mandibles, and its flexible tail, tipped with a yard-long stinger, flicked up threateningly. Naturally, a man couldn't expect anything good to come from being struck by that. As far as I know, there's no antidote to its venom.

"Shoot him!" yelped Luk.

The first and only arrow I shot struck the shpaguk in his mandibles. He shot up into the air and landed right next to me, spitting. I could do nothing but drop down and let the saliva pass over me. I didn't have time to jump up, and the brute was about to slam its stinger into me, but Ga-Nor leapt in front of me and used his sword to cut through the shpaguk's tail at the very base. Then the snap of a crossbow rang out—Layen was shooting.

The creature chirred, forgetting about me, and turned to face its new opponent. I rolled away, losing my arrows along the way. Luk resolutely stepped between me and the forest creature. It was occupied with raising its front claws as it prepared to attack the northerner. With a grunt, the soldier plunged his axe into the level back of the shpaguk, and a nasty substance spurted in all directions. Our adversary croaked hoarsely and began stumbling toward the trees on shaky legs, but it never reached them. It died at the very edge of the road.

Baring her knife, Layen rushed over to free Shen. Luk just stood there staring at the animal.

"Help her!" I quickly gathered my arrows. "Come on!"

"What a monster that was." The soldier's face was smeared with mud and the blood of the shpaguk. "I hit him good. What? Is he going to come back to life or something?"

"The male hunts. The female waits and eats," explained Ga-Nor as he walked past us.

"And she might put in an appearance," I added.

That made the man move. The three of them hacked into the strong cocoon of petrified saliva and liberated Shen from his imprisonment.

Just in the nick of time.

Only a deaf man couldn't hear that something was crashing toward us through the underbrush. Magpies soared out of the nearby trees with vile shrieks, and a new foe broke out onto the road about twenty yards from us. She was much larger than her mate. Unlike him, she was dark green, and she stood on bulky, barbed legs. Female shpaguks don't have a tail and they don't spit petrifying saliva, but a thing that size doesn't really need those kinds of weapons.

The creature saw its dead mate and headed for us, croaking menacingly.

"Little pig, little pig . . ." An arrow struck her in the leg.

"Where are you . . ."

In the eye.

". . . roving? Little pig . . ."

In the head.

". . . little pig, where are . . . you going? . . . Run faster, little pig . . . up to the trough. . . . Slops there, little pig . . . up to the . . . top."

On the eleventh shot, when the enormous female was already towering over me, I finally got her. Right in her gaping jaws. The shpaguk went into convulsions, striking out to the left and right with her claws, hoping to catch one of us. Only after several minutes did she deign to die.

Luk cleared his throat behind my back.

"Very impressive. I thought for sure she was going to rip you apart."

"Me too. Me too," I muttered, and peered into my quiver. There were only two arrows left in it.

"What was that you were singing?" Shen wasn't looking at me but at the green carcass lying on the road.

"That . . . It was a children's nursery rhyme."

"I didn't expect anything more intelligent from you."

"Then perhaps you should have helped me, instead of hiding behind my back," I said nastily.

"Enough!" Layen shouted at us. "When we make

camp you can bicker to your heart's content but right now we'd best get out of here. Sometimes they live in swarm."

"Shpaguks only swarm toward mid-fall." Ga-Nor shoved his sword into its sheath. "But it really is best if we leave."

I didn't bother cutting out my arrows. It would take far too much time, and plus the creature had broken almost all of them with the short claws that grew near her mouth. However, I did stop by the male's tail.

"You want to take the venom?" Ga-Nor asked as he noiselessly walked up to me.

"I'm thinking about it."

"It's a good thought," he approved. "It doesn't get old. Always works."

"I know." I cut into the flesh around the stinger. I pried up the plates with the edge of my dagger, revealing a refluent, blue sac that resembled a fish's air bladder.

"That's enough to poison an entire fortress." Luk peered at it over our heads. "It would have been handy to drop that in the cooking pot of a Nabatorian regiment."

"That wouldn't work. You could drink the whole thing and nothing would happen to you. It kills only through the blood."

"Ah," he drawled disappointedly and walked away to Layen, who was waiting impatiently for us.

I carefully pricked the wall of the bladder with my knife and held my flask under it, from which I had first emptied the water. A few drops of transparent venom landed on my hand but I didn't pay them any attention. My hands could be washed once the priceless poison had been transferred from its unstable sac to my container.

"You shoot fairly well, Gray." Ga-Nor was attentively observing my actions. "You've got good speed."

"I can't complain."

"Were you taught by a southerner?"

"I wouldn't have thought you'd have an eye for different styles of archery," I said, chuckling, in no hurry to reply.

"Somewhat." He did not bother to deny it. "The Imperials have a completely different stance. And they draw their strings differently. And if you had picked it up from my people, you would never carry a bow like that."

"You're correct," I capitulated. "A southerner taught me. A Sdisian, curiously enough."

"I figured as much." Ga-Nor nodded, not at all surprised. Then he asked, "Did you soldier in Sandon?"

"Is it so obvious?"

"I just recall that some Sdisian mercenaries served there. In the Arrows of Maiburg. One of those lads could easily have taught you a few lessons."

"That's ancient history." I smiled crookedly.

"I hope you aren't waiting for me to give my sword back to you." He swiftly changed the topic of conversation and I raised my eyes to him.

"So you won't give it back?"

"No."

"All right, carry it yourself." I shrugged my shoulders. "It'll be easier on Layen."

For some reason he laughed cheerfully and finally left me alone. I called out to him, "Hey, ginger!"

"Yes?"

"Thanks for saving my hide. I owe you one."

For a moment he looked at me intently and seriously, and then he broke into a smile, which caused his already threatening face to become downright predatory.

"I'll keep that in mind."

We passed through two hamlets, so small they didn't even have inns, came to the shore of a slow river overgrown with reeds, made our way across the river on a small ferry, and finally found ourselves on a low hillock overlooking a small town with an absurd name: Dabb's Bald Hollow. The road traveled down alongside a large cemetery, right beyond which the settlement began.

It grew up on the intersection of four roads. One came from the east—we arrived on it; another came from the west, from Al'sgara; the third came from the north, from Okni; and the fourth came from the south, from the mining villages that were located a week's ride away in the Boxwood Mountains. It was from the western part of that mountain range that merchants transported iron and silver ore to the southern part of the Empire. Essential goods passed through Bald Hollow and then traveled throughout the country. Before the silver mines near the Gates of Six Towers had been exhausted, the eastern road had been no less lively than the southern. But now it was desolate and the merchants who had lost their principal source of income in the region rarely traveled through the Forest Belt.

In my estimation, Bald Hollow should have been teeming with people, even though the Feast of the Name had long since passed and the main summer fair was over. People have a hard time dispersing to their homes after a weeklong drinking spree.

"It's as quiet as the grave," said Luk, looking around.

"Open your eyes! We are walking by a cemetery." Over the past few days Shen's mood had not taken a turn for the better.

"It's you who should open his eyes," objected the soldier. "The dead can not only make noise if they've a will to, but they can run quite quickly as well. I saw it myself, screw a toad."

"Be silent," I admonished him. "Do you want to draw them down on us?"

He shut up.

We traveled along the cemetery road, passed by the standing stone at the intersection of the four roads, and approached the town. Ahead of us was a low, gray wall, two wooden towers for archers (now empty), and the gaping panels of the gate. Three guards in beribboned jackets holding crossbows were next to them. They didn't pay any attention to us. Not even the presence of the northerner intrigued them. The men were dead drunk from too many toasts with reska (melon vodka).

"Good little defenders, aren't they?" Luk twisted up his face as if all his teeth had suddenly started aching. "Don't they know about the war?"

"It's very strange, all of it," said Ga-Nor.

"What's strange?" asked Shen.

"Where is the army? Why are there no patrols here and only three drunk degenerates? It's not all that far to Dog Green. The enemy wouldn't need much time to attack. A few swift assaults, and the road to Al'sgara is open. I don't see a single soldier. There wasn't even a measly roadblock."

"The army is keeping the enemy in check in the north. Apparently, they agreed that the Steps of the Hangman are more important than Al'sgara right now. Besides, why do you think anyone would care about this town? The army isn't deployed here, and all our fortifications are westward."

"I know. Crow's Nest holds the eastern road to Al'sgara."

"There you have it. It's no wonder that Bald Hollow has been left to its own fate. It's not the right place to stop the enemy."

"That's idiotic," disagreed the northerner.

"I think the Imperial commanders have a better idea of what's idiotic and what's not. You're nothing more than a soldier—"

"And you lecture too much. To each his own, Shen," I interrupted him.

"What are you insinuating by that?"

"There's no need for a Healer to meddle in the business of warriors. If you want to fight a war, enlist in the army."

"Perhaps I will do that. Unlike you all, I love my country."

"You all?" Luk scowled. "Just who do you have in mind, lad, screw a toad?"

"He means Layen and me. This has nothing to do with you. You can keep your peace." I chuckled meanly. "To the front, Shen! To the front! You do know that if you decide to go away no one will cry for you."

"Oh, no. We're getting to Al'sgara together."

"As you wish. But if you suddenly decide to go into soldiery, just give a whistle. I'll happily find a recruiter for you."

"You're very kind."

"I know." I stepped closer to him and whispered so that Luk and Ga-Nor wouldn't hear me, "But it would be better for you if you didn't test my kindness. Do we understand each other?"

"Entirely." His eyes were hard. "I'll remember your words."

"I really hope so. And I'll remember that you remember them."

At times we understood each other perfectly.

"Shen, do you have a dream?" Luk interrupted our conversation.

"What?" he asked suspiciously.

"Oh, nothing. I was simply trying to encourage conversation. I, for example, dream of a real bed, some chow, clean clothes, a barrel of shaf, and hot water."

"What a fastidious guy you are!" The Healer laughed. "I wouldn't have thought!"

"If you had crawled around forests and bogs with me, ran from the Damned, dead men, and Burnt Souls, well then, you'd want the same thing."

"You forgot about something, Luk," said Ga-Nor as he kicked a pebble in the road. "Where will you get the money from?"

"Well," he said, embarrassed. "I have one soren. I think it's enough for you and me."

The redhead raised his eyebrow in surprise, but he remained silent. It was clear that he hadn't expected his friend to have any money.

"If it's not enough, we'll happily treat you," offered Layen.

Now it was my eyebrows that crawled upward. I hadn't anticipated such sudden generosity from her. Of course, we had a lot of money; we could feed a whole squadron of northerners for five years, but Layen rarely offered help to outsiders. Should I take this to mean that she had decided to accept this pair into our team?

No matter. I was not against it. Unlike Midge and Bamut, they weren't too bad. And I didn't expect them to play any nasty tricks on us, unlike our Healer.

Even though Pork was rolled up in a warm blanket, he still shivered softly. The fire was no use at all and the forest hanging over the road seemed sinister. The cowherd was expecting a forest monster to come out of the darkness at any minute and devour him. The two horses standing by the stream whickered softly every once in a while, and each time the peasant flinched.

The village idiot was horribly terrified, and he very much wanted to cry, but he didn't, fearing that Mistress would wake up and he'd have to do things he didn't want to again. And then he'd wake from a trance in some nightmarish place. Like a graveyard. Or the lair of a man-eating gove.

He could not imagine how he found himself so far from his native village. At some point he'd heard Mistress command him to go to sleep and not bother

her until morning. But Pork couldn't get to sleep. Next to him lay the living corpse that used to be called Gry. The dead man watched the miserable cowherd with lifeless eyes. This made everything even more frightening. The half-wit recalled how the lady forced him to go up to the gallows and cut the rope, and then she disappeared from behind his left shoulder and the dead guy came alive and sat up, startling all the Nabatorians. Pork wanted to run away, but Mistress, who was crouched in the carcass of the hanged man, would not let him run far. The sobbing cowherd and the living corpse left the village together.

The first night, when the dead man stopped moving and was apparently asleep, Pork tried to flee. He didn't succeed. The enraged lady suddenly appeared behind his shoulder and then he was punished. After the insane pain, the pathetically whimpering cowherd crawled back to the fire on all fours; the terrible woman returned to the body of the dead man and he heard nothing more from her before morning. But the fool didn't even consider running anymore.

He just sat there, his eyes dilated in terror, peering into the darkness, waiting apprehensively for morning.

13

Layen and I had stayed at the inn, the Supreme Witch, several years ago and even though quite a lot of time had passed, I found the establishment without much difficulty. The sturdy two-story building had a sign, on which a fairly talented hand had painted a red-haired woman with a malicious appearance. True, it resembled a witch as much as a Je'arre looks like a butterfly. That is, they had nothing in common.

There weren't all that many people in the common room. But in about an hour, just when it started to get dark, the neighborhood residents would drag themselves in to toss back a mug of shaf or a glass of reska. Then it will get so crowded, people will be sitting on one another's heads.

Luk, as he had promised, urgently requested food, drink, and a bath. A servant boy was sent to the nearest shop for new clothing. When he found out that we were ready to foot the bill, the soldier got right down to it. But I didn't mind; I could spare the extra sorens.

Layen and I got a nice room—bright and clean. Through old habit, the first thing we did was check the door. It was hefty, with a good dead bolt. It wouldn't be easy to knock down. From the window there was a view of the inner courtyard, the stables, and the barn. That was also excellent—there was always the chance we'd have to leave without drawing special attention to ourselves.

I left my wife to rest and freshen up and went to a weapons dealer at the far end of town. There I grudgingly bargained with the surly dealer, who apparently didn't have such particular customers every day. I only stopped when I'd selected two dozen more or less decent arrows from the three hundred he had on offer. I had complete confidence in ten of them, while the remaining fourteen were of middling quality, but they'd do in a pinch.

After I paid, I returned to the inn, which was now crowded; the customers were piled high on top of one another, with servants rushing around between them with trays full of orders. It was one hell of a ruckus. It smelled pleasantly of cold mint and chamomile shaf, and the aroma of roast meat tickled my nostrils.

Our table was the one closest to the stairs that led up to the second floor. Happy and content, Luk was laying into his food assiduously. Shen, who had cheered up some, was sipping his cooling drink and playing with Midge's knife. I won't say that he impressed me, but the lad was somewhat skilled. Layen was listlessly watching the knife as it flashed through the Healer's fingers. Like I said, the Healer couldn't make an especially striking impression on a person who had earned her keep working risky jobs.

The northerner was looking around more than he

was eating. His interest was caught by a neighboring table, where some miners were sitting. There they were discussing important news—the war that was sweeping across the northeast of the Empire.

By the bar, the young, thickset innkeeper was arguing about something with a man who had just come in. This stranger's muddy cloak caught my attention. Regardless of the age of the fabric, the emblem sewn onto it was still discernible. It was the boots and cloud of the couriers' guild.

"Keep your mouths shut," I warned my companions, and then, without getting into particulars, I headed over to the disputants.

"Where should I seat you?" boomed the innkeeper. "You see how many people are here. All the tables are taken."

"Fine, no need to get nasty," said the courier soothingly. "Just bring me food in my room."

"It'll be a while 'til the room is ready. It's being cleaned now. You'll have to wait."

"If you want, you can sit at my table," I said, interrupting their conversation. "We have a free seat."

"I'd be honored." The courier bowed, making no secret of his pleasure.

"Bring him some food," I instructed the innkeeper, who immediately cheered up once he saw that the unpleasant situation had been resolved.

"I hope I won't be disturbing you," said the man I'd invited as we walked over to the table. "My name is Gis."

"Take a load off." Unlike the others, Layen had instantly realized that an excellent opportunity to learn the latest news had fallen in our laps. "Was the road hard?"

"It wasn't easy." Gis looked around at us curiously as the innkeeper set his plate down.

He was middle-aged, short, and lanky. He had a narrow, sallow face with a large, fleshy nose, a shiny bald head, and thick, unkempt mustaches. His eyes were dark, sharp, tenacious, and thoughtful. But his hands were strange; he had narrow palms with long, elegant fingers and well-groomed nails that would be more fitting for a musician or a juggler, but not for a man who spends his entire life on the road. Those hands perplexed me greatly, and at any other time I would have pondered their significance, but today, after our onerous journey, I was not up to it.

"Are you traveling?" he asked as he dug into the food.

"Yes," said Ga-Nor curtly, kicking Luk, whose mouth was wide open, under the table.

The kick didn't escape Gis's attention, but he in no way showed it. He meditatively broke a griddle cake in two, dipped it in gravy, and declared, "You're a colorful group."

"When you joined us, it became even more colorful." Layen smiled pleasantly. "Common room tables have a way of bringing all sorts of people together."

Gis returned the smile.

"True enough, my lady. I've seen it often during

my travels. Once I even saw a human, a Blazog, and a Je'arre amicably playing dice."

"All that and amicably? Flyers can't get along with each other, to say nothing of other races!" said Luk, and he dissolved into laughter.

Most people have no love for the Je'arre due to their pride, fierce tempers, and disdain for other races. Even the Highborn of Sandon do not elicit as much ire as the Sons of the Sky (what the Je'arre call themselves).

"Why would you call me lady?" wondered Layen.

Gis winked merrily.

"Have you not noticed how the entire common room is looking at you? Do you know the reason? You're wearing trousers. Our south is too stuffy. That which is normal in the north, here is considered an open invitation, if not a vulgarity. Even the whores wear skirts, to say nothing of the more dignified gentlewomen. Very few women can allow themselves trousers. Only the inhabitants of the northern parts of the Empire, and you don't look like them, or the nobles who disregard the opinions of those around them. I chose to place you in the second classification. Was I mistaken?"

Shen soundlessly repeated the word "classification" and raised his eyebrows in surprise. I also noticed that our guest was an exceedingly well-educated man.

"You're mistaken, in that you overlooked yet another possibility—it's far more comfortable to travel in trousers than in a skirt."

"I think that he"—Gis pointed at the impassive Ga-Nor—"might disagree with you. For the Children of the Snow Leopard, trousers could never compare for comfort with a kilt."

"A kilt is not a skirt," said the northerner. "But there is a snowflake of truth in your words."

"I thank you."

"You know the clan signs of my people quite well," said the northerner.

"I'm a courier." He shrugged. "I have to keep my eyes and ears open. Besides, only the Snow Leopards wear red and gold plaid. It's easy to remember."

"Are you bound for Al'sgara?"

"Yes, my lady." Our companion insisted on addressing Layen as a noblewoman.

"From the mining colonies?"

"From Gash-Shaku."

"Gash-Shaku!" Luk exclaimed, his mouth falling open. "But Bald Hollow isn't on the way! Why would you take such a detour?"

Gis's face darkened.

"If I'd had my way, I wouldn't have. But the prairies are enveloped in flames. The road between Al'sgara and Gash-Shaku has become too dangerous. Nabatorian and Sdisian soldiers. There are rumors of necromancers. I had to detour to the east, toward Okni. The battle hasn't taken hold there yet.

Our boys are keeping the enemy in check at the Isthmuses of Lina, so I was able to slip past. True, my journey was doubled."

"What's happening in Gash-Shaku?" Shen leaned forward.

"I slipped out of there a day before the city was besieged."

"But the army! Where is our army?"

"The Second Southern Army was completely destroyed. They say the Sixth and the First retreated to the Katugian Mountains for redeployment. Perhaps they'll try to lift the siege. The Third is mired in the Isthmuses, so there will be no help from them. I've heard nothing about the Fourth. The Fifth holds the Steps of the Hangman, so I don't think they're rushing off to save anyone. The most important thing is not to let the enemy break through to the north."

"Not good," said Luk, aghast.

He was right. It didn't seem like our troops were doing so well. The second-largest city in the Empire was under siege, and battle was raging from the forests of Sandon to the Golden Sea. The enemy, ignoring the untouched southwest, was striving to take the most important position—the Steps of the Hangman. If they succeeded, they would cut off reinforcements coming from the north and would have no fear of a sudden strike from behind.

"And all because someone was nodding off at the Six Towers," said the courier. "No one knows how such a thing could have happened."

Ga-Nor kicked Luk again, so he'd keep quiet.

"So it looks like we're losing?"

"Not yet. They have a hold on the eastern part of the country, but the Nabatorians have progressed no farther than the Isthmuses, even with the aid of the necromancers and the creatures of the Great Waste. Our boys are standing firm. Elite troops and reinforcements are coming closer through the Katugian Mountains. The Mineral Plains have been taken, Gash-Shaku is surrounded. Until it falls, the enemy is unlikely to strike the Steps. It's too dangerous. Plus, in the west we are resisting them. But the battles are hard fought. If not for the fortified citadels and stockades that constantly delay the enemy forces, who knows how it would all play out. And the land is also on our side. There are more than enough geographical hindrances for the Nabatorians. So maybe we'll be victorious."

"It's hard to believe there's a war going on. It's so quiet here," said Shen.

"A hundred leagues to the north would make you believe, lad. If you strike through the forests and swamps toward the Six Towers, you'll see it with your own eyes before the week is out."

"Do you have any idea what's going on in Al'sgara?"

"I'm just now headed there. But it seems like many in that city regard what's happening as something very far away. They think it doesn't concern them. And there are fools who don't believe the rumors at all."

"And there's no army to defend it."

"They've left Al'sgara to the dogs. You know what will happen if our forces are defeated. It's true there was a whisper that the Viceroy may be putting together a force to replace the Second Army, and it may even carry the same name, but it will essentially be a militia of irregulars, retreating troops, and mercenaries. It's just not enough. If the regular army couldn't do it, then how will they?"

"What about the Walkers?"

"They are fighting. They are battling with the Sdisian sorcerers and their creations. In some places successfully. But they won't succeed in burning out the entire infection. At times you meet evil where you least expect it. Four days ago I nearly lost my head."

"Nabatorians?"

"No. They haven't drawn so close yet. This was worse. Corpses were climbing out of their graves."

"A lot?"

"The entire village. There was no one living. If not for my horse, I wouldn't have escaped."

"And by a whole village, how many do you mean, sir? Ten? Twenty?" asked Layen.

"Two hundred."

My sun pursed her lips but said nothing. However, I did not keep my doubts to myself.

"It's strange that the necromancers have some sort of task in our villages when their strength is needed in the north."

"I agree." Gis was not put off by my skepticism. "But I've heard about no less than three such cases. Villages and townships where there are no survivors, but which are full of hungry corpses. And this in the very heart of the unconquered territories."

"The Sdisians are trying to add to our troubles," Shen said a second before I could.

"And to sow panic," I backed him up.

"Courier." The innkeeper walked over. "Your room is ready."

"Already? Well then, I suppose it's time for me to go. I need to rest. I'll be on the road again early tomorrow morning. Thank you for inviting me, friends."

"Thank you for telling us the latest news."

"There's nothing to thank me for." He smiled mirthlessly. "It's not the kind of news that causes joy. Good night."

Gis bowed and then quickly ascended the staircase.

"What will we do?" asked Luk, after clearing his throat for emphasis.

"You want to go to Al'sgara." I wanted to eat.

"Well, yes. But what then?"

"Then our paths diverge. Layen and I have our own problems, as do you."

Shen peered at me furtively, but I chose to ignore it. The redhead nodded in agreement, not disputing our right to look after our own affairs.

I knew how I was going to proceed even before

the conversation with the courier. Gis only strengthened my confidence in the decision I'd made. Right
now we had one vital goal—we would go to Al'sgara
and explain to Joch how wicked it was to offer
money for Gray and Weasel. That would spare
Layen and me from headaches in the future. When
no one is chasing after your head, life becomes so
much more tranquil. And then only one road will be
left—to the Golden Mark. The ships should still be
in the harbor while the war is still far off. They'd
overcharge us terribly, of course, but thank Melot
we had the money. We'd make it.

"Did you notice what he didn't talk about?"
Layen asked us.

All eyes turned to her.

"Not a word about the Damned. Not one. The
finest rumors, guesses, and theories, but nothing
about the Sextet. As if they don't exist."

"Perhaps they're in no rush to show their
strength," suggested Luk.

"Wasn't it you who told me that Rubeola tore
apart the Six Towers? And her friend was not exactly subtle in Dog Green. I think that, for the time
being, the Walkers don't want to frighten the common folk. For as long as they can attribute all the
displays of magic to the Sdisian sorcerers, they will
continue to do so. The Whites may be dreadful, but
they are nothing compared to the Sextet. Why spread
premature panic not only in the population but also

among the soldiers? I don't think the soldiers would fight as well as before if they found out that the old legends had come to life."

"That may very well be. I think our lads have more than enough on their plates if they have to contend with twenty thousand corpses," said Luk.

"There can't be more than a thousand," she corrected him perfunctorily. "However you calculate it."

"And why is that?" The soldier clearly didn't believe her words. "If there were no less than two hundred in that village the courier raced through, then there'd have to be just as many in other places, right? Something about that doesn't sit right with me."

"And something about that courier doesn't sit right with me. I think he's lying. It requires considerable power to raise a single kuks. Not all of the sorcerers can even manage such a feat. It's quite a difficult task to transfer a portion of your own spark into a dead body, to constantly keep it under control, to always be expecting your creature to attack you. It's not worth the waste of power. There are far easier and more efficient means of spreading terror or of creating obedient servants for oneself. A veteran necromancer can raise no more than ten bodies. The sorcerers of the Eighth Sphere can control perhaps thirty or forty zombies. But they'd use up all their power doing it. So, they rarely engage in such nonsense. They raise the dead when they have nothing better to do. Thus, thousands are out of the question. But to hear Gis tell it, there are two hundred living dead in one pitiful little village. For that you'd need five necromancers of the highest order! If not six. And there simply aren't that many in the world. And they'd be doing nothing more than sitting around a useless village, wrangling corpses while waiting for a chance passerby."

"Also, the courier said that this was not the first instance," I supported Layen.

"Exactly. If you count how many sorcerers you would need to fill three or four villages with the dead . . . I doubt Sdis would send so many Elects for such an insignificant matter."

During this discussion, Shen had been sitting with his fists clenched and his gaze lowered.

"So then how do you explain the existence of those dead men that attacked me at the old silver mine?" Luk insisted.

"I don't know. Perhaps there was a necromancer nearby, or perhaps he simply sent them away from the Gates, or maybe they killed their sorcerer. The spell of summoning doesn't usually vanish with the death of the conjurer. A particle of the spark remains in the puppets and they live on after their master has died. It's possible that you had the luck to run into just such wretches."

"I'm going out for a walk." Ga-Nor stood up from the table and, walking round the numerous customers, headed for the inn's exit.

"And I, if you don't mind, am going to bed." Luk yawned widely and, taking a full mug of shaf with himself for company, he went upstairs, satisfied and full.

The three of us remained. Shen was just sitting there, drumming his fingers on the tabletop. I enjoyed his behavior recently less and less. If earlier he behaved like a callow youth who flung insults around indiscriminately, now he spent a large portion of his time in contemplation. It always seemed to me that the lad was planning some kind of nasty trick.

"Why so gloomy?" I asked him.

He tore his gaze away from his hands and smirked. "I'm confused about a few things."

"What, if it's not a secret?"

The Healer leaned toward us so that none of those sitting at the nearby tables could hear and asked quietly, "How many of the dead can Layen raise?"

"What are you driving at, Healer?" she responded coldly.

"You know what I'm talking about. Not everyone can merge with a khilss, and you controlled Death easily. Why wouldn't you possess the other skills as well?"

Layen's face expressed nothing. "You're raving, boy."

"No. I just have a knack for drawing the right conclusions, that is all. I'd still be interested to know, who taught you?"

"Oh," I said, chuckling, having followed the discussion as it unfolded, "I see you've decided to turn back to that old subject."

"But surely someone taught you, right?" Shen paid me no attention. "Someone told you what the sorcerers call zombies. Kuks is a rare word. You also know what the necromancers are called in Sdis. No Walker would ever call them what you did. Elect."

"But you yourself know these words and you'll notice that I do not ask you how. Why shouldn't I know them as well?" Layen turned the accusation around on the Healer.

"And so I shouldn't ask either?"

"I would appreciate it. To tell you the truth, I don't even remember where I heard them. They came in handy today. There's nothing more to it."

"I see," he drawled. "Then allow me to ask that with which I began—how many of the dead can you raise?"

"None," she snapped.

For some time they stared at each other. Finally Shen took a breath and leaned backward.

"I believe you're lying," he said in a colorless voice. "And I also have an idea about what you would have done with that woman in the village if she hadn't caught you unawares."

"You can have an idea about whatever you like. As for the Damned, my power wouldn't have been enough to even cause her the slightest injury."

"Sure, sure. You already told me something to

that effect about the necromancer who came to your house. I'm going to sleep." And the Healer left.

"So how many?" I couldn't help myself.

She wasn't expecting such a question from me and she flinched.

"Don't start."

"Why not? I'm really curious to finally find out what you're capable of."

Now she was avoiding looking into my eyes.

"Like I told Shen . . ."

"None. And you weren't even lying. Until your spark flares up again, you can't do anything. But how many could you raise before?"

This conversation clearly displeased Layen. I was already expecting to hear that it was none of my business. It was all the more strange then that she answered, "Four."

Iron fingers encircled my throat; it became hard to breathe and a line of cold chills crawled up my spine. A completely childish terror of a person who could control the dead surged up in me. But I battled it down.

I loved her. And I knew that she was not like the necromancers are usually depicted. Many years of life spent side by side had taught us to trust each other. Well . . . or almost taught us. Layen was looking at me in dismay. She was already regretting her excessive candor and was awaiting what I would say to her now.

"Four." I savored the word. "That's not bad for

someone who taught herself. Turns out, you'd give a few of the Whites a run for their money. Thank you for finally deciding to tell me."

"I've wanted to for a while, but I didn't know how you'd take it," she answered hurriedly.

"I understand you completely." The specter of the living dead still dangled before my eyes. Truth be told, it wasn't a very pleasant sight. "Is there anything else I should know, my love?"

"Did they leave?" Ga-Nor returned at a completely inopportune moment.

"Yes. They went to their rooms." Layen was happy that this unpleasant conversation had been put on hold for a while.

"We should soon, too. Another round of shaf, Gray?"

"If you like."

The northerner waved his hand, and the girl set down three mugs from her tray.

"I wanted to ask what your game is, but I never got the chance." The redhead dipped his mustache into the dark beverage.

"I don't really know what you mean."

"How do you earn your keep? Are you a Shot?"

"No. I'm a carpenter."

The middle-aged war dog grinned. "I guess you must be the best carpenter in the world, to be carrying so much money on you."

"And you have sharp eyes." My smile came out crooked.

"No. I have keen ears. I heard how it jingled in Layen's pack. And it's quite a lot. I wouldn't mistake the sound a mass of sorens gives out for anything else."

"It's her inheritance."

"So I thought." He smiled openly. "An inheritance, of course. A carpenter couldn't amass that much in his whole life."

It was obvious that he didn't believe us, but it didn't matter to him who we were. This is why I love northerners—they never meddle in other people's business.

"I'm pleased that we could . . ."

"Ness." Layen called to me.

". . . clarify it for you."

"NESS!"

I cut short my blather and looked at her petulantly.

"An odd man." A hint of alarm had slipped into her voice.

I personally didn't see anything odd about the stranger she pointed out. He was a man like any other man. True, he was wrapped from head to toe in a cloak and he was looking around. He was clearly not from around here. He'd just walked into the inn and was now standing in the center of the room, between the tables, apparently wondering what to do next. I couldn't make out his face, as it was hidden by his hood, but when the man turned around a bit, his cloak fell open and I saw the dull flash of armor.

"Fish!" Ga-Nor barked so loudly that I nearly jumped from shock.

The next moment the northerner tipped the heavy table over on its side like it was a feather, and the plates and mugs fell to the floor with a crash.

"Come here!"

The redhead's face was so intent that I followed his order without thinking. Layen did the same. The startled faces of the miners flashed past my eyes and then something boomed deafeningly. It hit my ears so hard that I screamed in pain. Darkness swam before my eyes and my nose started to bleed.

When I regained the ability to think, I found myself lying on the floor. Ga-Nor was next to me on his hands and knees. He tossed his head and for some reason reminded me of a big red dog.

"Layen!"

I couldn't hear my own voice. The shrieks and groans of the wounded drowned out all other sounds.

"Layen!"

Tossing someone's severed hand to the side, I crawled across the blood-soaked floor toward a table that had been split in two.

"Layen!"

Strong hands grabbed me by the shoulders, and I was pulled to my feet with a sharp jerk. Of course, it was the northerner. He had recovered much faster than I had from the incident.

"There she is!"

Layen was getting to her feet. She had her hand

pressed to her mouth, and her eyes were dilated with horror as she looked around the room, which was a scene of immense slaughter. There were so many dead, it was like one of the legendary battles of the War of the Necromancers had just been fought. Several body parts were even hanging from the huge circular chandelier. This was not to mention the blood, which was not only on the walls, but on the ceiling as well. And everywhere there was the dull gleam of small scales, no bigger than silver coins, which had seemed like chain mail to me. They were embedded in all the wooden surfaces and in those unfortunate souls who had been unlucky enough to be standing close to the stranger.

"Layen, are you all right?" I ran over to her.

"Let's get out of here. Please," she whispered.

I grabbed my wife by the elbow and led her toward the stairs.

"Ga-Nor, grab my bow and quiver."

"Already done," the redhead replied behind my back.

"What happened?" An agitated Luk ran out from the second-floor corridor. Then he froze, speechless.

"Don't just stand there!" Ga-Nor roared at him. "Take the woman to her room! Help him, man."

These last words were directed at Shen.

"Luk can handle it," said the Healer. "I have to help the wounded."

"And what are we going to do?" I frowned. I didn't want to leave Layen.

"We're going to go out and find out where the Fish came from." Ga-Nor handed me my bow. "Get ready."

"I'm always ready. Layen, I'll be back soon. Come on."

Stepping over the bodies and avoiding the injured, around whom the survivors were already fussing, we went outside. It was already dark, but no thought had been given to lighting torches. It's always this way in small towns—no one wants to spend money on nonsense like streetlights. All six of the Damned could hide in such thick darkness, and you would see absolutely nothing until it was too late.

"What was that?" I asked Ga-Nor as he sniffed the air.

"A Fish."

"I didn't notice that he had either fins or tails."

"We don't know what they're really called. The creatures have been dubbed 'Fish' in the Border-lands. They're a product of Sdisian magic. They're corpses. They walk up to the living and then, bam! There's a bunch of dead people."

"Is it always like that?"

"Unfortunately. They have thousands of steel scales. Each cuts through flesh and bone like butter. When the creature explodes, the scales fly in all di-rections. It's best to hide before that happens."

"Hey, kid!" I cried out to a pale boy who was standing by the entrance to the inn, staring at all the blood and corpses in horror. "Did you see it, the thing that exploded, before?"

He didn't immediately understand what was wanted of him. Then he nodded frantically.

"It was Shkan. The local drunk. He died three days ago." It seemed like the boy was about to burst into tears. "He was buried yesterday."

There you go! Luk had spoken evil and now the dead were crawling out of the cemetery. Just great!

"Head home," I said to him. "You can't do anything here. Quick!"

The small boy ran so fast that his heels were on fire.

"He might not be the only one." The tracker was staring intently into the darkness.

"I'm not going searching," I said sharply.

"No one asked you to."

Suddenly two booms, muffled by distance, rang out into the night.

"We're leaving." I decided. "Right now. I'm taking Layen and getting the hell out of here. It's getting dangerous."

At the opposite end of the street a pair of green lights flashed. Then another. And another. And another. A startled cry rang out, but was immediately muffled.

"Into the inn! Now!" Ga-Nor, unlike me, knew what kind of attack this was. "The dead!"

My heart grew cold, and I sped back behind the

precarious cover of the walls. Again, the screams of terror. A warning alarm began ringing.

"Close the doors!" bellowed the redhead.

"What? Have you gone mad?" The landlord jumped up. "We've sent for the Healers. Stand back!"

"Idiot! It's full of the living dead out there!"

"Don't spout bullshit! Back, I said! Or else . . ."

He didn't have to finish because five wide-shouldered, gloomy men had stood up behind his back. The surviving miners stood behind their friend.

"Up!" I snapped. It's stupid to try and save those who don't want to be saved. They will drown and take you with them when they go.

No longer paying any attention to the locals, we rushed to the stairs. On the way, Ga-Nor scooped up the Healer, who was trying to staunch the flow of blood from one of the wounded. The lad began to fight back.

"Leave him! He's already a goner. Save your own skin!" I snarled.

Shen wanted to rebel, but my face, distorted by terror, made him stop playing the fool. No longer arguing, the Healer rushed behind us. We were flying up the stairs when the first of the creatures, apparently drawn by the thick scent of blood, burst into the room and, without delay, sunk its teeth into the neck of the nearest person.

The people didn't understand what was happening and rushed to help the unlucky fellow. Before they could do anything, death entered into the room once more. I was the first to see the creatures, and the impression they made was terrible. However, there's no point in staring. With every second, new "guests" arrived, and for now they were occupied with the living people by the door, but soon they would turn their attention to us. So, skipping over a few steps, we ran upstairs. There was still a chance for us to escape. But the growling behind our backs spoke to the fact that those who hadn't found enough food downstairs had decided to visit the upper stories.

The first room along the corridor belonged to Luk, Ga-Nor, and Shen. The Healer flew there, and I had to follow him because I wasn't sure if I'd have time to make it to my room. We tumbled in and slammed the door shut. Almost immediately something heavy struck it from the other side.

As I expected, neither Luk nor Layen was here. Excellent!

The panting Healer slid down the wall and began to mutter a prayer.

Why not? He had nothing better to do.

"The stubborn bastard," I said, listening as the corpse frantically tried to get into our room.

This had been going on for an hour, but the creature didn't calm down for a minute.

"Will the door hold?" asked Shen for the millionth time.

"I really hope so."

There were three of us in the room. But neither

Luk nor Layen was there and the uncertainty was terrifying me. I didn't know if my sun was alive, but I very much hoped that she had locked herself in her room and that she was all right. If it was so, we were now separated by an entire hallway. Twenty-five short and extremely long steps.

Ga-Nor had leaned his sword against the wall and was now standing by the window and looking out onto the street. I knew what he was seeing there. Ambling shadows and the green lights of dead eyes. Far more than two hundred of the dead were crammed into Bald Hollow. From what we could see, they had flooded the entire city. I wondered if anyone was alive but us. Someone had to have had time to slam a door, to hide in a basement or an attic.

The alarm had been silent for a long time. There were no longer any screams to be heard either. No one was rushing to put out the fire that had flared up on the opposite end of the street. Several houses had already burned down and all we could do was pray that the fire would not spread farther and engulf the inn.

"We can't stay here forever. They'll get us sooner or later."

"You said yourself that the door would hold." Shen frowned.

"I said I hope it will. Even if it does hold, we'll die of starvation. After all, they're not afraid of sunlight, right?"

"Right. But if you kill the necromancer—"

"To Ug with your necromancer!" I used one of Ga-Nor's few curses. "Didn't you hear what Layen said? You'd need five of the very best sorcerers to raise two hundred of the dead. But there are far more than five hundred of them. And it's not just the idlers from the cemetery that came out. Now those who they ate for dinner are running about as well. Just think how many Whites you would need to manage such a horde?"

"I won't think anything. I'll tell you one thing— I've no desire to go running around with them."

"What do you suggest?" asked the northerner calmly.

"First, we need to break through to my room."

"What a fool!" spat Shen. "I'm not planning to risk my head for the sake of your better half."

"We have a window that looks out onto the inner courtyard." Letting his words slip past my ears, I turned to Ga-Nor. "If we can break through to the stables, we have a chance of reaching our old age."

"And if the innkeeper left the gates open?" He rubbed his forehead.

"We'll never find out if we stay sitting here in this doghouse."

He thought a moment, weighing the options. Then he nodded decisively.

"You're right. I'm with you."

"Idiots!" Shen did not want to take a step out of this seemingly secure room. "Are you sure they'll open up for you? You won't be able to come back."

"You can stay here. No one's asking you to come with us."

He shut up, stood up off the floor, and grabbed his skeem.

"Can you help us?"

The Healer understood that I was asking about his Gift, and he shook his head no.

"I'm not sure that it will work."

Too bad. I'd actually been counting on his abilities.

"Does everyone recall that they need to be hit on the head?" the northerner asked us again.

We nodded.

"Then Ug help us. Let's begin."

"Don't get in the way of my arrows," I warned the Healer.

"Three. Two. One. Go!"

The Healer flung open the door and a stinking corpse immediately stumbled into the room. It didn't keep its balance, fell, and Ga-Nor chopped its head off. Another stiff, who I recognized as the landlord of the Supreme Witch, appeared in the doorway. I punched an arrow in his green eye. The northerner sliced through the creature's legs.

"Dead?" I asked just in case.

"He's long dead," said the redhead and, like a whirlwind with a head, he spun out into the hallway.

Everything turned out far better than we expected. There were only two of the dead remaining and they took no notice of us because they were trying to break through a door on the opposite end of the hallway.

While Ga-Nor and Shen dealt with them, I kept my eyes on the stairs, from which at any moment we might have to welcome new guests. Meanwhile, a short skirmish took place behind me. The nimble northerner dealt with his opponents with such speed that he didn't even require the Healer's help.

"Done!" I heard the Son of the Snow Leopard say, and I began to retreat.

"Layen, open up, it's us!" Shen banged on the door. "Layen! Open up!"

From below came the sound of wheezing and stomping feet. The first corpse practically flew up to the floor. My arrow pierced it right in the eye, causing it to fall backward and tumble down the stairs.

Ga-Nor appeared next to me and under his protection I felt much more sure of myself.

"If they don't open the door for us, we're lost," he said calmly, but his voice did not deceive me. Our situation really was rotten. Nine undead were already coming toward us. The same amount followed behind them. Even if we hacked our way back to the other room, we wouldn't get there whole.

"Layen!" I shouted as loudly as I could, drawing a new arrow. "Open up!"

The bolt snapped open immediately.

Smart girl!

"Oh, Melot! You're alive!" I heard the voice of my sun. "Faster! Faster!"

Yet another of the hunters of my living flesh fell with an arrow in his pupil. Then I turned around, jumped into the room right behind Shen, and immediately drew back to the wall to let Ga-Nor in. Layen slammed the door shut and put the bolt back in place.

"Finally!" said the Healer. "You dithered about long enough!"

"I see no reason why I should have let you in," she replied coldly, and then she walked over to me and hugged me fiercely.

"I was beginning to fear that you would not be saved."

"All is well," I whispered. "We're okay."

"Would you really have left us outside?" Ga-Nor frowned.

"Don't be silly, friend." Despite his pallor, Luk had lost none of his talkativeness. "It's just that we didn't believe our ears at first. Help me. We need to move this cabinet back in front of the door. Just in case."

Wheezing and blows could be heard from the other side of the door. There were a great deal more of them after our souls now. I was seriously beginning to fear that the door would not hold.

"Is there anything to drink?" After the short flight my throat was completely dry.

"I can only offer you reska, but I doubt that would be of any use to us."

Only now did I notice Gis.

The courier was sitting cross-legged on the floor like an easterner, wrapped in his battered cloak. Next to him lay a broadsword in a worn burgundy sheath, and a gray-green saddle bag.

"How did you get in here?"

"I was in the hallway when the undead appeared. I jumped into the nearest room and locked the door. Turns out, my lady and Luk were already here."

"Yes, indeed," confirmed the puffing soldier, who was dragging the cabinet with Ga-Nor. "If not for the courier, we wouldn't have known anything, screw a toad. The door was wide open."

"I wonder what's happening," I asked Layen quietly.

"I'd like to know myself. It would require tremendous strength to raise so many of the dead."

"Something like this has happened before." Gis, as it turned out, was not at all averse to talking. "Just very long ago. They say that when a very strong Walker dies, it rains heavily. So it was when Sorita died, for example."

"What is the connection?" Layen did not understand.

"When the bearer of a very strong Gift dies a violent death, after her departure a fraction of the magic does not disappear, but disperses into the world. It calls down the rain."

"So what are the dead here for?" asked Luk sulkily. "What are they, like mushrooms creeping out of the ground after a rain?"

"They say that when Cholera and Delirium died during the War of the Necromancers, for the entire next month, here and there, all over the lands of the Empire, entire cemeteries were raised."

"Do you mean to say that when the Walkers die, it rains, but when the Damned do, the dead rise?" Shen guessed.

"So the old legends say." Gis shrugged. "However, there is a small discrepancy—none of the Sextet have been killed in the last five hundred years."

I immediately thought of the woman we disposed of in Dog Green. It appears Gis was right.

"How do you know about all of this?"

"Old tales, my lady. When you travel your whole life, you learn a lot. Sometimes it is useful."

"And do the tales say when the dead will wander back to their graves?" asked Luk hopefully.

"Unfortunately, they do not. Just that it happened in various places and then subsided. Well, and that the Walkers no doubt helped."

"Well, we can't put our hopes in the Walkers," I said sharply. "We'll have to handle it on our own. Here's what I want to suggest. . . ."

"Careful. Don't make a noise," hissed Shen.

"I'm trying, screw a toad." Luk was clearly having a hard time keeping his voice down.

As I had hoped, the gates leading from the street into the inner courtyard, where the outbuildings and stables were located, were closed. Of course, someone was banging on them, but not too strenuously and for the time being unsuccessfully.

Without much difficulty at all, we had crept out the window and climbed down the chimney, which was not too high. While the Healer helped the soldier down, the rest of us did what we had agreed to earlier. I covered Ga-Nor, who was fortifying the door that led into the inn. It wouldn't be good if we were caught unawares and lost our souls. Layen and Gis went to the stables. I hoped there would be enough horses for all of us. Otherwise things might get a bit unpleasant. I really didn't want to leave anyone behind. Not even the Healer.

"It's done," said Ga-Nor as he returned. "I'm not sure it won't be torn down if they all press against it."

"I'll try to be very far away by then. Luk, you all right?"

"I've never understood people who creep into other people's houses through the windows." He panted, trying to catch his breath. "Same with creeping out, mind you."

"You just haven't got a taste for it."

Contrary to my expectations, he smiled and winked.

Gis ran up to us. "I need help saddling the horses. It'll take too long with just the two of us."

"Are there enough horses for all?" I asked with a transfixed heart.

"Yes."

"Then let's get going."

The animals could sense the dead, and they were in a sweat and trembling lightly all over, but thank Melot they obeyed us. I got a black, barrel-chested monster that I immediately dubbed Stallion. The beast was calmer than the others, and this inspired confidence in me that I might actually remain seated on his back.

"Now what?" Layen asked the question that had been disturbing me.

"We must open the gates."

"Brilliant, Luk! Can you do it?"

"I'm not so sure." He licked his lips nervously. "Will you help us, Layen?"

"Me?"

"You know you can do it." The soldier looked at her pleadingly. "Can't a Walker clobber them with a spell?"

I saw Gis's eyebrows go up.

"Who told you that I'm a Walker?" she asked, astonished.

"Well, or an Ember. Ga-Nor and I saw you send that hurricane at the Burnt Souls."

Oh dear! Turned out our friends knew far more than we thought.

"You're mistaken," said Layen unexpectedly gently. "Unfortunately, I'm neither a Walker nor even an Ember. And there is no way I can help us. Do you think if there were anything I could do, we'd still be sitting here?"

"I think—" Shen began, but I cut him off.

I began speaking with the utmost conviction and composure. "The gates must be opened. I will do it. But if there are far too many of the dead there; they'll pin us down and devour us right here. Along with the horses. They'll let none escape. We need to divert their attention. I think we should divide into two groups and make our way to the city gates separately and by different paths. The first group will distract the ones trying to break in here. I hope that the creatures will chase after them. They're not very smart."

"The ones who gallop off first are risking a lot." Gis thoughtfully stroked the face of his mare. "But it must be done. I'm with you, lad, and you're lucky I know this little town so well. I'll be able to lead you out."

"I'm also with you," volunteered Layen.

"No."

"But—"

"No!" I interrupted. "You will be with Ga-Nor, Shen, and Luk. We're not discussing this."

My sun's eyes flashed wickedly and she clenched her teeth in rage.

"I'll go with you and Gis," said the Healer unexpectedly. "You'll need help."

I hadn't expected him to be so resolved.

"Good. That's what we'll do. Let's not delay any longer."

"Ness. We need to talk," Layen called out to me. We waited until the others had left the stable.

"What are you doing?" An entire lake of resentment lapped against the shores of her blue eyes.

"I'm trying to save your life. Don't interrupt! Listen! You'll be in greater danger with me than with them. Right now, Ga-Nor is more reliable than I am. And Luk, despite his frivolity, is not a man to mess with. I alone cannot defend you. Neither Gis nor Shen would be of any help, but only a burden. With the soldiers you have a chance to escape."

"And what about you?" The corners of her lips fell down as she looked at the floor. "Do you have any chance?"

"I do. But you can't be there." I spoke the harsh truth. "Alone I will fly faster than the wind and defend only myself, without being distracted by anyone else. If you go with me and something happens, I can't leave you. As a result, we'll stay lost in this damned town forever."

She knew it was so and understood that what I was suggesting would help us both to live.

"You're right, even though I don't like it." She turned away, hiding her tears. "All I ask of you is that you don't stop if the courier or the Healer need help. Recall the rule of the Giiyans."

"I don't intend to stop." I hugged her. "Every man for himself. Everything will be fine. Keep close to the redhead. He won't let you come to harm. Just get out. I'll get out, too."

"Hey, are you asleep in there?" An agitated Luk appeared. "It's time. It'll be dawn soon."

"Let's go," I said, and then I kissed my wife and broke our embrace. "Be careful."

"And you. Try to survive."

"I'll put all my efforts toward it." I laughed. "Hey! Don't be sad. Everything will be fine. You don't really think I'd leave you for long, do you? If everything works out, we'll meet outside the town gates."

"And if it doesn't? If something happens to you?"

I sighed. "We've gotten out of worse scrapes."

"I had the Gift then. Right now I'm a helpless infant."

"That's why I want you to stay close to the northerner. You know that tribe. . . . But if I don't manage to get out, don't wait for me and don't look for me. Go immediately to Al'sgara. We'll meet at Nag and Leech's place. If I haven't appeared within a week after you arrive, take the money and sail to the Golden Mark. To Harog. Don't wait for anything."

"You'll find me?"

"Of course. Wherever you may be."

"Take care of yourself, Gray."

"Take care of yourself, Weasel. Everything will be fine."

We exited the stable side by side, leading our horses. Ga-Nor and Luk were already in their saddles. Layen touched her lips to my cheek one last time and went to them. I walked over to Gis and Shen, who were already standing by the gates. I gave Stallion into their care.

"I'll be quick."

"We have no time!"

"Wait! Damn you to the Abyss!"

They stopped arguing. I had one more unfinished piece of business. I needed to say something to the northerner. Seeing me walking toward him, he jumped off his horse. Tall, sinewy, morose. As reliable as a wall.

"As soon as we jump out, act, and no matter what happens, don't pay us any attention. We'll deal with it on our own."

He nodded. "Good luck."

"You too. Take care of my wife."

"Don't worry. Unlike Giiyans, my people have different rules. We don't leave our own behind."

"You really do have excellent hearing." I chuckled.

For the time being I decided to forget about what else he might have heard.

"I can't complain." He was serious.

"If anything happens to her, it would be better for you if you died, too. Or else I'll get to you, even from the Abyss. Do we understand each other?"

He looked into my eyes for a long moment and then gave a slight nod. "I'll bring her through."

Without saying another word, the redhead returned to his saddle. An amazing people, the northerners. They know that some people are complete bastards, but if they consider them their own, they'll help them even to their own detriment. I could only be thankful for the fate that sent such a man to Layen and me.

I ran to the gate, which was shaking from blows. The latch was heavy, but I managed to lift it up in one motion. I kicked the halves open and dashed back, leaping into my saddle.

The halves separated, and the first of the dead began to stumble into the courtyard. I shouted and drove the heels of my boots into my horse's sides.

The length of the courtyard allowed the horses to get enough speed for a respectable trot. Stallion was the first to crash into the corpses, scattering those who were hesitating with his broad chest and crushing a few others beneath his hooves. The scent of fresh blood and stupefying decay hit my nose. Grinning faces and glowing eyes flashed and then disappeared.

We broke through and rode down the dark street. The hunters of human flesh rushed behind us, empty-handed. I hoped that Ga-Nor, Layen, and Luk got out without any problems. I clung to the neck of my horse and didn't even have to urge him on. The animal wanted to get as far away as possible from the dead.

Gis's mare turned out to be a swift horse, and now the courier was galloping ahead, showing us the way. I remembered very little of this mad gallop.

Impenetrable darkness, the rustling of shadows, dark silhouettes with green eyes, the blaze of fires that arose from who knows where. Three times our path was blocked, and three times we broke through. The last time, a corpse managed to cling to the courier's stirrup, but he slashed at the undead with his broadsword.

When Gis suddenly reined in his horse, I saw that the street in front of us was blocked. A whole crowd of the dead was swarming around a house. Apparently, someone was still alive in there. One of the corpses saw us and rushed forward, forgetting all about the prey cowering behind the walls. After him came another three, and then the entire crowd swayed and began moving.

"Follow me!" Gis guided his horse into an alley.

I was afraid that Stallion would stumble and I'd come to my end right here, but Melot spared me. The wide-open city gates and a small torch-lit square appeared in front of us. Three riders on foaming horses flew out of a neighboring street, pursued by a few dozen undead. They didn't look around and so they didn't see us galloping toward the gates from the other side of the square. After a few seconds the people swept through the square and escaped from the town. My heart instantly became lighter. Layen had escaped the deadly trap. The dead didn't even bother to give chase. The creatures rushed at us instead.

"Damn it!" Gis tugged at his reins, causing his

horse to rear up on its hind legs. "We won't get clear!"

He was right. The dead had completely blocked off the exit. I doubt we'd be able to break through even at a full gallop. In such a crowd the horses would lose their way and that would mean our death. We couldn't hold out against so many adversaries.

"Is there another way out?" Shen was breathing as hard as his horse.

"Yes. Follow me!"

And again we had to zigzag through the streets to get away from the creatures that I no longer had the heart to call human. At one point I caught myself thinking that I'd ceased being afraid of them. It always happens when you're afraid for too long. The fear burns itself out. There is a surfeit of fear. You no longer feel anything except for dull fatigue. I know how my words sound from the outside—far too casual. But you can get accustomed to anything. Even to throngs of the dead.

It seemed like we had ridden right through Bald Hollow. We took off into a dark lane, rode to the end without encountering anyone, and found ourselves in a large square that served as the local market.

The courier reined in his horse and began looking around.

"Where to now?" I asked.

"Quiet. Let me think."

The sky was already getting light. Thin threads of mist glistened like silver in between the vacant wooden rows of the market stalls. The horses snorted and stepped from foot to foot.

"The river is close," whispered Shen.

"So is the cemetery," spat Gis. "We didn't come out where I expected."

"There's no point in worrying. All the inhabitants of the cemetery are in the town now. And leaving by the river would give us a real chance of getting out of this pit."

"Let's try to avoid swimming. There's a way through a field not far from here." The courier urged his horse forward. "Follow me!"

I could have argued and risked going on alone, but I didn't. The courier clearly knew where he was going. Not to mention that it was more likely we'd survive if we stuck together.

Back to the streets, back to the crowds of the undead. We raced on, paying no attention to anything. I followed immediately after the courier, and Shen was behind me. Sometimes we had to cut our way through. In these instances the might of the horses and Shen's skeem helped. Fate took care of me; I did not fall, and no one pulled me off my horse or even grabbed at me. *I don't know who owned Stallion before, but he was a fine steed. If I survive, I'll buy him a whole bag of oats. And I won't begrudge him.*

We zigzagged, swerved, doubled back, trying to shake the dead, who now and again pursued us, from our tail. At some point I realized that something had been bothering me for the last few minutes. I could no longer hear hoofbeats behind me. My blood went cold. I turned around in the saddle and saw nothing but a line of three of the undead straggling behind us.

Shen was lost. Whether he was delayed and missed a turn we'd taken, or something happened to his horse, or he was knocked out of his saddle, I didn't know. In any case, he was no longer with us.

"Gis!" I shouted. "Shen fell behind!"

The courier nodded, indicating that he had heard, but he didn't stop. He realized that it was useless to go looking for the lad in the dark streets teeming with the dead. We wouldn't find him and we'd be lost ourselves. He'd either get out on his own or die; we no longer had any control over his destiny. My companion knew this just as well as I did, and so he did not even look back.

Was I sorry that the kid was gone? Yes, I dare say. Despite all his impudence and his nasty disposition, he wasn't really all that bad. All in all, the Healer had saved Layen and me twice, so I hoped he had the luck to survive the night.

A short while later we broke out of the town and, driving our horses hard, we rushed away along a dusty road that led into hilly fields. Well, I was not mistaken about Gis. He really was capable of leading me out alive and unharmed. After galloping a bit more, we pulled in our reins and, standing up in the stirrups, looked back at Bald Hollow, which was wrapped up in the morning fog. If it weren't for the fires, nothing would indicate the tragedy that had befallen the town.

"We can't linger, man." Gis's face was glistening with sweat.

"Can we go around the town and get to the Al'sgara road?"

"I don't think that's a good idea." My companion shook his head. "Your friends are already far away. We'd need to catch up to them, and our horses are very tired. And I won't risk going closer to Bald Hollow. We'll make our way through the fields. I know the way. We'll be in Al'sgara in five days. We'll meet them there."

"Do you think the lad managed to escape?"

"I really hope so."

By his eyes I could tell that he simply didn't want to upset me. Casting a final glance at Dabb's Bald Hollow, I nodded at the courier, indicating that we should be on our way.

14

Tal'ki had not lied. The weave really was quite simple. The Damned had enough strength to pour herself into the hanged guardsman on the first try. As soon as she did this, her dormant spark, sensing the support of an uninhabited body, flared up and shone brightly, and Tia gasped in delight. She screamed so triumphantly that Captain Nai, who was green with terror, recoiled from the revived corpse, tripped over a swine trough lying on the ground, and fell into the manure.

However, Typhoid's rapture was premature. After a few tests, the Damned found that the capabilities of her temporary body were no match for those she had previously. Too much had been lost with the death of her true vessel. The feeling of ease vanished. Her delight plunged into a roaring, defiant deluge of destructive power. In a single moment, Tia had become the weakest of the Sextet. Even the despicable Mitifa could overpower her without any trouble.

The insult made her gnash her teeth.

Not even the knowledge that any of the Walkers would rend the clothes from their bodies just to enjoy the Damned's current abilities comforted her. Power like this would be a gift from the gods to the upstarts of the Rainbow Valley. But Typhoid felt cheated. All she could do was hope that in time it would all return.

Her primary objective was to catch that boy Healer. Tia had no doubt that she would catch the fugitives. In killing her body, the archer had placed a "mark" on himself without even knowing it. Right now it was pointing to the west and with each day she journeyed it burned all the brighter.

After Typhoid tightened her control, her issues with Pork lessened. She had never inflicted pain on others just for her own pleasure. Rovan loved to torture, and the Damned hated him for this. But in this situation, the murderer of Sorita found that this tool was not without its uses because as soon as her spirit flowed into the body of Gry, the half-wit discovered his will again. She had to resort to causing him pain.

That same day she took a horse and, together with the half-wit, rushed off in pursuit. Of course, she could have brought a pair of clods with her so that she could use their bodies when her current one became worthless, but the Damned would prefer a woman's form. She was already starting to feel nauseous from all these men.

As Typhoid had assumed, the idiot kept his saddle worse than a straw scarecrow. She always had to keep an eye on her ward. Despite the fact that she now had her own vessel, she needed rest and sleep. The first night, as soon as Typhoid fell asleep and relaxed her grip, the cowherd decided to run away. At the very moment when he got twenty yards away from her, Tia felt the full meaning of Tal'ki's words about being pulled out "like a dog on a leash." However, Leprosy could have just as easily compared it to the sensations of a salmon that has been hooked and pulled from the water. The bonds that connected her to the half-wit strained and Typhoid flew out of Gry's body like a cork from a bottle of sparkling Morassian wine.

It was not the most pleasant way to wake up. She was so angry that she almost crippled the imbecile. Pork didn't try to escape anymore. The half-wit's spirit gave up the fight over his body, stopped popping out like a Mort from a dark doorway, sat quietly, and became one less headache.

After three days Gry's body became unfit for her, and Tia once again had to hang over the shoulder of the moron. It truly irritated her. Suppressing his will, she took control over the other's body.

Sensing that she would catch up to the people who had caused her so much trouble, she drove both horses, hardly slept, and stopped only to let the animals graze and to feed the cowherd. The last thing she needed was for the fool to die.

On the fourth day, Tia broke free from the Forest Region.

She had the grim thought that in the populated areas she would get the chance to find a new body and once again touch her Gift. There had to be dead people in this backwater!

There turned out to be far more dead people in

the area than she had expected. The land was simply swarming with them. When four animated corpses jumped out onto the road in front of her, Tia acted without hesitation, regardless of her surprise. Because she was inside Pork she couldn't direct the kukses, let alone get rid of them. She needed a couple of seconds to create the weave that would put her in the body of a woman whose throat was torn. The Damned made contact with her Gift and, with a sharp slap of her hands, broke the ties of the summoning that was forcing the dead to live. The eyes of the three who were approaching the terrified horses extinguished, and the creatures fell like logs to the ground.

"Khsssand khup." Because of its torn larynx, this body had difficulty emitting the necessary sounds and was wheezing like a snake dying of apoplexy.

Pork had fallen from the saddle and was now crawling around in the dust, wringing his hands imploringly and sobbing. The sight of the half-eaten, living corpses had sent him into paroxysms of fear. He even wet his pants. Typhoid shuddered in disgust. Would her torment never end? Being with such a pathetic nitwit was trying her patience.

"Mistress," he babbled, wiping away snot. "Mistress, they . . . they . . ."

"Khsssand khup now."

It worked.

"Ffffollowkh khe khorsssesss khand kheep khlossse."

He obeyed. Typhoid was finally able to address more pressing problems. She wondered where all the kukses had come from. As far as she knew, none of the Elect were supposed to be in this area. The battles were being waged far to the north and the sorcerers had been strictly forbidden from coming near Al'sgara until Tal'ki gave the order. Had someone disobeyed the prohibition? Or was it . . . ?

She cursed herself for her own stupidity and quickly checked the amount of power gathered over the town.

"Khe Kkabysssss takhe me!" she gasped sharply, astonished.

The power around her was so great that it made her roar in ecstasy. She could swim in it, scoop up handfuls of it, waste it without a twinge of conscience. Without begrudging the expense. The most amazing thing was that there was no doubt who this outburst of power belonged to. Even a clumsy fool from the First Sphere could identify his own spark. All the power hovering around had once belonged to her.

It reminded her of fish flakes spilled from an enormous container. And now Tia swallowed the power like a hungry fish; she inhaled it, and with each passing second she became stronger and stronger.

She felt like exulting and singing.

This was why even in the bodies of the dead she felt so worthless. How could she forget about this? Indeed, in the ancient books such phenomena were mentioned! And this is exactly what happened after the deaths of Ginora and Retar—an enormous release of uncontrolled power into the world and unrestrained kukses arising from their graves in the hundreds.

Only now did Typhoid understand why Tal'ki had taken the time to visit such places then. The cunning creature had told them that she was going to get the kukses under control, but really the old snake had been gathering the others' power! That was the key to the growth of her power! She had fed off what remained of the two who had departed for the Abyss.

The sly, dangerous witch! She had fooled them all. She had stolen so much power, and they, idiots that they were, only rejoiced that Leprosy had taken on the onerous task of pacifying the kukses.

The old crone!

Not to worry! Tal'ki wasn't here, and Tia's spirit could absorb at least part of what it had lost through the death of her body. It rightfully belonged to her and would make her spark burn more fiercely.

The Damned rejoiced.

She was wandering through the deserted city streets, illuminated by the bright sunshine, collecting the scattered bits of her Gift. They did not just hover in the air, but also rested in the throngs of zombies. She had no problem drawing them out. The kukses sensed Pork and the horses and ran toward them in an attempt to assuage their hunger, but in obedience to Tia's commands, they died a second time, releasing her priceless strength.

There were far more of the dead than she had expected. Those who had surged up from the local cemetery had added those who had been alive the previous evening to their number. Typhoid only stopped and took a rest late at night, when she was as full to bursting with power as a wineskin.

She had done it. She had reaped a rich harvest. Her spark was rekindled almost to its previous level and she had freed the unfortunate town from the living dead. However, the latter was not part of her plan. That's just what happened, and she was far from considering it a good thing. As the Damned had assumed, nothing living remained in Bald Hollow. So there was no one to thank her. However, she needed this gratitude much less than Pork needed new pants.

Typhoid snorted irritably, and the cowherd standing in front of her cringed, fearing the wrath of Mistress.

What a great comparison! It wouldn't be a bad idea to get new pants for the fool. The ones he had on were rather off-putting.

"Ffffollowkh me," she croaked, and the cowherd, still shaking from the terrifying day he'd lived through, dragged himself after her.

During her wanderings around the town, Tia had seen a shop that sold ready-made clothes. She thought it was high time to dress the blessed fool in clean clothes.

The Damned entered the shop and looked around. It did not take her long to find the right clothes for Pork. Clean underwear, new pants, a shirt, and a good jacket transformed the fool. Typhoid studied him with a critical eye and, finding herself satisfied with the result, took control of his body, simultaneously leaving the corpse of the woman with the slashed throat. Now it was not quite so disgusting to stand behind the left shoulder of her servant.

As she expected, the spark faded after the transition, but the gathered strength remained. Typhoid may have lost an entire day, but her Gift was far more important than her enemies. With it, she had a chance to regain her former might. And the insects wouldn't escape her. Typhoid could sense them even now and she would have no problem catching them, even though they had decided to confuse their tracks and flee across the fields instead of along the decent road.

Tia-Pork leapt into the saddle and continued the chase.

"We'll get to the road in about an hour."

I nodded and buttoned my jacket. The early morning was overcast; the air was cold, not yet heated by the rising sun, but the earth was warm. Fog hung over the fields and covered the short grass. It had already filled the ravines and gullies to the brim, and was now flowing around them, threatening to rise up off the ground to its full height and plunge the world into a milky shroud.

The horses were walking very slowly. I looked around, standing up in my stirrups, but it wasn't possible to make out anything farther than ten yards away. After another twenty minutes I could barely see five paces in front of me. We were riding in a thick, syrupy, milky, cold fog.

"We're going to be wandering about here for more than an hour. More like three." My voice seemed unpleasantly muffled.

"Don't be afraid." The courier stroked his mustache. "We're in no rush."

I frowned, but said nothing. He might not be in a rush, but some of us were in a hurry to get to Al'sgara. After four days of traveling, I was entirely burned out. My attempts to call Layen had come to nothing. She still hadn't regained her power after the fight in Dog Green. I didn't know where my sun was, who was with her, or whether she'd made it to Al'sgara. What if something had happened along the road? The uncertainty was driving me mad. If I could have, I would have ridden day and night, but I wouldn't get very far without a change of horses, so I had to conserve Stallion's strength. Without him, I'd be traveling even longer. By my count, the city was three, maybe four days' ride away. We just needed to get out of these damned fields onto a regular road. Then it would get easier.

The only thing that warmed my heart was the thought that Layen had managed to escape Bald Hollow.

"Are you thinking about your wife?"

I scowled at Gis.

"Don't get mad." He smiled disarmingly, as if he hadn't noticed my disgruntled look. "I'd also be thinking about her. You're a lucky man, my friend."

"I know."

"Everything will be all right."

"All I can do is hope you're right."

"I never dared to tie the knot with any woman," he said, apropos of nothing.

"Why?"

Gis thought for a bit and then shrugged.

"Probably because I just didn't have the time. The life of a courier, if you know what I mean. One day here, the next day there. What kind of woman would agree to that?"

"You didn't look all that hard. Believe me, there are such women. . . . We need to stop and wait." I could not help it. "I can't see anything."

"Nonsense," replied the courier. "We won't lose our way, I'm telling you. Hey, I meant to ask you about what Luk said about Layen. . . ."

"No. She's not a Walker or an Ember," I replied in a steady voice.

"Then why'd he call her that?"

"I don't know. Ask him."

For some time we rode in silence, trying to catch a glimpse of the road through the fog. It was no use.

"Do you hear that?" Gis asked suddenly. "There! Again! It sounds like a bell ringing. Do you hear it?"

From afar, muffled by the distance, came a barely audible "ommm."

"You're right. Is there a village nearby?"

"I don't know, I don't know." He looked worried. "It seems we headed too far to the west. If it's Psar'ki . . . It's too early, don't you think?"

"Too early for what?"

"For services to Melot. Why is the bell tolling?"

"Ommm" was the response.

"Or for whom," I said, grinning crookedly. "I don't have a lot of arrows left."

Gis glanced at my full quiver. "You think it's the dead again?"

"And you don't? If they were in Bald Hollow, why wouldn't they be here, too? It's a really bad idea to get into that mess again."

"We have very little food left. And I'm a courier. I'm required to find out what's happening there so I can report it."

"Who requires it?"

He remained unfazed. "First of all myself."

"As you will. It's your own head on your shoulders. If you can't stand not knowing, stick your nose in there. I won't object. But I'm not going. And definitely not in such a fog."

It would be great fun when a dozen of the undead popped up out of nowhere. Why should I risk my own neck for nothing?

"Are you really that frightened of the ringing of bells?" He was astonished.

"Just imagine. I've been a coward since I was young," I replied coldly.

"Don't talk nonsense. I saw how you carried yourself in the city. Most so-called brave men couldn't handle something like that. I don't understand your fears. There are many reasons why they might have decided to sound the alarm."

"And I don't understand your lack of understanding. You yourself said it might be dangerous there. I have no need of it. Plus, the bell is ringing strangely, don't you think? Sometimes more than a minute passes between the strikes. And sometimes it rings one after another, with no time for the peals to stop. I wouldn't go there for all the sorens in the Empire. And I'd advise you against it."

"So our paths diverge."

My companion said this without malice, accepting my refusal as a matter of course.

"Hold to the west. After a quarter of a league turn north and you'll get to the road beyond the village. After about three hours you'll get to the Al'sgara road. I hope you find Layen, my friend."

"Good luck. If you change your mind, chase after me. I'll ride slowly."

The courier waved his hand, and after several seconds the fog swallowed both him and his horse. I listened to the random ringing of the bell a few more times; then I commanded Stallion, "Onward."

For some reason I recalled Shen at this moment. Did he survive? Why did he fall behind? Did he manage to escape Bald Hollow? He was an impudent pup, but I didn't want him to be dead.

Ommm.

Even if everything was all right in the village and they were just getting drunk over someone's wedding or funeral, I saw no reason to tarry. Gis was an utter fool. What came over him?

The sound of the bell and the density of the fog twisted into a nightmarish specter, and I was glad that I don't have a healthy imagination. That would be really bad. I'd be expecting something to jump out at me every second.

I'd been riding for quite a while, but I knew that I hadn't traveled very far. Every now and then we came across wide ditches and irrigation canals, and then the peasants' fields began. I had to circle around, holding to the right, and twice double back in order to avoid a shallow but long ravine. While I was bobbing and weaving, a light wind sprang up from the south, and the fog began to thin out. It no longer hung in a dense veil; gaps began appearing and the visibility improved. Now I could easily make out what was located fifteen yards away from me.

BOMMM!

The sound was so distinct that I flinched. I looked to the right. A dark spot stood out through the snow-white haze. Without realizing it, I had come far closer to the village than I wanted. I could see the houses on the outskirts.

BOMMM!

Damn that bell-ringer! Why didn't his kin drag him out of the bell tower? Did they really enjoy it? Cursing under my breath, I directed Stallion back into the field, away from the village. Every now and then I looked over my shoulder; then I couldn't take it anymore so I paused and strung my bow. Regardless of how large and unwieldy my weapon was for shooting from the saddle, I'd have to manage.

After a few minutes Stallion stopped abruptly and snorted irritably. Our path was blocked by a high fence. Right beyond it I could see some buildings.

BOMMM!

What bad luck! I still contrived to lose my way and once again enter the village. Turns out I was going in circles.

BOMMM!

It seemed I couldn't avoid Psar'ki.

"Shall we go through the village, my friend?" I asked Stallion.

He made no objection and peaceably jerked his ears.

"Well, so it's decided," I muttered and gently squeezed with my knees (my hands were occupied by the bow and I couldn't be distracted by the reins), causing the animal to move along the fence.

To the right and the left neat rows of low peasant houses appeared out of the fog. The doors were shut, the windows whole; there were no signs of destruction. Not even the flower beds were trampled. The street was empty. No children, no chickens, no cats, no dogs. It was as if everyone had disappeared at once. A loaded wagon was abandoned on the dusty road near a particularly nice house. Not even the smallest waft of smoke could be seen over the chimneys.

The gate that led into one of the houses was wide open. I cast a quick glance at the rickety shack, old and untidy, which seemed completely out of place on such a prosperous street. The door was torn from its hinges. The dark gap of the doorway yawned like the wide-open jaws of a demon. I quickly rode away. Just in case.

The fog thinned out more, the visibility improved, and I spied a wooden House of Melot and a bell tower, whose top was lost in the white haze.

BOMMM!

Amidst the deafening silence, the ringing of the bell was unexpectedly piercing. Wrong. Blasphemous. It was like screaming raucous tavern songs in a cemetery. I looked around but didn't see anything suspicious. I led Stallion to a fence and tied him up. I had to find out who was up there. My hands were itching with a burning desire to throw the idiotic bell ringer from the very top of the tower. So that he'd land face-first on the ground.

The door of the bell tower was wide open.

BOMMM!

"Hold on, you louse," I hissed. I put my bow in my left hand, as it would be useless in such a cramped space, pulled the axe from my belt, and began to climb the narrow spiral staircase. The boards under my feet creaked treacherously, and I winced, annoyed at the old building. Whoever was on the bell platform could probably hear me.

All that remained was one flight of stairs. I scaled it in three jumps, burst out onto the landing, and nearly crashed into the bell ringer. Or more precisely, his legs.

Some clever prankster had hung the unfortunate man by a rope attached to the clapper of the small bell. Gentle breezes caused the body to sway slightly. That's where the ringing of the bell was coming from.

It was all so much worse than I had thought. If you go around hanging bell ringers in Melot's House, then you are a very daring and fearless person indeed. What had they done with the others?

I had to tinker about before I could cut the rope from his scrawny neck. The corpse thudded down onto the boards below and the bell finally fell silent.

I stood on the platform, visible to all. Unfortunately, below the railing the fog was thick and I couldn't get a good look around. I'd have to ride onward blindly, but I had to get to the road as soon as possible. The people who so thirsted to hear the ringing of the bell might show up here at any moment to find out why it had been silenced. I needed to get back to the fields to avoid the people who hanged that poor soul. I started to make my way down, hoping that Gis was still safe and sound. While I was fooling around up top, nothing had changed on the village street. Stallion was waiting for me where I'd left him. The horse trod lightly, the fog muffling the sounds of his hooves so well I had no fear of being overheard.

A saddled horse suddenly jumped out from behind the tall fence and almost flew right by me, but at the last moment I managed to grab it by the halter. The beast belonged to Gis. Melot! What had befallen the courier? Fly could have escaped if she was poorly tied up. But there was a worse possibility; Gis could have been killed. The whole question was, who or what did it? The courier had clearly fallen on some bad luck, but he had only himself to blame for it. I wouldn't search for him to find out what happened. He had his own concerns, and I had mine. I didn't need to lay another's idiocy on my own head.

I had almost exited the village when I spotted figures in the fog. I sharply reined in Stallion and slipped from the saddle.

Had I been seen?

I led the animals backward, praying to Melot that

they wouldn't inadvertently start neighing. Now the sound of their hooves didn't seem as quiet as before. Leaving the horses in the care of the nearest fence, I armed myself with my bow and, not taking my eyes off the foggy veil, walked forward.

There were six of them. Swarthy, with black mustaches and shaved heads. Wearing saffron-colored robes and turbans. Costly, wide belts, curved sabers, small composite bows. I hadn't expected an encounter with Sdisian warriors in the heartland of the Empire. There was no time to think about how they came to be here or what they wanted. I saw Gis in the midst of the six soldiers. He was lying on the ground, bound hand and foot, and the bald men were standing over him, apparently having a lively debate in their guttural, melodious language about the best way to finish him off. The men were so engrossed in their conversation that they didn't notice me in the slightest. It would be a sin to throw away such a chance.

Before they came to their senses and realized where the arrows were flying from, I killed one and seriously wounded another. Two of them rushed toward their horses, and while a third reached for his bow, the fourth drew his sword, clearly intending to finish Gis off. I had to hurry.

My cheek felt the momentary brush of feathers and a soldier dressed in saffron fell to the ground next to the courier.

One less.

I outpaced the archer by a second. He had just about completed taking his aim at me, but my arrow caught him in the chest and he didn't get me. His short bow, which was no match for mine, trembled in his enfeebled hands.

Meanwhile, the two horsemen were rushing at me, howling and waving their sabers. It was useless to run, too late to shoot. At the last moment, right before I was crushed by a charging horse, I jumped to the side and ducked to avoid a blade. Both my opponents flew by me and disappeared into the fog before I had a chance to take aim.

Of course, they did return.

As soon as a dark splotch appeared in the white shroud, I shot and a Sdisian fell from his horse. The last of this bizarre company was a cunning fellow. He did not rush right at me, but dismounted and almost got me, leaping out from a completely unexpected direction. Only Gis's outcry warned me of the danger. I didn't have time to use my bow. I had to scamper away from the saber of the dark-skinned freak in the most comical manner. He charged after me, bellowing challengingly, but I have to say that the bandy-legged klutz didn't run nearly as fast as he should have. As soon as there was enough distance between us, I shot the man easily.

"I didn't expect to meet you here," said the courier in lieu of a greeting.

I silently cut the rope from his hands. Then from his feet.

"You dispatched them handily." He nodded toward the dead men. "Something you're used to?"

"How were you caught?" I ignored his question.

"Uh . . ." My companion paused to rub his wrists. "They nicked me with a stupid arrow, and took me down like a duck. I fell off my horse, and they trussed me up. Your help was most welcome. Thank you."

"Not at all," I said dryly. "I wasn't planning to look for you."

"I understand," he said, and chuckled. "I can only thank Melot that you saw the light."

"Get up. We have to leave."

"I'd be happy to, but my head's still buzzing." He groaned, taking out a flask of reska.

"Do you know what happened here? Where everyone went?"

"No. Perhaps they ran, perhaps they were chased, killed, eaten, turned into butterflies, who knows," Gis said morosely. "There's no one here except the Sdisians. No bodies, no traces."

"Well, on the matter of bodies—you're way off. There was one ringing the bell."

I quickly told him about the hanged man.

"That's just the kind of trick they like to play." The courier looked at the dead archer with hatred in his eyes. "They say they are masters at arranging such nastiness."

"Nonsense. The Highborn of Sandon could put

them to shame. And our lads from the frontier garrisons played such tricks on the bastards from the House of Butterfly (one of the Houses of the Highborn. Notable for their cruelty toward human prisoners of war) almost every day."

"You were involved in that war?" he asked with interest.

"I had to be," I replied reluctantly, waiting for a barrage of questions. But he only nodded.

"Right now we are fighting in the north and east, and I didn't expect to see a Sdisian patrol so far to the west of the Empire. How did they manage to penetrate so deep, and to bypass all the patrols and outposts?"

"That's easy. Through the fields and forests. Another thing—what do they want here? Why in the Abyss have they wandered in so far, and just six of them?"

"They could be a preliminary reconnaissance squad. They are marching not far from Crow's Nest. Al'sgara hasn't been attacked yet; perhaps it's her time. We don't actually know how many of them there are."

"And I don't plan to find out." I pulled him to his feet. "Let's go."

"I'm afraid I can't go anywhere until I find Fly. She gave me the slip."

"You're lucky. Your mare didn't run far. I'll be right back."

Having left Gis, I went after the horses and stopped in my tracks when I saw that two more animals had appeared next to Stallion and Fly.

Before I could figure out where such a miracle had come from, something struck my legs and I fell straight on my back, so hard that my teeth clacked. Ignoring the pain, I rolled to the side, began to get to my feet, and once again got a whack to the legs from the invisible something. I fell again, tried to jump up again, simultaneously turning my head in the hopes of seeing my unseen enemy.

This time I was lucky and I saw a man running out of the fog. I raised my bow and almost instantly tossed it aside with a yelp. My weapon flashed with a bright flame and it was only by some miracle that I didn't burn my hands. Meanwhile the stranger was right in my face. He once again struck me down to the ground, and then he pinned me there with his weight and began clawing at my neck with his hands.

"Gotcha!" he wailed in a sepulchral voice.

I tried to resist, but some strange force wouldn't let me move a muscle. Steel fingers squeezed relentlessly at my throat.

"Where are they? Where are the boy and girl? Speak!" yelled the lunatic. He obviously didn't grasp the fact that in just a little while I would never be able to speak to anyone again.

Not once in my life had I fallen into such a bind. Even being led to the gallows was easier. Lungs burning, I tried to pull in just a drop of air. My ears

were buzzing. It was just at that moment that I recognized my enemy—it was none other than the
half-wit Pork from Dog Green. He had changed
greatly, and his eyes were glowing with a white
light.

Coming to my rescue, Gis kicked the idiot in the
face, and this forced him to let go of my neck. I immediately took the opportunity to fight back, and
threw my opponent off of me. He snarled, jumped
at me, and then something unheard-of happened.
The courier took a short, twisted wand inlaid with
red stone from his bag and pointed it at our assailant. Pork twitched once and then froze. His face
contorted, and the next second he fell facedown on
the ground, twitching with convulsions.

"You alive?" Gis asked me as if nothing were the
matter.

I coughed desperately and rubbed my poor neck.
The fool was surprisingly strong. I considered it a
miracle that he hadn't broken my spine.

"Hey! Are you alive?" Gis asked again.

"Thanks to your efforts, wizard," I croaked.
"Thanks to your efforts."

"Well then," he said after a pause. "I'm glad I
don't have to explain anything to you."

"Only a fool . . . would not understand . . . what
kind of people . . . carry twisted wands with rubies."

Gis grinned and suddenly asked, "Do you know
him?"

"Yes. Pork. From the village where I lived for the

last few years. I can't imagine how he came to be here."

At that moment the fool groaned, sat up, shook his head, and looked at us. His eyes were no longer white, but had become blue once again.

"Well, now we'll have a chat." I turned toward him with a determined air.

The cowherd, realizing that he would be beaten, squealed thinly and clasped his hands.

"No! Don't! It wasn't me!" he whined. "Please! I'm good!"

"Ness!" Gis called to me quietly.

"What?" I stopped halfway and looked at him angrily.

"Leave him alone. He's not to blame."

"Not to blame!" agreed Pork and for some reason began looking around cautiously. "It's all Mistress. She made me. Yes!"

"How do you know?" I asked Gis, ignoring the fool's words.

"It's obvious. Your acquaintance shows all the signs of possession. And it's very strange."

"Do you mean to tell me that one of your friends has taken up shop in him?" I asked him incredulously.

"Well, first of all, demons are not my friends. Get that into your head. And secondly, the one bound to him is not a demon. I've never encountered anything like it."

"But now he looks . . ." I wanted to say "normal"

but I realized that such a word didn't really fit the village idiot.

"Not possessed?" continued Gis. "That's not at all surprising. I managed to save the young man from his companion in time. . . . Hey! Hey! Stop!"

I turned around and saw that Pork was running away from us so fast that his heels were on fire. Well sure, why would he wait around until we were done chatting and decided to give him a drubbing? Gis and I ran after him.

The cowherd was quick. He disappeared into the damned fog and for some time we ran aimlessly, hoping to catch him.

"It's useless!" I said finally. "He must have turned aside and we ran past him. Shit! It's like looking for wind in a field!"

I was beginning to regret that I hadn't stabbed the fool in the back with my axe. I wanted to take him alive, and this was the result. Gone, like water in sand. No way would I catch him now.

"I don't mean to upset you, but we need to get out of here as soon as possible." Gis had not parted with his wand.

"Why such haste?" I asked irritably, angry at both him and myself for having lost Pork. "An hour ago I couldn't persuade you to pass this place by."

"You've got to understand the situation, lad." He drew out the words, staring into the fog. "Of course I am not at all averse to staying here, but your friend, or rather, the one who controls him, is weak for the moment, but has quite a bit of real magic. And I, for all my considerable experience, would not want to face him when he finally takes control of that poor man again. So I ask you kindly, stop baring your teeth at me and let's go."

His expression was very troubled, and I decided not to argue.

Less than three hours later we found the road, and by evening we were sitting in a decent roadside tavern and everything that had happened that morning might have seemed like a dream if not for one thing—the fingerprints of that hapless strangler on my neck.

The incident with Pork seemed very, very strange. I kept wondering how he found me and what he wanted. Why did he attack? Who was he asking about? Where did I come into it? At first I didn't recognize him at all. He was dressed far more nicely than usual, and his appearance had changed. It was as if someone fashioned a new face for him. There was quite a noticeable difference between the Pork from before and the current Pork. He little resembled the idiot I'd seen almost every day I was living in Dog Green. He was a completely normal man, if just a little bit off. That, and he had impossibly white eyes.

What? What, the Abyss take me, was going on?

And why did Gis say that the moron was possessed and had magic? The perpetual laughingstock of the whole village—a mage? Don't make me laugh! However, the wizard probably knew better.

That's another of today's surprises—the dusty, gray mouse turned out to be a lion.

I put down my completely untouched mug of shaf and stared grimly at the man who I'd gotten used to calling a courier. He caught my gaze and grinned.

"What is it?" I asked irritably.

"You're a very patient man. You've been silent all day, like a stubborn Je'arre or a proud Highborn. But I can see in your eyes that you have more questions than a Nirit has teeth. Ask me."

"Who are you?"

"Hmm. I thought you already had an idea."

"Pretend I'm ignorant. I don't even know your name."

"You can call me Gis. That's a real name."

"And you—"

"Just talk quieter," he swiftly interrupted. "Why bother these nice people?"

Here he was right. The tavern was full of customers, and if these farmers, traders, travelers, and soldiers from the nearest garrison found out that someone from the Scarlet Order was sitting next to them, who knows what would happen? I think they'd probably only be more alarmed at meeting a necromancer. While the Walkers, the Viceroys, and the Emperor himself recognized the existence of the wizards as a necessary evil, the common folk were afraid of people like Gis.

It is said that the Scarlets possess their own, very strange magic, which has no effect on ordinary people, but works perfectly well on various demons and spirits. It's quite easy to understand why someone who could control such fierce and terrible beings would be dreaded even more than the Damned. The Damned were far away. Beyond the Boxwood Mountains, Nabator, and the Great Waste. But the Scarlets—here they are. Right next to you. And the darkness knows how strangely they'll behave. One thing's for sure—it won't be anything good.

I didn't think that way. I'd never seen the wizards do anything wicked. Even if they wanted to, the Walkers would quickly take them under their authority, since even the strongest tamer of demons was no more dangerous than an ordinary man without his amulets, wand, and books of Invocation. As for the magic, even the weakest Ember could easily overpower a wizard. The wearers of scarlet cloth did not possess the spark. All their abilities were based on long study, good memory, and plenty of artifacts. As some wiseasses joked, with due diligence, even a monkey can learn to master demons.

"You don't really look like a wizard," I said, lowering my voice. "More like a . . ."

"A courier?" His narrow face looked inordinately satisfied.

"Just a little. Why the masquerade?"

"Have you ever tried traveling in scarlet clothing?"

"No."

"I wouldn't recommend it."

As I already said, people have very little love for those who rub elbows with demons. The roads are long and all sorts of nasty things can happen on them. Including a crossbow bolt from the bushes. And not all the demons of the Abyss could save you from that. So here Gis was correct—it would be better to have something more modest than red silk and velvet in reserve for long travels. Like the costume of a courier, for example.

"What compelled the Magister to hit the road?"

He was astonished but he did not hide it. He yanked at his walrus mustache and said, "You never cease to amaze me, lad."

"Right. A simple acolyte would never have a wand with gems of that size."

"Allow me to keep silent about my business."

"But is everything you told us about Gash-Shaku true?"

"Yes. The city is under siege. I barely managed to get out. And everything else is also true."

I nodded grimly.

"I'm glad that you, unlike so many others, do not shy away from me," he said suddenly.

"Should I?"

"Many people do just that."

"Actually, I don't really care who you are, and I care not a whit for the causes of your journey."

"So much the better for both of us. Tell me, that man who squeezed your throat with such abandon, does he always act like that with his friends?"

"I don't really know. I never noticed him do anything of the sort before. I don't understand what happened at all. You said he was connected with demons."

"Did I? I don't recall that."

"I thought you said something about possession?"

"Possession is not caused by creatures from the Abyss, but by spirits."

"What difference does it make to me? Do you have some way of explaining what happened to him?"

Gis frowned, clasped his fingers together, and cracked his knuckles.

"The lad is possessed, as I said. But it is somehow strange. I"—he made a point of highlighting the word—"have never encountered anything like it. And such a case is not mentioned anywhere in the book of Invocation."

"The real question is, where did our village idiot manage to unearth such foul trash?"

"I really don't know. He could have encountered it anywhere. Or it him, for the minds of the mentally ill are always open to such creatures. Are there any ancient burial grounds near your village, or abandoned settlements or anything like that?"

"No. But I think a pig will always find a way to get dirty."

He nodded thoughtfully; then he remembered his plate and looked with dismay at his cold food.

"At first, when I saw the boy, I thought he was a bandit. Then something made me look at him differently. I'm telling you, what I saw amazed me. It was like someone was standing behind him and pulling the strings. And this one had the Gift, no doubt about it. More than enough to incapacitate you. So I didn't hesitate."

"You took your wand and finished the wretch," I concluded for him.

"I'm afraid not," he said gloomily. "I wasn't able to kill it, or even drive it out completely." It was clear that Gis was wounded to the depths of his soul. "It was so far from everything I've experienced before that not a single one of my formulas of expulsion worked. Do you understand what I'm talking about, or should I speak more simply?"

"I understand. Go on."

"Well, anyway, I managed to cut the thread for a short time and give the lad his freedom. You saw how he came to."

"What happened to the spirit?"

"It's keeping its head down for the time being, I suppose."

"And you can't beat it?"

"You can beat anything. The question is how. I suppose if you destroyed the physical shell that holds the spirit, there might be some chance of getting rid of it."

I just ground my teeth. This was the second time I was regretting that I hadn't sent the cowherd to the Blessed Gardens. I should have done it the moment Midge dragged him out of the bushes into that accursed glade.

"In fact, we were lucky. If I hadn't caught the spirit by surprise, it could have all ended badly. I had a thought. Were there any Walkers or Embers in your village?"

"What would they have to do there?"

"Hmmm. . . . Well, they could just be passing through. I'm just trying to figure out where such a strange entity came from. I'd bet my wand it was a mage in life."

"Anything's possible."

"So you haven't seen anyone like that? Strange." He lowered his bushy eyebrows.

"What's so strange?"

"I have a hypothesis, a guess," he immediately corrected himself, thinking I didn't know the meaning of the first word. "If a mage died next to your Pork, then his spirit could very well have made use of the opportunity and . . ." He didn't finish and, sighing bitterly, started in on his cold food. But I sat there, neither living nor dead. Unlike Gis, I knew what kind of mage had died in Dog Green.

A Damned!

The murderer of Sorita!

Typhoid!

And Pork, as far as I recall, was not very far from her at the time.

Was I right? Did that snake really manage the impossible and survive after the attack of the Healer and my arrows? Rumor has always had it that the Damned cling to life, but that's just insane! And if she really did survive and shift herself into Pork, then it's quite clear just who the "cowherd" was looking for. Shen and Layen!

"Hey! My friend. Are you all right?" Gis inquired solicitously, while pouring gravy over his meat.

"Yes," I said, and I forced a smile.

The cowherd stopped glancing back over his shoulder every second the day after that horrible Mistress, who had wronged and terrified Pork for so long, disappeared. After he ran into Pars the carpenter, who had nearly beat him, his lady no longer appeared. At first Pork didn't believe in his good fortune and kept waiting for the terrible woman to return at any moment. He shivered like an aspen leaf in a strong fall wind from anticipation. He was scared, hungry, his whole body hurt, and he wanted to go home.

For a while the half-wit hid in the village, fearing to bump into the savage carpenter who was chasing after him, but when the danger had passed he even dared to sneak into one of the empty houses and steal a few onions. That somewhat assuaged his hunger and Pork set out to return home. Even though there he had to deal with his father's beatings and the ridicule of the villagers, he was always well fed and not terrified by the horrible living dead.

Having come to this decision, he left the village, but he headed in the completely opposite direction from that which would lead him to Dog Green. Unaware of this, the half-wit confidently walked through the endless fields. He didn't meet a single living soul along the road, not counting the multitudes of squirrels to be found in this region. Pork was so hungry that he tried to catch at least one of them. Regardless of the fact that the animals seemed fat and clumsy, they ran quickly and immediately hid in their holes. Pork shoved his hand into the nearest hole and his finger was bitten mercilessly. Just then he happened to look over his shoulder and see Mistress's face, deformed with fury.

Then the pain came.

15

The last time I beheld these legendary walls was seven years ago, after Layen and I assassinated the Walker and hastily fled from the southern capital. In the rays of the rising sun the strong fortifications, towers, and temple spires of Al'sgara seemed carved out of rose marble. It was a captivating sight, to say the least. Especially for those who were seeing the great thousand-year-old city for the very first time.

The Sculptor himself had once had a hand in the construction of the defensive walls and towers. He imbued these ancient stones with so much magic that no one in the entire history of the Empire had taken the city by storm or destroyed the great mage's creation. Al'sgara had survived the Nabatorians and the navy of the Golden Mark, rebellious Viceroys, the Dark Revolt, and the War of the Necromancers.

The enormous city was surrounded by six fortified rings. The three outermost rings were built several centuries after the death of the Sculptor—Al'sgara had grown in prosperity with each passing year, and had long since passed beyond the first three rings. The growth continued and now the current Viceroy was not in much of a hurry to empty the coffers to defend the soft underbelly of the district that the locals call Dovetown, and visitors call Newtown. However, until this past year there had been no need to defend this part of Al'sgara—the Empire hadn't been at war with anyone for a long time. Now there was fortification, but it was too late. They wouldn't have time.

The Pearl of the South is spread out along the wide, green valley of the river Ors, which originates in the Boxwood Mountains. Narrow and fast near the peaks, here its banks stretch a quarter of a league across before it flows into the sea at a leisurely, dreamy pace. The city itself is located between the sea and the Ors. The western part abuts Moon Bay, where the port is, and the southern part stretches along the river.

I was riding along the river bank, now and then glancing at Al'sgara, which was located on the opposite shore. Despite the early hours, quite a few people had gathered at the ferry. The motley crowd was discussing that most important of topics—the war. They were speaking of the newly reassembled Second Army, which was stationed one march away from the city, and about whether the Nabatorians and the frightful necromancers would reach here or if they could be stopped at Gash-Shaku, the Isthmuses of Lina, or the Steps of the Hangman. Judging from the conversation, not much had changed since the moment we met Gis. He had told us the same news and it all boiled down to one thing—our forces were still standing and were not planning to retreat.

As I had expected, not a word was said about the Damned. I don't know if it was because the Sextet were in no hurry to show themselves or if the Walkers were in no rush to announce to the common people who they had to face. In my view the latter was very wise. Fear defeats an army no less than swords and magic.

I was able to cross quickly; three sols to the ferry guard allowed me to skip the line.

"From the south?" he asked, checking one of the coins with his teeth.

"Yes."

"And how's it there?"

"Quiet as a swamp. And here?"

"The same. Get going. I don't have time for chatter."

I led a recalcitrant Stallion onto the gangway. The ferry smelled of damp wood, oil for the chains, horses, and fish. My neighbor was a thin man with a wart on his nose—a petty trader of cloth. During the leisurely ride, I questioned him well and heard much of what was going on in the city. The situation was not good. But I didn't care. I just had to take care of business and then slip away, letting all of it go up in blue flames.

"Prices are three times as high as they were in the spring. The Viceroy increased taxes. The Guards are acting up." The trader continued his complaints.

"And what about the port. Is it closed?" I asked, my heart freezing in my chest.

"The port? No, the ships are sailing. But not often. Very few foreigners are visiting right now. They don't want to get stuck here. Only those who are greedy. They make a lot of profit on their goods. Mostly sailors from Sino and smugglers. The strait of the Golden Mark is blockaded by the Nabatorian fleet. They say they're letting through all the ships except for ours."

I had learned everything I cared to, so I listened to the rest of the unnamed trader's complaints with half an ear. I could take a breath and relax a bit. Take a load off. The port was open; the sea lanes, for the most part, were not in danger. There are other places to sail besides the Golden Mark. At least the ships were sailing. And that meant I'd be able to convince some captain to take us onboard and get us far away from here. Just a trifling thing remained before our departure—to find Joch and convey Layen's and my displeasure with his actions.

The ferry wheel dragged the thick chain out of the dark water with a thunderous clanging, and the shore came closer and closer. I could already make out the faces of those standing on the pier.

There were a lot of people there to greet us. Among them were those who wanted to go to the opposite shore, mainly merchants transporting goods. There were also porters, barkers for the city inns, and, of course, Guardsmen. Only a blind man could ignore the dozen lads in red-and-white uniforms. Four had crossbows, while the rest carried formidable glaives. The sun was shining at our backs and in their faces, so the Guardsmen could only make out our faces once the strong men on the ferry stopped rotating the lever that caused the wheel to gather the chain.

"Here we are then, people!" yelled the old ferryman rakishly. "Please step out onto the shore. Kuha, change the team!"

I waited for the pedestrians to leave the ferry, and then they opened the horse corrals and I took Stallion's reins. He was clearly annoyed that I'd forced him to ride on such an unreliable vessel and he nearly took a bite out of me. I had to keep an eye on him.

One of the Guardsmen bestowed a serious gaze on me but, not noticing anything suspicious, lost all interest. I'm sure the Viceroy put men at all the entrances to the city just in case enemy spies tried to get into Al'sgara. Or a necromancer. One or the other would cause all sorts of trouble. And if they started a siege, life in Al'sgara would go down the drain.

Somehow I doubt that the Guards could detect even the worst spy, not to mention those wearing white robes. And if one of the Damned should deign to come here . . .

I shuddered at this last thought. The face of the beautiful Typhoid, disfigured by Shen's magic, appeared before my eyes and then . . . the half-wit Pork. If he (or she) came to the city, I'd be almost afraid to imagine what might happen. To me. To Layen. I could feel it in my soul—we were far more interesting to her than the fall of all the cities in the Empire. I'd have to move fast to avoid such an unpleasant encounter.

Joch, Joch, right now you're the biggest bone in my throat. You couldn't conceive of leaving us alone, and thus the heads of Gray and Weasel will never be safe. If you offer up ten thousand sorens, you can always find people willing to kill a thousand people, let alone just two. And that means we'll never be left in peace and we'll have to be always on the alert, looking over our shoulders, waking up in the night and waiting, waiting, until that happy man comes who will catch us and pull in that most deserved jackpot. Personally, I would like to live to a ripe old age, and any three-fingered cretins standing in my path will just have to be dealt with.

Apart from the main road that leads to the Lettuce Gates of Al'sgara, Dovetown was an insane maze of alleys, lanes, side streets, and thoroughfares. If you were not a local, it was easy to get lost. The majority of this part of Newtown (the dirtiest, by the way, of all those that have grown up under the Outer wall) consisted of one-story buildings placed at random, with no sense of order. So any kind of reasonable route was out of the question. There were homes, stores, workshops, stables, cattle yards, and the Abyss knew what else. The Viceroy really was a fool for having drawn out the question of fortifying Dovetown for so long. After all, only a fool could hope that Nabator and Sdis would bypass Al'sgara altogether.

I wasn't planning on taking a long stroll through the district. I had absolutely nothing to accomplish here; my goal was beyond the walls. So I kept to the main road, taking no turns, merely looking from side to side. Over the past seven years, this suburb had grown in breadth, taking over the entire right shore of the Ors, and it had become even more dirty, chaotic, and unpleasant. I held no love for this little neighborhood, even though I had to work in it a few times for the guild. Those who settle here don't have enough money, experience, success, or luck to move beyond the Wall, as it was simply called here. I stuck to the main street so that I could get to the Lettuce Gates as soon as possible.

I noticed the man walking behind me accidentally.

By an ancient shop that sold all sorts of rubbish, I had to duck so as not to hit my head on the iron sign. It turned out brilliantly, even though the shopkeeper smothered me with abuse for stumbling into his wares. When I turned around to say something vile in reply, I saw the sneaker who was tailing me out of the corner of my eye. I'd had the honor of beholding this short lad when I exited the ferry. He'd been leaning against the wheel of a wagon sunk into the mud, blinking from the morning sun hitting his

face. A man like any other. I didn't notice anything
unusual about him, so I ignored him. But I shouldn't
have.

I didn't show that I'd observed my shadow and
turned onto the next curving side street. I stretched
until my back cracked, "accidentally" turned
around—and my tracker had disappeared. Was it really as it seemed, and he was simply walking the
same route as I? Odd. It had been a long time since
my intuition failed me.

For the next several minutes I rode along the side
street as it curved in front of a line of wooden houses
on the right, until it led me back to the main street.
My unknown friend was already here, hanging
about a shop that sold sausages.

Gotcha!

We made brief eye contact. As soon as I rode a few
dozen yards away, the lad once again trudged after
me.

Not too smart!

I started whistling a dissolute tune, trying to figure out who had set a tail on me. Why was he following me and what did he want? Had he taken a
liking to Stallion and decided to deprive a visitor of
his superfluous livestock? Or was it something else?
This was the first time I'd ever seen him, that's for
sure. Who would he be running to after he found
out where I'd stopped? Joch? Mols? Bounty hunters? The Walkers? Or did he prefer to do it all on
his own, without worrying about others' greedy

mouths? That's what I would do. But that's me, and that is him. After observing how the greenhorn followed me, I came to the conclusion that this was one bird who didn't fly very high. In any case, he didn't possess a talent for surveillance. Nor any brains either, if he had the brilliant idea to take me on alone. Even old Midge wasn't prone to such idiotic behavior.

I'd have to ask this man a few questions. Just letting him go might be fraught with serious consequences, especially if the half-wit got it into his head to ask around about a certain man's arrival in town.

It was less than two blocks to the gate, and I decided not to wait. I directed Stallion to the first more or less decent inn I knew. I liked the owner of the establishment—he wasn't too much of a crook. So I quickly rented a room and a stall in the stables, paying a month in advance, and asked him to look after my horse and to give him the bag of oats I'd promised him. Then I told him I wouldn't be back anytime soon and limped out onto the street.

My tail was waiting for me. I had to go in the opposite direction of the one I desired. By the Wall there was little chance of coming across a vacant passageway where no one would interrupt our conversation, but I'd find a likely place closer to the river. And there I'd get to ask some questions.

Knari, nicknamed Hamster, had a good memory for faces. So he almost jumped up when he saw the blond man who was arriving on the ferry take a black horse from its pen. The lad could barely force himself to sit in place as he tried not to look at the newcomer. Despite the fact that almost ten years had passed since the time when he, still a very young boy, had caught a glimpse of the man while he was talking to Stump, there was not the slightest doubt—it was Gray.

Knari had heard that a whole lot of money was being offered for the Giiyan's head but until today he hadn't believed he was alive. Seven years had passed since they found the burnt bodies of Gray and his girlfriend, and until last month no one had any doubt that the people who had ordered the hit on the Walker had done away with the assassins. Now though, upon catching sight of the Giiyan, Knari not only believed that the man was alive, but he believed in his own lucky star as well.

He waited until the horseman rode away from the river and then hastened after him, at first fearing that the Giiyan would notice him. But minute after minute passed, and the rider had no idea he had a tail. Knari sneered contemptuously—turns out Gray wasn't such a dangerous man after all. As always, rumors were exaggerated far more than they should be. And it seemed like he didn't have any weapons on him: no bow, no sword. True, he could be hiding a knife under the fabric of his dirty green jacket, but

Hamster wasn't all that worried. He'd heard over and over that the Giiyan was a great shot, but no one had ever given any indication that he could do his work with another weapon. Plus, Knari had two knives on him—a throwing knife up his sleeve and a straight Nabatorian knife under his shirt. He'd used the latter many times, and he rightly considered himself a consummate master of knife fighting.

At one point Gray left the main street, but Hamster didn't bother to follow him. He knew that those side streets would lead the Giiyan out onto the main street and that it was better to wait than to take a risk. He didn't have to wait long. From the side street the rider appeared, looked around in surprise, clearly not understanding how he got there, and after a short hesitation directed his horse toward the Lettuce Gates.

Hamster came to a decision. He wouldn't tell anyone that he'd found the blond. Neither Mols nor Joch. The crumbs they'd pay him for the news were nothing compared to the five thousand sorens he'd get for the murder of this dolt. That Gray was a dolt, he had no doubt. Knari had no idea where the rumors that he was dangerous had come from. Judging from all he saw, he'd be easy to take care of. Then he could bring his head to Joch in exchange for the reward. The littlest thing was required for a cushy life—to wait for an opportune moment and cut the blond's throat.

Who, by the way, was acting like a complete

hayseed. He was looking around ceaselessly, as if he'd never been in a city before. Then he did something completely idiotic; he decided to stop at some rundown inn, as if he couldn't just go through the Wall and find decent lodgings in Outer City. Apparently, he was really bad with money.

When Gray leaped from his horse, Knari was delighted to see something he hadn't noticed at the ferry landing—the man was quite lame in his left leg. He wouldn't be able to move very quickly at all. Knari had it in the bag.

He prepared himself for a long wait, but that's not how it happened. The blond left the inn quite quickly and, still limping, headed toward the river. After a while he turned off the main street, and now Knari had to work so as not to lose sight of his victim, nor to be seen by him.

Gray wandered aimlessly through the streets for some time, getting deeper and deeper into Dovetown. There were fewer people around, and the stench of sewage and garbage thrown into the street became stronger. Then Hamster heard the cries of seagulls and realized that they had strayed into the fishing quarter, not far from where the Ors emptied into the sea.

Suddenly the assassin stopped (Knari had to cling to a wall) and then turned into a narrow alley between two houses. He had to wait a moment so that he wouldn't come face-to-face with Gray if he decided to turn back.

He didn't.

So without wasting any more time, Knari went after him. He passed into the alleyway and walked forward a few steps; then he stopped short. He was in a small channel that was enclosed on two sides by the walls of the stone houses. Fifteen steps in front of where Knari now stood, the river began. Gray wasn't there.

It seemed that the blond had managed to dupe him. He'd jumped into the river and now he could be anywhere. The Abyss! He's gone. Disappeared without a trace. Knari cursed.

"Hey," came a soft voice from behind him. "Aren't you looking for me?"

Hamster didn't choke, and as soon as his throwing knife slid out of his sleeve into his palm, he whipped around and flicked the weapon with his wrist without raising his arm. The Giiyan turned out to be far more skilled than his unfortunate stalker thought. He was no longer in the same place and the throw was for nothing.

Knari swore a second time and grabbed his knife.

"Not smart," said Gray.

A small axe appeared in his hands and then everything happened very quickly. The blond was no longer limping and he moved so fast that Hamster missed the moment when his enemy appeared next to him. The unlucky killer lunged at Gray's stomach with his knife, but by some miracle he had already turned to the side, and at the same moment Knari felt a strong blow fall on his right wrist. The Nabatorian knife fell into the muck. The lad stared dully at his useless weapon and then turned his gaze to his hand. His wrist was disfigured. His little and ring fingers were missing.

Only now did the pain come.

He groaned, but even then he didn't lose his self-control. He reached for the knife lying on the ground with his left hand and instantly felt a terrible pain in his right knee. His vision went dark; he howled and, without understanding how it came to be, he found himself on the ground.

"Are you from the guild?" The blond didn't raise his voice.

Hamster had enough stubbornness to tell the Giiyan off in fairly colorful language. Another wave of pain pierced his hand.

"It seems like it's your intent to do stupid things. Tell me who sent you and we'll part as friends."

Knari was gasping for breath, and a deluge of tears was rolling down his cheeks. He'd never experienced anything like this. Finally, through his coughing and tears he managed to gasp, "My friends will be here at any moment, and then you'll be done for."

He raised himself up on his elbows and a crushing blow came down on his nose. Something crunched ominously. His face instantly became hot and wet. Blood started dripping down his lips and into his beard. Knari had no strength left to scream, so he whimpered softly.

"You're being stubborn for nothing, lad." The Giiyan was standing right over him. "I'll still find out what kind of beast you are and who feeds you."

Again, the pain in his crippled hand.

"I don't like doing this, but you leave me no choice. You still have one finger on your right hand and five on your left. I had to hone my skills in Sandon. Believe me, the Highborn screamed even louder than you. I promise you, it will be quite unpleasant. And don't lie and tell me that you have help—I saw that you were working alone. No one will interfere with us. Sooner or later you'll tell me everything."

I was just concluding my conversation with the sheep when some conscientious person called a patrol of watchmen. I had to finish the hapless killer off quickly and get out of there. I missed the guardians of order literally by a minute. I heard the clatter, dove into a convenient doorway, and five watchmen ran past me. I waited for a moment and then walked away. I needed to leave the fishermen's quarter as soon as I could.

Fairly swiftly but without drawing attention to myself, I made my way to the main street and then headed for the Wall at a leisurely pace. From here the Lettuce Gate was a stone's throw away.

You could say that I was lucky. The lad had been working without support and had been too stupid and greedy to run for help. He decided to do it all by himself. A small fry, one of Mols's hangers-on. Hopefully the head of the guild wouldn't be too upset that I cut up one of his employees. Unlikely, as old Mols didn't take too kindly to those who tried to conduct business behind his back.

The most important thing I learned from my chat with that stupid, stubborn ass was that it was nothing more than chance that he ran into me. No one was waiting for me in Al'sgara. And he'd heard nothing of Layen.

The Lettuce Gates were the last ones in the southern Wall and the closest to the sea and the river. Unlike the other five gates that led into the city, there was rarely a crowd near these and it was much quicker to pass through them. The Guardsmen there had never been known for their vigilance or zeal.

The sun was high in the sky and the outer Wall was no longer rose-colored, but had taken on its customary yellow-gray color. Though the Sculptor had not had a hand in its construction it looked sufficiently solemn and reliable. It rose high above me, built from massive stone blocks. It would not be easy to take such a wall by storm, and if you did, there were five more fortified walls beyond it, and three of them had been built by the strongest mage in the history of the Empire. The enemy would have a very difficult time getting into Al'sgara. Of course, that was unless someone decided to let them in. It's well known that most towns and castles fall not by storm, but by hunger, disease, and the fools who rush to open the gates and throw themselves on the mercy of the victors. The capital of the south might be saved by the fact that even if the first walls fell or traitors allowed the enemy into the Outer City, the inhabitants could always take cover behind the next stage of defense. Hightown and Second City, where the main warehouses, the palace of the Viceroy, the Tower of the Walkers, and the Guards' barracks were located, were practically impossible to take by force. Probably the only thing that could cause Al'sgara to fall was hunger. And that's why a continuous stream of wagons full of provisions was flowing into the Gates. Apparently, the city elders were buying up all the food in the province.

During the time I was away, some changes had occurred. Six guards had been added. In addition, a few swordsmen in full armor were standing by the gate, and beyond them was a crowd of a dozen crossbowmen. No one was paying them any heed, and they were playing dice on a barrel of reska. If there was this much security at the entrance of the gatehouse, then I was willing to swear by my right hand that there was just as much on the other side of the Wall. If not more.

The Guardsmen, irritable from the heat, examined each approaching wagon critically. As they should. The Abyss knows what the Whites might bring into the city. The undead or one of those Fish. If it burst somewhere in Hightown, there would be hell to pay.

I stood in a barely moving line. I wasn't too happy about that, of course, but in this case I preferred not to rush things. There was no reason to attract attention to myself.

Today, it seems, everyone was talking only about the war. Each rumor was more absurd than the next. While I was waiting my turn, I had more than enough time to get tired of these conversations.

When only five people remained in the line ahead of me, I noticed someone I should have taken note of from the very beginning. Behind the dice-playing crossbowmen, hidden in the dense shadows of one of the two massive gates, stood a middle-aged woman wearing a blue mantle with a red circle on her chest. She was talking unreservedly to the captain of the Guards and casting intent looks at the people walking by her.

A Walker!

Things were taking a bad turn. I had to keep as far away as possible from bearers of the spark despite the fact that seven years had gone by. Certain people have long memories. I'd learned that well enough this morning, when that filthy little toad got on my tail. He'd seen me only once, and he recognized me even though I'd acquired a beard during my travels from Dog Green.

Leaving the line would be too conspicuous; then they'd really notice me.

"State your name, where you're from, your destination," the exhausted Guardsman asked me.

It was too late to run.

"I'm a craftsman. Pars the carpenter. From Oglad. I'm here by invitation."

I named one of the less important lords of the city council. As I expected, he didn't bother to check.

"Do you know the way?"

"I've been here before."

"Then get going." The soldier lost all interest in me.

I thanked him and entered the coolness of the gatehouse. The Walker slid her eyes over me and continued her conversation with the captain. I breathed a sigh of relief. The first thing she checked for was the Gift, and only then did she examine faces. I was lucky.

There was a massive corridor running through the Wall. Footbridges trailed along under the ceiling, where archers could be placed if the enemy swept through the outer gates. There were arrow loops in the walls, and two raised steel portcullises. After fifty paces I got through the corridor, passed by the interior gates, which were in no way inferior in terms of strength to the exterior gates, and found myself in Outer City. As I'd assumed, there were just as many guards at the exit of the Lettuce Gates as at the entrance. If a commotion suddenly arose near where the Walker was standing, then the lads here would have time to either go help or lower the portcullises.

My beloved city can sleep peacefully. For the time being, at any rate.

My goal lay beyond the second wall, between the harbor and Birdtown. This part of Al'sgara was called Birdtown because a community of Je'arre had lived there for quite some time. Their neighborhood began at the top of a giant hill and slowly descended toward the sea.

The flyers had an unquenchable passion for construction. They erected a vast assortment of towers in the district. Thick, thin, tall, short, spired, steepled, stone, wood, finished, and under construction. There was one every thirty yards or so. As the more spiteful critics said, Birdtown had long since surpassed Hightown when it came to the number of towers. Perhaps that's true. The Je'arre love to take off from high perches.

The quarter was surprisingly empty. I didn't see a single representative of the race. Only the numerous inhabitants of other parts of the city and, of course, the sullen Guardsmen. Of the latter, however, there were a surprising number. What happened to have driven so many keepers of the peace here? In my memory there was never a time when the Je'arre sat in their homes and the skies over Al'sgara were empty.

According to legend, the flyers came to the lands of the Empire from somewhere beyond the Great Waste many centuries ago. I have no idea what forced this nation to flit from their ancestral roost and come visit us, but they were accepted, albeit without much enthusiasm. It had seemed like a good idea to the current ruler to use the winged folk as messengers and flying archers. The beggarly Sons of the Sky dealt with this, but they were often at one another's throats and they liked to create minor havoc among the other peoples of the Empire. As a result, they were politely asked to leave Al'sgara, Gash-Shaku, and Okni, and were given a fairly large plot of uninhabited land between Sandon and Uloron. People mockingly called the place where the Je'arre had been sent to live the Promised Land. Everyone knew full well that the birds were caught between the rock of Uloron and the hard place of Sandon. The Highborn would undoubtedly chew up the Empire's untrustworthy allies and spit out their feathers.

To universal surprise, the Sons of the Sky withstood the pointy-eared elves. More than that, they eventually helped our army drive them from the Country of Oaks (another name for Uloron) into Sandon. And when the Emperor finalized a perpetual peace with the Del'be (the King of the Highborn. Currently, the Del'be is Vaske of the House of Strawberry) twelve years ago, life in the Promised Land became completely calm and carefree. A few clever people even wanted to take the fertile territory back, but the Je'arre showed their teeth and were left in peace.

However, not all the Sons of the Sky went to live in the east of the country. A large community remained in Al'sgara. The City Council agreed to tolerate them because a quarter of the revenues in the city treasury came from the textiles the flyers wove. Just as splendid as eastern silk, they are worth a staggering amount of money and ships sail into port for their sake from all around the world. Part of the proceeds, of course, fall into the greedy hands of the City Council and the Viceroy. It would be foolish of the powerful, self-satisfied fellows to turn away such a remarkable cash cow.

Birdtown came to an end. I stopped and looked at the sloping pavement, the white homes of the harbor, the distant port, and the dark blue haze of the sea. To my right, wedged in between a tall tower with three spires and a ramshackle tavern, stood a two-story building. On the first story was a shop selling Je'arrean silk, and three of its four windows were shuttered.

Strange.

I walked to the end of the street and then paused. I waited a bit to check if someone was following me or not. After five minutes, sure that I was not being followed, I turned and pushed on a heavy door.

A brass bell over my head rang contrarily, and I found myself in a murky room. There was obviously not enough light from the street, and the owners were in no hurry to light all the torches they had. Only two were lit—the one hanging to the left of me and the one located at the far end of the shop, by the stairs leading to the second floor. I could not help but appreciate the beauty and elegance of this solution. On the one hand, all those who enter from the street fall into a circle of light and are visible at a glance; on the other hand, the distant light strikes the visitor in the eyes, and it takes a bit more than a second to become accustomed to it. That's more than enough time for the owners hiding in the shadows to decide if the stranger is dangerous or not. And to take appropriate action.

I quickly stepped to the left, leaving the illuminated circle, and blinked several times as I'd been taught, chasing away the multicolored specks in front of my eyes.

A quiet laugh came out of the gloom.

"You haven't lost your skills over the years, have you, Gray?"

"That would be an impermissible luxury for me, Jola."

Another laugh.

"If you'd be so kind as to lower the latch. I don't want us to be bothered by casual shoppers."

"Nonsense." There was a dry cough to the right. "After your kvinsmen played such a dirty trickva, you won't entice anyone here for all the kvold in the Empire."

"I swear by the wind!" Jola squealed. "No wingless leech is going to tell me anything!"

"Hey, I'm your partner, chickvadee." The one who had so infuriated the Je'arre spoke the words strangely. Human speech was very difficult for him. "I'm tellinkva you akvain. The ones livinkva in the Promised Land have lost their minds."

"I've never regretted that we are partners." She calmed down quickly. "As for the clans, it's their business. I'm not going to pay for others' mistakes."

"But you will, sister. The humans are very ankvary at those who have winkvas."

"Has there ever been a day when they haven't spat at the Sons of the Sky? This is not the first time, nor the last, I swear by the wind."

"Now it's all much more serious."

Listening to the squabble of the old partners, I lowered the latch and, walking past the bales of scarlet and silver cloth, each worth at least eighty, if not a hundred sorens, I made my way to a massive table. One of the chairs was free, the other was taken.

A small woman was seated in it. I knew her height very well—if she stood up the crown of her head would barely reach the middle of my chest. Jola was a Je'arre, and like all members of her race she was fragile, thin boned, almost airy. A narrow, unattractive face, tapering to her chin, sharply defined cheekbones, an aquiline nose, and black eyes. Her shaved head was covered in complex and incomprehensible (to me) tattoos, which indicated that Jola belonged to the Fire Clan; it seemed absurdly large for such narrow shoulders in the dim light. The fingers of her thin hands were long and tipped with violet finger-nails. Or claws. Depends on who you ask.

And of course, she had wings—massive wings, covered in red feathers. Right now they were folded behind her back, but I could well imagine how the Je'arre would use them to soar through the sky.

Jola was frowning so that the corners of her eyes wrinkled, observing me.

"Come closer. I swear by the wind, I don't believe my old eyes. Have you really come here from the Abyss to annoy me again? Ktatak, do you see who's come to our humble abode?"

"I do." The voice again came from the gloom. "It seems the rumors were not false."

"So it seems. Gray wound everyone round his fingers and disappeared for many years. Didn't even warn his best friends. Ai-ai-ai. How mean, don't you think?"

"Indeed."

I remained silent, allowing them to have a bit of fun at my expense.

"And now, after I wept all those tears I harvested over my long life, you show up like a Mort out of the sand, grinning brazenly! That's gratitude for you!"

"Indeed," agreed Ktatak.

"I'm sure you were delighted at my death, you old crow."

She clucked indignantly, shifted her wings, collected her cards from the table, and began to shuffle them briskly. Meanwhile, I sat down, spied a jug of wine and without asking permission, poured some for myself into an empty mug. Jola twitched her eyebrows in displeasure, but, uncharacteristically, said nothing. She handed me a deck. Following the usual ritual, I took the topmost card. I looked at it. The Key. I showed her. She nodded and took it.

"The past? The future?"

"The future."

"Near? Distant?"

"Near."

"Choose a deck."

I picked the fourth to the right of the ten lying on the table. All the others were sent away. She began laying out the spread.

"It's very arrogant to return to a place where you are considered dead," said the Je'arre.

"And stupid!" Ktatak couldn't resist adding.

"They're looking for you, Gray. And not so that you will return the money. Mols, Joch, the witches from Hightown. Not to mention the throngs who want to earn a little cash at your expense."

"A lot of kvash," said her partner.

"So much that I'm tempted to fly up there and sing in someone's ear."

"Singkva!" There was a scuffling in the dark corner, and then a jarring laugh rang out. "Don't flatter yourself, partner. You kvan only kvaroak."

"May you be blind in both eyes, you miserable

leech!" she muttered wickedly, waving her fist at Ktatak. "The spread isn't very good, Gray."

I looked at the table. The Key was striving toward the Knife, but was overpowered by the Fortress. The Tower loomed over them.

"There's something to think about, huh?" muttered Jola.

"I don't understand any of this." I could only shrug.

"What a fool. You could have learned it a long time ago. Something"—she tapped a purple claw on the Fortress—"is preventing the implementation of your plans. The Tower stands over everything. Oo-oo-oo," she whined in disappointment, realizing that I was in no hurry to gasp. "My dear, I'm beginning to wonder how you managed to survive after that debacle you arranged in this wretched town. Even a blockhead like Ktatak knows what the Tower signifies. What does the Tower signify, Ktatak?"

"The Walkvers, oh wise one!" said the Je'arre's partner with obvious sarcasm, but she chose to ignore it.

"Oh," I said profoundly.

She hissed angrily, thinking that I didn't have a sufficiently respectful attitude toward the magical cards. And it's true; I didn't really believe in the bullshit on multicolored pieces of thick paper. It's not magic, but charlatanism. However, among the Sons of the Sky the art of fortune telling is highly valued, and it wasn't all that difficult for me to indulge the old winged witch.

"It's all so much worse." Jola clicked her tongue woefully. "Never in my life have I seen such a bad spread. One card is superimposed over another and bound to the third. You, no doubt, are the Key."

"I'm flattered," I muttered.

"And here are five new guests." She flipped over more cards that were laying facedown. "The Fool and another four Knives. All very close to you."

"I'll be careful."

"And another Tower! A white one!"

"You sure it's not another Walker?" I frowned.

"You're makving a muddle of your kvame, chickvadee," said Ktatak. "You always insist that the Tower kvan only play one role."

"I'm not muddling anything. It's possible in this combination."

"Stupid kvarows." He couldn't help himself.

"Be silent, you leech!"

"What about that kvard?"

"A white Tower may not signify a Walker. In this position it can be interpreted as life, virtue, health, or a priest, a Healer, a virgin—"

"And yet another thousand thinkvas," Ktatak interrupted.

Jola snorted in disdain, her fingers flashing with unimaginable speed. For several minutes the flyer placed out cards until a fanciful spread was laid out on the table. She inverted the cards, laid them one on top of the other, shifted them, piled them, and spread them out until the final product was worked out.

The path from the Key to the Knife was, as before, overlapped by the Fortress. Over all these hovered the Tower. Next to the Key, fit snugly against it, lay four Knives, the Fool, and the Tower the Je'arre called white. Nearby were two Swords, two Demons, and seven facedown cards. One of the facedown cards was located next to the Key (as far as I could recall, according to the rules it should cover the other), five surrounded the central part of the spread, and the last, alone, was on the very edge of the table.

"Well then, let's see what the pattern will show us."

Out of the corner of my eye I saw a movement in the gloom. Ktatak was also curious.

A lilac nail hooked the card lying next to the Key and turned it over.

"The Maid." Ktatak laughed hollowly. "I don't doubt that at all, partner."

Jola chuckled knowingly and laid the new card on top of the Key.

"The Maid casts out the Fool. He's too weak to resist her. Though now the little lady is dependent upon the Tower," she said, and then she moved the Fool to the circle where the five facedown cards were still lying. Now there were six. "Well? Should we reveal them?"

"Don't tease," was the grumbled reply from the gloom.

The first of the five inverted cards was Death. The second, to my great surprise, was also Death. Ktatak cleared his throat quietly. Jola thoughtfully shook her head. The third card—Death. The fourth—Death. I had no doubt about the fifth. I knew what it would be.

"Death."

Now the center of the spread created by the Je'arre was surrounded by five Deaths and one Fool.

"I swear by the wind! It cannot be! It. Can. Not. Be," whispered the winged one.

"Do you really mean that?" her partner protested.

"Yes! I! You're an idiot, you leech! In the Great Cards there are ten decks. In each deck there are a hundred cards. The spread involves no more than forty. Death is a high card. Like the Tower, it rarely comes into play. And to have two Towers and five Deaths all at once, and in the company of the Fool! Next to them he becomes very strong. Strange."

"I guess you made a mistake," I comforted her.

"I'm never mistaken in this, Gray!" she snapped, and then returned her gaze to the pattern. The Je'arre stretched out her thin hand and, holding her breath, turned over the last, solitary card that was lying beyond the boundaries of the spread.

"The Thief!" grunted Ktatak. He sounded shocked.

"The Dancer!" She gasped.

"Excuse me?" I asked for clarification.

None of the other cards had made such an impression on her as this one did. Jola was far too overwhelmed by what she saw, so Ktatak had to step in.

"It's a kvomplicated kvard, my friend. One in a thousand. And if it kvomes out in the spread, it usually has no effeckvat. Actually, it never has any effeckvat. All previous times my partner kvast it aside. But apparently now the Thief is in the spread."

"This time you're right, leech. Death, the Fortress, three Knives, and the Tower with the Key in this position gives life to the Thief."

"And why is it a Dancer?" I frowned.

Once again it was Ktatak who explained. "It's the birds' little idol. The Sons of the Skvay believe that he kvareated this world. The Thief symbolizes their kvod."

"I see that you've become a true expert on the Great Cards," I joked.

"If you'd lived side by side with her for as longkva as I have, you'd be full of it, too."

We both thought this joke was funny enough to laugh. Jola did not join in. She was muttering under her breath, checking the position of the cards, trying to determine if some error had crept into them.

"Well, what should I expect in the near future?"

The Je'arre looked at me irritably and replied reluctantly, "I don't know."

"Ah! Ah!" Ktatak was simply bursting with joy. "Has Kvagun really kvandescended to hear my prayers and kvive me such a kvift in my old age? I kvan die happy now that you've finally kvanfessed your own inadekvacy!"

She jerked her wings in irritation, glanced at me and again, uncharacteristically, said nothing in reply.

"I was wrong. The spread can't be true." The Je'arre swept the cards from the table, in one motion destroying the complex pattern she'd created with such care. "Today is not the best day to learn your fate. Come back another time."

"You know that I didn't come here for this."

She smiled bitterly.

"For a man you are terribly patient. I kept wondering when you were going to ask about your Maid."

"Is she here?"

I waited for her answer with bated breath.

"Go up the stairs. The second door on the right."

I stood and Jola roused herself.

"By the way! You owe me a hundred and fifty sorens. Since you and Weasel were so kind as to set fire to our place and put burned corpses in it, then you can pay."

"I'm sure that as soon as Layen appeared in your doorway, you immediately gouged her for all you're owed."

Ktatak burst out into deafening laughter.

"I swear by Kvagun's eyes! Today's really not your day, partner!"

"Stop braying! You'd better go with him and make sure that he doesn't filch anything along the way."

"Okvay, okvay, don't be ankvary, birdie. I'll do it," he replied, still laughing, and then he finally condescended to come out into the light.

Ktatak was a Blazog. He had ash-gray warty skin, fantastically long, muscular arms, and a stooped posture. On his massive, round head the first thing that caught one's attention were his enormous hazel eyes and his wide, toadlike mouth. Blazogs weren't the most pleasant things to look at. Especially for those who were seeing them for the first time. The inhabitants of the swamps located in the south of the Empire usually lived in isolation, in small floating villages, and very few of them ever ventured out into the wider world.

Blazogs are usually considered strange and stupid, mainly because human speech is difficult for them. And because of a few behaviors that would seem insane to the average human. However, rare was the man who would tell a swamp dweller to his face that he was stupid. Given the strength and agility of the Blazogs, for all their external absurdity, an idiotic comment like that would have dire consequences. I would never try to take on Ktatak, especially when he has two axes or swords in his grasp. I once saw Jola's partner at work; he ripped three experienced robbers, greedy for free silk, into tiny pieces before they had time to put up any kind of resistance. Since that time, thieves have avoided this shop for three blocks.

"I'm kvalad to see you alive, Kvaray. I'll tell you a sekvaret. We were a little upset when our shackva in the harbor was turned into a piece of kvoal. You and Weasel, even though you're fishy kvids, you're not so bad. Even old Jola mourned when we found your remains."

"Don't be a fool," muttered the Je'arre. "I was mourning the loss of a decent house that we were stupid enough to lend to that pair."

"I have no doubt about that," I hastened to assure her. "You haven't changed at all since our last meeting, Ktatak."

"Still skvary and awful?" the Blazog said, chuckling. "It's too soon for me to kvet old. I'm just in my seventh dekvade."

"There you go. And still going strong. Are you still amusing yourself at the Fights?"

"Ockvasionally," he replied humbly, and then his hazel eyes were momentarily covered by transparent lids. "Right now that business is in Jokva's hands. I'm not too friendly with him."

"So he's alive and well?"

"Unfortunately for you, yes, he's alive and well. Well enough to stand, anyway. Let's kvo. I'll lead you."

He walked forward with a deliberately slow and awkward gait. The steps creaked mournfully under his weight. For a Blazog Ktatak was very sturdy. He was wider than me in the shoulders and in terms of weight I lost to him outright.

"Jola's out of spirits today," I said, when we were upstairs.

He chuckled, pushed open a door, and invited me in.

"She's always out of spirits. As if you didn't know her."

"How is business going?"

"Kvarappy. Especially in the last two days."

"Did something happen that I should know about?" I looked around the room.

It was large and cozy, with expensive furniture, a king-size bed, and bands of thick fabric curtaining the windows. Ktatak didn't conceal his grin when I walked over to the window and looked out into the courtyard. What can you do? Old habits. All too often I've had to leave without saying good-bye.

"Possibly. Did you notice what was kvoinkva on in Birdtown?"

"The flyers didn't seem to be seeking out fresh air."

"Just so." He yawned lingeringly, opening wide his enormous jaws and displaying a few yellow teeth. "The day before yesterday, we kvot the news that the Je'arre have flipped to the side of Nabator and Sdis."

I whistled.

"They kvan't stand it, you see, that the Empire wants to take their land from them and send them north. Jola's kvinsmen don't really find the prospeck-vat of freezing their asses off all that tempting, and really, who kvould blame them? And what did they expeckvat would happen? That race is as fickvale as the wind that kvarries them."

"It'd be better if it dropped them. I'm surprised the rest of the city hasn't ripped their wings off yet."

"It already happened. Yesterday eveninkva some avengers kvaught two of the Sons of the Skvay and kvut off their heads. They would have done even more nasty thinkvas, but the bloodthirsty kvarowd was dispersed by the Viceroy's Kvuard. Everythinkva is quiet for now."

"Not for long."

"I know." Ktatak frowned and his entire face was covered in comical folds. "Less than a weekva will pass before the Viceroy askvas all the Je'arre to leave the city. And that's the best-kvase scenario. The worst kvase is that he'll send them to the sckvaffold. As traitors."

"Not even the fact that the city coffers are fattened year after year thanks to those like Jola will stop him?"

"When you're talking about the fackvat that some birdie might open the kvates during a siege, money is forkvotten."

"Oh really? Hightown has forgotten about money?"

"Well, let's say so. They can akvaree to the lesser

evil. If the city falls, they'll lose all their money. And now, only a part."

"A fairly reasonable approach, it seems to me. What about Jola?"

"Many of her relatives have already left Al'skvara. Only the most stubborn and most stupid remain. I don't know which kvaroup to put our old lady in. She doesn't want to leave her shop, so she'll wait until her feathers have been pluckved."

"I'm sure you'll take care of her."

Ktatak smiled. "I already am. The kvoods left to-day for the Kvolden Markva. I've hidden money away. There's nothing to hold me here. If I kvatch a whiff of smoke, I'll kvarab that silly chickven in my arms and we'll sail far away to the horizon, even if she will kvaluck and resist me."

"A ship can be found?" I seized on this immedi-ately.

He frowned again. "For now, yes. But the prices have risen sharply. Are you planninkva a van-ishinkva ackvat?"

"After a chat with Joch."

The Blazog chuckled. "You never did kvet alonkva with him."

"True. He's a nuisance."

"And Mols?"

"Mols never bothered me."

"Unlike Jokva, he's very kvautious and not very kvareedy. But I advise you to hurry. After seven or eight days, thinkvas are kvoinkva to tighten up around here."

"How are you so sure?"

"First of all, when half the city sleeps it dreams of settlinkva skvores with the Je'arre. For the time beinkva the watch and the Kvuard are holdinkva them backva, but sooner or later they'll pluckva up their nerve and riot. I don't know if you heard or not, but Nabator is in talks with the Kvolden Markva so they'll open the passage through the Straits to them. If the merchants kvomply, the city will be under siege from the sea and there'll no lonkver be any way out of the Empire. Sooner or later Al'skvara will be encirkvaled."

"Our troops are holding them back, aren't they?"

"That's old news," he dismissed me. "Here's somethinkva fresh for you. The Je'arre hit the Third Army from behind. Then it was attackved head on by a force of Nabatorian troops, nekvaromancers, and Sdisian soldiers. Not to mention the Highborn."

"The Highborn?" I exclaimed.

"Just so. The pointy-eared elves also decided to makva use of this opportunity and pay us backva for all offenses. The Isthmuses of Lina have been takven. The remains of our troops fled to the Steps of the Hankvaman or to the west, toward Al'skvara. And at their heels . . ."

He didn't finish. There was no need. Everything was clear. It would get hot here very soon.

"We fought the Highborn for three hundred years and eventually concluded that damned peace treaty! We should have finished them off right after Gem's Arch, but instead of that we gave them a whole decade to recover. I hate that race!"

He nodded understandingly. He knew that I'd served in Sandon for a number of years. "I'm surprised you're without your bow."

"It was ruined," I replied, and recalled Pork, thanks to whom my weapon was burnt.

"Buy a new one. Okvay, I'm kvoinkva downstairs or else some rioter's kvoinkva to stumble in and butt heads with a very ankvary Jola. And another thinkva." He stopped at the door and was no longer smiling. "You are of kvourse our friend and we have history, but it would be best for you if you didn't stay here too lonkva. You understand."

"I understand." I nodded seriously. "You don't have to worry. We won't expose you and we'll be out of here today."

"Do you have a place to stay?"

"We'll find one." I avoided a direct answer.

"I'm sorry that it's kvotten so—"

"Drop it. I'm not going to drag you in with Joch. We'll leave. No offense taken."

"That's kvood, Kviiyan." He obviously relaxed. "Rest well."

"Can you do me one favor?"

"Anythinkva I kvan."

"I need a bow. I'm sure you understand, it wouldn't be the smartest thing for me to go around to the weapons shops myself."

I couldn't use the weapon of the Sdisian archer I'd killed in Psar'ki. It would draw the attention of people in the know. A far too remarkable bow.

Ktatak nodded and smiled.

"That's not too diffikvult. I know your preferences. And your measurements. I know a kvood dealer. Do you have any wishes?"

"No. I have complete faith in you in this matter."

The Blazog grinned one last time and tightly closed the door behind himself. I listened to his retreating footsteps.

By the bed stood a chair, on which I placed my throwing axe. My dagger went under the pillow. We had some time until evening. Then we should leave. Ktatak and Jola were old friends, and Layen and I had pulled them out of a sticky situation once, but it would not do to abuse their hospitality.

The door creaked quietly and I instantly jumped up and grabbed the knife I'd hidden under the pillow and concealed it behind my back. The woman who walked into the room had short blond hair and was wearing a colorful skirt. I was so startled that it took me a second to realize that it was Layen.

16

She smelled faintly of jasmine. I reached out for her and wrapped my arms around her. Humming softly, she bit my earlobe. A cat. A warm cat. And predatory. From time to time even too predatory. The scratches she left on my back always ached sweetly though.

"I can't get used to you."

"Really?" Sharp little teeth sank into the side of my neck. She growled. "Then I guess I'll just have to do something to get you used to me again."

Much later, when we were lying in the bed after this most recent onslaught of passion, I still found it necessary to explain, "Your hair is much shorter. I didn't recognize you at first."

"You don't like it?" My sun smiled.

"How could I not? I've just never seen it like this."

"I had to sacrifice it. We're being looked for, and any sign might give us away. I was afraid they'd recognize me at the gates."

For some time we lay there in silence, thinking our own thoughts.

"I kept thinking that I'd never see you again," Layen said suddenly. "You delayed too long."

"I'm sorry." What else could I say to her?

"It's a miracle we got out."

"I know. I saw. You were ahead of us by a few seconds and were able to escape. We had to find a different route and sneak through the fields. Did the rest of your journey pass without incident?"

"Yes. I said good-bye to Ga-Nor and Luk at the gates and came here. You can't imagine it, being locked inside four walls, every second wondering whether you survived or not."

"I can imagine it, my sun. I can imagine it all too well. I wondered the same about you. It's a good thing the redhead crossed our path. He was able to bring you out of that mess. Did our friends object to you leaving them?"

"The tracker, no. He understood that I wouldn't give in to entreaties and immediately let me go where I wished. But Luk was truly upset, and kept urging me to stay. But I washed my hands of them. We have our business here, and they have theirs. We shouldn't get them involved. Plus, our soldiers were going to meet the Walkers."

"Why?" I was on my guard.

"From what I gathered, Luk was the only one to survive the storming of the Gates of Six Towers. And he saw Rubeola. That might interest the Walkers."

"He also saw Typhoid."

"She's dead."

"I'm not so sure. It seems she's a tenacious creature and managed to return from the Abyss."

I told her about running into the lad who used to be Pork. With each passing second her face became grimmer. When I was done a tense silence hung between us. Layen was lying motionless with her eyes closed.

"Is such a thing possible?" I asked finally, unable to contain myself.

"You want to hear the truth? I have no idea. Anything's possible with the Damned. They are stronger than anyone else in our world. Their bodies are very difficult to destroy, and that's to say nothing of their spirits. It's entirely possible that destroying the latter requires more than ordinary steel. You need to disrupt the essence, the foundation, to burn out the spark. Do you remember that arrow?"

I nodded tiredly, realizing what she was talking about. I remembered it well—the strange bone arrowhead, the green shaft, and the lilac radiance before it hit the Walker.

"If Typhoid is alive, we're in for trouble."

"Cunningly observed," she said, laughing, and began to get dressed. "I would say that we're in for a great deal of trouble. She may just want to break your neck, but I'm sure she has much more to talk about with me and the Healer. It's possible she just has a desire for revenge. It's possible. But I wouldn't rule out the idea that she wants us for something else."

"Like what?"

"Perhaps to find a more fitting body than the one she has now. Or to get back her Gift. Did Gis actually say that she was very weak?"

"He did. Or at least, that's how it seemed to him. Who knows what's in the mind of a wizard?"

"So our mutual friend, the courier, is a Scarlet? Hmmm . . ." She lifted the hem of her colorful, recently purchased skirt and fastened a knife in a long, narrow sheath to her right shin. "You're lucky he was there."

"And he's lucky I was there."

She suddenly broke into laughter. "I'd give much to see the look on the Damned's face when she realized who she was dealing with! It's unlikely Typhoid ever thought she'd come across a demon charmer! She'd be particularly defenseless. Just imagine; I'm starting to regret that Gis isn't with you. Where did you leave him?"

"At a wayside tavern. About two days' travel from Al'sgara. I crept away in the middle of the night, while he was sleeping. I have no liking for such companions. With all due respect toward demonologists, I like to stay as far away from them as possible. It makes my soul rest easier."

"Did the boy stay with him?" She hid another dagger in her left sleeve.

"The lad disappeared in Bald Hollow. We left without him. Whether he survived or not, I don't know."

This news upset her. "I'd be sorry if the Healer died. He had some good qualities."

"Sure, like arrogance and stubbornness."

"Other than those," said my sun. She was already fully dressed. "But it's possible the world lost the next Sculptor."

"Why are you getting ready? Shouldn't we wait 'til dark? I already had to quiet one bounty hunter this morning."

I told her about what happened in Dovetown.

"So soon?" She was surprised. "At times I marvel at your ability to get into trouble. Not a day passed, and you were already recognized. Who was he working for?"

"For himself. He was fed by Mols on a case-by-case basis. So, where are you going and wouldn't it be better for us to wait 'til it's dark?" I asked again.

"Don't you know that a curfew has been declared in Al'sgara after nightfall? It's not a good idea to go out onto the streets. Military patrols, the watch, and the Viceroy's Guards together with Walkers and Embers. I really don't want to get caught by the last two, so I'd prefer to risk it during the day, and sit inside at night. We need to see Mols. Don't you think it's time to visit our old friend? After all, he was kind enough to send Whip and his team to warn us about Joch's bad behavior."

I smirked. "Perhaps you're right. They'll be glad to see us."

We both laughed and I began to get dressed.

"Did you find out anything about Joch?" I asked in passing.

"I couldn't stick my nose outside, so Ktatak and Jola were my eyes and ears. From what I could find out—the task will be hard. Joch is well guarded."

I shrugged. "Sooner or later we're all sent to the Abyss. Unfortunately, we don't have a lot of time. We need to be on a ship by the end of the week. Perhaps sooner."

"I know. I heard that the Isthmuses of Lina have been taken. We'll smell smoke soon enough."

I nodded and took my axe from the chair. "What about your Gift?"

Layen's face instantly darkened. "It's not going as well as I'd hoped."

"But still?" I insisted. "Can I count on your help?"

"In that sense, no. Not right now, anyways. My spark is flaring up, but very slowly. For right now there's little I can do. Let's wait a few days, okay?"

I nodded, trying not to show my disappointment. The Damned! It was all her fault! If we'd never crossed paths with her, the hunt for Joch would have been much easier.

"Okay, don't worry about it, my sun. We'll manage on our own. It's not the first time, right?"

She smiled gratefully. "Let's go. I'll tell you about our target on the way."

"Wait a moment. What about the money?" I didn't see her pack.

"I left it with Jola."

"Now I'm really starting to worry," I joked sourly.

"What if the old woman flies away with our so-rens?"

"She knows where her interests lie, of course, but in this I trust her."

"Just like in fortune telling," I said even more bitterly.

"Just like in fortune telling," Layen concurred. "By the way, what did your cards say?"

"Nothing. Our prophetess was at a loss. She said she made a mistake. The spread was incorrect."

"She made a mistake? An incorrect spread?" my sun echoed. "Are we talking about the same Jola?"

"And now just imagine how surprised Ktatak was. I thought he'd croak from happiness."

She laughed loudly. "That would have been wonderful to see."

"I wouldn't want to miss the chance to see it a second time. The winged one almost plucked all her feathers out from vexation. Come on. We need to say good-bye to them. I hope walking around with weapons hasn't been prohibited in the city?"

"No. With that, praise Melot, everything is as it should be."

We went downstairs. There were still only two torches burning in the shop. Jola was ignoring us and muttering curses under her breath, laying out her fortune-telling cards on the table for the hundredth time that day. And the Blazog was attending his own business, too—he was pulling a hefty sword from the back of a dead man. Another corpse was lying under the Je'arre's table. As far as I could tell in the gloom, he had been split by a single powerful blow from his collarbone to the middle of his chest. A whole lake of blood was flowing out of him.

"Guests?" I inquired politely.

Jola launched into a series of shrill imprecations, which placed primary emphasis on the mothers who gave birth to the bastards that dared attack her shop.

"Are these on your souls or on ours?" Layen was watching as the Blazog wiped his sword on the clothes of the dead man lying by the door.

"Don't worry, Layen. There's absolutely no kvonnection to you." Ktatak laughed. "This kvouple of children of fish decided to tickvale my partner's feathers. And at the same time as their little prankva, they were kvoinkva to make a profit."

"The damned bastards!" confirmed the Je'arre without looking up from her cards. "May the skies fall upon their rotten families. May their children's eyes dry up. May maggots devour their despicable guts alive!"

"That's the right approach," agreed the swamp dweller, not hiding his sarcasm. "Why didn't you tell them that to their faces when they were still alive?"

"You stole my chance, you leech!" Jola snorted irritably and finally put her cards aside. "I didn't have time to open my mouth before you swatted them like mosquitoes from your swamp!"

Ktatak laughed deep in his chest.

"You did your work quietly," I said in a low voice. "I see your grip is as strong and quick as ever, you old trunk."

"I take pride in the praise of a master." He stretched his lips into a smile.

It wasn't all that difficult to imagine what went on here. The two men obviously weren't from the neighborhood, nor did they make their living as professional evaders of the law, otherwise they would have found themselves some friendlier victims. The lads were just eager to get their hands on a Je'arre. If they weren't blinded by the torch hanging by the stairs and saw the winged woman, then it's unlikely they had time to take note of Ktatak hiding in the gloom. So they'd stumbled right by him. I wondered if they had any idea who it was that jumped out at them?

Trying not to step in the blood that was seeping along the floor, Layen walked over to the door and lowered the latch.

"That's right, girl," said Jola approvingly. "If another dozen stop by, I'll be cleaning the floor for the rest of my life."

"Since when do you mop the floors, chickvadee? I'm always the one doinkva it," said Ktatak indignantly.

"Stuff it, you leech."

"What are you going to do with the bodies?" asked Layen.

"That's our business. Don't worry your pretty little head. Are you leaving?"

"We'd like to."

"Go out through the back door." The flyer had buried her nose in the cards once more. "Ktatak, show them the way. Then you can take care of these bodies. They're not going anywhere."

Layen kissed the Je'arre on the cheek. "Thank you for everything."

"Not at all, Weasel. Not at all. I was happy to help." For the first time since their conversation began, Jola smiled. "Take care of yourself. And good luck."

The Blazog brought a quiver full of arrows and a bow out of the darkness—it was an exact copy of the one I'd had before. Four curves, composite, black. A good weapon.

"Nicely done. Just what I needed." I endorsed his choice, carefully examining the merchandise.

Ktatak grunted in embarrassment and quickly said, "I'm just sorry for the arrows. I don't know how to choose the right ones."

"It's okay," I comforted him. "I'll manage."

"Takva your sorens." He handed Layen her pack. "We kvan't answer for their safety. We'll be out of here any minute now."

"Farewell, Jola."

"Until we meet again, Gray. Until then." She didn't even raise her head from the cards.

We walked behind the Blazog, passing through a succession of half-lit rooms, brimming with bales and boxes. It's hard to believe they'd sent off all their goods. To me it looked like there was still something here that could turn a profit. Disorder prevailed all around, and no one was planning to contend with it. In one place the floor was strewn with reels of expensive multicolored Sdisian thread. The dust in the room shone in the rays of the evening sun, which was peeking through one of the windows.

Finally, Ktatak stopped at a door, removed the dead bolt, inserted a beautiful key into the keyhole, unlocked it, and looked out.

"All kvalear. Kvo through the backvayard, to the right of the pikvasty. There's a kvate there. There's a kvey under the tile with a frokva painted on it. Don't forkvet to put it backva. Then kvo alonkva the alleyway, it'll lead you right to the harbor. I hope fate will brinkva us backva tokvether again. May Kvagun help you."

"The god of the Blazogs is unlikely to pay attention to humans."

The swamp dweller smiled. "If the kvod of the Je'arre kvan kvome to you in the fortune-telling kvards, why kvan't my kvod look after my friends?"

"That reminds me! Do me a favor?"

I told him about Stallion. I had no need of the horse now, but I didn't want to leave him to the innkeeper.

"Okvay. I'll put your horse in kvood hands. Farewell."

We walked outside and the door slammed behind us.

"You got the Thief?" inquired Layen curiously.

"Yes," I replied, studying the backyard. "Is it important?"

"No. I'm just curious. As far as I recall Jola's tales, that card is very rare, and even if you come across it, it doesn't affect the spread."

"It affected the Je'arre's spread today."

"That's why I'm curious. It's too bad I didn't get a chance to talk to her about it."

"What for?" I shrugged. "The flyer said that the spread was incorrect. You know that. She made a mistake."

In truth, I didn't really think that. I was very disturbed by the Fool and the five Deaths that formed a circle. You didn't have to be all that clever a man to look at that and see the six Damned, one of whom, by some miracle, had survived and seized the body of a village idiot.

The western region of the city, which was laid out just beyond the community of the Je'arre, adjacent to the sea, was called Haven, or simply the harbor. It stretched along the shore of the huge bay, gradually growing wider and subsuming into itself the smaller neighborhoods of Whitehand and Eunuchtown. Now Haven rivaled the city's largest district, Midtown, in terms of size. Right now we were north of the port, in a neighborhood of wealthy artisans. The streets here were quite wide and clean, so you didn't have to flinch away from trash on the street or dread being doused with slops from above. But the tidy, low houses with white walls were depressing. They were so repetitious and identical that it made you want to hang yourself. There is no way I'd want to live in a place like this. I'd much prefer the riotous streets of Eunuchtown, the cheerful bedlam of the docks, or the quiet calm of the Gardens.

Unlike Birdtown, Haven was bustling with life. The servants of the law all ignored my bow. In liberal Al'sgara, as opposed to the capital of the Empire, Corunna, there was no ban on weapons. Not in Haven, at any rate. Many men wore daggers on their belts.

"We ought to take a look at the port," I said, casting a glance at the street leading to the docks.

"We don't have time." Layen shook her head. "It'll get dark soon."

"You're right. So today we have Mols. We can deal with the rest tomorrow."

My sun smiled and took my hand. "How about some pastries?"

I smiled back at her. "I wouldn't refuse."

We smelled the scent of bread long before we saw the baker's shop. The magnificent aroma of fresh baked goods wafted along the entirety of Old Coin Alley. I thought the sign, which was shaped like a pretzel, was completely unnecessary. A blind man could find where bread was being sold. The trays were stuffed with goods, but there were few customers—it was late, and everyone who wanted to had already made their purchases. The fools. In their place, I would have been squirreling away breadcrumbs. When the siege began, prices would soar sky-high, and goods would disappear within a few days. Then they'd be sorry they didn't increase their food reserves whenever possible.

There were two people behind the counter. They looked dashing, like they should have been aboard a pirate ship, not behind a counter. I didn't know them.

"What would you like?"

"A doughnut and a crescent roll with cinnamon."

I laid out small change and handed the doughnut to Layen, who immediately sank her teeth into it.

"Anything else?"

"Call Mols."

They immediately tensed.

"We don't know anyone of that name."

"Search your memory." My rude words did not correspond to my polite smile.

Layen was busy with her doughnut, pretending not to follow the conversation.

"You're mistaken," said one of the bakers dully. "There's no Mols here."

"Of course." I was not about to argue. "His real name is quite different."

"It'd be best if you left." Now the face of the thug nearest to us was radiating "goodwill."

His companion drew a knife out from behind the counter. "Be off with you. We're up to our necks in work."

I sighed in disappointment, took out my utak, saw that these fools were ready to fling themselves at us, and with a disarming smile tossed the axe onto the counter.

"And what's that supposed to mean?" The one with the knife frowned. "Have you decided to give up?"

"No, he just doesn't want to crack your empty skulls," Layen answered for me, having finally finished her doughnut. Without asking, she took a crescent roll from the nearest tray. "Which of you is smartest? Take what you've been given and go look for Mols. When you find him, show him the weapon. We'll wait."

"There is no Mols here! Get out of here or we'll call the watch!" The baker with the blade was standing his ground.

"What's your name?" I asked softly, in no hurry to leave.

"What's it to you?" he snapped.

"Well, if Mols should ask me why I didn't come to the meeting, I need to tell him something."

That made them stop and think. If I was speaking the truth, they wouldn't get a pat on the back for not letting us in.

"Fine." The husky one finally made up his mind and took the utak. "Wait here. If you're lying, I'll rip you a new one."

"Don't get bent out of shape too soon, little boy." Layen smiled. "Just do what you were put here for."

He cast her a spiteful glance full of promises, muttered to his comrade not to take his eyes off us, and disappeared into the depths of the shop. I had a free minute so I took a bite from the pastry I'd bought. Layen had finished before me and grabbed another bun from the tray. As I understood it, just to annoy the man.

"Are you going to pay for that?" he spat.

"I doubt old Mols will begrudge us some crumbs. His good friends shouldn't die of hunger." She grinned.

"Good friends, huh?" muttered the thug, but he didn't utter another word about payment, wisely deciding that he should wait for his comrade to come back and clarify the situation.

A customer entered, and the lad quickly hid his weapon under the counter. He was clearly nervous while he served the client, even though we were behaving ourselves. At that moment the second baker came back—without the utak, but with a sour face. He caught the inquisitive glance of his coworker and shook his head almost imperceptibly.

"Come with me. They're waiting for you," he told us reluctantly.

We followed him and found ourselves in a long corridor.

"You see, kid, everything worked out just fine," Layen teased him.

He flinched and hissed, "I don't know who you are, but you shouldn't annoy me."

"I'll bear that in mind, kid, oh yes I will." Layen turned to me and winked cheerfully. I made an upset face so that she'd stop taunting the fool. Why the stupid game? She stuck out her tongue at me in reply.

We walked into an interior yard, which had not changed at all over the years. Except that the trees were much taller than they had been before. The bakery was to our left, and we tramped along a neatly swept path through a small orchard to a nice three-story house. It wasn't visible from the street, and many of the inhabitants of this part of Al'sgara would have been quite surprised to find out how their bakers lived.

Four men were standing by the entrance, near which torches were lit. This was the first time I had seen something like this here as well. It seems there had been quite a few changes over the past seven years. New people all over the place. One of them, tall and broad-shouldered, got up from the grass and walked over to us.

"Now then." The broad-shouldered man smiled. "Gimme your bow. Me and my friends gotta search you. Just so we have an understanding. Don't want no disagreements."

The threesome remaining on the grass got to their feet as if on command.

"I'll check the wench," quickly offered the kid who'd led us.

"She'll tear off your arms, Luga," said a mocking voice.

A red-faced, heavyset man stood by the door. He had immense, shaggy sideburns that melded into an untidy salt-and-pepper beard. A leather vest was thrown over his bare and, despite his advanced age, muscular torso. He wore short pants that stopped at the knee, a wide belt with a silver belt buckle in the shape of a snarling wolf's muzzle, and a curved Sdisian dagger in an expensive sheath. In his left hand he was casually holding my axe. His thick lips were smiling, but his brown eyes were watchful. He anticipated a trick from us at any moment. He was paying special attention to Layen.

"Hi, Stump." My sunshine greeted him first.

"Hello, hello. How was your trip?"

"Successful."

"I don't see your escort. Where did you lose them?"

"They had a bit of bad luck," I replied.

Our questioner was no longer smiling.

"Stump." The broad-shouldered man jumped into the conversation. "Should we look for them?"

"Shut up," snapped Stump, and that order worked

on Mols's people like the crack of a whip. "Bad luck," he said, as if savoring the words. "All of them?"

"Yes."

"Did Whip bite off more than he could chew?" Nasty undertones had slipped into his voice. Stump was friends with my old acquaintance. Simply put, they were like brothers.

"No. He really was unlucky. He ran into a clever Nabatorian."

"A pity." It was unclear whether he believed me or not. "Midge and Bamut as well?"

"Not quite." Layen looked him in the eye. "They did bite off more than they could chew."

"Oh," he said slowly. "That's a shame. They were good people."

"Beyond a shadow of a doubt." I was uncommonly serious.

"The Abyss take me!" suddenly cried out the one who was called Luga. "Gray!"

This announcement made quite the impression on the thugs surrounding us. They all finally made the connection between the mysterious absence of Whip, Midge, and Bamut, the utak in Stump's hands, and the arrival of a man and a woman.

Now they were looking at us with wide eyes, and Luga stepped as far away as possible from Layen. It was obvious that he now took Stump's words about having his limbs torn off in a literal sense. When she'd been working, Weasel didn't have a reputation for being the calmest person in Al'sgara.

"You're too quick on the uptake," said Stump in a deceptively quiet voice. "It bodes you no good, you get me?"

The kid went paler than before. "Yes."

"I know that the temptation to gossip about this on every street corner is very great, just as is the desire to earn a few sorens, but before you open your mouth, think about this. You still need to get the money; Joch is far away, but I'm close. And your family, too. You're a smart lad, aren't you?" asked the red-faced Giiyan insinuatingly.

"I'm not going to talk."

"That's nice. Go away. Be about your business. My warning goes for all of you. I hope no one here thinks that ten thousand sorens is better than my displeasure and family troubles? That's wonderful. Gell, you're responsible for your lads' heads."

"We won't talk idly. You know that," said the broad-shouldered one resentfully.

"I know. Gray, Weasel, come into the house."

"You're harsh with them," I said once we were inside.

"There's no other way."

"You don't think that such treatment might do harm?"

"Nonsense!" spat Stump. "They know that I bark often, but I bite only when I have to."

"You don't bite. You rend."

He chuckled softly and returned my utak, warning me just in case, "Be good."

It was already rather dark outside, and candles were lit inside the house. The expensive burgundy rug lying on the floor muffled our footsteps. Stump stopped by a set of double doors and shoved them open.

"In you go."

The room was large and brightly lit by candles, which were standing on a large table covered by a white tablecloth.

We heard three soft handclaps. A tall middle-aged woman was applauding us. She had a pleasant face, a large mouth, and a strong jaw. Her graying hair was hidden under a white starched cap. Her clothing was simple, one could even say modest. Looking at her, the sweet and kind mistress of a bakery, you would never think you were seeing the head of the southern guild of Giiyans and one of the most influential people in the criminal world of Al'sgara. She who took the name of Mols. Only a select few, who could be counted on the fingers of both hands, had ever seen her. She always preferred to stay in the shadows, communicating with all those who worked for her through Stump. And he tried his best to make sure that everyone believed Mols was a man. Even people in the know, while talking with one another, preferred to speak of Mols as a he. It was more familiar, and much less dangerous.

"Bravo, my dears. Bravo." She stood up from the table. "You almost managed to dupe them all."

"Almost doesn't count, Mols," I said.

She was calm, smiling, and everything about her indicated that she was happy to see us. A kind aunt, meeting with her niece and nephew after a long separation.

"So you say. But you managed to fool even me with that fire, for a time."

"But not the Walkers."

"Oh, yes. They were born suspicious, but after a year or two they calmed down. In any case, so it seemed to me. Sit down, don't stand around like strangers. We'll have supper now. Stump, see to it. I'm glad we're all back together again. I always said that Gray and Weasel were a lovely couple. And the work you did—a thing of beauty! Do you remember those times? Not the times, but the gold!"

We caught her meaning well enough. Layen took a prepared purse from her pack and put it on the table—fifteen coins worth one hundred sorens apiece. It was Mols's share from our last job. We could have dispensed with the guild and refused to pay them a tenth of our fee, but there was no sense in being greedy. It was simpler to pay out what was due and maintain good relations. One and a half thousand sorens—some people couldn't even earn such a sum in five lifetimes. And what's funniest of all, I didn't begrudge them at all.

Mols took the purse, loosened the strings, and looked inside.

"So that's how much the life of a Walker is worth. When I heard about what happened I thought you stupid. But, as I see, it was worth it. By the way, you did good work. And it was pulled off beautifully. The Embers smashed the neighboring houses, but after four days they found the bow and it turned out that you shot from quite the awkward position. Someone tried to repeat your trick for fun, but it didn't work."

She put the money on the edge of the table and, it seemed, forgot about it, absorbed in the conversation. While the table was being set and supper served, Mols chatted incessantly on various topics, starting with the weather and ending with the price of flour. Occasionally we were able to put in a remark. Stump frowned often and drank more than he ate. Only after the dirty dishes were taken from the table did we get down to business.

"Are you in the city long?" asked Mols.

"That depends," I replied evasively. "Aren't you planning to leave?"

"Where would I go? I've spent my whole life in Al'sgara; now it's too late to leave my home. I'm too old."

"A siege doesn't worry you?"

"Are you talking about hunger? I have enough supplies to feed both myself and my boys. Anyway, a siege is long off. The Nabatorians have to get through our army."

"For some reason, I have no doubt that they will get through. And if there's famine, they loot a bakery first thing."

"Just let them try," growled Stump, pouring another glass of wine down his throat. As always, he wasn't getting drunk.

"I'm sure you'll strangle all the looters," crooned Layen. "But what if the soldiers come? Or the Viceroy's Guards? Against them, and I say this with all due respect to your lads, you won't hold out for long."

"If they come on the orders of the Viceroy and the City Council, I'll open my cellar," declared Mols calmly. "I wouldn't begrudge it for my hometown."

"Especially when there is a secret cache twice the size of the one everyone knows about," Stump said, chuckling. "I'm at ease about my stomach."

The head of the guild cast her assistant a disgruntled look. I recognized her usual initiative. As his detractors, now dead, said, if normal people have one secret passage in their homes, damned Mols has more than ten.

"I didn't expect you to return."

"You sent for us yourself."

"And all the same, given the circumstances, I wasn't expecting it. I'm glad that my warning reached you. I was truly worried."

I made a wry face, showing how I felt about her words.

"Let's be honest with each other. You didn't start all of this to help us. You're just tired of Joch and we are among the few who would undertake such a task. We simply have no other choice."

"You've turned into a terrible cynic these past few years, my boy." She was not at all put off by my words. "Do you really mean to tell me that you aren't grateful for the timely news?"

"I'm grateful."

"Then I don't see any reason for your dissatisfaction."

"How did you find out that we were alive, and how did you find us?" asked Layen.

"Well, I guessed that you were alive. You're not such fools as to do in a Walker without preparing a means of retreat. Take a pastry, treat yourselves."

"Thank you, but I've eaten enough of them today. I'll get even fatter."

"Nonsense. You've got a great figure. So"—she returned to the topic at hand—"I suspected it, but searching for you like the Walkers was too long and difficult. If they couldn't do it, what could a simple bakery owner do? The Empire is vast, and you had clearly hid yourselves so well the light of day couldn't find you. You could have been lying low in the Golden Mark, Urs, Grogan, Sino, or anywhere else. The world of Hara is large. You owed me money for your last job of course, but I preferred to wait. Gray has always been honest in such matters. As you see, the waiting, though it was long, justified itself." She glanced at the purse lying on the table. "And when, for no apparent reason, Joch put a price on your heads, I no longer had any doubt. Threefingers is not such a fool as to throw money into the wind. I had to put my best foot forward to pinch the nephew of our mutual acquaintance. Stump was so kind as to have a word with the young man, and was able to pull something out of him after a few days. Before he died, the boy named a village. A certain Dog Green."

"He didn't say how Joch found out about it?"

"He didn't know who told Joch. Even after you crossed him and deprived him of a couple of fingers, he waited quite a long time to try and take his revenge on you. The fact that he bothered at all means there's profit in it for him. That or he had no choice."

"Who could force Threefingers to dance to their tune?" asked Layen, frowning, and she cast a quick glance in my direction.

I knew of whom she was thinking. The Walkers.

"If you think about it, there are many who could, Layen. Joch is influential and powerful, but there are those who are more influential than him. They could very well exert pressure on him." Mols ignored the glances we exchanged. "In any case, he's already done it. Your heads are in the balance against ten thousand sorens."

"Decent money." Stump took an empty bottle of wine from the table and replaced it with a full one. "Many would be overjoyed to earn that much."

"But not us." Mols stressed the last word. "The amount is large, but I won't play dirty with you."

"It's more profitable for you to get rid of Joch than to fill your treasure chest a bit more." I grinned enigmatically.

"As always, you are right." She did not look aside. "Joch has always been a bone in my throat, and he's flown very high recently. The Viceroy's good friend, he arranges all sorts of stylish diversions for him and his nobles. You should have seen the master of fireworks displays he got sent here from Grogan. All of Al'sgara was harping on about it for a month. New friends, new opportunities, new power and influence. He's got a large part of the city under his thumb. Joch has tried to meddle in the business of the guild and my people. There were a few skirmishes, but thank Melot it hasn't devolved into a war. But I'm not sure we'll be able to hold out if he really turns his attention to crushing us. Threefingers can now set the Viceroy's Guards on us and then enlist the help of the Tower. For now he's being cautious, but how long will that continue? And I can't strike at him; the old beetle cares too much for his health. In recent years, he's become almost untouchable."

"Not even for a good price? A thousand sorens and a pair of desperate men could deal with this easily." Layen gestured to Stump to pour her some wine.

"I don't have an extra thousand, Weasel." It was unclear if Mols was joking or speaking seriously. "And desperate men have long since gone extinct. No one will risk their necks on such a hopeless job. I wasn't joking when I said that Joch is not easy to get to. He sits in his house, which is more like a fortress, and if he travels around the city, it is with such a guard that even a small army couldn't break through. They'd be devoured."

"I don't believe it."

"You'll believe it when you see it for yourself. Tomorrow is the fourth day of the week. Joch is in the habit of going to the Fights, which now take place in the Cucumber Quarter. If you're curious, you can take a look. Why are you grinning, Gray?" She raised her thin eyebrows.

"You said that you don't have money or desperate men. Isn't that why Whip and his comrades come to us? We'll do everything for free. Did you decide to use our hands?"

"Of course," she said with dignity. "It's in your interests because of the price on your heads. And at the same time, you'll be helping me. I'll support you in any way I can, but relieving Threefingers of his soul is not my concern."

I nodded. "A fairly honest answer."

"Did my people really misbehave?" she asked suddenly.

"Just Midge and Bamut. The money turned their heads."

"Bamut was a fool. I've no doubt he was obeying the runt. Well, it serves him right. But it's too bad about Whip. He's been with me since the very beginning. I hope his soul is in the Blessed Gardens. And what about the boy?"

"That's what I wanted to ask you about."

"What do you mean?"

"About Shen, who you added to the threesome. Who is he and where did you dig him up?"

"I felt that a walkabout would be good for the boy's soul. Let him gain some experience." She didn't flinch under my gaze. I could only envy Mols's cold-bloodedness.

"Experience in what? In assassination or in healing practice? You know that he did not belong to the guild. The lad is a Healer, and you should let those who know how do the killing. Why did he go with Whip?"

I was not about to say that Shen had the Gift or that he was a Healer. It's unlikely Mols knew about it, and it should remain a secret for now.

"It was asked of me." She did not move her gaze.

"Who asked, if it's not a secret?"

"It is a secret."

"Allow me to insist."

"I won't allow it." Steel was rattling in her voice. "It's not connected to you in any way. I had a choice of where I could place the healer, and I chose Whip. Perhaps Shen could shed some light on all this. Where is he now?"

"We don't know."

"Is he dead?"

"I told you, we don't know. He fell behind on the road."

Mols was a clever woman. She deftly moved from

defense to attack. She began to ask questions and I had to answer, taking the heat off her. She was clearly not planning to tell me where she had found the Healer.

"When do you intend to start?"

"As soon as we get a look around."

"Just don't draw it out. You'll be recognized. If you need anything, Stump is at your disposal. At any convenient time."

"We'll take that into account. Thank you for supper." I stood up from the table and nodded a good-bye to the grim Stump. "We'll talk when I've got a feel for the situation."

"Do you have a place to spend the night?"

"Yes."

We weren't about to tell her about our hideout.

"Stump, see our guests out." Mols was clearly pleased with the conversation. "I will pray for your success."

And again, I did not know if she was mocking us or not.

The wine in the glass was the color of pigeon blood. Mols took the glass in hand and sipped. She tasted the tart yet at the same time heady aroma of ripe grapes. She didn't like this drink, but today she felt the need for something stronger. The woman didn't even dilute the wine with water. The incomparable taste of ripe berries flowed over her tongue, but Mols grimaced as if she were drinking vinegar.

It was dry. She couldn't stand dry wine. And furthermore, it was red. How could Stump drink such shit, and how could it cost five sorens a bottle? Still grimacing, the head of the guild of Giiyans placed the glass back on the table; then she thought better of it and drained it in one gulp. Now she wasn't grimacing anymore. As she had assumed, it didn't get any better. A glimmer of dismay had settled somewhere in the depths of her soul.

The door opened and Stump entered the room quietly. He was sullen and agitated. He sat opposite her, took some beef tongue onto his plate, salted it generously, stuffed it into his mouth, and began to chew grimly. Mols remained silent, ignoring her assistant and the man with whom she had lived for twenty years.

"This is unprecedented." Stump broke the silence. "You decided to reverse yourself and drink wine?"

"Right now's not a good time for taunts, Olna."

"For me, it's the best time. Soon we won't have any time for them. They left, if you care."

"I don't."

"Did you really expect something different?"

Mols looked at the man angrily; then she sighed. "Yes. They might not have been so agreeable and compliant."

"Gray had no cause. Plus, I would not allow—"

"And Weasel as well?" she interrupted him. "How would you have stopped her, if she had decided to boil your brains?"

"But she didn't do that."

"She simply didn't want to. Like all intelligent people, they prefer to fight only when there is no other recourse. I didn't thwart them and I didn't drive them into a corner. She had no reason."

"And yet you're uneasy."

"They know about the boy."

"Oh," said Stump emphatically, and then he reached for the bottle.

"Knowing Gray's stubbornness, I'm surprised he didn't insist on a direct answer."

"Ness could have grown wiser over the years. Or it's just not that important to him, Katrin."

"With all his suspicion and caution?" Mols spat. "Don't be stupid. It's very important to him. He wants to understand why Shen went with Whip. Why a man outside of the guild was needed."

"I thought you gave an adequate explanation."

"Everyone makes mistakes." She sighed and stood up from the table. "I wasn't counting on them knowing that the lad is not part of the guild."

"Do you think you acted correctly, giving in to that request?"

"I wasn't fool enough to risk it. I was told directly that stubbornness on that matter would be fatal to me. And for you as well, by the way. I had to agree."

"Why did they need to send the boy, and an untrained one at that? Did they not trust us?"

"Go and ask them."

"No thank you, Katrin. I'll somehow manage to live without the answer. I'm worried about what will happen if Gray comes and asks again. More aggressively. Will you tell him the truth?"

"The truth is dangerous. In this instance, for us. They paid us well and left the guild alone. I won't give anything away."

"And if Ness insists?"

Mols gazed coldly at her lover.

"For the time being everything is going according to plan. But if Gray starts kicking up a fuss, I myself will bring Joch his head and collect the ten thousand. Believe me, that would be much safer than crossing these people."

"We can now honor the contract. When Gray and Weasel come again, we'll be ready."

"No. I'm in no hurry to finish what was started so long ago. Joch is in our way, and Ness and Layen can get rid of him. Then we can consider the contract."

For some time he was silent, but then he said softly, "So be it."

17

It was dark, but I was not about to light the candle Layen had in her pack. The light would disturb the pigeons sleeping in the rafters, and then things would get really crazy in here. A commotion among the birds at such a late hour might draw unnecessary attention.

We did not need that.

It smelled strongly of bird droppings, and somewhere over our heads the birds, not quite woken by our cautious steps, rustled and cooed discontentedly. Fortunately, the dumb creatures did not realize that uninvited guests had come to their attic. I held Layen's hand and slowly moved toward the open attic window, through which I could see the half moon.

Something fell onto my left shoulder with a disgustingly savory plop and Layen, unable to restrain herself, giggled quietly. I swore through my teeth, cursing the bird who so cleverly managed to shit on my jacket.

"I'm sorry," whispered my sun. "But don't you recall the same thing happened to you once before? On the day we met?"

I snorted good-naturedly and almost tripped over a wooden circle of Melot that was resting on the floor by the window. Swearing again, I glanced out the window, saw that all was quiet, and jumped out onto the roof. The tiles under my feet were secure, so I had no fear of falling. However, I had no desire to look down. We were very high up. After all, it was the second tallest temple to Melot in the city, built by the Sculptor himself.

I extended my hand to Layen, helping her out onto the roof. The light wind blowing in from the sea smelled of salt and iodine. The half moon was swimming through the sky like a sleepy fish. Now hiding behind low clouds, now appearing again, it flooded the flat roof of the temple, its domes and seven spires with silver light. We needed the third spire from the central cupola.

"It's a good thing the priests rarely come up here. They'd consider us sacrilegious." Her smile gleamed in the night.

"They're too fat and lazy for that," I said. "What do they have to do up here, anyway? The bells are somewhere else. Melot wills that once or twice a year they send workers up here to make sure the roof isn't leaking."

"Did you notice that Mols wasn't disposed to discuss Shen's history?"

"I'm not an idiot. I noticed. It worries me."

"But you didn't insist? Even though you could have."

"Yes. But I didn't. Of course, he fears you and your Gift. But it wouldn't be a good idea to take advantage of this fear without real power backing it. That could end very badly. I'll still find out why the Healer came to him."

We stopped by the spire. It had a huge, square base, which turned into a steep cone about thirty yards above our heads.

"We want the eastern part." I was trying to orient myself.

"Then it's on the opposite side," said Layen without hesitating. "Come on."

Each side of the spire was about ten yards long. We had to go west and north before we arrived at the place we needed.

"This isn't the central temple. There might not be anything here."

"They were built at the same time and by the same man, my dear. It's just that the central temple is in the Hightown and this one is in Haven. The sanctuary should be here. I'm sure of it."

I began searching to the right of where the base of the Sculptor's enormous spire passed into the roof. It wasn't all that easy. Finally, by a wall, under the sixth tile from the edge, I found a faint image depicting an arch.

"Can you do it?" I asked Layen.

She licked her lips nervously. "I'll try. I hope whatever spark I have left is enough."

"Don't fret. If it doesn't work, we'll find another place to hide."

"I'm not going to give up that easily." She smiled. "Slipping past the priests won't be any fun."

I winked encouragingly at her. My sun stretched out her palm and covered the partially faded symbol, which the Sculptor himself had put there a thousand years ago. After a few seconds the arch began to shine a ruby red color, and part of the wall by the eastern side of the spire moved aside, revealing a dark, narrow passage. You needed to go sideways to squeeze into it.

"Excellent," I praised her. "I see you can already do some things."

M . . . Gi . . . . . . ee . . . . ck ev . . . d. . . .

"I'm sorry? I didn't understand." I was smiling like an idiot. After so many days I could hear her again.

"My Gift keeps coming back every day. Faster and faster. It just lacks strength," she concluded apologetically.

"The fact that you can do anything at all is good enough for me."

We squeezed through the opening. It was as dark as if our eyes had been plucked out.

"Light," Layen requested softly.

I winced from the bright light that flooded in on us from all sides. It was radiating from white spheres.

"I don't like this place," I muttered.

Layen, also a bit nervous, put her hand on an arch inscribed on the wall, an exact copy of the one I found on the roof, and the secret door slid into place.

"Does it seem to you that it's much bigger on the

inside than it appears from outside?" I asked nervously.

"It's one of the Sculptor's tricks. I've heard of it."

Nine years ago Layen showed me a secret sanctuary, created by the Sculptor, in the spire of the central temple of Melot. How she knew about the secluded nook and why none of the Walkers or Embers had heard of it, I didn't ask. Just as I didn't ask who taught her the Gift or where she was from. In our life there were topics we tried not to touch upon.

In those days we used the sanctuary my sun showed me as a hideout. It was small, but fairly comfortable and cozy. And, most importantly, no one knew about it, and getting into it without the Gift was impossible. The only place that would be safer would be under the Mother's skirts, if you can forgive the blasphemy.

This space seemed enormous. Six yards from the entrance, ten steps down, and it became a spacious hall that extended at least a hundred yards, with a high, domed ceiling, powerful buttresses, and rows of massive hexagonal columns along the walls. All in gloomy gray stone, with no thought toward beauty.

"I don't understand!" I finally exclaimed. "How can the outside be so small, and the inside so large? How does this hall fit in the spire?"

Layen was distracted from her contemplation of the space. It was obvious that she was no less shocked than I was.

"It's a game with space, with the world. Something may seem smaller than it actually is. The mages of the past knew how to do such things."

"And the Walkers?"

"Of today, no."

"What about the Damned?"

"Their power and knowledge isn't sufficient either. Only those who lived at the time of the Sculptor could do things like this. Then the Great Decline came. The War of the Necromancers finished off that which had not yet been forgotten."

"That means—"

"Do you know why the Walkers are so afraid of the Damned?" she asked suddenly. "Because they were born five hundred years ago and they possess knowledge the likes of which none of the current spark-bearers could ever possess. Knowledge, not power, that is the main weapon of the Sextet."

"Do you mean to say that the Damned aren't really all that powerful?"

"No. They are strong enough to crush most wielders of the Gift. But there are those who compare to them in terms of power. The Mother, I believe, could very well match Rubeola—she was considered the weakest of those who started the Dark Revolt. But the Mother has much less knowledge than Mitifa does."

"Is Mitifa Rubeola's name?"

"Yes."

"I didn't know that."

"The Tower prefers not to spread it about. But

any bearer of the Gift knows the real names of the Damned. In the Rainbow Valley they don't consider it necessary to conceal the history. Or at any rate, the history that benefits them."

I could hardly refrain from asking Layen if she had been to the Empire's most illustrious academy, where those who have the spark are taught.

"I'm afraid we'll never know why the Sculptor created this space," she said, apparently not noticing my hesitation. "Come on. Let's have a look around."

"You could fit a whole lot of people in here," I said, running my hand along one of the columns.

"You know, I wasn't sure we'd find a hiding place here," she confessed suddenly.

"So you didn't know about it before?"

"Of course not. But going to Hightown at night made no sense. You know that no one would let us in. So I thought of the temple in Haven. The Sculptor built it and at that time this structure was beyond the city limits. Why not give it a try?"

"And if you were mistaken?"

"We'd have spent the night in the refectory attic. With the pigeons." She giggled.

I raised my eyes to heaven. That would have been so much fun!

"Hey! Look here! There's a hatch in the floor!" Layen exclaimed suddenly. She fell to her knees and began trying to pry the heavy lid up with her fingers.

"So this place is even bigger than I thought." I shook my head.

"Instead of standing there trying to look smart, you could help a poor woman!"

"I'd prefer to stand a bit farther away. This place isn't hidden for nothing. A hungry monster could crawl out of that at any moment."

"You said the same exact thing when I opened the passage into the central temple for the first time. Nothing jumped out at you then." She was beginning to get angry.

I got down to work.

The cover was wedged in tightly, and I could only just get my hands into a crack.

"Watch your fingers!" Layen warned.

I strained my muscles and threw the heavy steel lid to the side. It fell on the stone slabs with a clang, and we looked down into the dark gap in the floor. Only the first five steps leading into the darkness were visible.

"Shall we climb down?" I asked, already knowing her answer.

"As if you have to ask! Light!"

At the bottom, magical lanterns flared up, but they didn't shine as brightly as those in the hall.

"Wait." I grabbed Layen's hand as she was about to descend and at her perplexed look explained, "I'll go first."

"I swear by my Gift," squeaked my sun when we

got to the bottom. "I swear by my Gift! It's . . . it's . . ."

She didn't finish. She just paused on the stairs, frozen with wonder.

We were in a small heptagonal room with a flat ceiling, rose-colored walls, and a floor of the exact same color. A wide circle was inscribed on the floor (ten people could fit comfortably inside it), and inside the circle seven mosaics were cleverly laid in the shape of large petals. Each petal corresponded to a wall. All seven of the petals of the flower exceeded the boundaries of the circle, and seven tips sprung up from the floor where they ended. Half as tall as a man, the steeply curved petals pointed back toward the center of the circle.

I'd never seen anything like it before.

"The Paths of Petals!" Layen finally recovered the ability to speak. "Ness! It's the Paths of Petals!"

"Oh!" I said profoundly.

A legendary creation, made by the Sculptor himself. According to all the myths and tales, which I have heard more than once, it was possible to travel unimaginable distances almost instantly with the help of the magic embedded in the Paths of Petals.

"He was a great man. And a great mage." She passed her hand over the nearest petal tip.

I didn't bother to ask who "he" was.

"Sure. So great that he took the secret of their creation to his grave. As far as I recall, from the moment of his death, not one of the Walkers could even come close to the creation of this miracle. Nothing they did worked."

"You're correct, my dear. But that doesn't over-shadow his greatness."

"I don't know." I watched with apprehension as Layen entered the circle. "Call me greedy, but I don't understand why he didn't share this knowledge with his descendants."

"Perhaps he didn't find them worthy. Or maybe he just didn't have the time. Who knows? So many centuries have passed. It's all forgotten."

"Hey," I said, unable to restrain myself. "Could you get away from them? I'm not sure it's safe."

"Don't be silly," she dismissed me. "None of the Petals have worked for the past five hundred years or so."

"I know," I grumbled resentfully.

"Then I don't know why you're worried. When the Damned left the Council and staged a revolt, Sorita managed to close the Sculptor's works before she died, and since then they've been dead."

"Dead, huh?" I walked over to the nearest tip and touched it. The stone was unexpectedly warm and smooth. "I'm not so sure of that."

"Dormant, then. What difference does it make?" Sometimes her complacency amazed me. "All the Walkers in the world, including the Damned, could not wake them up. We're certainly not going to. Believe me, Sorita strived to make it so that the Petals would be lost forever. Not a single Walker will ever walk through them again. Unless, of course, a wise person is found who can revive stone."

"Do you know how they work?" I was curious to hear what she had to say because I'd heard many different theories about how the Petals worked. From the simplest, such as uttering a word, to the most ridiculous, like bat dung and donkey urine.

"I've read in books"—she had stopped looking around and came to stand next to me—"that people stand in a circle, a Walker imagines the place they need to be, and with the help of the Gift she makes the Petals come to life and then—you're already in another place."

"Uh. Um . . ." I stuttered, trying to formulate a thought. "So without Walkers it's impossible to make do?"

Layen looked at me somewhat strangely and gently asked, "Ness, do you know why the Walkers are called Walkers?"

I'd never thought about it before today, but I saw what she was getting at quite quickly.

"Oh!" That simple word was becoming my trademark. "They're called that because they operated the Petals."

"Clever boy." She kissed me on the cheek. "You're absolutely right."

"Wait, wait! What do the Embers do then?"

"What do you think?" She answered my question with a question.

"I don't know," I said honestly. "I always thought

they were weaker than the Walkers. Something along the lines of pupils or schoolchildren."

"Not at all. You understand . . ." She lapsed into thought; then she smiled, caught my surprised look, and quickly explained, "I'm sorry. It's just strange to have to explain common truths to you."

"Common?" I was indignant. "Go out on the street and ask a hundred people what differentiates one mage from another and why they are called what they are, and you'll see what they tell you."

"You're right. Of course you're right." She nodded. "No one gives any thought to why they are named so. It developed over the centuries, became habitual. And because the Walkers were more important and sat at the Council, the Embers were instantly placed on a lower step. In terms of power, of course."

"And it's not so?" It was strange to learn something new on a subject I'd thought I'd known since childhood.

"Do you remember what I told you about the Healer? About the fact that he has a different Gift from the inhabitants of the Rainbow Valley? Just so, between the Walkers and the Embers there are a few differences. The first could travel with the help of the Paths of Petals, could force them to submit, could so clearly imagine a place that it became almost real to them. Also, they are more adept at weaving spells. Adept, I said, not more powerful. It's like knitting. If they are working with complicated patterns, then the Embers can't create very serious spells, although they may be powerful. But the Embers have a different ability; they can share their spark, their warmth. They can transfer a part of their strength to a Walker, enhancing her Gift for a time. This is very crucial, especially in battle."

"Like a quiver of arrows held in reserve?" I chuckled.

"Just about. If we take two Walkers of identical strength, who for whatever reason decide to fight each other, the one with the stronger Ember on her side would win. Or the one with a few Embers. They strengthen exponentially when added atop one another."

"I think I understand," I said thoughtfully. It's funny to say! I lived my whole life, and here now such a revelation! "Embers can be stronger than Walkers?"

"In terms of power, yes. But not skills. Also, Walkers are always women, but Embers can be men. Excluding the Healers. Male Healers could command the Petals. The Sculptor was a Walker."

"I already knew that. But other men couldn't talk to the stones?"

"It seems they couldn't." Layen smiled cheerfully. "But I don't think this was very frustrating to Plague, Delirium, and Consumption. Especially after Sorita lulled the Petals to sleep."

I recalled that three of the eight original Damned

were men. And two of them were still alive. But one question was still bothering me.

"And how is it, now that the Petals have stopped working, that they determine who is a Walker and who is an Ember?"

"I don't know." She shrugged. "I've never seen it happen. But I can assume that all that's required is to check how complicated the spells are that an applicant can weave and whether she is able to give a bit of her spark to another bearer of the Gift. For myself, I'm curious as to why the Petals are in such an odd place. You have to agree, it's a strange find. I doubt anyone knows they are here except for their creator. Did the Sculptor have a reason for secreting away one of the Petals in this place? What for?"

"I'm afraid we'll never learn the truth. Come away from here. We only have a few hours for sleep. Tomorrow will be a hard day."

She nodded reluctantly and was already beginning to climb the stairs, when I saw something curious on one of the walls.

"Layen, that drawing is here, too!"

We walked over to it.

"The arch, the sign of the Sculptor. It seems we haven't found everything he hid here. The lock is exactly the same as the one by the entrance on the temple roof."

"Do you want to take a look?"

"No," she replied resolutely. "Otherwise, we'll be

here too long. Right now I'm not strong enough to squander my spark. Next time."

"We'll definitely return here."

"You promise?"

"I promise."

Her smile was tired.

"Lights," my sun whispered softly when we had settled into our travel blankets, and the spheres hanging on the walls plunged the room into darkness.

Ga-Nor awoke because the door creaked. He jumped up, grabbing the dagger lying next to him on his pillow.

"Calm down, buddy. It's just me," said Luk quickly, and just in case he held up his hands to show he was unarmed. Who knows what kinds of things the Son of the Snow Leopard imagined in his sleep.

"I can see that it's you," grumbled the tracker and, letting go of his weapon, he fell backward onto the bed. "Don't stand in the doorway, come in. And shut the door behind you. Where have you been for half the night?"

"Bah! What's this I hear! Were you really worried about me?"

Ga-Nor cast an evil glance at his comrade, but he ignored it.

"Why did Ug send such a punishment to me?" groaned the northerner suddenly. "For what sins?"

"What are you on about?" Seated on the other bed, Luk even stopped tugging off his boots.

"I'm talking about you. You were dumped in my lap and now I have to babysit you."

"Excuse me!" said the soldier, offended. "I didn't ask you to make a fuss over me. That was your wish. If you'd passed me by, I wouldn't have said a word."

"You act all high and mighty now, but then you were barely holding your own against the dead. If I hadn't helped you, you'd be with them now."

"Nothing of the sort. I could have dealt with them myself."

"I swear by Ug!" Ga-Nor was so indignant he sat up. "You're the most ungrateful pig on the face of the earth, Luk! It's not enough that I saved your hide and we tramped through half the south to get to Al'sgara. What am I doing here? The war is going on in the east and in the north, but I've been lazing around here, futilely knocking on the doors of the Tower for the past week."

"Do you know why you are so angry?" Luk collapsed into his bed, which creaked under his weight. "Because you're used to the northern forests and trekking through the snowy tundra, and the city frightens you."

"Ass. Where would I be without you?" Ga-Nor sighed.

"The Nabatorians would probably be playing catch with your red-haired noggin. You heard what's happening, screw a toad! Gash-Shaku is under siege; Okni has been taken and given over to fire and the sword. In less than two weeks, battle will break out at the Steps of the Hangman. From there a straight path will be opened to the center of the Empire and the capital. Don't think I'm a coward, but it's better here than in that inferno, with necromancers all around."

"I've never considered you a coward," said the tracker and then immediately added a spoonful of vinegar to his compliment. "Just a fool, and those are very different things. I'm a warrior. It's my business to wage war, not to crawl on my knees to the Walkers, waiting for the silly quails to hear us out. How many times must we ask for this, for your audience? Do you really not get that no one wants to see us?"

"If you're so eager to fight, the war will descend upon us soon enough. Then you can swing your sword around until you burst, friend."

Or until a Nabatorian more clever than you cuts you down, Luk concluded to himself.

"Let's do this," said Ga-Nor, gazing at the ceiling. "If after five days everything is just the same as it is now, and we are being shown the door every time, I'm leaving."

"Where, if I may ask?"

"To where our troops are fighting. And if that

doesn't work out, I'll go home. I swore an oath to my clan; let the elders decide how I should serve."

"Don't be dumb, Red. Your north is too far away from here, and the Nabatorians are at the Steps of the Hangman. You won't break through."

"There's always the sea."

"I don't think the situation's much better there. They could have besieged the Cape of Thunder on the western passage from Losk. There are two good routes into the center of the Empire, and both may be closed. You can't get anywhere from the south. Not right now, at any rate."

"I'll try, man. You know I can do it."

"Maybe," Luk agreed reluctantly. "The Children of the Snow Leopard are a persistent people. Do what you will. But I'm going to do what I came here for. I must tell the Walkers about Rubeola."

"Do you really think they don't know?"

"What does that matter? I must."

"I swear by Ug. You're a real soldier," said Ga-Nor mockingly. "Stupid and stubborn."

"Not like you, that's for sure." Luk didn't get angry when the northerner taunted him, although he himself didn't know why. "Okay, I want to sleep."

"You didn't tell me where you were."

"I was playing dice," the soldier replied unwillingly.

"Of course. With the money Layen left us?"

"Yes."

"And what will we live on when it's all drained away?"

"I won, screw a toad!"

"Really?" Ga-Nor was surprised. "I don't believe you. You usually lose."

"Not always."

"I suppose you cheated."

"A little bit." Luk couldn't deny it.

"Tomorrow you will give all the money to me."

"Why?" The soldier shot up like a scalded cat.

"Because at any moment you might sit down to play with someone who cheats better than you. And I don't want to be stuck in Al'sgara with empty pockets," said the northerner adamantly. "Besides, you still owe me."

The mention of his debt caused Luk to shut up. He huffed aggrievedly, wiggled around on his bed to find a comfortable position, and then settled down for the night. Ga-Nor silently thanked Ug that his talkative companion had finally quieted down. The northerner lay there for some time, thinking that they needed to head out for Hightown earlier tomorrow, and that if the secretary of the Tower once again tried to lead them around by the nose, he'd grab him by his throat and squeeze until Luk was sent to someone in the Council.

But the quiet didn't last long.

"Ga-Nor, are you asleep?"

"I'm trying," the northerner hissed without opening his eyes. He was silently calling down all the curses he knew on Luk's head, up to and including the icy axe of Ug.

"I was thinking about Layen. I regret letting her go. How do you think she's doing on her own?"

"I think she's doing just fine. Far better than us. Sleep."

"I wonder if she met up with Ness? Did they even escape Bald Hollow at all? We really don't know anything about them. Not about Ness or Gis or Shen. What do you think, were they lucky like us?"

"I don't think anything, Luk. I want to sleep. Their fate is in Ug's hands. He usually protects good soldiers."

"You might laugh, but I got used to their company. I think it would have been easier together—"

"There was never any 'together.'" Ga-Nor abruptly broke off his friend's musings. "It's unlikely the assassins would have stayed with us for long. And from what I understand, they have their own business in the city. And you have yours."

"Who are you calling assassins?" asked Luk, dumbfounded.

"Ness and Layen."

"What for?"

"They are Giiyans."

"What?"

"They are masters. They kill for money."

"I know what Giiyans are. It just seemed to me that you called—"

"Our acquaintances are Giiyans," the Son of the Snow Leopard interrupted him.

A brief silence hung over them. Luk was digesting this news.

"You're sure?"

"Yes."

"But—"

"I swear by Ug, I'm telling the truth. Can we sleep now?"

"Sure. Listen, is Shen one, too?"

"I don't know."

After a minute Ga-Nor was already asleep but Luk kept staring at the ceiling, still unable to believe his companion's words.

18

Tia got to the Ors when it was getting dark. She stopped in a grove of willows along the bank, a few yards away from the water, and sat down without taking her eyes off the opposite shore. The mighty river was leisurely flowing toward the sea and it gleamed with the nighttime lights of Al'sgara reflected on the water. Right now the southern capital reminded her most of the great city of Sdis, Sakhal-Neful, when it was being approached after sunset from the Great Waste.

Typhoid gazed through Pork's eyes and could not believe what she saw, even though she should have expected it. The last time she had beheld these walls and towers was five hundred years ago, on the day when one part of the Council rebelled and decided to destroy the other. Twenty of them opposed the Mother and her supporters, and only eight, those who would later be known as the Damned, survived the night to leave the city, fleeing after the failed rebellion. Yes, they killed many, including the Mother herself, but they wasted too much energy fighting those who came from the Rainbow Valley to help Sorita.

Pork gritted his teeth and clenched his fists, remembering that time along with his Mistress. Since then none of the Sextet had seen the great city. The War of the Necromancers devastated the Empire over the course of fifteen years, and then they had to go beyond the Boxwood Mountains and Nabator. To Sdis. To the Great Waste and beyond.

And now, after so many years, here she was on the shore of the river, looking at the city once more, the city in which she had lived a part of her former life. Al'sgara was the same and yet completely different. Foreign. True, even from this shore it was possible to see the walls, towers, and spires of Hightown. The Sculptor's walls and the temples to Melot were the same as before, but much that was new had appeared. The city had grown. It had expanded along the coast, overgrown its walls, spawned new districts, new buildings, new homes, new people, and had become much more unsightly, dangerous, and frightening. Typhoid felt like this enormous creature was breathing, defecating, and seething with thousands of people, alive with the magic of the Walkers. If Retar were alive, he would have put it differently. But he was long gone, even though she could still recall his face and his smile quite well. She had loved him more than life—she'd followed him into the Abyss and been left alone.

Deep-rooted hatred toward the idiots sitting in the Tower stirred within her, and Pork, twitching with fear, began whimpering. Typhoid suppressed his will. Once again she contemplated the Walkers and stared grimly at the city. She was sure that the archer, who had unfortunately escaped her, was beyond the walls that towered over the other side of the river. And the girl with the spark and the boy Healer would be with him. That meant she needed to get into Al'sgara.

But it wasn't that simple. Tia was sure that the gates were being watched by the Tower and she wouldn't be able to pass through them. The Walkers might sense her Gift, even though her spark barely glimmered in Pork's body. Even the smallest hint of a spark was enough for some experienced mages. And then . . .

Tia knew that she would not be able to deal with all the Walkers and Embers of Al'sgara when they inevitably descended on her, drawn like wasps to molasses. And descend on her they would, if she so much as touched the gates. That meant there was only one way—by water. It was unlikely the entrance to Haven was guarded as closely as the walls. She had a greater chance of sneaking in there. But even if she succeeded, she would still need to be on the alert and not be seen by the bearers of the Gift. Or by the Scarlets, for that matter. Though the Damned could more or less fight against the former, she would be completely powerless against the wizards. Anyone wearing a red robe could bind her hands and feet with a snap of his fingers. It had already happened once in that foggy village and, if she were honest with herself, she was still shocked at how easily the old man had bested her.

At the time Tia had been out of her wits because she had finally caught the archer who killed her body, and so she saw the twisted, ruby-covered wand too late. It seemed to the Damned that she'd been hit over the head with something heavy. Her vision darkened and she only regained consciousness after a day, when the fool was wandering through a field. Typhoid was so enraged that she vented all her anger on Pork.

She had to go back to the deserted village on foot, and there she found out that the horses had disappeared. The archer and the wizard had probably taken them. In an extremely foul mood, realizing that with every minute she was falling farther behind the people she was pursuing, the Damned walked on, and in the next village she stole a horse.

Suddenly a nasty burning sensation pierced Pork's

spinal column and Tia grimaced as if she had a toothache.

A Summons!

The Abyss take her, a Summons! One of the Sextet wanted to talk to her. The burning increased, spread from her back to her shoulders to her neck, and then it started creeping up the back of her head.

Typhoid knew, of course, who was calling her.

Rovan.

Only his summons burned like the venom of a red scorpion or a fiery hot brand. Curse him three times over! What did that tomb worm want? They didn't talk often and tried to be as far away from each other as possible. Consumption was a dangerous opponent. Especially now, when the Damned had lost most of her powers. Rovan would gleefully take advantage of this opportunity to destroy her.

The burning increased.

Rovan was not going to give up. He was demanding a conversation, and with each passing second resisting him became increasingly difficult. Before Typhoid could have simply brushed aside his intrusiveness, tearing up the weave, but not now. She didn't have enough strength, and the damned maggot would not let up. The burning sensation was bordering on pain. Rovan strengthened it and then suddenly eased up on the pressure, and when her body relaxed, the next painful sting hit her. Tears poured from Pork's eyes, and Tia realized that this pathetic shell simply could not withstand such abuse.

She forced the half-wit to stand up, and she hurried over to the river on his trembling legs. Falling to her knees at the water's edge, she looked around. There was no one. With all her strength she struck her fist on the surface of the water. A splash shot up into the air and hung there, the drops shimmering with silver in the uneven light of the half moon; then they merged together and formed a wide, flat mirror in front of the Damned. It was translucent, but, in obedience to her command, it shone with a dull light, and Typhoid saw her interlocutor.

Rovan was reclining on soft satin pillows scattered haphazardly over an expensive Sdisian carpet. Next to him was a cuirass, polished until it gleamed, and a sword with an expensive hilt; a bit farther away was a table piled high with papers. Enough candles were burning that Typhoid could see that he was in his tent.

Rovan Ney, Lord of the Tornado, Son of the Evening, Axe of the West, known as Consumption, seemed about five years older than Tia. He had a purebred, somewhat pale face, large brown eyes, arrogant, thin lips, and a perfectly straight nose. Very light blond hair and eyebrows, a neatly trimmed beard and mustache. Thick, long eyelashes that any woman would envy and a dazzling smile. He was of average height, fairly broad in the shoulders and well muscled enough to be intimidating. He had narrow, elegant hands with long fingers, such that you rarely encounter in good soldiers. And yet, he could run rings around any living thing when it came to his mastery of the blade. Only Retar had been able to compete with him before.

Consumption was dressed in a black silk shirt, which was lying open on his broad chest, and loose trousers of the exact same color. No jewelry, no weapons, no shoes. At his feet was perched a short, and quite young, woman of the Je'arre nation. She could have been called beautiful, even taking into account her shaven head, but one of her snow-white wings was broken and, apparently, it had happened recently. The flyer did not take her adoring gaze off her master. In contrast to the Damned, a small knife hung on her belt, but she obviously had no thought of putting it into action.

It was a familiar scene. Rovan delighted in the pain of others. He elevated it to a kind of worship, a daily requirement of gratification. He loved to torment, loved to feel the terror of his victims. He loved to hear them beg for mercy, choking on their tears, crawling at his feet. But most of all Consumption loved to subjugate. To convert pain into blind love, adoration, slavishness. With magic and pain he broke others' wills and reforged them to bend only to his own. He turned the proud into sycophants and ciphers, his enemies into servants and the dead. Oh! No one in the world knew how to surround himself with dead bodies and to derive true pleasure from it like Rovan did!

"You took your time answering," he said by way

of greeting. "It's not very polite of you to treat your friends like that. Don't you agree?"

"I see you're not at all surprised to see me looking like this." She ignored his question and forced Pork to stretch his lips into a smile.

"Just imagine." Rovan barely moved his finger, and the Je'arre was already offering him a cup of wine. A well-trained girl. "Although you must permit me to say—you looked much better before."

At this Typhoid could only smile sweetly. Or at least try to. Right now she was occupied with a far more important matter—she was feverishly wondering why the maggot was so calm and sarcastic, and why he didn't even raise an eyebrow at seeing the stupid mug of a village cowherd instead of Tia's usual face. There could only be one answer—Rovan knew what he would see before he made the Summons.

Damn Tal'ki!

"What do you want?" she asked sullenly.

"You don't sound very happy to see me."

"Enough!" she snapped. "Tell me what you want!"

"I see that some things never change. You're just as rude as before, Typhoid. Even in that body. I just wanted to inform you that I'll arrive soon."

"Where, if it's not a secret?"

"In Al'sgara. I'm hastening there as fast as I can."

"As far as I recall, you're stuck in the east."

"You have outdated information. Leigh and I

managed to conquer the Isthmuses of Lina. He went to Okni to meet up with Alenari and head for the Steps of the Hangman, while I and my army are going to crack the sweet nut that is Al'sgara."

Rovan smiled blindingly and stroked the cheek of the Je'arre. She shivered with delight.

"I don't recognize you, Son of the Evening. You were never so unreasonably flippant. The nut is sweet, but hard. Or do you think that the walls, delighted by your beauty, will fall and the gates will fling themselves open? You'll meet an army of the Imperials. Plus, there are no fewer bearers of the Gift here than in the capital."

"My regiments will capsize the army into the sea." Rovan shrugged nonchalantly. "Don't look at me like that, Rider of Hurricanes. I know they are good soldiers, but the battles have not been going in their favor. And there are far fewer of them. The Sdisian spies did their job well. Soon I will crush Crow's Nest and open a direct route to Al'sgara. How do you like my friend?" he asked suddenly.

"You prefer boys."

"Slander." His eyes were laughing. "At any rate, no more than girls. So?"

"She's pretty," she answered dryly. "You educated her well."

"Education is something you have never lacked. She would do anything to please me. If you want, she can die."

"It makes no difference to me."

"Yes, I think you're right. I still haven't played with her enough. I want you to cut your face," he snapped at his handmaid.

She eagerly bared her knife and without a moment's hesitation drew it from her temple to the corner of her eye and down her cheek, passing though her lip to her chin. Blood began to flow. A lot of blood. The Je'arre smiled, oblivious to the blood and pain. She was happy that she pleased her lord.

He didn't pay the slightest bit of attention to the winged girl. Instead, he watched Tia intently the whole time. She lived up to his expectations; Pork made a contemptuous face.

"I'm always amazed that such a repulsive maggot like you could have had such a remarkable brother," she said bitterly.

Rovan's beautiful features contorted instantly, and his brown eyes flashed with fury.

"You filth! Don't you dare talk about my brother!" he roared, jumping to his feet and grabbing his sword. "Retar was the best of us and he died because of you! You stupid, insignificant painted whore!"

His pale face was flushed, and he took out his fury on the Je'arre. The unfortunate girl's head rolled under the table, her body collapsed to the floor, her wings were shorn off, pouring blood over the satin pillows and the expensive carpet. Rovan stood over her, breathing heavily, trying to control himself. He succeeded. He ran his hand over his face, tossed the bloody sword into the farthest corner of the tent and shoved the body away with his foot. He sat down and said, drawing out his words, "Let's get back to our conversation."

"You're a pervert, Rovan." Tia shook her head. "But I'm sorry you ruined your toy."

He smiled tightly. "A trifle. I'll find myself another."

"One would think you had an entire regiment of Je'arre." She deliberately led the conversation astray.

"Well . . . for some time I did."

"What do you mean by that?"

"The flyers came over to our side. Their elders sold out their own people."

"That's news."

"Yes. They provided us with a little help at the Isthmuses, where they struck the Imperials from behind. But a few days ago there was a little trouble— the birds got into a serious argument with the Shay-z'ans. You know how they have their history. The Burnt asked for blood. I consider the Shay-z'ans more important than the feathered. So now the numbers of the Je'arre are a bit, shall we say, curtailed. But I'll find something for myself."

Typhoid gritted her teeth. What an idiot! He'd grown stupid from the smell of blood and decay. How could Leigh have entrusted the leadership of an entire army to him? He couldn't just play the two formerly unified peoples against each other and deprive them of new allies! Now others, knowing what fate befell the Je'arre, would think ten times before moving to the side of the Overlords.

"I want you to help me with Al'sgara," Rovan said suddenly.

"Did I just imagine it, or did you really just say that?" Typhoid didn't know what to think.

"Don't make me ask twice," he replied, his blond eyebrows converging.

That would be fun, Tia thought to herself, but just said, "What do you want?"

"I want you to sneak into Al'sgara before the rumors fly that I'm coming to visit. You'll open the gates for me."

"A single set of fallen gates won't do you much good. There are many walls in the city."

"I'll think of something. Just do it."

"What do you want?" asked the Damned a second time.

He drilled her with his eyes for a moment and then said, "A book."

"I don't understand." Hearing this from Rovan was a novelty.

"Don't play the fool. I need the same thing as Tal'ki does, or else Leprosy wouldn't have sent you there, still in that form. I need a book. I need The Book. Have you got it? I want to know where it is when we storm the city. It would be a very bad thing, if we unknowingly burned down the library. Don't you agree?"

"What reason do I have to help you?"

"You're not helping me, but yourself. If the library burns down, every Overlord will lose a great deal. Plus, I'm willing to share with you if I get there before Tal'ki. We can help each other."

"I simply don't recognize you."

"Don't think that I've forgotten." He smiled promisingly. "I haven't forgotten or forgiven. You hate me, and I pay you back in the same coin. But right now we should work together. I give you my word that we'll divide everything evenly, and I won't stab you in the back."

"How very generous of you."

"Have I ever broken my word?" He frowned.

"No," she said, and finished to herself, *In this you and your brother were always alike.*

"Then I want to hear your answer."

"If it's possible," she replied cautiously.

"That's enough for me. I hope you won't waste time. When I arrive, I'll contact you."

The mirror darkened, and the water flowed back into the river.

Typhoid clenched her teeth. The Abyss take her, but what was going on here? Melot knew what kind of book, what library? What was the maggot talking about? What had Tal'ki told him? It was obviously something important if Rovan, who considered Tia to blame, albeit indirectly, for Retar's death, had decided to enlist her support for the first time in all these centuries. She had to know. And quickly.

It took her a lot of effort to create the Silver Window. Leprosy answered almost instantly. Typhoid saw her sitting on her bed in a cap and nightgown. She had clearly just been woken up, but there was no resentment on her face over the late Summons. Her faded blue eyes studied Pork steadily.

"I see, my dear, that you are handling him well. And you've even tuned him up a bit. He's not as ungainly as he was before. You're making progress. That. I. See." She narrowed her eyes and with a plump hand pushed the cat sleeping on her legs to the side. "I see that some of your power has returned to you. But you can only use it when you're in a dead body, am I right? How did you manage that?"

"The same way you did." Tia was angry. "When Ginora and Retar died, you drank up their power. I just took back my own."

"Very good." Tal'ki was not going to deny anything. "Very good, my dear. I'm happy for you."

"You didn't even tell us, Tal'ki!"

"Why should I have done that?" The Healer was sincerely amazed. "We all have our little secrets. Did you wake me up for this?"

"No! I just had a conversation with Rovan! You told him about me!"

She didn't even raise a brow.

"Not all that much. He knows that you are near Al'sgara and that you changed bodies. As for the fact that you are as weak as a kitten, no one but me even suspects."

"But why did you need to involve him in our affairs? You know how much he hates me!"

"Well, he's hated you for five centuries, so you're coming to your senses far too late. He still can't forgive you for his brother. That boy always thought he loved him far more than you did. I don't see why I should explain this to you. You think that I blabbed to him for nothing? What do you take me for, a silly, gossiping old goose?"

Typhoid was choking on her indignation, but Tal'ki curtailed her wrathful tirade with a question. "What did he want from you?"

"He offered me a deal. He needs a book."

"Naughty boy." Tal'ki bit her lip in chagrin. "And what would you get in return?"

"He's prepared to share."

"Well . . . that's not so bad. I hope you agreed?"

"Yes."

"A wise course of action."

"Perhaps you could explain to me what it is we're talking about?"

"Mitifa is still stuck in the library of the Walkers at the Six Towers. She's a smart girl. She found much that is interesting. This includes what may very well be the Sculptor's notes."

"How did the Walkers miss them?"

"You wouldn't be all that surprised at it if you saw the state they keep the books in. The parchment was practically impossible to handle. It crumbled. But Mitifa read a part of it."

"I'm quivering with anticipation to hear what was written there."

"It seems that the Sculptor hid his old journal in Al'sgara. It tells how to create the Paths of Petals."

That explained a lot. Including the fact that Rovan had decided to make a deal with her. Such knowledge would mean vast power. Enough power to become higher than the other Overlords. To create new Paths to replace those destroyed by Sorita. To rule the entire world. If it was true, there would be a real hunt for the book.

"I don't believe my ears!"

"I too did not believe at first, my dear. But then I thought about it for a bit, and why not? It's entirely possible."

"Where is the journal located?"

Tal'ki smiled sadly. "Do you think if I knew, I would tell you? The book is somewhere in Al'sgara. In the older buildings, possibly in Hightown. What makes you smile so, if I may ask?"

"Mitifa's idiocy."

"There's nothing to be done about it—she's terribly naïve when it comes to such matters."

The stupid fool! If Typhoid had found such a parchment, she would have kept silent about it. Not a word to anyone. But her? She instantly spread the news around the entire world!

"Who did she gossip to?"

"Only to me. I've always taken care of her, so she trusts me a bit."

"How did Rovan find out?"

"I mentioned it in passing, but he's a clever boy. He understood." Tal'ki was smiling contentedly, but Typhoid could no longer keep up with the thoughts of the mad old hag. "Well, I also said that you had gone to Al'sgara. Of course, I couldn't be exactly sure that you were headed there, but what is said cannot be unsaid. You understand."

The old witch! Of course, all it took was mentioning the book to Consumption and hinting that Tia had already been sent to search for it, for him to immediately head for the city. He would have no desire to give Typhoid and Leprosy such a valuable prize. The latter didn't have anything to lose. The city was vast, and the secret cache of the Sculptor had not been found for a thousand years (albeit no one knew about its existence to this day), so Rovan would not find anything right away. It had to be well planned out, but Consumption was incapable of that. He was a warrior, not a thinker. Retar, yes. Retar could have done it. But not his brother. So there was no need to worry about the safety of the book that spoke of the creation of the Paths of Petals.

Tal'ki had acted wisely. With the help of a false rumor she had made Rovan decide to do that which had been put off for so long—the assault on Al'sgara. No one wanted to start it, fearing to break their teeth against the great walls, and so the city had not yet been touched, had been left for later. But now

Consumption would brave the whirlwind, and perhaps he would be lucky. In any case, he would be kept busy and wouldn't hinder Leigh and Alenari from breaking through the Steps of the Hangman.

"Very well done," approved Tia.

"Thank you, my dear. I knew you would appreciate it."

"And what about Mitifa?"

"She's at the Towers. Finishing her work."

The Abyss! Rubeola really was a complete idiot, for still choking down book dust after revealing such a secret. In her place, Typhoid would have been rushing toward Al'sgara like a lunatic.

"The Son of the Evening is sure that you know where the Sculptor hid the book, and he said as much. He offered me half. What do you offer me?"

Tal'ki coughed out a dry laugh. "I think the same thing he offered you—nothing."

"That's not very generous of you."

"But honest. Rovan doesn't know where the book is. You don't know where the book is. I don't know where the book is. It could take us a century to find it. So all his promises are empty. Right now you should have little interest in the Sculptor's secrets. You've clearly forgotten that you are in no state to go chasing after phantoms. Judging by the fact that you are already at the great city, you haven't managed to catch either the Healer or that talented girl. And yet they are your only chance for getting back your strength and a satisfactory body, if, of course, that is what you still want. I see that it is. So redouble your efforts. They, not the book, are your main goal. You've gotten around just fine for five centuries without the Petals, and you'll live as many more, but without your power and a body, even Mitifa could crush you. You'd agree that would be a humiliating way to end such a long life. The Healer. The Healer, my dear. You can even forget about the girl, she's not that important, but the boy—bring him to me alive and unharmed. He is your only hope. Is he in the city?"

"I don't know. It's possible."

"Find out! And don't waste time! When the army arrives, madness will ensue. It will be very difficult to escape."

"Escaping is not the problem. Getting in will be virtually impossible."

"I suppose. But the harbor is always more poorly guarded. You should try a boat, my dear."

"I was thinking that. That's just what I'll do."

"Wonderful. Everything is ready. Bring the Healer and I will try to return what was lost. I found one interesting weave in the old books. It will help make it so that your ward's eyes are a normal color. You agree that white pupils would attract too much attention to you. Look."

She drew a few fine lines in the air.

"Thank you. That will help."

"I have no doubt. Good luck, my dear."

Without waiting for a reply, she liquidated the window. Tia muttered a curse, forced Pork to his feet, and set off in search of a boat.

19

Alms for a poor cripple. A-a-a-lms for a poor cripple."

Since morning, I'd drawled out the same exact phrase about a thousand times. Pretending to be a cripple was difficult of course, but a pound of dirt, tattered and vile-smelling clothes, a hood pulled down over my eyes, and a clay bowl with a broken rim lent credence to the idea that I was in need of money. Or that I was too lazy to work, however you looked at it. At any rate, the townsfolk completely ignored me. Though a few tenderhearted souls dropped a coin or two into my cup.

Over the course of three hours sitting on the pavement, I'd earned twelve coppers from my honest panhandling. The role of a lowly beggar had its benefits.

However, it also had its downsides. First, a group of the watchmen who patrolled Cucumber Quarter became interested in me. The lads offered me two choices—I could either get sent to the slammer, or I could share what I earned. Without thinking twice, I slipped two sols into their clutches and they left me alone for a while. Then came the local beggar, a hulk whose like I'd never seen and, of course, a true cripple. You could plow half the Empire on his hunched back. The man was very offended that I'd taken his rightful place, and he grabbed me by my lapels and vowed to beat out my soul. I had to get angry and press my dagger against his manhood. He shut his trap, unclenched his fists, and made himself scarce, which suited me just fine.

The sky was overcast, and it was drizzling from time to time, on the verge of turning into a downpour, so the hood over my head didn't cause any suspicion. Joch should be passing by soon, making his way to the arena where the Fights would be held this evening. This was why I had to resort to the attire of a beggar. While I was begging the nice folk of Al'sgara for money, Layen had gone to Second City to check on how Joch's lair was guarded.

I hadn't seen the yellow mug of Threefingers since I'd deprived him of two of the fingers of his right hand. Since that memorable day, the man's dislike of me grew stronger and a few times he had tried, by various means, to get to me. But he was not successful. At that time Joch did not have the power to confront the guild, and for a while he got off my back. But he forgot nothing. Now he was sure in his safety and had decided to try his luck. A good time for it, especially if you're friends with the Viceroy, whom you bribe well. Threefingers was the shadow advisor to the Viceroy, the organizer of displays and balls for the upper elite, the sponsor of festivals and celebrations. He'd also taken control over gambling, the Fights, the whores, and the petty thieves. . . . He started small, and finished big. The Viceroy's "best friend"—it's a most remarkable title. No one would bother him while he held it. Perhaps only the guild would dare, but then again, it's unlikely. Those in the guild are people, too, and they have no desire to be in that much trouble with the authorities, even less with the Walkers.

While Mols quietly conducts her business and eliminates people the Council deems undesirable, they look through their fingers at a series of other murders, a benefit of having the majority of contracts come from the stewards of this world. Plus, a portion of the well-earned sorens regularly finds its way into the pockets of the City Council, the head of the Guards, and other luminaries. And so for the time being, they know nothing, but should Mols overstep the line, they'd have her by the throat right quickly. Right now my dear baker so desperately wants to get rid of Joch, who yearns to subjugate the guild and to take a cut of the money, but if she does it with her own hands there would be a whole heap of trouble, including the Viceroy's dissatisfaction. He too knows everything, but he always forgets to give the necessary orders to his subordinates.

But then Layen and I turned up for Mols. If the affair went south, guess who the scapegoats would be? That's right. It'd be us. This was exactly what Mols was counting on. Joch would be sent off to feed the worms, and the hands of the guild would be clean. We didn't have a choice—we had to put Threefingers into the ground or else, as I had already said, we wouldn't be left in peace for the rest of our lives. In former years I would have killed myself for ten thousand sorens. What can be said about others?

A cavalcade appeared. I tugged the hood low over my eyes and huddled into my corner. His greatness Joch was deigning to inspect his domain and personally prepare everything for the evening's Fights.

First a foursome of horsemen with light crossbows pranced by. It was telling that they had their weapons on hand. Then I got an unpleasant surprise—Threefingers's bodyguards were kinsmen of Ga-Nor. Severe, red-haired men with grim, whiskered faces and the habits of experienced predators. A dozen Children of the Snow Leopard surrounded the carriage in a tight ring, and another three brought up the rear. I noticed they were carrying short bows.

The carriage should be given special mention. It had no windows, so there was no hope that a stray arrow could pass through a curtain. Also, I was sure that the doors locked from the inside. While you were wasting your time trying to get into that snail's shell, you'd be killed ten times over. Yet another crossbowman sat next to the driver.

The carriage passed by me and disappeared into the tangled streets of Cucumber Quarter. I sat there for a while, and then I stood, gathered my coins, and walked away. I knew everything I needed to.

A heavy rain began just when I had changed into more respectable clothes in a deserted alley.

Layen was waiting for me in the very heart of Haven, under an awning where cold shaf was served. Having a roof over our heads was a good thing—the raindrops were digging into the pavement like mad. There were almost no customers. No one wanted to sit in a puddle. Streams of water flowed right under the tables and stools, and you could count those who desired to soak their feet on your fingers.

My sun was grimly sipping the cold drink from an oaken cup while sitting at one of the driest tables. When she noticed me, she smiled in relief.

The serving girl brought another shaf and a hot pork sausage. I ate in silence while Layen stared off into the distance, in no hurry to begin our conversation. Her lips were compressed tightly, and her short blond hair was wet and sticking to her forehead. I finally finished my food, wiped my hands, set aside the empty dish, and recounted to her what I'd managed to spy out.

"He's very cautious. It won't be that easy to take him," she said in a whisper.

"Force won't work. We'd never make it to the

carriage; we'd be cut to pieces before that. I might be able to finish him off with an arrow when he steps out of the carriage, but even if I don't miss, there's the northerners to consider. They're a bit different from ordinary people. Once they're on your tail, you can't shake them. It's a very risky option."

"So we have to do it when Threefingers is at home," Layen concluded.

"Is it possible?"

She thought for a moment. "Perhaps. But with a whole host of reservations."

"Like what?"

"In the last seven years, our friend has managed to change his lair. The picture is bleak. He bought a mansion in front of the wall of Hightown. In the hills, in the part of Second City where the orchards are almost continuous. Getting there will be very difficult. It's a real fortress, and also right next to the barracks of the Viceroy's Guards. The main gate and the servants' entrance are guarded. The wall is also under surveillance. By his people and even more northerners. I can't even imagine how many there are inside."

"We don't know the schedule of patrols. We don't know how many men he has. We don't know where he sleeps, where he eats, or where he spends most of his time. We don't have the layout of the building. Sneaking into his home is practically suicide."

"We don't have a choice. If I had a bright spark it would all work out. It's flaring up with each passing day, but we don't have those days. Either we do it or we give up."

"I didn't come to Al'sgara for that, my sun. We'll think of something."

"Or Mols will. He may well know something. I think he and Stump have been calculating how to get Threefingers for many years. We should visit them again."

"Not the worst idea. He might be able to help us. After all, it's in his best interests."

"Let's do it, but only after a walk around the port."

The main street of Haven abutted the portside docks and the piers. Despite the bad weather, work was at full tilt here. I wouldn't say that there were many ships docked, but provisions were being unloaded from nearly all of them. The Viceroy was stockpiling food in the event of a lengthy siege.

Hustling near the docks was useless and depressing, so we went to a port tavern and tossed the landlord a soren, asking a few questions. He quickly grabbed the money and nodded to a table where two men with tanned faces, hardened by the sea winds, were sitting. Judging by their black hair, high cheekbones, and beards without mustaches, they were inhabitants of the Golden Mark. They were obviously smugglers or those who warm their hands on the fires of impending war. Right now you could get really good money for the sale of food and medicine.

We sat at their table uninvited. The older one grunted and looked pointedly at the bottom of his empty cup. I got the hint and ordered shaf all around. When the serving girl had brought the frothy beverage, the sailors raised their cups and the older one turned to Layen and said, "To your smile, beautiful! I swear by the great octopus, she's a wonder!"

They drank. We followed their example.

"I am Captain Dazh. This"—he pointed to his companion—"is my first mate. As I understand it, you were sent to us by that corrupt individual at the bar? And I even know why. You're not the first he's sent to us."

"I think that's why you pay him money." I couldn't resist.

Dazh bared his teeth, and I decided to interpret it as a smile.

"A witty fellow, eh, Riuk? I love those. And so. These last few days there's been no end to people wanting to take a ride on the *Lightborn*. So many people want to leave this wonderful city."

"We are just such people," I assured him.

"So I thought." An anchor and an octopus were roughly tattooed on the back of the captain's left hand. "The trouble is that when people find out the cost, they immediately shuffle off to look for another tub. Let's agree on this. I'll name a sum, you will agree or disagree. No bargaining, no persuasion, no 'we'll think about it.' And twenty percent of the payment up front."

"How much?"

He grinned. "A hundred sorens a soul."

"The price of sea travel has soared high in these hard times." I returned his grin.

"War has a wholesome effect on our wallets." Dazh shrugged. He was not about to make excuses. "What's your answer?"

Layen and I looked at each other. Two hundred sorens was quite a large amount. We could, of course, look for different passage, but I wasn't sure the prices there would be any lower.

"We agree."

"Wonderful," said Dazh in a dry, businesslike tone.

"Where is the guarantee that we won't be left on shore once we give you the forty sorens?"

"I have a reputation, and believe me, it's worth far more than forty coins. I swear by the great octopus that I do not cheat my passengers. As they say, rumors fly faster over the sea than schooners."

"When will you ride away?" asked Layen.

"We'll *sail*, beautiful. It's called sailing. As soon as we finish our business. After five days, if you count this one. We'll sail in the morning, as soon as the wind is suitable. So I ask you not to hold us up and to be on time. I won't wait; I give you fair warning."

"That suits us." Layen stretched out her fist, in which money was clenched.

Dazh held out his calloused palm, and before the people around us had time to notice the sparkle of the four coins, each worth ten sorens, the money had become the property of its new owner.

"Outstanding. When Al'sgara is pinned down, you'll be far away, I swear it by the great octopus! The *Lightborn* is at pier thirty-six. By the new warehouse and the fish market. The best way to get there is by taking Hemp Street. You'll recognize it at once—I have a two-masted schooner. The fastest in Hara. And I remind you once again, don't be late. We won't wait for anyone. I hope this is understood?"

"It is." I was not opposed to such conditions. "May I ask what's going on at sea right now?"

"Waves and wind," said Riuk grimly.

Dazh chuckled.

"Don't pay any attention to my mate. He has a poor sense of humor. The sea is calm right now. But everyone is carrying full sails. Darting about, they are. For now the lanes are free and even calmer than usual—the pirates are acting up far less than before. The Nabatorian fleet is stuck at the Straits. The Brotherhood of Merchants (the Golden Mark is ruled by the Brotherhood of Merchants, which is composed of the most respected and wealthiest traders in the country) is still bargaining, but it's just a question of time, money, and power. Sooner or later they will give in. The Imperials are settled in at White Cape. They're waiting for their guests to arrive."

"Will we slip through?"

"You may rest assured."

We said good-bye to the sailors and left the tavern. It had started to rain again. It became gloomy, as if evening were already setting in. But it was still a ways off. We walked through the mud; it always seemed that there was more of it near the port than in Dovetown. All around there were puddles with floating debris and little floods of water from the hills streaming toward the sea, trying to carry off heedless passersby, or at least their shoes. The smell of damp earth, wet straw, horse manure, the sea, the rain, pitch, fish, soured shaf, and the Abyss knows what else was so disgusting that it took my breath away. The port wasn't the cleanest part of the city. We tried to get out of there as quickly as possible, but our boots and cloaks were hopelessly soiled by filth.

"We have five days," Layen muttered from under her hood.

She had a firm grip on my arm, and kept slipping on the wet ground.

"Four." I was trying to keep my balance. "We can forget about today. If we don't have time to get it done, Dazh and his impudent mate will be waving their fingers at us from White Cape."

"Hurrying could damage our undertaking, my dear."

"And delaying will shove us into the Nabatorians, the Sdisians, and the Whites. And don't forget about the Damned. She won't just desert us."

"If it was Typhoid."

"I don't think that Pork could have become such a fool as to search for you and Shen."

"Shen is probably long dead."

"He's a slippery lad. I'm guessing that the Healer is not yet in the Blessed Gardens."

She almost fell while stepping over the next puddle. Swearing softly, she wiped her nose.

"We're in the crossfire, aren't we?"

"Don't worry, my sun. We won't get caught in it," I comforted her. "We'll make it. Joch is not immortal. We'll get him."

"Yes. But I beg you, let's not rush it. We have to think things through."

"In order to think things through, we've got to have at least a rough plan. And for that we need a bit of knowledge."

"Are we going to Mols?"

"Clever girl." I smiled and kissed her.

"It's all ruined, screw a toad." Luk sighed and, ignoring the rain, sat down on a wet bench not far from the Tower of the Walkers.

Ga-Nor, grim and angry, stood next to him and looked at the majestic building with hatred.

"Get up. You need a drink of hot shaf, my friend. You'll catch a cold," the tracker said finally.

"What a business! And you couldn't have spared a thought for me before?" Luk hissed venomously as a raindrop flowed off his upturned nose. "It's all because of you!"

Ga-Nor kept his silence, even though he had something to say.

"What got into you?" the soldier persisted. "I had almost convinced that goon! He'd already given up! And then you came in. I told you to stand quietly while I settled everything."

"You've been 'settling' for a whole week without any results." The northerner could not help himself. "I'm sick to death of this cursed city and its stupid people. They look at me like I'm some kind of wild animal!"

"But you are a wild animal, screw a toad! Come on, tell me, explain to me, why did you have to go and grab the secretary's throat? Do you think he'd let us in to the Walkers after that?"

"I don't. But he has such an arrogant mug. I couldn't help it."

"I would have happily punched him in the nose myself, if not for my task," Luk growled, and then immediately pounced on his comrade: "And where did your desire lead us, huh? They kicked us out. Thank Melot we weren't roasted on the spot. And now entrance into the Tower is closed to me forever."

Ga-Nor silently chewed on his waterlogged mustache. He had no desire whatsoever to talk about the Walkers. Luk continued to drone and complain until the northerner noticed a horseman riding along the path. The tracker poked his friend on the shoulder.

"Look."

Luk stared in astonishment. "I swear by the Abyss! It's Gis!"

The courier drew in his reins and smiled at the two friends like they were old acquaintances.

At one point Luk felt as though he had thrown the dice and the Seal of the Abyss (a combination of four dice, each of which shows a five. It's a winning roll.) came up. Ten times in a row, no less. Stumbling upon Gis, who surprisingly turned out to be not at all what they thought he was, changed so much.

The friends had no cause to suspect that the man they'd bonded with in Bald Hollow was the Magister of the Scarlet Order. At first Luk was a bit afraid of him, but over the course of dinner he got used to it and after only ten minutes he was wagging his tongue just as much as before. And he didn't stop.

Of course, at first they asked him about Shen and Ness. The wizard knew nothing about the first—the lad had disappeared while they were fleeing from the living dead. But the second had run away from him a few days before Gis's arrival in Al'sgara.

"He decided that he and a wizard had different paths." The "courier" smiled into his mustache.

After the news and food were finished, Gis asked

his friends what they were doing in Hightown. Luk instantly became sorrowful, complaining that he needed to speak to the Walkers, but no one wanted to listen. Then a frowning Ga-Nor said dully that he'd like to see the secretary, who sat like a spider in the Tower's reception room, damned by Ug.

"I think I can assuage your grief and arrange a conversation with one of the Walkers. But not right away. It will take a day, perhaps two. And in the meantime you can stay with me, if, of course, you don't have any prejudices against those who commune with demons," said Gis.

"My people have respect for those who wear scarlet," said Ga-Nor, scowling.

"Screw a toad!" exclaimed Luk, who had thrown off all reserve and was delighted at the possibility of a meeting with the Walkers. "It certainly doesn't scare me."

"Well, excellent," said the wizard, laughing. "Right now I have some business to take care of and I'll disappear for a few hours. My student will take care of you. Make yourselves at home."

"Something's different, isn't it?"

"You're right," I said, assessing the situation. "There's very little bread. Mols has reduced his inventory. That can only mean one thing—he's saving grain and flour. And judging by the price of rolls, bad times are upon us." The familiar pair of "bakers" were standing behind the counter. Luga caught sight of Layen and me, and he almost died of a heart attack. He went all green in the face and began looking around frantically. His comrade, who clearly had not yet learned our names, just looked hostile.

"We've come for a visit," I greeted them. "It's been set up."

This time Luga didn't even think about baring his teeth at us, and he quickly led us to Stump, who met us in the dining room and offered us something to eat.

"Mols isn't here right now," he said as he invited us to the table. "He's on business."

We nodded understandingly, though we both thought that the head of the guild was avoiding us so that there wouldn't be a repeat of the conversation about Shen. I must confess that I wouldn't have been able to resist that topic. The baker appeared to have something to hide.

During the meal we talked about this and that. Stump complained about joint pain due to the bad weather. Layen sympathized with him and recommended several concoctions. This meaningless chatter went on for quite a while, as Mols's assistant was in no hurry to ask what made us visit. This time he was polite and courteous. But he drank the expensive wine just as quickly as before. And as always, without getting drunk.

"Today Gray took a stroll through the Cucumber Quarter," Layen said finally.

"Was the walk enlightening?" He drank deeply from his glass.

"Quite so."

The Giiyan grinned knowingly. "With the red-heads around him, Joch feels like he's in Melot's bosom. Getting at him when he sticks his nose out of his lair is difficult."

"But possible," I interjected.

"It's possible." He did not deny it. "But afterward I wouldn't pay a copper coin for your hide. People have already tried. The northerners ripped the fools to shreds. I don't think you should take such a risk."

"That's exactly why we came here today. I'm sure that you and Mols have thought more than once about how to get to Threefingers. Layen and I would be extremely grateful if you would share your thoughts on this matter."

Stump perked up, and a happy smile blossomed on his red face. "Oh yes! You can believe me, we've knocked ourselves silly over this. And spent a whole lot of sorens to find out what's what."

"I dare to hope that you won't take money from us."

He ignored my jibe.

"Right now the only chance to get that louse is at his home. Sure, it looks like a fortress, but it's probably a lot less risky than finishing Joch off in public. There, if you're lucky, you can do everything quietly and then leave just as quietly."

"Then why is he still alive?" asked Layen snidely.

"Because besides you, no one wants to tangle with Threefingers. Too many influential muckety-mucks stand behind him to expose your neck."

"You're wrong. You just need to put decent money on his head. There are always hunters to be found."

"We're too greedy for that." He smiled grudgingly, though the reason, of course, was quite different—unless the guild was backed into a corner, Mols wouldn't tangle with the mighty of this world. "In general, you can only swat an annoying yellow jacket in its hive."

"For that you need to know how its hive is constructed. Do you?" Layen looked at him expectantly.

"Believe it or not, I do. We were able to buy a rough plan of the house from someone. As a friendly gesture, I can lend it to you."

"We're indescribably happy."

"No doubt." Stump chuckled and scratched his belly.

"Just one thing remains. How do we get in?"

"You could do it brazenly—knock on the gates and then send everyone you come across to the Abyss until you get shot down. Or you could do it the smart way. Which option do you find more appealing?"

"The second." Layen picked up a bunch of claret grapes from the table.

"That's what I thought. Permit me to astonish you. Many people know that most of Hightown and Second City were built by the Sculptor. But did you know that not only did he erect the walls, towers, and temples, but he also dug under the ground?"

"Yeah, we know," I said, not feeling all that enthusiastic about what I was hearing. "I've been in that tunnel. It's under Freedom Square, right by the old fountain. Two corridors leading nowhere, with rats and low ceilings. They're blocked after about fifty yards. You can't go any farther."

"Oh, I remember those." Stump nodded, smiling widely. "I used to crawl around in there when I was a boy. Searching for treasure. Yes, many went there and searched, what can I say! But the thing is, the Sculptor built outlet canals under Hightown. On the cliff, where that part of the city stands, there used to be a spring. They built the Tower and the Palace of the Viceroy right next to it. They say that there used to be a lake there and the water rushed from it in a waterfall that went straight off the cliff on the western side, into Second City. Then it turned into a small river and flowed to the sea. But the Sculptor decided that the Ors was enough for Al'sgara—a second river wasn't needed. He suggested that it be hidden underground."

"Are you planning on telling us a fairy tale?" I was indignant. "Get to the matter at hand."

"I will! I will!" he growled. "Just shut up and listen!"

I decided not to be stubborn and waved my hand at him, indicating that he should go on, and then I poured myself some wine.

"The Sculptor dug a canal into the cliff on which Hightown stands, which the water would flow through. Then he built a whole underground system of aqueducts under Second City. The water flowed out near Birdtown. It's in the Pipe District. You get it?"

"I don't recall any rivers or pipes there," I muttered.

"Of course you wouldn't remember them!" He snorted. "They are long gone. About sixty years before the War of the Necromancers the spring dried up. The lake, of course, has been preserved up until this day in the orchards of the Tower, but how the Walkers keep it filled is beyond me. Maybe they haul buckets of water from the Ors." He laughed at his lame joke and then continued. "For a while the empty aqueducts stood vacant. Then some clever folks started using them for storage instead of their cellars, and the poor lived there. But after the Damned swatted down Sorita and the war began, the Tower realized that the canal might be a really convenient way to pass under the wall to Hightown. If an enemy took Al'sgara and made it all the way to Second City, he'd have a readymade tunnel. So they filled it in. But the work was done haphazardly. They broke the stone arches supporting them, but not all of them. They were mainly concerned about the canal that passed under Hightown, and the rest were destroyed carelessly. And the tunnel under Freedom Square is proof of that."

"Come on then. Tell us that yet another passage exists, and that goes right into Joch's lair."

"Perhaps it does, and maybe more. Why not? But you're thinking along the right lines. It's entirely possible to get into Joch's compound from under the ground."

"You must be joking!" I exclaimed.

"Do I look like I'm joking?" he asked grimly. "There is a passage. It's just that very few know about it. We found it by accident and didn't think that it would ever come in handy. It's just a coincidence. The passage starts under the wine cellar of the Pig's Snout. Then it goes under the street, turns south after two hundred yards, and passes under the barracks of the Viceroy's Guards and right under Threefingers's land. There are a few branches, but they are all dead ends. It's fairly roomy and for the most part dry and clean. So there won't be any special inconveniences."

"And does Joch know about this rat hole?" Layen asked a very important question.

"He does," Mols's assistant replied calmly. "But he hardly expects trouble from that quarter."

"Do you just think that, or do you know?"

"I hope. He discovered that it was there, under one of his barns, but he made sure that rats wouldn't climb out of it. He bricked up the passage."

"The cautious bastard." My sun finished her grapes and took a new bunch.

"Not so very cautious. I don't know if it was him

or one of his people who left the bricklayer alive. But he came here one day, told us this very story and showed us the hole."

"Wonderful. All we need to do now is learn how to walk through walls."

"Not at all. Mols made sure the path was unobstructed. The very same bricklayer made it so that the five lowest bricks could be easily removed. Enough so a man can crawl through."

"Is the man still alive?" I was curious.

"Alas." Stump sighed sorrowfully. "He died in a completely senseless accident."

It was like I thought. Mols, unlike Joch, rarely made mistakes.

"So the way is open?"

"Not entirely. Threefingers did not rely solely on stone. There's an iron grate there, too. Good and strong. Our lovely friend would never skimp on his own safety. And the lock is, shall we say, difficult. You take the hint?"

"I do. Without a decent lock picker you won't get around it."

"That's right. Layen, you know how to work with locks, right?"

It was clear what kind of know-how Stump was talking about. He thought that with the help of her spark my sun could break down doors.

"No."

"Then you'll need an experienced person."

"Do you have anyone in mind?"

"Hmm . . ." Stump gave it some thought. "I was hoping Layen would be able to do it. . . . There aren't that many experienced men. Even in Al'sgara. That kind of work isn't all that easy, as you know. I know four; I'm sure of two of them, but I have some reservations about the other two. But not one of them would risk going up against Joch. Threefingers bites very hard, and no one needs that. No one will agree to it, even for a lot of money."

"What do you propose then?"

Stump chewed on his thick lips and then sighed reluctantly.

"There's one man that comes to mind. He's a strange sort. He hasn't been in town long, but it's rumored he's pulled off a few jobs. And pulled them off well, even stylishly, I'd say. It wasn't the easiest job, but the head of the City Council was deprived of a beloved and fondly cherished bauble, and the wife of the captain of the Guards lost a well-guarded necklace."

"Who does he work for?"

"I don't know. Probably for himself. I tell you, he's strange. Some of the housebreakers wanted to pin him down, but it didn't work out. They were found in a dump. The man knows how to stand up for himself and get people to leave him alone. Mols has been trying to send out feelers, but let's just say they were sent back to her politely."

Unlike us, Stump did not hesitate to mention in private conversations that his boss was a woman.

"And he's still around?"

"Like I said, he did it politely. Plus, this thief could come in handy for us. As you can see, she was right."

"He's not at all useful to us. The man might not agree."

"Maybe. But I'll think of something and get back to you. Where shall we get together?"

I thought for a moment and then named a time and place.

"Don't delay," said Layen as we were getting ready to leave. "We don't want to stay in Al'sgara forever."

He nodded his understanding and waved a hand at us, telling us to leave. We happily followed this advice.

20

The night was warm and full of stars. The moon was waxing, and it had grown brighter than a few days ago. It was yet another reminder that time was not standing still, and that we had to get a move on. We didn't have many nights left (more precisely, we had two nights and one day) to finish our task.

A fresh wind was blowing in from the sea, and the waves were striking against the pier with a soft splash. Besides this sound, and the barely audible creaking of the rigging of a potbellied merchant vessel anchored about fifty yards from the shore, complete silence reigned. On this side of the port, where all there was nowadays were empty warehouses and little fishing boats, there was no one but me. Not a single person had passed by in the entire hour I'd spent in the dark between a warehouse with a sunken-in roof and an overturned cart without its left rear wheel. Not even the watch had honored this place with their vigilant presence. Who would they catch here anyway? People seldom came here at night, if only because the filth and stench that dominated in the old parts of the docks deterred even those who'd been accustomed to filth and stench since birth. There weren't even any rats. What would a self-respecting rat do in a place like this? Gnaw on old salt-covered fishing nets? All the stocks had been transferred to a different part of the port about ten years ago.

We had met with Stump early that morning in a small shop that smelled of smoked meats, located on the very edge of Second City. The Giiyan arrived dressed as a wealthy artisan, cheerful and ruddy. He'd been able to arrange a meeting with the man we would need to wage a successful campaign against Joch. The thief hadn't said yes or no, but he had agreed to hear us out, and to that effect he set up a meeting in the old part of the port. At night.

Plus, he commanded that I come alone and, although Layen wasn't very happy about it, I accepted his terms.

I arrived an hour earlier than the agreed-upon time and walked around the neighborhood just in case Mols or this unknown craftsman had got it into their heads not to play fair. And then, tucked in a secluded spot, I watched the pier.

A soft chime swept over the sleeping city—the bells of Melot's temples. It was three in the morning.

I almost missed his arrival. The man came from the direction of the Crab District, passed by about thirty yards from me, walked down the pier, and stopped at the water's edge. The stranger stood with his hood thrown over his head, his back to the shore, looking out at the sea.

The man was my height but a bit narrower in the shoulders. He was dressed in a short, well-fitted jacket, tight trousers, and soft boots. All in gray and black tones. On his right hip hung an impressively large knife, and a canvas bag was thrown over his shoulder. He didn't even bother to turn around when I walked up to him. He just stood there, staring somewhere beyond the horizon, as if all the treasure of the world were hidden there.

I coughed.

"You're late." The man's voice was unpleasantly dry.

"Does it bother you?"

A slight shrug. "No, I suppose it doesn't. People who are late for a good reason do not deserve any special blame. I'm sure you had to make sure that everything was all right."

He turned his head slightly.

"You're a sharp-sighted fellow."

"And you're cautious and patient. Not everyone would spend an hour in such a pigsty."

It seemed to me that he was smiling.

"Well, we're standing here together, so apparently I'm not the only one spending time in such a place."

"You have a way with words, Ness."

"I didn't think that Stump would have told you my name."

"Stump? Ah . . . the red-faced assassin. No. He didn't say who wanted to meet me."

"Then how do you know my name?"

"I have my own ways of learning what intrigues me, Gray."

I grabbed my hatchet but then froze, not daring to raise my hand to throw it.

My companion had moved very quickly. Before I even had time to blink, he'd already aimed a miniature crossbow at me. It looked like the thing was loaded with two bolts.

"Put it away." His voice was just as dry, but his tone was also benevolent. "You didn't come here for this, am I right?"

Slowly, without taking my eyes off the crossbow, I returned the utak to my belt.

"Don't be nervous. I don't care who's looking for you or how much money you have on your head," he said, lowering his crossbow, and he once again turned his back to me.

"Are you so rich?" I hadn't been able to make out his face—it remained hidden in the shadows of his hood.

He laughed.

"I'm not as greedy as you might think."

"But you're rude. You know my name, but I don't know yours."

A pause.

"Call me Harold."

"A strange name. I've never heard one like it."

"It is what it is."

"Do you know why I need your help?"

"Yes. Stump mentioned it."

"What do you think?"

"It's going to get too hot, Giiyan."

"Is that a no, thief?" I spat in irritation, suspecting that I'd wasted time coming here for nothing.

"Far from it." He turned around and threw back his hood. Finally, I could get a good look at him.

He was perhaps five years older than me. He had a lean, tanned face with extremely sharp cheekbones. A high forehead. A straight, slightly bony nose, bushy eyebrows, and two days' worth of stubble on his chin. Short black hair that was surprisingly gray at the temples. The man had obviously been worn down by life. I would have said that the man standing before me was the dark and dangerous type, if not for his eyes. They were completely out of place in his face—lively and full of laughter. It seemed like the thief was having a wonderful time, though at the moment I didn't see cause for celebration.

"Far from it," he repeated. "It will be intriguing."

"I'm afraid that first and foremost, it will be dangerous," I said coldly.

"Sometimes danger and intrigue go hand in hand. When are you planning to send Joch into the Darkness?"

"Tomorrow night."

He nodded.

"Well, then. That works for me."

"I hope you can help."

"When it comes to locks, you can count on me."

"How much?" I wanted to finish this deal as soon as possible.

He thought for a moment and then grinned, his eyes glinting mischievously. "Like I already said, I'm not greedy. Five sorens should do it."

I lost the power of speech. It seemed that fate had brought me a lunatic. Layen and I expected that the bargaining would begin at three hundred minimum, and we were prepared to pay good money for his services. And he says five measly coins!

"What's the catch?" I had to ask.

Harold raised an eyebrow. "Seems to me you should be jumping for joy that I didn't rip you off for five hundred."

"Five hundred?"

"I place a very high value on my skills," he said cheerfully. "But consider yourself lucky today. I've decided to play for charity."

I didn't really understand his last words, but I said, "All the same, I'd like to know why you're so generous."

He chuckled and began walking along the pier back to the shore. I had to walk next to him.

"I'm interested in this matter," he said cautiously. "That's all. It's a challenge to my skills. And a chance to shake things up. You can't imagine, man, how boring it is to live sometimes." He paused and then suddenly added, "Especially if you live for a very long time."

It's not a problem for me if a person doesn't need money and is tired of living when he's barely thirty. I wasn't about to insist that he raise his price.

"That's your right. I have nothing against it. Especially if it entertains you."

"Entertains?" The thief laughed wholeheartedly. "Yes. I suppose you chose the right word."

He sniffed the air and remarked randomly, "I can just smell that the coming Game will be impossibly interesting."

"When would you prefer to receive the deposit?"

"Tomorrow. Before the job. And not the deposit, but the whole sum."

"Okay."

"I have some conditions. First. I work with locks and I don't hurt anyone. You'll have to deal with Joch's people yourself. When I'm handling my business, I'm the boss. You will not interfere. I'll let you in, but I won't go into the house. I'm not interested in that. Second. I've heard about your woman. Be so kind as to keep her on a short leash. We will carry out the commission and then disband. All the rest doesn't interest me. Third. If it gets too hot, it's every man for himself."

"It's a deal."

"I'll be waiting for you tomorrow. At the same time. At the entrance to the cellar."

I nodded and hurried away without saying goodbye.

Tia snuck into Haven by hiring a fisherman. He was snoring away in his tub when the Damned woke him, and he doused Pork in the choicest language. Typhoid ignored this completely and asked him to carry her to the port of Al'sgara. The drunkard laughed in her face and called her crazy, but Typhoid thrust some gold under his nose. This sobered him up right away, and he plopped down at his oars hastily.

All her fears proved unfounded. No one stopped them or even hailed them. As Leprosy had implied, this way of getting into the city wasn't guarded very vigilantly. For now, at any rate. So less than an hour later the faint lights of the port appeared. When the boat came alongside a wooden pier, Tia stabbed the man with her dagger and walked away, leaving the body in the boat.

Now she had to find the blond archer who would lead her to the Healer. She'd been wandering around the city since early morning. Typhoid walked at random, hoping she would be lucky and her spark would bring her to the archer. She didn't dare go to Hightown or Second City—the chance that she would run into one of the Walkers, Embers, or Scarlets there was too great. And it wouldn't do to forgo caution in the other neighborhoods either. A second encounter with a wizard might not end as well as the first.

Tia started with the lowest districts, the ones right by the sea. Of course, not an hour passed before she was lost—Al'sgara was completely different than it had been five hundred years ago. Many of the streets and alleys hadn't existed in her time. As a result, the Damned was not an inch closer to her goal and, angry at herself and Pork, returned to the port, deciding to look for lodging in an old warehouse.

The next day also came to nothing. All that Tia knew was that the blond was in the city. Al'sgara was too big, and her inability to use her Gift openly was oppressive. Without her abilities she couldn't do anything. Every minute she was tempted to call upon her power. And time after time she restrained herself, whispering that it was not yet time. She still had a few days left to her, and for the time being she just needed to search and not despair.

She should be lucky. All her life, Typhoid had walked hand in hand with luck. Suffice it to recall the day when Retar died saving her from Sorita's jackals—it was a miracle she escaped. And she had left Ginora's side the day before the woman was brought to bay in the Marshes of Erlika. Or . . . she didn't want to recall how she had survived but lost her body.

Despite these internal arguments, the Damned fell into deeper despair with each passing hour. She was afraid that she wouldn't succeed before Rovan arrived.

But she was lucky again. And as always, when she least expected it. That night something caused her to wake up and crawl from the warehouse toward the sea. Pork was whining quietly somewhere on the edge of her consciousness, begging her to leave him alone and to let him go home. She ordered him to shut up, and just at that moment she saw two people standing on the pier. Tia didn't need any light to recognize the blond archer, whom she'd been vainly searching for these past few days. The mark hanging over his head spoke for itself.

Her first impulse was to grab the bastard and shake the information out of him. But Typhoid never made the same mistakes twice. She remembered what happened the last time she allowed her fury to prevail over her reason. There was no rush. He would not escape retribution. She just had to take her time.

The Damned began to scrutinize the archer's companion. His back was toward her, but he didn't seem to be the wizard who had dealt with her so deftly. Just in case, she inspected him using a small shred of her Gift.

Her breath caught in her throat.

Multicolored spots danced before her eyes. Her temples began aching with a throbbing pain. The stranger had the Gift. And what a Gift it was; it made Tia want to hide away and pray to the gods in whom she did not believe. The man was bursting with power inside; Tia had never seen anything like it. It wasn't light, and it wasn't dark. It was primal, incomprehensible, and so powerful that the magic of the Damned was like a raindrop in the ocean in comparison. He could casually crush them all with one finger as if without a care in the world. The thing that the mages of this world since time immemorial had called the spark, hot and bright, should in him be called a "tangle"—it was constantly changing shape, pulsating as if it were alive. It seemed to be woven from a multitude of dancing shadows. Typhoid watched this breathtaking dance, and the pain she was feeling intensified. It was like looking into the Abyss itself, but she couldn't tear her eyes away.

Tia was torn in two. She wanted to wail and run away, if only not to see, not to feel this impossible, mighty, ancient, primordial force. But she couldn't force herself to move. She was drawn to the majesty of the shadows, like a moth to a flame.

Then it all ended, as if someone had blown out a candle. The pain disappeared. The member of the Sextet could no longer see the tangle. She had stopped sensing the Gift that was as old as the world; it was as if someone had slammed the door leading to the Abyss in her face. The blond was walking away, in the opposite direction from where the Damned was hiding. She watched his retreating back in despair but remained where she was. The stranger stood between her and the archer. He blocked Typhoid's path, and she didn't dare walk past him.

A few more seconds and the man she'd so tenaciously pursued vanished into the night. A wave of hopeless despair swept over her. And then the terrifying man with the tangle of shadows in his chest turned his head in her direction.

She couldn't see his face, hidden as it was by his hood, but she felt his gaze. It was burning, tormenting, painful and . . . mocking? The stranger looked at her, and Tia forgot how to breathe, terrified of what he would do next. He took a step toward her and Typhoid couldn't stand it anymore. She ran away.

21

The last night of our stay in Al'sgara we changed hideouts. Layen was hoarding her strength for the job, and every time she opened the secret door to the Sculptor's sanctuary her scanty reserves were devoured. That was unwise so we moved to an inn, despite the considerable risk. It was located not far from Second City on quiet, sleepy Chestnut Street.

We got a clean, comfortable room on the third floor. From the window there was a wonderful view of the hill that was bounded by the wall of Second City. There were virtually no guests; people preferred the much cheaper establishments located by the outer walls and the sea. But good food, regular sleep, and a reliable door—that was what we needed, and so we weren't bothered by the price.

My sun was studying the plans of Joch's compound. Stump had been kind enough to share them with us. I don't know how Mols managed to get hold of something so valuable (no doubt someone was slaughtered), but the papers were very helpful to us. Early in the evening I had to leave Layen to her occupation and go to a last meeting with Stump before the job. We needed to discuss a few details.

I took a roundabout route. I had to make a big circle and lose a certain amount of time, but I knew what I was doing. It was far better to lose an hour than to draw trouble down on my ass. A few times I checked if anyone was shadowing me, but it was all clear.

They came at me just when I was walking through a vegetable market. A tall, gray-haired man lost interest in a tray of cucumbers and turnips and appeared next to me. He had a kind face, a thick, fluffy beard, and bushy eyebrows, which made him look even more good-natured, as well as laughing blue eyes and a very steady hand with a short Groganian knife, which he held to my liver.

"Hi there." Greybeard grinned at me.

Nothing good could come of this. He was not at all worried by the crowd. He held his knife well. From the outside, it gave the impression of two old friends meeting. Yet this "friend" could drive a few inches of excellent steel into my liver at any second. This was the first time I'd seen the man. Judging by his accent, he was from the north, probably from the capital, and that meant he was just passing through and was not under Mols's command.

A small blond man with a mass of freckles on his cunning face slipped out of the crowd. I noticed that his left wrist was held tight to his body, and there was a small bulge in the sleeve of his loose shirt. Probably a throwing knife. He came up close to me and put his arm around my shoulder.

"You have a chance to live a little bit longer. Where's your woman?"

"What reason do I have to answer?" I looked into the crowd, trying to figure out if they were just working in a pair or if there was someone else.

"You don't have a wealth of options. If you don't agree to help us, you'll be writhing in pain for a long time. Believe me, my friend here will make sure of it. Then we'll find your woman ourselves and think of a way to do her in good. Or, if you're accommodating, you can die with her. But quickly and without pain. I give you my word that you'll both be sent to the Blessed Gardens without feeling anything."

Some doubt obviously showed on my face, so Greybeard explained, "We try to do our work cleanly and not to drag it out. Believe me, we don't take any pleasure in causing our targets pain. We're professionals."

He wasn't lying. It really was the case. They were very calm, they didn't flinch, they weren't nervous and they were completely unafraid of me. They worked skillfully and harmoniously. These two were Giiyans. Masters. Much better than me. Much better than most that ever worked for Mols.

I had no choice. If I refused now, I'd die right away. If they had managed to catch me, then sooner or later they'd find Layen. It was far better to take the risk. Perhaps I'd get lucky. Al'sgara is large, and anything could happen along the way.

"Okay. I'll help you."

"The right choice," said Greybeard. "Well done, lad."

He spoke softly and kindly, but he didn't shift the blade. I felt the shallow wound oozing blood under my shirt.

"Where is she?"

I hesitated.

"Don't get jittery. Relax."

"Near Second City."

"Let's take a walk. Do we have to tell you what will happen if you think of doing anything stupid?"

"No."

"I'm liking this lad more and more." Greybeard smiled broadly. "Good. Walk next to me. Don't rush. If you make a move, call out, or make a scene, I'll finish you. If you intend to take a chance anyway and run away, my friend throws knives quite well. Am I explaining myself clearly?"

"Yes."

I knew I would have to take a risk along the way. There were two of them, and one of me. They were better. But I didn't have any choice.

"Limp. A lot. Please don't forget about it." Freckles was walking behind my back. "Move."

I diligently limped on my left foot as if it had just been sprained. Greybeard amiably supported me under my arm with a steely grip, and not for a second did he ease up on the pressure of the knife. The lads trusted in their skill so much that they didn't even think it was necessary to relieve me of my utak or my bow. However, the latter didn't present the slightest threat to them. I wouldn't have time to draw the string back. But I was happy that they hadn't touched the Blazgian throwing axe.

However, it seemed my happiness was premature. Someone's deft hands slipped under my jacket and a second later I was left unarmed.

"That's Marna," Greybeard explained to me kindly.

I didn't know what Marna looked like; she was somewhere behind me, with Freckles. One thing was clear, though—there were three of them.

We left the market and went out onto Jennet Street. Out of the corner of my eye I observed movement to the right and above us. I raised my head and managed to see something interesting.

"Jakan." My companion smiled. "I heard that you're a good shot, but my friend is quite good, too. He's there just in case we make a false step."

So, now there were four in the team. A Je'arre, an archer. This was really quite bad. The winged one flew from rooftop to rooftop and was ready to shoot me at any moment.

"Truthfully, Jakan really wants to use you as target practice," said Greybeard confidentially. "Some friendly advice—don't give him a reason."

"Why such a dislike?" I cast a bored glance at a squad of Guardsmen. As one would expect, they ignored us. And thank Melot that it was so; otherwise I'd already have one foot in the Blessed Gardens.

"You killed his boyfriend in that forest. So Jakan isn't your biggest fan."

It took me several seconds to figure out what the Giiyan was talking about.

He meant the forest glade not far from Dog Green and the attack on Layen when she went to collect our money. Besides those monsters who were rotting under the open sky, there had also been a flyer, who stunned my sun. He was the only one who managed to get away.

"The team he was on then wasn't distinguished by their experience."

"I have no doubt, since you're still alive." He winked at me. "They were amateurs. That's why you beat them."

"Why are you working with him?"

Greybeard sighed sorrowfully. "You have to make sacrifices, buddy. Jakan knew your face. He's been a great help to us."

"How did you find me?"

"Don't worry about it. You did everything right, friend. Just the usual bad luck, that's all," he comforted me. "Neither I nor my partners have anything against you personally. It's just a job that will pay out a decent amount of money. Well, you understand."

I did understand. But for some reason I wasn't particularly thrilled that Joch was going to send ten thousand their way for our souls.

I could feel Freckles's attentive gaze on my back. Invisible Marna's skirts were rustling. The winged freak was following me somewhere up above. The fourth man's knife could punch a nice hole in me at any time, piercing my liver. I could already hear Melot's servants singing to me near the gates that led into the Blessed Gardens.

"What are you going to do with the money?" I asked.

"Buy a house by a lake. I'll angle for fish and bring my grandkids to visit. I love them very much."

Greybeard chatted incessantly. While we were walking, I got to hear his opinion about the weather, the war, gambling, and fishing. He paid special attention to the last topic. Grandpa was an avid fisherman. So avid in fact that I began imagining how I would plant him on a big hook instead of bait and cast him far out into the sea, where perhaps some monster would devour him.

"We've been walking for a long time," said Freckles.

Greybeard smiled into his mustache and pressed on the knife a little harder than before. I gritted my teeth so as not to groan.

"My friend thinks you're trying to dupe us."

"I'm not."

"And yet, we've been walking for too long. If we haven't arrived in the next ten minutes, we're going to have to part ways with you, even though you are a wonderful conversationalist. I don't really want that." He clucked his tongue sadly. "What about you?"

"Me neither."

"Don't let me down, lad. Where to?"

"On the left," I said without batting an eyelash.

When I had left, Layen was sitting at the table near the window. All I could do was hope that she was still busy there, and that she would look out the window by chance. Of course, it was a foolish hope, but I clung to it with all my might. There was nothing else I could do. I even started to walk a little slower, so I could stay in sight for as long as possible, but Greybeard noticed this and without lengthy consideration, he gently poked the knife into my side.

"Thinking about something?"

"Yeah. My last request."

"Sorry, we don't fulfill those," he said sympathetically. "Speed up."

And then it dawned on me!

You stupid ass! You should have thought of this earlier! I could speak to Layen! I could, but over the past month I'd gotten used to her being silent. Only a few days ago, in the secret refuge of the Sculptor, she'd tried to say a few words and had almost succeeded. I remembered what she said, about how her Gift was coming back to her every day. It was very possible that my sun now had enough power to hear me.

Layen! I called. *Layen!*

For an entire, infinitely long second nothing happened, and then a warm wave ran along my spine.

Ness?

Afraid that her ability would run out at any second, I babbled, *Look out the window! Carefully!*

The curtain stirred faintly on the third floor.

I understand. Her words came to me, and then she was gone from my head.

I felt relief sweep over me. Now Layen was warned, and whatever happened to me, she wouldn't be so easy to take.

"Here?" Greybeard glanced quickly at the inn.

"Yes." I nodded.

"Security?"

"I didn't notice any."

It wasn't clear if he believed me or not.

"Are there any guests?"

"Yes."

"But I don't think there are very many." He chuckled. "You picked out an expensive little nest. We're in luck. Change places with me."

Freckles pressed a blade to me, giving his partner the chance to withdraw. They did it very deftly. They'd clearly practiced it out more than once.

"I'll take a look," said Greybeard. "Marna, stay."

He walked into the inn. The Je'arre was sitting on a nearby building. Noticing that I was looking at him, he grinned wickedly. I shifted my glance to the woman who was standing next to the Giiyan. They were obviously relatives—she was just as short, blond, and freckled. A large bag was hanging over her shoulder.

"What are you looking at?" she asked sullenly.

"What have you got there?" I nodded at the bag.

"You'll find out soon enough," the woman promised.

Greybeard returned.

"It's clear. Listen to me, lad. You're doing everything right. Our agreement remains valid. If you keep your word, we'll keep ours. Where do we go?"

"The third floor."

"Onward, friend." Freckles added a poke with the knife to these words.

They thought they were leading me to the slaughter. Well. I could only hope that Layen had thought of something. And just at that second she let herself be known.

I'm ready. Our floor. Eight paces from the stairs. The door to the left of you.

Got it, I said, walking into the inn.

The common room was empty. Not a soul. The owner was also absent. Greybeard noticed my glance toward the bar and disarmingly threw up his hands.

"He could remember our faces. The price of doing our work."

"Do you intend to free the souls of anyone we meet along the way?"

"You don't approve?" He stepped behind my back, letting the woman pass by.

"You work dirty," I chided him.

"No one asked you," said Freckles.

Marna took a crossbow out of her large bag. Of course, it lost in terms of size when compared with Harold's, but it was also very small. It was clearly the work of the Morassian masters. They make very nice weapons in that country.

"We'll go up slowly. When we get to the door, you'll knock. You'll say you've come back. Me and my friends will be off to the side. Any careless gesture or word, and you'll take a long time to die. Your woman too. Understood?"

"Yes."

"Marna, you need to get her with your first shot."

"I remember that she has the Gift." The girl's voice was unexpectedly low.

"Let's go, buddy."

Marna and her crossbow went up first, followed by Freckles and me. Greybeard brought up the rear. On the second floor we ran into a servant carrying a tray of empty dishes. Before the man had a chance to understand what was happening, the girl sank a bolt into him and Greybeard shot forward, moving very swiftly for his age, plucked the tray from the man's enfeebled hands, and carefully placed it on the floor. Then he finished off the wounded man by snapping his neck.

"Let's hurry, folks. Let's hurry."

And once again a staircase.

"You're not as terrible as people say you are, Gray," Freckles said suddenly. "I heard you're a good shot, but up close you're weak. I was expecting more."

"We're all masters of one thing," announced Greybeard. "And why are you complaining? Do you think it would be better if he head-butted you?"

The third floor. Marna had already reloaded her

dangerous toy and was stealthily creeping into the hallway.

"Which door?" Freckles asked me quietly.

He was tense, and he was holding me tightly by the elbow, his knife threatening to release my soul at any moment.

"The last one," I whispered, trying to ignore the pain in my side. "On the right of the hallway."

"No stupid moves."

I walked forward, counting my steps. While I was still on the stair I had shifted my center of gravity slightly to the left and just a bit (so that there was no way my escort would notice) began to inch my elbow toward the hand holding the knife.

Six.

Seven.

Eight.

Now!

Click! The sound came from behind me.

I dropped my weight onto my left foot, simultaneously pushing my elbow at the Giiyan's hand. At the same second a short bolt came flying from somewhere behind us and hit Freckles in the base of his skull. The knife, which should have pierced my liver, only slid along my side, tearing through shirt and skin. Ignoring the pain, I jumped to the left and slammed into the door with all my weight. At that very moment, Marna turned at the noise and shot.

The door was not locked, so I stumbled into the

room (barely avoiding the bolt), couldn't keep my balance, fell to the floor, and rolled, almost crashing into a table. I jumped up and turned toward the door just as Greybeard popped in with his knife.

Behind his back something resembling a gray cloud of flies passed by with a roar. Frankly, I had no idea what it was. Greybeard was not distracted by the strange noise, and he walked toward me swiftly and quietly. The knife flashed in his large hands. For some reason he thought I was unarmed. For some reason he thought that I would defend, not attack. For some reason he thought I was going to lose to him.

In order to play with him on equal terms, I had to exert myself. I almost jumped out of my skin in order to dodge his blade. Greybeard clearly didn't expect such swiftness from me and missed his mark. An arrow pulled from a quiver is no worse than a dagger. I slid up next to him, struck him in the clavicle, close to his right shoulder, and he immediately opened his fingers. The knife fell out of his hand, but I didn't leave it at that. I kicked him in the shin and slammed my open palm under his chin. He fell to the floor with a thud.

Layen, disheveled and bristling like a thousand berserk cats, flew into the room. A discharged crossbow was in her hands.

"Are you okay?"

"Yes," I said, picking the knife up from the floor and with my other hand pressing the bleeding wound in my side. "I think so. Hold this. I'll be right back."

I still had one piece of unfinished business. I ran past Marna's body (or rather, what was left of it) toward the staircase that led to the attic. I climbed it quickly, strung my bow, and cautiously climbed out onto the roof. A chimney hid me from the house on the opposite side of the street.

The evening sun was shining behind me, so the lovely Jakan never saw it coming. To tell the truth, I took special pleasure in shooting down the winged louse.

On the way back I picked Marna's crossbow up off the floor. The girl had been deprived of her head and the upper half of her torso, so she no longer had any need for personal belongings. And we could use a little thing like that. In any case, it would do Layen nicely. Without pausing to think, I also grabbed the bolts. I loaded the weapon—it was fairly easy—and took my utak back.

When I returned Greybeard had already woken up and managed to break off the arrow shaft sticking from his shoulder. He was discussing something with Layen. She had her crossbow aimed at him and was replying amiably. The Giiyan took note of me and smiled, but there was not the slightest hint of joy in his eyes. They were tense and watchful. Fear splashed in their depths.

"You turned out to be a lad who doesn't miss."

"I'm glad you appreciate my skills," I said dryly. "Stand up."

He raised himself up with a groan.

"Old age is not a joy." His smile came out crooked.

"You had a pretty unlucky day today, didn't you, my friend?"

He swallowed and then nodded. "I've had better."

"I sympathize."

"It's just a job, lad," Greybeard said suddenly. "Nothing personal."

"I understand. It's all about taking care of your grandkids."

"I have two." He looked at Layen beseechingly.

He knew that I was feeling far from kind today.

"Get out of here," I said, pointing the crossbow toward the door.

"What?" Greybeard clearly couldn't believe his ears.

"Get out of here," I repeated.

He didn't linger any longer, nor did he wonder at my unearthly kindness. "It was nice to meet you, Gray."

The Giiyan headed for the door. As soon as he crossed the threshold, I hit him with a bolt in the same exact place where not too long ago Freckles had taken it. The assassin fell to the floor without making a single sound.

"It's just a job. Nothing personal." I repeated his words, thinking that getting a house by a lake wasn't as easy as it seemed.

22

"There, that's better," said Layen quietly as she finished bandaging the deep scrape on my side.

"Thank you."

We'd already been stuck in this small, old graveyard, not far from the Pig's Snout, for more than an hour. It was late evening, almost dark, and no one had bothered us. We were hidden by the ivy-covered graves.

"At one point I was scared for you."

"I too almost lost hope, my sun. They were good."

I smiled, but she remained serious.

"Believe it or not, I noticed." Layen put her arm around my shoulders. "Where did they capture you?"

"At the vegetable market. Apparently, they came all the way from Corunna for our souls. Stump will be unhappy that I didn't come."

"I wonder who handed us over to them?"

I chuckled and kissed her on the cheek.

"Ask me something easier. It could have been anyone. One of the pissants surrounding Mols, for example. Hey, tell me, how did you end up behind us? As far as I recall, the stairway was empty."

"Not one of you bothered to look up." Her eyes

gleamed triumphantly. "The innkeeper built something there, a pantry of sorts. I was able to hide myself there and shoot the one holding you."

"You didn't just get Freckles, you got the woman, too. You handled her nicely. I wasn't expecting it." I praised her work.

"I was so scared for you that I acted without thinking," she said guiltily. "The truth is, now I'm completely empty. The strike took away everything I accumulated over the last few days. I have to start again."

"It's okay," I comforted her. "The main thing is that your spark is flaring up. We'll use steel to deal with Joch."

"He knows we're in the city. I'm sure of it."

"Do you think it's not worth the risk?"

She thought for a moment and then reluctantly shook her head. "No. He has to be removed or else our lives will go to the Abyss. Do you think there are more than these three today who want to make a grab for the money?"

"There were four of them."

I told her about the Je'arre.

"Good riddance," she said. "It's already dark. How long until we move?"

"Another two hours," I said hesitantly, and then I made a proposal. "We need to go back into town and get something to eat."

We made it back to the Pig's Snout just in time for the chiming of the bells that indicated it was three o'clock in the morning. The wine cellar was located in the basement of the old building.

As soon as we walked up to the door, a man stepped out from behind the corner.

"It's the thief," I said softly to my sun.

"And it's the Giiyan," said Harold in lieu of greeting. "I must say, you don't waste any time."

"What are you talking about?" I asked grimly, thinking I already knew the answer.

He smiled crookedly. "I'm talking about the four corpses, found about five blocks away from here. The whole underworld is seething. Some joker overwhelmed three masters and one petty winged crook."

"What does that have to do with us?"

The thief shrugged. "I'm not a fool. And neither is Mols. I imagine the lady is on a rampage right about now. Goons from the capital trespassed onto her turf and almost twisted off your heads."

"Are we going to wag our tongues or are we going to get down to business?" Layen was starting to get angry.

He laughed without malice. "We'll get to business as soon as I get my money."

I counted out five sorens and tossed them to him. He flashed his smile again and put the money away.

"Wonderful. I'm entirely at your disposal."

Layen knocked briefly on the door. For a long moment nothing happened; then the bolt clanged, the hinges creaked briefly, and the light of a lantern struck our faces.

"Come in," said Stump, stepping aside. "When you didn't come to our meeting, I started to worry."

He didn't say a word about Greybeard and his friends. So much the better.

"Is everything ready?" I looked around.

Rough masonry on the walls, small windows right under the ceiling, and huge wine barrels along the walls. A small table in the corner, a cabinet with lopsided doors, and a cracked stool. Besides Stump, there were two of Mols's ruffians in the room.

"We politely asked the landlord to leave the door open. He knows Mols, so he didn't mind. Let's go."

He beckoned us to follow him. As it turned out, there was a narrow opening between two of the barrels. Stump barely squeezed himself through it; we followed after him and came out into a narrow closet. On the floor was a hatch, which opened up onto a surprisingly sturdy wooden staircase.

"Why are you standing there with your mouths open?" muttered Stump. "Go down."

The basement was stuffed with racks of wine bottles and, just as above, barrels. Harold walked along an impressive row of wine racks, selected a bottle, and meticulously studied the label.

"Not a bad selection at all. It's worth remembering this place."

"To buy or to fleece?" sneered Layen.

"However it works out," he replied, not offended at all.

"I would never have taken you as a lover of wine."

"A connoisseur, actually. And only of good wine. It's one of the few things that can still afford me joy."

"Can we put a stop to the idle chitchat?" Stump said irately. "When you return, you can carry off as many bottles as your heart desires."

"I'll remember your words," said the thief. "Where's the rat hole?"

"In the corner."

A lantern stood by a hole dug in the floor. Previously it had been covered with a wooden lid, which was now pushed to one side.

"The shopkeeper stumbled upon it accidentally. He wanted to dig another cellar for the colder wines, but it didn't work out. He got this legacy of the Sculptor instead."

"I don't see a reason why he couldn't have used it for his own needs." I peered into the hole.

It was as dark as the Abyss. I wondered if the bottom was far away. Judging by the thickness of the floor beneath us, it was built soundly. And also, if magic and just a little bit of brains were applied to the construction, it was not surprising that after a thousand years these vaults still hadn't collapsed.

"It's not very high." Stump seemed to read my thoughts. "A bit more than three yards. My lads and I will lower you down on a rope."

"And who will lift us back up?" asked Layen suspiciously.

Indeed. What would prevent him from lowering the cover and forgetting about us for all eternity?

"We'll wait until morning. After that don't blame me."

"Naïveté is a great virtue, Giiyan," said the thief, laughing.

"Are you trying to say that you don't trust my word?" Stump scowled.

"I don't even always trust my own, to say nothing of others'. What do you think, Gray?"

"I don't think Stump would do something so nasty," I said slowly, looking into the eyes of Mols's helper. "It's . . . grotesque. Isn't that right, Layen?"

"Oh yes! That's not how you behave with friends," she said. "But if you do decide to leave, I'll have to smash in the ceiling."

A bluff as clear as water. She couldn't even squash a mouse right now, let alone smash through a thick layer of stone.

"That's also an option," I supported her, and turned back to Stump, who was still frowning. "Believe me, she's capable of it. Especially when she's angry."

"You don't scare me," said the red-faced assassin, scowling, even though his eyes spoke to the fact that he was feeling quite uncomfortable. "We'll wait as long as we can."

Harold found the entire situation amusing, and he

was smirking. I got the impression that the man really had agreed to participate in this adventure just for the sake of entertainment.

I was first to be let down by the rope, carrying the lantern; then came Layen and the thief. Finally, Stump's shaggy head appeared in the hole above us.

"Go straight all the time. Don't take any turns. This is the main tunnel, it will take you to Joch's compound. Give my regards to Threefingers."

"And where, in your opinion, is straight?" Harold asked sarcastically. "There?" He pointed in one direction, turned, and then pointed in another. "Or there?"

"There." Stump pointed to the left. "Don't get lost. Now be gone with you—my head is already starting to ache from looking at you."

I walked in front with the lantern. Behind me came Layen, clutching her crossbow. The thief brought up the rear, humming an unfamiliar song under his breath. His behavior was really irritating, but I endured it stoically.

I hoped we weren't taking him with us for nothing.

When the lantern light disappeared in the distance, Stump got up from his knees, brushed off his trousers, sighed, and walked to the exit. Halfway to the stairs he stopped and glanced at the racks where the dusty bottles were resting. He walked over, took one at random, and looked at the label. The wine wasn't one he needed to stand on ceremony with, so Olna tugged his favorite Sdisian dagger from its sheath and with one blow cleaved the top off of the bottleneck. It was faster and easier than trying to tug out the cork without a bottle opener. Gulping it down, he walked up the stairs, came out into the closet, and nodded to one of his subordinates. The man jumped up immediately, as if he'd been waiting just for this, and darted out onto the street.

Stump sat on the pitifully creaking stool and occupied himself with the wine, getting grimmer by the minute. Olna didn't like what Katrin had set in motion, but he knew she was right. If they didn't do what they were told, there would be trouble. They'd simply be crushed.

The door opened and Mols walked into the wine cellar with six assistants. She looked at Stump inquiringly.

"They've gone," he said succinctly.

"We'll wait," said Mols.

"Do you think they'll get it done?"

"Joch won't live through the night."

Stump nodded grimly and brought his lips to the bottle once more. He needed some way to pass the time.

The tunnel was dry but the river that had flowed through in the past had left its mark on the walls.

They were so smooth they looked polished. It was obvious the water level had never reached the ceiling, for that was rough. It smelled of cold stone and centuries of dust. I didn't see any rats, nor any other small creatures. There were no echoes either.

The wound Freckles left on my side was aching contrarily, but I tried to cast it from my mind for the time being.

"Now we're somewhere near the barracks," said Layen when we had walked two hundred yards. "If Stump is to be trusted, there'll be a turn soon."

And indeed, the tunnel did take a sharp turn and begin to slope upward, climbing the hill under the cliff on which Hightown stood. We passed by four side tunnels. The thief couldn't resist and stuck his head into one of the tunnels, but as expected, he didn't see anything interesting.

"Just think of it! So many glorious things used to be made with the help of mages . . ." said Layen, coming up to walk next to me. In the lantern light her face was pensive and very beautiful.

"What?" I asked her gently.

She sighed. "None of the Walkers living now could dig underground aqueducts that not only led the river to the sea, but also brought water to the houses along its path. In Hightown and Second City it's just below the ground."

"Fairy tales." I didn't really believe in such stories.

"Judging from what I heard, no."

"She's right," came the thief's voice. "In one of the

wealthy houses, not far from here, I saw a bath. It was old. Just the kind of thing that would have been filled by an underground river. Although I must say, I'm not all that impressed by this dungeon."

"One would think you'd managed to get into a lot of them and that you've seen so much better," murmured Layen.

Harold grinned but didn't respond.

"Imagine all the frustration of the rich when the spring dried up," I said, chuckling, and raised the lantern higher.

"The river began to dry up, and it was only then that they destroyed some of the arches."

"To break is not to build," concluded Harold philosophically.

"That's not the point," I disagreed. "Here's the heart of the matter. If they hadn't, parts of the houses would have collapsed into the ground."

"Is it just me or is the ceiling getting lower?" said the thief thoughtfully.

Indeed, the farther we walked, the lower the ceiling became. After some time I could have touched it if I wished to do so. Finally, a brick wall blocked our way.

"We've arrived," I said, and I put the lantern on the floor.

"The masonry is six years old, no more," Harold estimated. "Compared with all of this"—he gestured around the tunnel—"it's very fresh."

"Old Joch took pains so that not a single rat

would slip in to pay him a visit," I said and, plying it with my dagger, teased out one of the lower bricks.

The mason who betrayed Threefingers did his work excellently. Without the mortar to bond the bricks together, they were easy to pry out, but to a person who was not in the know it would seem that there was a solid structure in front of him. The bricks were heavy, and Harold's help came in very handy. Finally, we opened up the passage—a hole so small that you could only squeeze through it lying on your back.

"Lower the wick. We don't need the extra light right now," said the thief as he crawled through first. After a few seconds he called back, "It's clear."

We followed after him and once again found ourselves in the tunnel. The ceiling here was even lower, and we had to stand hunched over.

"Take a seat," invited the thief. "This will take some time."

Right above us was the hole closed by the grate.

The entrance to Joch's lair.

The darkness of the Abyss reigned beyond the thick bars. The place we were supposed to enter was some kind of barn, according to Stump. I hoped that the servants were not in the habit of sleeping here, but Joch probably wouldn't allow everyone to know about the grate that covered the entrance under the ground.

"And now would be a good time for light," Harold suggested.

I raised the lantern and whistled softly. The lock was largish, black, constructed in the form of a snarling dog's muzzle, and the keyhole was located down its throat. The work of Morassian masters. To any knowledgeable person such a trifle said, "Go away! I bite!"

And it really did bite! It would bite anyone who failed to open it. The cunning Morassians had crammed this thing with so many tricks and snares that only a true master could open it. And even then not always.

Stump hadn't spoken a word about what awaited us. But he had to have known, the bastard!

"A charming little thing," the thief said, chuckling.

"Joch didn't spare any money for the trinket," I agreed.

"Trinket!" Layen said, outraged. "Are all men such idiots, or is it only you two? It's more dangerous than an irritated cobra! If you make even the slightest mistake it will kill you. Why else do you think the Morassian craftsmen ask so much money for the things?"

"I can handle it," said Harold simply.

"And if you can't?"

"Then for a start the jaws will snap shut, and these delightful, razor-sharp teeth will bite off my fingers. Or the lock will spit out a poisoned needle, but in that case I'm not too worried. I won't be in front of it, but behind. But it'll be worst of all if I make a mistake with the last pin. Most often they make it the toughest, and if it stops halfway or slips, the lock might spit out some poison that will turn our lungs into tattered rags after a few seconds. There'd be quite enough for all three of us."

"You know how to explain it all superbly." I coughed. "My sun, maybe you could turn back and wait for us behind the wall?"

She was immediately on her guard. "What for?"

"So that if he makes a mistake, all three of us don't die."

"Why me?"

"Because I have to hold up the lantern. And you're just sitting there doing nothing. So shoo!"

She grumbled for show, but agreed with my arguments. "If you're thinking of dying, warn me in advance, dear."

"I love you, too."

She snorted loudly and crawled under the wall.

"Get twenty paces away," I called after her, lowering myself on all fours and sticking my head into the hole. "When we're done, I'll call you."

She pecked me on the lips and, still grumbling in irritation, walked away into the darkness.

The thief was studying the lock, humming that same unfamiliar tune.

"What are you singing?"

"Oh, never you mind." Harold grinned without taking his eyes off the Morassian Cur. "A silly old song. A good friend of mine sang it. One could say, in another life."

Well, if he didn't want to tell me, he didn't have to.

"Have you ever worked with such things?" I asked, nodding toward the dog's jaws.

"A couple of times," he said in a bored tone of voice, and then he put on a pair of gloves with the fingers cut off. "Don't worry, it's not as difficult as people think. With the right amount of experience, this toothy little toy can be cracked like a nut."

"I hope you have that experience."

"I should also hope so." A shadow of a smile passed over his lips. "Most fail by going too fast."

I don't know. Morassian Curs have killed a lot of good thieves. The things were too capricious and dangerous, and their masters made them too well. Most people who saw black canine jaws on a door or coffer preferred to get out of harm's way and find themselves easier pickings.

"You're going to have to work blindly. The lock is on the other side."

"As if I didn't notice," he muttered. "By the way, I really don't need the light. I'll do it all by touch. So, before it's too late, go take a stroll with your girl-friend. When I've opened it, I'll give a shout."

"I want to watch."

"Well, have it your way." Harold shrugged.

He took a bundle of finely crafted lock picks from his bag.

"Morassian made?"

"No. By far better craftsmen." He grinned, and

then he put his hands through the bars of the grate. "Well, let's . . ."

"Let's what?"

"Pray to Melot." He snickered and on his first try got the pick in the keyhole. "I hope the god is on our side today."

For some time he worked in concentrated silence, and only the gentle click of metal against metal could be heard. His face was tense, his lips tightly compressed, but his hands never trembled. Harold didn't need to look at them to know what they were doing, so the thief studied the toes of his boots instead. I anxiously watched the dog's jaws, which could turn into a trap at any moment and snap shut. Or even worse, spit out a poison cloud.

"There's the first pin," he said.

Personally, I hadn't heard anything. The click must have been very quiet, but the keen ears of thieves are hard to deceive.

"How many more?"

"However many it takes to open it."

"So that means you don't know?"

"I don't know," he said. "One. Two. Ten. This is piecework. Every Morassian master creates a different number of pins, tricks, and traps. There are no identical Curs. That's why they're such a bother."

While he was talking he didn't stop working, and over the course of the next several minutes he disarmed three more pins. I was beginning to have respect for this strange man. Behind all his jokes, laughter, and carelessness, a genuine master was hidden—calm, experienced, and aware of his own value.

"Why did you stay with me?" he asked suddenly.

"I told you, I wanted to watch. Do you mind?"

"Not at all. Watch all you like. I'm flattered that you have such faith in me."

"Faith?"

"Well, yes. If I made a mistake now, you wouldn't hold out for very long." He grinned crookedly. "Nothing I could do about it. So you're really just moved by curiosity to see what I'm capable of?"

I pondered his question and then answered honestly, "I don't know. I just hate sitting still. At least there's something going on here."

"Many of the present generation hate sitting still. They're always rushing off somewhere, hurrying, striving to get something, trying to change, even though most of them have no idea what they want."

"We're simply moving." I smiled.

"I call people like you 'chasers of the wind.' You chase after it blindly, but what will you do once you find it? Not one of you thinks about where that search will lead you. You may find something completely different than what you are looking for and, instead of catching the wind, you'll get lost in the storm. Are you ready to meet it face-to-face?"

"You're a philosopher, aren't you?" I laughed quietly.

"I try to think." He chuckled. "It keeps me from turning into an idiot. And you should meditate on what I said at your leisure. If you, like many others, chase the wind, without even knowing why, there is still time to stop. To avoid the storm."

"I'm not afraid."

"Being unafraid is stupid. And not fearing for the fate of your loved ones is doubly stupid. If you're lucky, you might survive, but the storm will devour someone else. A person dear to you. Is that what you want?"

"No."

"So don't run. Stop and think about the consequences. Decide, do you need this?"

"Why are you saying all this?" I frowned.

"It makes it easier for me to work." He shrugged. "If you don't like it, I can shut up. However, more conversation isn't really necessary."

He abruptly twisted his left wrist and something clicked in the lock.

"Opa!" said Harold triumphantly.

"Did it work?" I exclaimed.

"As if you have to ask!" The thief pretended that he was offended and, pushing the grate upward, showed me how easily it opened. "It may be that this world came out a bit flawed, but I know all about locks. Harold's more than a match for Morassian Curs. Call your wife; the path is clear."

While Layen was returning, he pulled himself up

with his arms, and then he helped us up. I opened the lantern window a bit, increasing the light so we could look around. We were in a large but completely empty barn. Joch wasn't about to store anything here. The floor was made of earth, and the walls were constructed from thick logs. There were no signs of a window. There were transverse beams under the roof. On one of them hung a thick chain, which ended in a frightful butcher's hook, the kind that serves quite well for stringing up undesirable people. By the ribs. As I heard it, Threefingers sometimes entertained himself thus with those who did not pay back their debts.

The first thing the thief did was dash over to the door. Then he returned to us, smiling happily. "I underestimated the master of this house. He's not just cautious, he's very cautious. I tip my cap to him. Go see for yourselves."

"Damn. It. All," hissed Layen through clenched teeth when we got to the door. Then she turned to me. "Do what you want, but I'm not crawling back. I'm staying with you."

I nodded reluctantly. I hadn't thought Joch would have enough brains to hang a second lock worked by Morassian masters on his barn. But that's what he did! The dog's jaws with the sharp teeth and the keyhole in its throat grinned warningly at us.

"I'll have to work a bit longer." Harold was not at all dejected by what he saw. "You still chasing the wind?"

"Yes."

"As you will. They're your lives," he said indifferently, and once again took his picks from his bag.

"What are you talking about?" Layen half whispered to me. "What wind?"

"Later, okay?" Now there was neither time nor need to explain it to her. All my thoughts were occupied with the lock. "Harold, what if there's a dead bolt on the other side of the door?"

"Is your Joch an idiot or a coward?"

"No," I replied, not knowing what he was driving at.

"Then there won't be any dead bolt. Only a complete fool would place something else on a door with a Morassian Cur. The dog's jaws are reliable all by themselves. And here there are two of them—one on the inside and one on the outside. I've never seen anything like it."

My heart beat painfully.

"How do you know that it's double?" Layen asked, surprised. "Can you see through the wood?"

"No. I can just feel it." He smiled thinly. "Also, sane people usually put a lock on the outside of such places, not on the inside."

"Sane people don't usually put Morassian playthings on barns," my sun argued with him.

"It makes no difference to us right now, whether your friend is sane or insane. I just have to open the first one without knocking aside any pins, and then I'll tackle the second, though they probably have some bits in common. It's going to take some time."

"I hope you'll get it done before dawn."

"Sure," said the thief, and then he got to work.

He managed it in less than twenty minutes. When the lock clicked, there wasn't a drop of sweat on Harold's forehead.

"I'm impressed."

"It's cats who thrive on flattery." Harold grinned. "Now it's your turn to show what you can do."

"You're staying?"

He thought about it. Then he chuckled, and the miniature crossbow appeared in his hand.

"Are we going to tug the storm's beard? Perhaps I'll join your team, after all. It's too hospitable a home to leave it so quickly."

"All right." Layen and I donned black half-masks. "Follow us and don't get into any fights. Do you have something to cover your face?"

"No. I have no need for it. Just watch out for dogs. Right now dogs are our biggest threat."

Well, if he didn't want to cover his face, that was his right. I didn't care.

I opened the door and looked around. I saw no one. We slipped through and, clinging to the wall, crept from the moonlight to thick shadow. Now I could really have a look around.

The barn from which we'd successfully escaped was neighbored by two identical structures. There were also mismatched sheds, a chicken coop, a pigsty, a small silo, and a few other buildings whose purpose I couldn't guess. Twenty yards away there were some low, squat stables. Beyond it was a narrow strip of orchards, consisting of large shadowy apple, apricot, and mulberry trees.

We swung wide around the stables and plunged into the orchard. Harold plucked an apple from a nearby tree, rubbed it on his jacket, and sank his teeth into it. He immediately grimaced and tossed the unpleasant fruit aside. We approached the house from the rear.

The Viceroy himself could very well live in this four-storied palace. The large lancet windows were dark, and the only lights burning brightly were in the far wing of the ground and fourth floors.

"That's the kitchen." Layen pointed at the lighted windows on the ground floor. "Going through there would be faster, but more dangerous. There's always someone there. And that's Joch's bedroom." She pointed to the fourth floor.

"Not sleeping at such an hour. Obviously his conscience is not clear," muttered Harold. "I suggest we go through that door there."

"It's lit by torches," I objected.

"Does light frighten you? Never mind," the thief dismissed me carelessly.

"We'd just need to get through the greenhouse, and we'd be in the right wing," Layen supported him. "Otherwise we'll have to walk through the entire house, and we're bound to get an unwelcoming reception then and—"

"Look at the balcony," I interrupted her softly.

A man with a crossbow on his knees was sitting there.

"He's sleeping," objected Harold. "Some guard."

"He could wake up. Also, we don't know how much security there is around the house."

"Most of it should be at the gate and the front door. No one expects uninvited guests to crawl out of the barn."

"Okay," I decided. "We'll do as you say. I'll cover you."

As two shadows they slipped out from under the cover of the trees. Trampling the flowerbeds, they broke out into the open and appeared near the door. Harold busied himself with the lock, and Layen peered intently at the corner of the house, from which someone could appear at any moment. The guard with the crossbow didn't even move. Truly, the deep sleep of fools is our best ally. It came my turn to run. The thief had just finished with the door.

We were in a dimly lit gallery on the ground floor, where every fifth oil lamp on the walls was lit. Their flames wavered timidly, thickening the gloom. The floor was covered by a plush carpet. To the right were a series of closed doors, and to the left, tall windows.

I went first, behind me came the thief, listening

intently and for once serious. No more jokes or strangeness. Cool and collected, just like us. Layen brought up the rear, glancing behind as she walked.

The gallery led us to the greenhouse.

Joch loved flowers, especially rare ones. It was one of his many passions, and he purchased rare plants from distant lands for astronomical sums.

I passed by some kind of mangy palm, suspiciously rustling vines, a miniature tree, and an enormous flower that reeked of rotten flesh; the leaves of one furry plant were burning with a dim light like fireflies. I really wanted to sneeze from all the unusual smells. Layen was staring at the glowing bush and almost overturned a pot holding some kind of thorny plant that bore a distorted resemblance to a rotten cucumber. Harold grabbed the tilting pot in time and put it back in place, looking at us reproachfully.

"Watch where you're walking," he whispered.

We left the greenhouse and came out into a small room with a fading fireplace and pictures on the walls. Right opposite the exit was a staircase lined with white marble, which led upward. Like all the floors in the house, it was covered with carpet.

"Beyond there is the kitchen. We need to go up," said Layen quietly.

"I'll go first. You two follow."

Holding my bow at the ready, I left the room and began slowly walking up the stairs. I stopped on the second floor and looked around. I waited for my companions. I walked up to the third floor. Then the fourth. In all this time, we didn't encounter a single soul. I've already mentioned sleep. It's a great ally. It was the hour when it was too late not to sleep and too early to wake up. There was minimal risk.

"Joch's bedroom is there." Layen pointed in the direction we needed. "Down the hall, through two rooms and a parlor."

"You still with us, thief?" I asked.

"It's too hot." He frowned. "With your permission, I'll snoop around a bit. I might find something interesting."

I shook my head doubtfully. "You'll get caught."

"Not likely. I just need a few minutes. I'll catch up."

"Leave him. We have our own concerns," said Layen, and then she warned Harold, "Mind you, we won't search or wait for you."

He nodded and walked away from us. I followed him with my gaze and sighed. "We shouldn't have let him go."

"He might hinder us. Let him go."

I frowned uncertainly. If he stumbled upon someone, it would definitely hinder us. But I didn't argue. The next two rooms were empty, but there were three men in the parlor. One was standing idly by the door, and two were sitting by the fire at a small table laden with fruit. They were playing dice.

The lad at the door caught sight of me, opened his mouth in shock, and instantly got his throat slit. This guaranteed that he wouldn't cry out and raise the alarm. Blood flowed in all directions from the ghastly wound in his neck that I'd made with the edge of my arrow. The guard fell to his knees and was dead a second later, laid out on the carpet that had muffled the fall of his heavy body. Layen's crossbow snapped harshly and the man sitting with his back to us fell face-first into a bowl of Morassian grapes. For some reason, his companion threw his dice at us and then grabbed a short sword lying on the table. He jumped up—and died from a second arrow.

A few seconds and three corpses. None of the guards had a chance to make a sound. After seven years of retirement, we hadn't lost our skills and we still worked seamlessly and quickly. Layen reloaded her crossbow and nodded toward the double doors made of oak with bronze handles, which led into Joch's bedroom. Through the slits in her mask, her eyes shone with a hostile blue light.

I nodded in reply, took a new arrow from my quiver, rested it against the bowstring, and went to stand opposite the entrance. Layen walked over a corpse, trying not to step in the blood soaking into the carpet, and headed toward the bedroom. She took hold of the door handle and pushed the door open gently; then she gracefully slipped to the side, leaving the path free for me. After a moment I was in the room, which was fairly well lit with burning candles.

Joch was on an enormous bed with bloodred curtains and white sheets, too occupied by a red-haired girl to realize right away what was happening. The wench saw us first and squeaked in fear, shying away from us to the far corner of the bed, drawing a blanket up to her chin. Joch Threefingers, a tall, broad, middle-aged man with a handsome, refined face, a neat beard, and the yellow skin of a native of Urs, cursed filthily and then, catching sight of us, froze.

The masks didn't fool him. He knew who had come to him and why. For several long seconds we looked at each other. Joch smiled crookedly with paled lips, sat down on the bed, and looked at me defiantly. He had decided to take revenge on me for severing two of his fingers; he took a risk, set his life against ours, and lost. I had nothing to say to him. No pompous, malevolent, or triumphant words. There was no need for it. He was a smart fellow and he read the verdict in my eyes.

I shot, hitting him in the heart. The arrow passed through his chest, and fine drops of blood fell onto the sheets and pillows. Threefingers fell onto his right side and died a moment later. The girl sniveled submissively.

"Don't even think of screaming," Layen told her sternly.

The girl squeezed her eyes tightly shut and whined softly, "Please don't kill me. For Melot's sake! I haven't even seen your faces! I'd never recognize you. Please! Please! Have mercy on me!"

Layen went over to her and lightly struck her on the neck with the side of her palm. That was quite enough to make the red-haired girl lose consciousness for a long time and so we didn't have to fear that she'd raise the entire house against us. I checked Joch's body just in case. Convinced that he was really dead, I indicated to my sun that we should leave. We had nothing more to do here.

We found Harold in the parlor. The thief was leaning against the doorjamb, looking at the corpses lying in their own blood with gloomy interest.

"Not very clean work. It'll never come out of the carpet. And you could easily get three hundred sorens for that one."

"Enough yakking," I said. "We can talk when we're out of here."

"As you wish. I just made a circuit of several of the deceased master's rooms, may he rest in peace, so I can live without the carpet."

We quickly made our way to the stairs and began to descend, but on the second floor luck turned her back on us. A door opened and two men ran right at us. The first, with a sword, was one of Joch's thugs. The second looked very similar to Ga-Nor—a redheaded northerner.

Harold spun to the side and under the protection of our backs. Layen drove a bolt into the belly of the Son of the Snow Leopard, rightly considering him the more dangerous of the two. Despite the wound, he drew his sword, roared so loudly the ceiling rattled, and threw himself at us. Harold helped by shooting two bolts one after the other from behind our backs. Both men were on the floor, but they'd done their job, alerting the entire house.

With soft catlike steps another two redheads stepped out of their doors. A third northerner was coming up the stairs from the first floor.

Terrific!

The thief obviously didn't plan on waiting for further developments and he took to his heels, choosing a somewhat unconventional path of retreat. Tossing the discharged crossbow, he dashed over to a window and leaped through it, and together with a hail of wooden framing and fragments of glass, fell somewhere outside. Given the fact that the second floor was fairly high up from the ground, Harold's act could only be considered suicide. But he left this world beautifully, there's no doubt about it. Even our opponents froze, completely stunned, for a moment.

I took advantage of that pause and shot down the one who was coming from below. One of the remaining warriors rushed at me with a roar. I raised my utak. Fortunately for me, the redhead slipped in the blood of his fallen comrade and fell to his knees, letting his guard down. My strike was glancing and not very strong, and the northerner, even though he was wounded, almost chopped off my legs with his sword. I had to dodge it and finish him off with a second blow.

When I was done with my opponent, I turned to Layen, but she was coping without my help. The redhead thought that a woman posed no threat to him. He grabbed her and lifted her up into the air.

Bad idea.

The dagger hidden in Layen's left sleeve slipped into her hand, and she jammed her weapon right under her opponent's chin. Then she pulled down sharply, ripping open his neck.

Somewhere on the floor above us alarmed cries rang out. Once we made it to the room on the ground floor, I threw a hefty little end table at the window. The glass burst with a resounding crash, and, slipping over the fragments underfoot, we leaped out.

The thief was not there. To be honest, I was expecting to see his body smashed to pieces, but all that remained on the ground was the twisted frame and broken glass. Our companion who'd fled in such a timely manner was a surprisingly resilient man.

We rushed through the flowerbeds, ruthlessly trampling the unfortunate tiger lilies and Groganian roses. The house was waking up more with each passing second, lights were flashing in the windows of the upper floors—people were running with torches up there. For now they thought that the assassins were in the house, but they'd soon start scouring the grounds.

We'd almost reached the orchard when I saw three men running toward us from around the corner of the house. Two of them had short bows in their hands. The archer closest to me shot but missed.

"Under the trees! Quickly!" I yelled at Layen.

The archers were no more than eighty paces away.

Twang!

I laid out one of the archers, but his companion was a nimble fellow. A shattering blow in my right thigh blinded me with pain, and I collapsed into the grass. The archer screamed triumphantly and rushed toward me. A guard armed with a club was running with him.

That bastard actually managed to hit me!

The arrow had pierced through my thigh, and the leg of my trousers was quickly soaked with blood. I had to rest on my left knee to take the shot, practically blind because of the pain.

Twang!

A repulsive rattle informed me that I had not missed. There was one opponent left, but Layen got there in time. She tore my axe from my belt.

The axe flew through the air with a zing, a dull thud, and a falling body.

"Oh, Melot!" she groaned, grabbing me under my armpits and dragging me under the cover of the trees. "Hold on! Everything will be all right, my love!"

The pain had receded a bit, and my vision gradually cleared. My throat was dry and I was terribly thirsty.

"It's not fatal," I croaked. "The arrow needs to be pulled out."

"I'll do it."

"No. I'll do it myself."

Clenching my teeth, I broke the shaft sticking out of my leg. I groaned and swiftly yanked out the part that was sticking out of the other side of my thigh. Then I almost passed out.

"We need to stop the blood." Layen had been squeezing my shoulders the entire time.

"Not now and not here." Tears were rolling down my cheeks. "We need to clear out of here, before it gets any worse. Help me stand."

Hopping on my uninjured leg and leaning against her shoulder, I hobbled away. I don't know how long it took us to get to the barn; sometimes the pain took over and I was unable to keep track. Fortunately for us, no one was chasing after us anymore.

Layen picked up the lantern we'd left behind, lowered herself into the hole first, and supported me as I awkwardly dropped down.

"It seems the thief didn't get away," I said. "Or he was so kind as to leave us the light."

My sun lowered the grate. I barely squeezed myself under the dismantled wall and lamely helped her put the bricks back where they should be. This gave us a bit of hope that we'd briefly confuse the pursuit. My ears were buzzing and my head was spinning. Before we dealt with the wound we had to get as far away as possible, but I knew that if we delayed treating it, I would lose consciousness very soon from blood loss.

Layen ripped open my bloody trouser leg with her dagger. She quickly retrieved clean cloths from her pack and a vial of strong-smelling antiseptic liquid.

She wiped away the blood.

"It went through cleanly," she said, referring to the arrow, and suddenly poured half the vial on me. I howled from the burning pain and almost jumped out of my own skin.

She skillfully dressed the wound, tying the ends of the bandages together. Multicolored specks floated before my eyes, and the sound of bells was ringing in my ears. I passed out for a while. When I came to, I saw that my leg was already bandaged and that Layen was crying silently.

"Don't," I begged. "I promise not to die for the next hundred years."

She dutifully wiped away her tears and smiled. "I'm okay. I just got scared."

I'm not going to relate how I hobbled back along the underground tunnel. But I can congratulate myself on the fact that the walls, constructed so long ago by the Sculptor, heard so many curses and oaths from me that they'd easily be able to hold their own against an entire crew of sailors.

The only weapons we had left were my bow and our daggers. Layen had lost her crossbow while we were fighting the northerners, and my trusty utak remained in the skull of one of our opponents. Neither I nor my sun had bothered to pick it up at the time.

A pity. I'd had that thing with me since Sandon.

When we saw a dim light pouring in on us from the ceiling, I cried out, "Stump!"

"Well, finally!" he replied with evident relief. "Damn! What's with you?"

"Perhaps you could pull us up first and then ask questions," I retorted sluggishly.

He dropped the rope.

"Did you succeed?"

"Yes," said Layen shortly.

"Thank Melot!" sighed the Giiyan with even more relief than before. "Let us pull you up. Where's the thief?"

That meant that Harold hadn't come back this way. Smart. He realized that Mols might get rid of him. Or maybe he just preferred another route. I hope he got out.

"You go first," I said quietly to my wife. "They are afraid of your Gift, but still, be careful."

"Can you manage on your own?" she asked just in case.

"Yes. Stump, pull!"

While she was going up, I extinguished the lantern and checked my dagger. It was unlikely they were planning to play some nasty trick on us, but Melot protects those who protect themselves.

"Come on!" called Stump.

I tied the rope around me securely and then walked my way up the wall, ignoring the pain in my leg. Two of the red-faced Giiyan's assistants swiftly pulled me up.

"That's unlucky," Stump said, glancing quickly at my leg. "You need a Healer."

"I was just thinking that myself."

"Lads, help him to the door."

"There's no need. I'll do it myself."

"You don't trust me?" sneered Stump.

"Would you?" I returned his sneer.

"As you wish. Hobble along on your own. Follow me, boys."

Huffing resentfully, he headed for the staircase, leaving Layen and me alone.

"He seems fairly peaceable," she said uncertainly.

"But a dagger up the sleeve doesn't hurt. Help me up there, please."

I somehow managed to climb up, and when we got to the main room—that's when it happened.

Layen cried out in warning, and in the same instant translucent lilac chains appeared on our wrists. The next instant we were on the floor, bound hand and foot by magic. All I could do was watch.

Besides Stump and his henchmen, there was Mols and six of her people, five of the Viceroy's Guards and some Walkers—three women in long blue dresses with red circles sewn into their chests, and white veils over their hair.

I looked at Mols furiously. "This is foolish, Katrin!"

Her face remained impassive. "I didn't have a choice. You understand."

I did. But I wouldn't forgive it. Sooner or later she would pay for her betrayal, I swore by the Abyss!

"Is this them?" asked the oldest of the Walkers.

"Yes," said a familiar voice from somewhere to the right. I shifted my eyes and saw Shen. He was alive and well. "Yes," he repeated. "That's them."

And then darkness came.

23

All Typhoid could think about was that night-time encounter by the pier. She kept getting lost in her conjectures: who had fate brought into her path, and how was that strange man with the incomprehensible power connected to the archer? She stayed trapped in her mind until evening when she sensed a surge in the magic of the girl-prodigy. The one because of whom all this started.

The Damned quickly rushed to the place where magic had been used. But before she got there, the wretched girl had already disappeared. But the inn where she had apparently been staying was swarming with Guardsmen. The Damned sensed death, and a Walker approaching in the darkness. Staying any longer would be risky, and Tia cleared out while she still had a whole skin. She couldn't get back to Haven before curfew, so she decided to spend the night under the open sky. She chose an old cemetery in Second City, the exact same one where Ness and Layen had hidden not so long ago.

Making herself comfortable, Typhoid lapsed into thought.

The girl was even more foolish than she would have thought, for even once using her Gift within sight of the Tower. The Damned hoped that she might beat the Walkers, that she might be the first to get to the prodigy. Closer to morning, the sudden flash of three sparks caused her to wake up. Typhoid's fears were entirely justified. When she ran to the right street, the Viceroy's Guards were carrying two unconscious people out of a small wine cellar, located in one of the nondescript buildings. In the light of the torches she could make out the faces of the archer and the girl perfectly. She nearly tore her hair out with frustration when she saw the three Walkers following them. There was no way she could deal with them in her present condition. Then a man appeared, and to her infinite surprise she recognized him as the Healer. The lad was a Walker, which hadn't happened since the time of the Sculptor!

The prisoners were taken away, and all Tia could do was gnaw on her own fingernails. The only thing that Typhoid was sure of was that now she would have to search for them in Hightown. In the Tower, where she was forbidden to go. She had to wait for the dawn and slip into Cliff (the former name of Hightown).

She went back to the cemetery and patiently observed the swiftly brightening sky.

I woke up because sunlight was striking me in the eyes, and I lay there for some time without raising my eyelids. It was quiet. Then I moved and an awful pain flashed through my right leg. Trying not to groan, I opened my eyes and, perching on my elbows, looked around.

A stone cell with a low vaulted ceiling. Strong bars instead of a door and a tiny window opposite where I was lying. The warm rays of the sun were passing through the opening and falling on my face. We could say good-bye to the Golden Mark. Captain Dazh was unlikely to wait for us. He'd probably long since gone to sea. And we remained here. In the clutches of the Walkers.

Layen? I called.

There was no answer.

Harold was a prophet. To our misfortune, we caught our wind, and fell into such a storm that it was unlikely we would get out alive.

After about an hour steps rang out, there was the jingling of keys, the lock clicked, and Shen walked in accompanied by two guards and a jailer. The Flame (the Flame, like the Red Circle, is a symbol of the Walkers) was embroidered with silver thread on his black velvet jacket.

"Leave us," he said curtly.

"If something happens, we're right nearby," said the jailer, and he and the soldier stepped out.

Shen waited until they had gone far enough away and then he smiled. "Hello, Ness."

"How's Layen?" I hissed instead of a greeting.

"You don't have to worry." He allowed himself another cautious smile. "You'll see her soon."

"How soon?"

"As soon as we've finished talking."

"About what? About our impending doom?"

"I want to examine your wound," Shen said suddenly.

"Just try it."

He laughed quietly and sorrowfully. "You look like a dog who's dreaming of eating the cat, Gray. Don't be foolish."

"And what would happen then?" I asked challengingly. "Would you fry me, Walker?"

"I'd be happy to, but I don't know how. Listen, there are many in the Tower who want to extinguish Layen's spark. I'm trying to keep them from doing it, and I'm going to talk to the Mother. Now then? Will you help me out or are you going to keep baring your teeth at me?"

"To the Abyss with you. Do what you want." I gave up.

"There, you see, we can always come to terms." He was already next to me.

"Somehow I don't recall you ever being in a rush

to come to terms during our journey from Dog Green."

He didn't answer, so I changed the subject. "Gis and I decided that you'd been gobbled up by the dead. How did you manage to get out of Bald Hollow?"

"I was lucky." The boy was trying to unravel the bandage, which was stiffened with dried blood.

"Ah!"

"Don't move," said the Healer sternly. "You were galloping on like crazed cats, and my horse fell behind. So then I had to act on my own. I returned to the river, crossed to the other side, and rushed through the cemetery to a field."

"What a hero," I said, and then I howled because he put his hand right on my wound.

"I said, don't move!" snapped the Walker.

I hissed and showered him with curses. He ignored me completely. After a second the wound became cold, as if he'd pressed ice against it. The cold spread through my leg, and I could no longer feel my toes. The frost, for it could not be called anything else, began to gnaw ruthlessly at my bones.

All at once it was over. A pleasant warmth flowed through my body and I opened my eyes. I cautiously moved my leg, realizing with astonishment that there was no more pain. The wound wasn't there anymore. All that remained was a pale, white scar. Shen, somewhat paler and sweating, grinned in satisfaction.

"Sometimes the Gift of a Healer has its uses. I can't do everything the Embers and the Walkers can do, but I can heal. This skill can come in very handy."

"You're being unexpectedly kind."

He scowled. "I just really didn't want to have to drag you everywhere. That's all."

"You'd prefer that I walked to the scaffold on my own?" I asked.

The Healer gave me a level look and said reluctantly, "You killed a Walker and you deserve to die. But right now they just want to talk to you. In particular, to Layen."

"I'd be interested in having a look at the one who'll honor us with conversation. The poor wretch's brain probably swelled, coming up with such an absurd and complicated plan to return us to Al'sgara."

"Have you guessed?"

"Not completely. Perhaps in the spirit of friendship you could explain what's what to me?"

He nodded reluctantly. "The search for you never stopped for all these years. But it was as if you had disappeared into the ground."

"I can imagine how that would enrage the Tower," I interrupted.

"Suffice it to say, you were finally found. And quite by accident. Mols's people were trying. She was indebted to us."

"I'm disappointed in her."

"Well, it's better than hard labor in the copper mines, so the baker agreed to assist us. You must understand that Layen is of some interest to the Tower. But if Walkers or Embers had appeared in your backwater, no conversation would have happened. No one knew what your wife was capable of, so the Mother decided not to risk it. Until today. After the encounter with the Damned, Weasel's Gift faded a bit. As for Joch, it was Mols herself who made it so that rumors came to him that you were not yet in the Blessed Gardens. He'd long been gnashing his teeth over you and, to his misfortune and our luck, did not spare money for your head."

"A brilliant plan," I said sarcastically. "And what if someone had killed us?"

"The risk was small."

Uh-huh. Go tell that to Greybeard and his friends. They almost nailed us.

"But since you risked it, that means we weren't all that important to you."

"I'm just a Healer, and I am not part of the Council." He shrugged. "The Mother decided everything."

I was beginning to think that the Walkers were out of their minds.

"Is that why you came with Whip?"

"Yes. A few words were spoken to Mols, and I was taken into their company. No one can see the spark of a Healer until he uses his Gift. So I was beyond suspicion. Layen shouldn't have been able to sense anything. I was just supposed to learn her abilities and make sure you got to Al'sgara without any problems."

"And if we hadn't come?"

"But you did."

"Hmm," I said thoughtfully. "The actions of the Tower baffle me."

Shen broke out into laughter. "Yeah, okay. Everything was going fine until the Nabatorians arrived, and then you know the rest. Also, I lost you in Bald Hollow. So all the hope rested on Mols. You had to come to her sooner or later."

"Yes," I said dryly. "Only she was in no hurry to do right by us. First we burned our hands on hot chestnuts and then she betrayed us."

Oh, Mols, Mols. You old bitch.

"Let's leave this conversation for the time being. We need to go." Shen stood up, walked over to the bars, and called out to the jailer.

It was bright and clean in the carriage. Expensive seats upholstered in red velvet, gold-plated handles, wide windows with burgundy silk curtains. These folks don't begrudge themselves anything. I had the honor of sitting in it while dirty, and in fairly ragged and bloody clothes.

Shen was sitting across from me, and on either side of me were unsmiling, broad-shouldered Guardsmen. An unneeded precaution. While they had my sun in their hands, I wasn't about to budge.

"Where is Layen?" I asked again.

"Show a little patience. I beg you. You'll see her as soon as we get there."

The carriage started moving, and Shen, having lost all interest in me, began looking out the window. The Guardsmen were silent, but as soon as I shifted, the lad sitting to my right began to get nervous. This diverted me very much until the second Guardsman lost patience with me and punched me in the side with his fist. I lost my distraction and felt a wave of anxiety wash over me. I was worried about Layen. I didn't know what the Walkers would decide.

I kept glancing out the window. Soon we passed through a park and the carriage stopped by a small lake.

"Remove his shackles," Shen ordered.

He stepped out, and one of the Guardsmen followed him and the other tapped me gently on the back so I wouldn't delay. With the clinking of chains, I hopped down.

Outside a dozen soldiers were waiting for us. One of them liberated me from my bonds.

Another carriage approached. Three Walkers and Layen came out of it. The lilac bracelets still shone on her wrists. My sun was pale, but when she saw me, color returned to her cheekbones and her blue eyes sparkled. Ignoring her escort, she walked up to me.

"Are you okay?" I asked.

"If you don't count this abomination." She twisted

her lips and twitched an eyebrow at the magical shackles. "But more or less. And you?"

"Just the same." I laughed and immediately saw a smile on her lips. "Shen condescended to heal my leg."

"Don't mention it," said the Healer modestly.

"It's a pity my hands are tied." Layen's eyes sparkled maliciously. "I'd happily smack you in the face, you filthy little toady."

"Then I'm in luck," he said quite seriously. "Let's go; they're waiting for us."

Well then. The storm awaited us. We would have to pay for what we did seven years ago. The question was, what price would be asked of us?

"Take her shackles off," I said to the Healer.

"No! Her Gift—"

"Get them off her, the Abyss take you, or you can forget about us talking!" I barked.

Shen blinked and then nodded to the Walkers. They weren't excited about it, but for some reason they obeyed the boy. The light went out.

I wondered how things were with Layen's Gift? I didn't think these old maids would be able to release her spark. I shifted my eyes to the right.

There was the Tower. A massive structure shoring up the clouds, it loomed over us like a gloomy giant. Despite the bright, pink-veined stone from which the Sculptor had erected this majestic building, an indefinable menace emanated from its statuesque majesty. Those walls had seen too much over the past thousand years. They remembered the blood of those who died inside them during the Dark Revolt; they experienced the pain, fear, despair, and insane hope of the mages battling one another. They absorbed their souls, compressed them into their stone, and did not release them into the Blessed Gardens or the Abyss, forcing immortality on the souls to invest themselves with strength. Normal people rarely entered the enormous spire crowned with seven spikes. This was the preserve of the Walkers and the Embers; all others were allowed to pass only by special invitation. And it is extremely regrettable that we found ourselves among those miserable few.

What awaited us? What did the mages want from us? I didn't believe the Healer. It was unlikely they searched for so long simply to have a talk. Almost no one who passes through the Gates of Light ever returns.

"Can we go now?" asked Shen venomously.

For a few seconds Layen and I looked into each other's eyes. Then she gave a slight nod and, grasping me firmly by the hand, turned toward the Tower of the Walkers, which overshadows the entire world.

GLOSSARY

Abyss   Where, according to belief, the souls of sinners fall. It is populated by demonic creatures, who sometimes manage to break out into the outer worlds. The Abyss gives warmth to the sparks of those who have turned to the dark side of the Gift.

Al'sgara   The largest city in the south of the Empire. It was founded more than a thousand years ago on a rocky cliff near the Oyster Sea. It was developed under the Sculptor, who built two large temples to Melot, the first three rings of defensive walls, the Tower of the Walkers, the underground aqueducts, the Palace of the Viceroy, and much more.

Blazogs   A race that lives in the Great Blazgian Swamps in the south of the Empire. Most Blazogs never leave their homeland and very rarely do they come to a human city. They have a repulsive appearance and human speech is very difficult for them, so only a few master it.

Blazogs are considered excellent warriors. During the War of the Necromancers they sided with the

Empire and formed the Marsh Regiment, considered one of the most effective and battle-seasoned units of the Second Southern Army.

Blessed Gardens   The place, according to legend, where the souls of the righteous go. It is from the Gardens that bearers of the light side of the Gift draw strength for their spark.

Book of Invocation   A foundational book of the wizards; it contains fundamental spells for battling demons.

Borderlands   The territory between the Empire and Nabator. It is considered part of Nabator, but the region is uninhabited because of the huge amount of goves that live in this part of the Boxwood Mountains.

Bragun-Zan (Dead Ash)   The rocky, lifeless wasteland to the north of the Empire that emerged as a result of the War of the Necromancers. It is nominally a part of the Empire, although the race of Nirits that live there consider themselves a free nation. In the center of Bragun-Zan is the Groh-ner-Tohh (Belting Mountain), a dormant volcano.

Burnt Souls (Shay-za'ns)   A race related to the Je'arre. They live in the Great Waste, and are unsurpassed archers. According to the legends of the Sons of the Sky, the Shay-za'ns went against their god, called the Dancer by these peoples, and were punished. Both their souls and their wings were taken away.

Children of the Snow Leopard (Sons of the Snow Leopard) The name of one of the seven clans of northerners, who live in the Icy Lands in the northern part of the Empire. Besides the clan of the Snow Leopard, there exist the clans of the White Squirrel, the Bear, the Owl, the Marten, the Elk, and the Wolf.

Council of the Towers The governing organization, which includes the most influential Walkers.

Crow's Nest A mighty fortress that guards the road to Al'sgara from the east.

Damned Eight rebel Walkers who escaped after the Dark Revolt: Rubeola (Mitifa), Plague (Leigh), Delirium (Retar), Consumption (Rovan), Cholera (Ginora), Pox (Alenari), Leprosy (Tal'ki), and Typhoid (Tia). Delirium and Cholera died during the War of the Necromancers.

Dark Revolt Initiated by a group of Walkers who wanted to change the rules of training and the possession of magic. After the Revolt, the eight remaining rebel mages came to be called the Damned.

Elect A person who has passed through the Sphere of the Necromancers, the Sdisian magical academy.

Feast of the Name   A celebration of the Emperor's birthday.

Fish   A corpse that has scale armor grown onto its body with the assistance of a necromancer's magic. It is able to explode on the orders of its master, destroying everyone who is nearby at that moment.

Forest Region   The territory at the base of the Boxwood Mountains; it occupies a large part of the Empire's south.

Gash-Shaku   The second-largest city in the southern part of the Empire. The city's fortifications were built by the Sculptor.

Gates of Six Towers   An impregnable citadel that guards the only traversable pass through the western part of the Boxwood Mountains. This is the most convenient way into the Empire from the south.
   The fortress was built by the Sculptor about a thousand years ago. It has never been taken by storm.

Gem's Arch   The name of the countryside near Sandon. The last major battle between humans and the Highborn occurred there; it ended in victory for the Empire. The signing of the peace treaty between the two races took place there as well.

Gerka   A city in the Boxwood Mountains. It was abandoned during the War of the Necromancers. It still nominally belongs to the Empire, but has been neglected for the past five centuries.

Giiyan A master assassin. The word comes from the Blazgian word *Giiyanragganrrattanda,* which means "a murderer who receives a reward."

Golden Mark The Golden Mark is ruled by the Brotherhood of Merchants, which is composed of the most respected and wealthiest traders in the country.

Great Decline The period between the death of the Sculptor and the War of the Necromancers. It lasted about five hundred years. It was during these years that the Walkers lost most of the secrets of the Art and were deprived of their ability to create new spells.

Great Waste An enormous desert beyond the Kingdom of Sdis.

Grogan Western country, behind Oyster Sea.

Highborn A race of forest-dwelling elves. They live in the forests of Sandon and Uloron. For several centuries the Highborn fought with the Empire for the eastern part of the Boxwood Mountains and the passes that led to the southeast, into the Uninhabited Lands, which now belong to the Empire. The series of wars ended with the elves first being driven from Uloron and then pressed in Sandon and routed near Gem's Arch. The King of the Highborn, Del'be Vaske, had to sign a peace treaty, even though some of the Houses of this race were against an alliance with the Empire.

The elves consider archery unbecoming to males, so only females use this weapon. (The Black Lilies.)

There are seven Great Houses among the Highborn: the House of Strawberry (currently ruling), the House of Dew, the House of Willow, the House of Fog, the House of Butterfly, the House of Lotus, and the House of Spark. Fifty Highborn families belong to each House.

House of Scarlet (The Scarlet Order) Subject to the Viceroy. The wizard-demonologists who are affiliated with the Order struggle against the creatures of the Abyss who have broken through the reality of the world of Hara, and also against spirits and ghosts. Unlike the Walkers, the wizards don't have a spark; their abilities are based upon ritual magic, elixirs, formulas, and symbolic ruins. The head of the Scarlets is the Magister of the Order.

Isthmuses of Lina Two rocky passes that traverse the Bogs of Shett. A natural barrier to the Steps of the Hangman and Okni, it protects the southeast of the Empire.

Je'arre A race of winged creatures who came to the lands of the Empire after a part of their race was transformed into the Burnt Souls. Previously, they lived beyond the Great Waste.

The Je'arre have lived side by side with humans over the course of many centuries. The fabrics made by this tribe are highly valued in many countries, and they have gained great wealth thanks to these products.

Krylgzan A winged predator.

Kukses Slang for a revived corpse from necromancer.

Marshes of Erlika Located beyond the Katugian Mountains, they occupy vast reaches of the northeastern part of the Empire. They are famous for the fact that one of the Damned, Cholera, perished in them together with her army during the War of the Necromancers.

Morassia A small country renowned throughout Hara for its masterful weapons-makers, jewelers, and inventors.

Mort A product of the magic of the Sdisian sorcerers. These creations are not alive, but they are not dead either. They cut off their own noses, ears, and tongues, and they carve monstrous scars into their faces. Legends abound about the cruelty, resilience, and resourcefulness of these creatures. They have not appeared in the lands of the Empire since the War of the Necromancers.

Nabator A large and powerful kingdom beyond the Boxwood Mountains. It wars with the Empire over the south, which at the dawn of time belonged to Nabator.

Nirit A race inhabiting Bragun-Zan. They are fairly tolerant of humans, but they do not recognize themselves as citizens of the Empire. The Nirit are ruled by their Queen, or Zan-Nakun (The Ash Maiden). The Nirit worship Mount Groh-ner-Tohh.

Okni A large city located between the Katugian Mountains and the Isthmuses of Lina.

Overlords A title the Damned give themselves.

Paths of Petals Portals created by the Sculptor, capable of moving people unimaginable distances in a few moments. Only a Walker can activate a portal. The Sculptor did not reveal the secret of the creation of the Petals before his death, so no one else had the ability to create a new portal.

During the Dark Revolt, the Mother of the Walkers, Sorita, managed to lull the portals to sleep, and since that time they have ceased to operate. All attempts to awaken them have been unsuccessful.

Rainbow Valley The magical school of the Walkers is located in the Rainbow Valley.

Sandon Forests to the east of the Empire, near the Boxwood Mountains. They are inhabited by the Highborn.

Sculptor The greatest mage in the history of Hara. He created many of the most prominent buildings, as well as the Paths of Petals.

Sdis Southern country, supporting necromancers.

Shot A bounty hunter of those who are declared criminals by the city magistrates.

Snow Trolls A race that lives in the Icy Lands. There are very few of them. They are allies of the northerners.

Sorita A Mother of the Walkers; she perished during the Dark Revolt.

Steps of the Hangman Created by mages three hundred years before the Sculptor. It is a man-made pass through the Katugian Mountains in the form of a narrow stairway with an enormous number of steps and fortifications. It leads to the north of the Empire from the southern provinces.

Superiors The sorcerer-necromancers of the Eighth Sphere, the most powerful mages of Sdis, who go through their training under the supervision of Leprosy.

The Superiors hold all the power over their country, subject only to the Damned.

Uloron (The Country of Oaks)   The first homeland of the Highborn. It consists of the forests near the Katugian Mountains, conquered by the Empire from this race and returned after the conclusion of peace in exchange for the eastern part of the Boxwood Mountains and the Eastern Lands.

War of the Necromancers   Broke out after the Dark Revolt and swept through the whole of the south and part of the north of the Empire. The Army of the Damned fought against the armies of the Empire and the Walkers. Later, Sdis and Nabator allied themselves with the mage-apostates. The war lasted for fifteen years. It bled the south of the country dry and incinerated Bragun-Zan during a terrible magical battle between the Walkers and the Damned.

The outcome of the war ended with the defeat of the Sextet (one of the causes for the loss was the death of Cholera) and they departed for Sdis, and then beyond the Great Waste. For its part, the Empire lost the territories beyond the Boxwood Mountains, which were transferred to the Kingdom of Nabator.